About

Award-winning author
contemporary romances.
books translated into mor
a two-time winner of the ,
Reviewers' Choice Aw
Reviewers' Choice Award. Now living her dream, she
resides with her very patient husband and Writer Kitty.
When she's not plotting out her next romance, you can
find her with a mug of tea and a book. Learn more at
www.jenniferfaye.com/

Deborah Fletcher Mello has been writing since forever
and can't imagine herself doing anything else. Her first
romance novel, *Take Me to Heart*, earned her a 2004
Romance Slam Jam nomination for Best New Author,
and in 2009, she won an *Romantic Times* Reviewers'
Choice Award for her ninth novel, *Tame a Wild Stallion*.
Born and raised in Connecticut, Deborah now considers
home to be wherever the moment moves her.

Caroline Anderson's been a nurse, a secretary, a
teacher, and has run her own business. Now she's settled
on writing. 'I was looking for that elusive something
and finally realised it was variety – now I have it in
abundance. Every book brings new horizons, new
friends, and in between books I juggle! My husband
John and I have two beautiful daughters, Sarah and
Hannah, umpteen pets, and several acres of Suffolk that
nature tries to reclaim every time we turn our backs!'

Italian Playboys

Italian Playboys:
Nights

JENNIFER FAYE

DEBORAH FLETCHER MELLO

CAROLINE ANDERSON

MILLS & BOON

First Published in Great Britain 2021
by Mills & Boon, an imprint of HarperCollins*Publishers* Ltd,
1 London Bridge Street, London, SE1 9GF

www.harpercollins.co.uk

HarperCollins*Publishers*
1st Floor, Watermarque Building,
Ringsend Road, Dublin 4, Ireland

ITALIAN PLAYBOYS: NIGHTS © 2021 Harlequin Books S.A.

The Playboy of Rome © 2015 Jennifer F. Stroka
Tuscan Heat © 2016 Deborah Fletcher Mello
Best Friend to Wife and Mother? © 2015 Caroline Anderson

ISBN: 978-0-263-30063-5

MIX
Paper from
responsible sources
FSC C007454

This book is produced from independently certified FSC™ paper to ensure responsible forest management.

For more information visit: www.harpercollins.co.uk/green

Printed and bound in Spain
by CPI, Barcelona

THE PLAYBOY
OF ROME

JENNIFER FAYE

For Ami.
To a wonderful friend who has kept me
company as we've walked a similar path.
Thank you for your friendship and
unwavering encouragement.

CHAPTER ONE

"*Scusa.*"

Dante DeFiore stepped into the path of a young woman trying to skirt around the line at Ristorante Massimo. Her long blond hair swished over her shoulder as she turned to him. Her icy blue gaze met his. The impact of her piercing stare rocked him. He couldn't turn away. Thick black eyeliner and sky-blue eye shadow that shimmered succeeded in making her stunning eyes even more extraordinary.

Dante cleared his throat. "Signorina, are you meeting someone?"

"No, I'm not."

"Really?" He truly was surprised. "Someone as beautiful as you shouldn't be alone."

Her fine brows rose and a smile tugged at her tempting lips.

He smiled back. Any other time, he'd have been happy to ask her to be his personal guest but not tonight. Inwardly he groaned. Why did he have to have his hands full juggling both positions of maître d' and head chef when the most delicious creature was standing in front of him?

He choked down his regret. It just wasn't meant to be. Tonight there was no time for flirting—not even with this stunning woman who could easily turn heads on the runways of Milan.

He glanced away from her in order to clear his thoughts. Expectant looks from the people waiting to be seated reminded him of his duties. He turned back to those amazing blue eyes. "I hate to say this, but you'll have to take your place at the end of the line."

"It's okay." Her pink glossy lips lifted into a knowing smile. "You don't have to worry. I work here."

"Here?" Impossible. He'd certainly remember her. By the sounds of her speech, she was American.

"This is Mr. Bianco's restaurant, isn't it?"

"Yes, it is."

"Then I'm in the right place."

Suddenly the pieces fell into place. His staff had been cut in half because of a nasty virus running rampant throughout Rome. He'd called around to see if any business associates could loan him an employee or two. Apparently when Luigi said he might be able to track down a friend of one of his daughters, he'd gotten lucky.

Relief flooded through Dante. Help was here at last and by the looks of her, she'd certainly be able to draw in the crowds. Not so long ago, they hadn't needed anyone to draw in customers; his grandfather's cooking was renowned throughout Rome. But in recent months all of that had changed.

"And I'd be the luckiest man in the world to have such a beauty working here. You'll have the men lined up down the street. Just give me a moment." Dante turned and signaled to the waiter.

When Michael approached Dante, the man's forehead was creased in confusion. "What do you need?"

In that moment, Dante's mind drew a blank. All he could envision were those mesmerizing blue eyes. This was ridiculous. He had a business to run.

When he glanced over at the line of customers at the door, the anxious stares struck a chord in his mind. "Michael, could you seat that couple over there?" He pointed to an older couple. "Give them the corner table. It's their fortieth anniversary, so make sure their meal is on us."

"No *problema*."

Lines of exhaustion bracketed Michael's mouth. Dante couldn't blame the guy. Being shorthanded and having to see to the dining room himself was a lot of work.

Dante turned his attention back to his unexpected employee. She had her arms crossed and her slender hip hitched to the side. A slight smile pulled at the corners of her lush lips as though she knew she'd caught him off guard—something that rarely happened to him.

He started to smile back when a patron entered the door and called out a greeting, reminding Dante that work came first. Since his grandfather was no longer around to help shoulder the burden of running this place, Dante's social life had been reduced to interaction with the guests of Ristorante Massimo.

After a brief *ciao* to a regular patron, Dante turned back to his temporary employee. "Thanks for coming. If you give me your coat, I can hang it up for you."

"I've got it." She clutched the lapels but made no attempt to take it off.

"You can hang it over there." He pointed to the small cloakroom. "We can work out everything later."

"You want me to start right now?"

That was the plan, but perhaps Luigi had failed to make that part clear. "Didn't he tell you that you'd be starting right away?"

"Yes, but I thought I'd have a chance to look around. And I didn't think I'd be a hostess."

"Consider this an emergency. I promise you it's not hard. I'm certain you'll be fantastic…uh…" Did she give him her name? If she had, he couldn't recall it. "What did you say your name is?"

"Lizzie. Lizzie Addler."

"Well, Lizzie, it's a pleasure to meet you. I'm Dante. And I really appreciate you pitching in during this stressful time."

"Are you sure you want me out here? I'd be a lot more help in the kitchen."

The kitchen? With her looks, who would hide such a gem behind closed doors? Perhaps she was just shy. Not that anything about her stunning appearance said that she was an introvert.

"I'd really appreciate it if you could help these people find a table."

She nodded.

An assistant rushed out of the kitchen. "We need you."

By the harried look on the young man's face, Dante knew it couldn't be good. He turned to his new employee. There would be time for introductions and formalities later. Right now, he just needed to keep the kitchen from falling behind and giving the patrons an excuse to look for food elsewhere.

"Sorry for this rush but I am very shorthanded." When the girl sent him a puzzled look, he realized that Luigi might not have filled her in on the details of her duties. "If you could just get everyone seated and get their drinks, Michael can take their orders. Can you do that?"

She nodded before slipping off her long black coat to reveal a frilly white blouse that hinted at her willowy figure, a short black skirt that showed off her long legs and a pair of knee-high sleek black boots. He stifled a whistle. Definitely not the reaction a boss should give an employee, even if she was gorgeous enough to create a whirlwind of excitement on the cover of a fashion magazine.

He strode to the kitchen, hoping that nothing had caught fire and that no one had been injured. When was this evening going to end? And had his grandfather's friend Luigi been trying to help by sending Lizzie? Or trying to drive him to distraction?

Once the kitchen was again humming along, he retraced his steps just far enough to catch a glimpse of the blonde bombshell. She moved about on those high-heeled boots as if they were a natural extension of her long legs. He swallowed hard as his eyes followed her around the dining room. He assured himself that he was just doing his duty by checking up on her.

When she smiled and chatted with a couple of older gentlemen, Dante's gut tightened. She sure seemed far more at ease with those men than when he'd been talking with her. How strange. Usually he didn't have a problem making conversation with the female gender. Lizzie was certainly different. Too bad she wouldn't be around long enough to learn more about her. She intrigued him.

Obviously there was a misunderstanding.

Lizzie Addler frowned as she locked the front door of Ristorante Massimo. She hadn't flown from New York to Italy to be a hostess. She was here to work in the kitchen— to learn from the legendary chef, Massimo Bianco. And to film a television segment to air on the culinary channel's number-one-rated show. It was a dream come true.

The strange thing was she'd flown in two days early, hoping to get her bearings in this new country. How in the world did this Dante know she was going to show up this evening?

It was impossible. But then again, this smooth-talking man seemed to know who she was. So why put her on hostess duty when he knew that her true talents lay in the kitchen?

Her cheeks ached from smiling so much, but all it took was recalling Dante's flattering words and the corners of her lips lifted once again. She'd heard rumors that Italian men were known to be charmers and now that she knew that it was true—at least in Dante's case—she'd have to be careful around him. She couldn't lose focus on her mission here.

She leaned her back against the door and sighed. She couldn't remember the last time her feet ached this much.

Why in the world had she decided to wear her new boots today of all days?

Oh, yes, to make a good impression. And technically the boots weren't new—just new to her. They were second-hand, like all of Lizzie's things. But in her defense, some of her things still had the tags on them when she'd found them at the gently used upscale boutique. And boy, was she thankful she'd splurged on the stylish clothes.

Her gaze strayed to the wall full of framed pictures of celebrities. There were black and whites as well as color photos through the years. Massimo was in a lot of them alongside movie stars, singers and politicians from around the world. As Lizzie scanned the many snapshots, she found Dante's handsome face. In each photo of him, he was smiling broadly with his arm around a beautiful woman.

"Pretty impressive?"

She knew without looking that it'd be Dante. "Very impressive." She forced her gaze to linger on the army of photos instead of rushing to ogle the tall, dark and undeniably handsome man at her side. "Have all of these people eaten here?"

"Yes. And there are more photos back in the office. We ran out of space out here." His voice was distinguishable with its heavy Italian accent. The rich tones flowed through her as seductively as crème brûlée. "We should add your photo."

"Me." She pressed a hand to her chest. "But I'm a nobody."

"You, my dear, are definitely not a nobody." His gaze met hers and heat rushed to her cheeks. "Is everything wrapped up out here?"

Her mouth went dry and she struggled to swallow. "Yes…yes, the last customer just left."

Lines of exhaustion etched the tanned skin around his dark eyes. His lips were lifted in a friendly smile, but something told her that it was all for her benefit and that he didn't feel like doing anything but calling it a night.

"I can't thank you enough for your help this evening." His gaze connected with hers, making her pulse spike. "I suppose you'll be wanting your pay so that you can be on your way. If you would just wait a moment."

Before she could formulate words, he turned and headed to the back of the restaurant. Pay her? For what? Playing hostess for the evening? She supposed that was above and beyond her contract negotiations with the television network.

Dante quickly returned and placed some euros in her hand. His fingers were warm as the backs of his fingers brushed over her palm, causing her stomach to quiver. She quickly pulled her hand away.

"Thank you so much. You truly were a lifesaver." He moved to the door to let her out.

She didn't follow him. She wasn't done here. Not by a long shot. "I'm not leaving. Not yet."

Dante shot her a puzzled look. "If this is about the money, this is the amount I told Luigi I was willing to pay—"

Lizzie shook her head. "It's not that. I came here to meet with Chef Massimo."

"You did? You mean Luigi didn't send you?"

"I don't know any Luigi."

Dante reached in his pocket and pulled out his smartphone. A few keystrokes later, he glanced up. "My mistake. Luigi wasn't able to find anyone to help out. Thank goodness you showed up."

"And I was happy to help. Now if you could introduce me to Chef Massimo."

Dante's forehead creased. "That's not going to happen." His tone was firm and unbendable. "He's not here. You'll have to deal with me."

"I don't think so. I'll wait for him."

Dante rubbed the back of his neck and sighed. "You'll be waiting a long time. Chef Massimo is out of town."

"Listen, I know I'm here a couple of days ahead of time, but we do have an agreement to meet."

"That's impossible." Dante's shoulders straightened and his expression grew serious. "I would have known. I know about everything that has to do with this place."

"Obviously not in this case." Lizzie pressed her lips together, immediately regretting her outburst. She was tired after her long flight and then having to work all evening as a hostess.

"You're obviously mixed up. You should be going." He pulled open the front door, letting a cool evening breeze sweep inside and wrap around her.

She couldn't leave. Her whole future was riding on this internship, and the money from participating in the upcoming cooking show would pay for her sister's grad school. She couldn't let her down. She'd promised Jules that if she got accepted to graduate school she'd make sure there was money for the tuition. Jules had already had so many setbacks in her life that Lizzie refused to fail her.

She stepped up to Dante, and even though she was wearing heeled boots, she still had to tilt her chin upward to look him in the eyes. "I did you a big favor tonight. The least you can do is hear me out."

Dante let the door swing shut and led her back to the dining room, where he pulled out a chair for her before he took a seat across the table. "I'm listening."

Lizzie wished it wasn't so late in the evening. Dante looked wiped out, not exactly the optimal position to gain his understanding. Still, she didn't have any other place to go.

Her elbows pressed down on the white linen tablecloth as she folded her hands together. "Chef Massimo has agreed to mentor me."

Dante's gaze narrowed in on her. "Why is this the first I'm hearing of it?"

"Why should you know about it? My agreement isn't with you."

"Massimo Bianco is my maternal grandfather. And with him away, I'm running this place."

This man wasn't about to give an inch, at least not easily. "When will he return so we can straighten things out?"

Dante leaned back in his chair and folded his arms. His dark eyes studied her. She'd love to know what he was thinking. Then again, maybe not. The past couple of days had been nothing but a blur. She'd rushed to wrap up her affairs in New York City before catching a transatlantic flight. The last thing she'd wanted to do was play hostess, but she figured she'd be a good sport. After all, Dante seemed to be in a really tight spot. But now she didn't understand why he was being so closemouthed about Massimo.

"All you need to know is that my grandfather won't be returning. So any business you have with him, you'll have to deal with me. Tell me about this agreement."

Uneasiness crept down her spine. This man had disbelief written all over his handsome features. But what choice did she have but to deal with him since she had absolutely no idea how to contact Chef Massimo? The only phone number she had was for this restaurant. And the email had also been for the restaurant.

"The agreement is for him to mentor me for the next two months."

Dante shook his head. "It isn't going to happen. I'm sorry you traveled all of this way for nothing. But you'll have to leave now."

Lizzie hadn't flown halfway around the globe just to be turned away—she'd been rejected too many times in her life. Her reasons for being here ran deeper than appearing on the television show. She truly wanted to learn from the best and Massimo Bianco was a renowned chef, whose name on her résumé would carry a lot of weight in the culinary world.

"Surely you could use the extra help." After what she'd witnessed this evening, she had no doubt about it.

"If not for this virus going around, Massimo's would be fully staffed. We don't have room for someone else in the kitchen."

"Obviously Chef Bianco doesn't agree with your assessment. He assured me there would be a spot for me."

Dante's eyes darkened. "He was mistaken. And now that I've heard you out, I must insist that you leave."

These days she proceeded cautiously and was always prepared. She reached in her oversize purse and pulled out the signed document. "You can't turn me away."

When she held out a copy of the contract, Dante's dark brows rose. Suddenly he didn't look as in charge as he had just a few seconds ago. Funny how a binding legal document could change things so quickly.

When he reached for the papers, their fingers brushed. His skin was warm and surprisingly smooth. Their gazes met and held. His eyes were dark and mysterious. Instead of being intimidated by him, she was drawn to him.

Not that she was in Italy to have a summer romance. She had a job to do and this man was standing between her and her future. He may be stubborn, but he'd just met his match.

CHAPTER TWO

WHAT WAS IT about this woman that had him feeling off-kilter?

Could it be the way her touch sent currents of awareness up his arm? Realizing they were still touching, Dante jerked his hand away. He clenched his fingers, creasing the hefty document.

Or maybe it was those cool blue eyes of hers that seemed to study his every move. It was as though she could see more of him than he cared for anyone to observe. Not that he had any secrets to hide—well, other than his plans to sell the *ristorante*.

His gaze scrolled over the first lines of the document, pausing when he saw his grandfather's name followed by Ristorante Massimo. He continued skimming over the legalese until his gaze screeched to a halt at the mention of a television show. His gut twisted into a knot. This was much more involved than he'd ever imagined.

"You said this was for an internship. You didn't mention anything about a television show."

Her lips moved but nothing came out. It was as though she wasn't sure exactly how to proceed. If she thought he was going to make this easy for her, she'd have to think again. She'd tried to get him to agree to let her work here under false pretenses when in fact she had much bigger plans.

When she didn't respond fast enough, he added, "How

long were you planning to keep that little bit of information a secret?"

Her forehead wrinkled. "Obviously I wasn't keeping it a secret or I wouldn't have handed you the contract."

She had a valid point, but it didn't ease his agitation. He once again rubbed at his stiff neck. It'd been an extremely long day. Not only was he short-staffed but also the meeting with the potential buyers for the *ristorante* hadn't gone well. They didn't just want the building. They also wanted the name and the secret recipes that put his grandfather's name up there with the finest chefs.

Dante didn't have the right to sell those recipes—recipes that went back to his grandmother's time. They were special to his grandfather. Still, selling them would keep them alive for others to enjoy instead of them being forgotten in a drawer. But could he actually approach his grandfather and ask for the right to sell them? Those recipes were his grandfather's pride and joy. In fact, employees signed a nondisclosure agreement to maintain the secrecy of Massimo's signature dishes. The thought of selling out left a sour taste in Dante's mouth.

"As you can see in the contract, the television crew will be here on Tuesday." Her words brought Dante back to his latest problem.

"I also see that you've arrived a couple of days early." He wasn't sure what he meant by that statement. He was stalling. Thinking.

"I like to be prepared. I don't like surprises. So I thought I'd get settled in and maybe see some of the sights in Rome. I've heard it's a lovely city."

"Well, since my grandfather isn't going to be able to mentor you, perhaps you can have an extended holiday before heading back to—"

"New York. And I didn't come here for a vacation. I came here to work and to learn." She got to her feet. "Maybe I should just speak with one of the people in the kitchen. Perhaps they can point me in the direction of your grandfather."

"That won't be necessary."

His grandfather didn't need to be bothered with this—he had more important issues to deal with at the moment. Dante could and would handle this woman. After all, there had to be a way out of this. Without reading the rest of the lengthy details, he flipped to the last page.

"It's all signed and legal, if that's what you're worried about." Her voice held a note of confidence, and she sat back down.

She was right. Right there in black and white was his grandfather's distinguished signature. There was no denying the slope of the *M* or the scroll of *Bianco*. Dante resisted the urge to ball up the document and toss it into the stone fireplace across the room from them. Not that it would help since the fire had been long ago extinguished.

He refused to let the sale of the *ristorante*—the deal he'd been negotiating for weeks—go up in smoke because of some promotional deal his grandfather had signed. There had to be a way around it. Dante wondered how much it'd take to convince Lizzie to quietly return to New York.

"I'm sure we can reach some sort of agreement." He was, after all, a DeFiore. He had access to a sizable fortune. "What will it take for you to forget about your arrangement with my grandfather?"

She sat up straighter. "Nothing."

"What do you mean nothing?"

"I mean that I'm not leaving." She leaned forward, pressing her elbows down on the tabletop. "I don't think you understand how serious I am. I've cut out months of my life for this internship. I've said goodbye to my family and friends in order to be here. I had to quit my job. Are you getting the picture? Everything is riding on this agreement—my entire future. I have a signed agreement and I

intend to film a television segment in that kitchen." She
pointed over her shoulder.

She'd quit her job!

Who did something like that? Obviously someone very
trusting or very desperate. Which type was she? Her beautiful face showed lines of stress and the darkness below
her eyes hinted at her exhaustion. He was leaning toward
the desperate scenario.

Perhaps he'd been too rough on her. He really hadn't
meant to upset her. He knew how frustrating it could be
to be so close to getting what you wanted and yet having
a barricade thrown in the way.

"Listen, I know this isn't what you want to hear, but I'm
sure you'll be able to land another job somewhere else—"

"And what are you planning to do about the film crew
when they arrive?"

Dante's lips pressed together. Yes, what was he going
to do? This situation was getting ever so complicated. He
eyed up the woman. Was she on the level? Was she truly
after the work experience? The opportunity to learn? Or
was she an opportunist playing on his sympathies?

He certainly didn't want to spend his time inflating her
ego in front of the camera crew for the next two months—
two very long months. But he was getting the very unsettling feeling that there was no way over, around or under
the arrangement without a lengthy, messy lawsuit, which
would hold up the sale of the *ristorante*.

This was not how things were supposed to go.

Lizzie resisted the urge to get up and start pacing. It was
what she usually did when she was stuck in a tough spot.
While growing up in the foster care system, she'd found
herself in plenty of tough spots. But the one thing she'd
learned through it all was not to give up—if it was important enough, there had to be a solution. It'd worked to keep

Jules, her foster sister, with her through the years. She just had to take a deep breath and not panic.

Dante appeared to be a businessman. Surely he'd listen to logic. It was her last alternative. She sucked in a steadying breath, willing her mind to calm. "If you'll read over the contract, you'll see that your grandfather has agreed not only to mentor me but also to host a television crew. We're doing a reality spot for one of the cooking shows. It's been in the works for months now. Your grandfather was very excited about the project and how it'd give this place—" she waved her hand around at the restaurant that had a very distinct air about it "—international recognition. Just think of all the people that would know the name Ristorante Massimo."

Dante's eyes lit up with interest. "Do you have some numbers to back up your claims?"

She would have brought them, if she'd known she'd need them. "Your grandfather is confident in the value of these television segments. He has made numerous appearances on the culinary channel and has made quite a name for himself."

"I know. I was here for every one of those appearances."

She studied Dante's face for some recollection of him. His tanned skin. His dark eyes. His strong jaw. And those lips… Oh, they looked good enough to kiss into submission… She jerked her attention back to the conversation. "Why don't I recall seeing you in any of them?"

"Because I took a very small role in them. I didn't understand why my grandfather would sign up for those television appearances."

Her gaze narrowed in on him. "Do you have something against people on television?"

"No." He crossed his arms and leaned back, rocking his chair on the rear two legs. "I just think in a lot of cases they misrepresent life. They give people false hope that they'll be overnight successes. Most of the time life doesn't work that way. Life is a lot harder."

There was a glimmer of something in his eyes. Was it regret? Or pain? In a blink, his feelings were once again hidden. She was locked out. And for some reason that bothered her. Not that it should—it wasn't as though they were friends. She didn't even know him.

Not about to waste her time debating the positive and negative points of television, she decided to turn the conversation back around to her reason for being here. "Surely your grandfather will be back soon. After all, he has a restaurant to run."

"I'm afraid that he won't be returning."

"He won't?" This was news to her. Surely he couldn't be right. "But we have an agreement. And he was so eager for us to begin."

Dante rubbed his jaw as though trying to decide if he should say more. His dark gaze studied her intently. It made her want to squirm in her seat but she resisted.

"Whatever you're thinking, just say it. I need to know what's going on."

Dante sighed. "My grandfather recently experienced a stroke. He has since moved to the country."

"Oh, no." She pressed a hand to her chest. This was so much worse than she'd imagined. "Is he going to be all right?"

Dante's brows lifted as though he was surprised by her concern. "Yes, it wasn't as bad as it could have been. He's getting therapy."

"Thank goodness. Your grandfather seemed so lively and active. I just can't imagine that happening to him."

She thought back to their lively emails and chatty phone conversations. Massimo's voice had been rich and robust like a dark roast espresso. He was what she thought of when she imagined having a grandfather of her own. "He was so full of life."

"How exactly did you get to know him?"

Perhaps she'd said too much. It wasn't as if she and Massimo were *that* close. "At first, the production group put us in touch. We emailed back and forth. Then we started talking on the phone, discussing how we wanted to handle the time slots. After all, they are short, so we couldn't get too elaborate. But then again, we didn't want to skimp and do just the basics."

"Sounds like you two talked quite a bit."

She shrugged. "It wasn't like we talked every day. More like when one of us had a good idea. But that was hampered by the time difference. And then recently the calls stopped. When I phoned here I was merely told that he wasn't available and that they'd give him a message."

Dante's eyes opened wide as though a thought had come to him. "I remember seeing those messages. I had no idea who you were or what you wanted. I was beginning to wonder if my grandfather had a girlfriend on the side."

"Nope, it was me. And now that you know the whole story, what's yours?"

"My what?"

"Story. I take it you run this place for your grandfather."

His brows furrowed together as though he knew where this conversation was leading. "Yes, I do."

"Have you worked here long?" She wanted as much information as possible so she could plot out a backup plan.

He hesitantly nodded.

"That must be wonderful to learn from such a talented chef." There had to be a way to salvage this deal. But she needed to know more. "When did you start working with your grandfather?"

"When I was a kid, I would come and visit. But it wasn't until later that I worked here full-time."

She noticed that his answers were vague at best, giving her no clue as to his family life or why he came here to work. Perhaps he needed the money. Still, as she stared across the table at him, his whole demeanor spoke of money and culture. She also couldn't dismiss the fact that most women would find him alarmingly handsome. In fact, he'd make some real eye candy for the television spot. And if that was what it took to draw in an audience, who was she to argue.

She'd been earning money cooking since she was fourteen. Of course, being so young, she'd been paid under the table. Over the years, she'd gained more and more experience, but never thinking she'd ever have a shot at owning a restaurant of her own, she'd taken the safe route and gone to college. She'd needed a way to make decent money to keep herself and Jules afloat.

But then Jules entered her application for a reality TV cooking show. Jules had insisted that she needed to take a risk and follow her dream of being a chef in her own five-star restaurant.

Winning that reality show had been a huge stepping-stone. It gave her a television contract and a plane ticket to Rome, where she'd learn from the best in the business. Jules was right. Maybe her dream would come true.

All she needed was to make sure this deal was a success. One way or the other. And if Chef Massimo couldn't participate then perhaps his grandson would do.

She eyed him up. "Your grandfather must have taught you all of his secrets in the kitchen."

His body noticeably stiffened. "Yes, he did. How else would I keep the place running in his absence?"

She knew it was akin to poking a sleeping bear with a stick, but she had to confirm her suspicions before she altered her plans ever so slightly. "But do your dishes taste like your grandfather's?"

"The customers don't know the difference." The indignity in his voice rumbled through the room. "Who do you think took the time to learn every tiny detail of my grandfather's recipes? My grandfather insisted that if you were going to do something, you should learn to do it right. And there were no shortcuts in his kitchen."

From the little she'd known of Massimo, she could easily believe this was true. During their phone conversations, he'd made it clear that he didn't take shortcuts with his recipes or with training people. She'd have to start from the beginning. Normally, she'd have taken it as an insult, but coming from Massimo, she had the feeling that he only wanted the best for both of them and the television spotlight.

"Will you continue to run the restaurant alone?"

Dante ran a hand over his jaw. "Are you always this curious about strangers?"

She wasn't about to back off. This information was important and she had learned almost everything she needed. "I'm just trying to make a little conversation. Is that so wrong?"

There was a look in his eyes that said he didn't believe her. Still, he didn't press the subject. Instead he surprised her by answering. "For the foreseeable future I will continue to run Massimo's. I can't predict the future."

"I still wonder if you're as good as your grandfather in the kitchen."

"Wait here." He jumped to his feet and strode out of the room.

Where in the world had he gone? She was tempted to follow, but she thought better of it. She'd already pushed her luck as far as she dared. But her new plan was definitely taking shape.

The only problem she envisioned was trying to keep her mind on the art of cooking and not on the hottie mentoring her. She knew jet lag was to blame for her distorted worries. A little uninterrupted sleep would have her thinking clearly.

This arrangement was far too important to ruin due to some sort of crush. She pursed her lips together. No matter how good he looked, she knew better than to let her heart rule her mind. She knew too well the agonizing pain of rejection and abandonment. She wouldn't subject herself to that again. Not for anyone.

She pulled her shoulders back and clasped her hands in her lap. Time to put her plan in motion.

One way or the other.

CHAPTER THREE

How DARE SHE question his prowess in the kitchen?

Dante stared down at a plate of *pasta alla gricia*, one of his favorite dishes. The fine balance of cured pork and *pecorino romano* gave the pasta a unique, tangy flavor. It was a dish he never grew tired of eating.

He proceeded to divvy the food between two plates. After all, he didn't need that much to eat at this late hour. As he arranged the plates, he wondered why he was going to such bother. What was so special about this golden-haired beauty? And why did he feel a compulsion to prove himself where she was concerned?

It wasn't as if he was ever going to see Lizzie again. Without his grandfather around to hold up his end of the agreement, she'd be catching the next plane back to New York. Still, before she left, he needed to prove his point. He'd taken some of his grandfather's recipes and put his own twist on them. And the patrons loved them. This meal was sure not to disappoint the most discerning palate.

He strode back into the dining room and placed a plate in front of Lizzie. She gazed up at him with a wide-eyed blue gaze. Her mouth gaped as though she were about to say something, but no words came out.

He stared at her lush lips, painted with a shimmery pink frost. They looked perfectly ripe for a kiss. The urge grew stronger with each passing second. The breath hitched in his throat.

"This looks delicious." She was staring at him, not the food. And she was smiling.

"It's an old family recipe." He nearly tripped over his own feet as he moved to the other side of the table. "The secret to the dish is to keep it simple and not be tempted to add extras. You don't want to detract from the flavor of the meat and cheese."

He couldn't believe he was letting her good looks and charms get to him. It wasn't as if she was the first beautiful woman he'd entertained. But she was the first that he truly wanted to impress. Safely in his seat, he noticed the smallness of the table. If he wasn't careful, his legs would brush against hers. If this were a casual date, he'd take advantage of the coziness, but Lizzie was different from the usual women he dated. She was more serious. More intent. And she seemed to have only one thing on her mind—business.

"Aren't you going to try it?" Dante motioned to the food. Just because he wasn't interested in helping her with her dreams of stardom didn't mean he couldn't prove his point—he could create magic in the kitchen.

He watched as she spun the pasta on her fork and slipped it in her mouth. He sat there captivated, waiting for her re-action. When she moaned her approval, his blood pressure spiked and his grip tightened on the fork.

"This is very good. Did you make it?"

Her question didn't fool him. He knew what she was digging at—she wanted him to step up and fill in for his grandfather. Him on television—never. That was his grand-father's dream—not his.

"It's delicious." She flashed him a big smile, seemingly unfazed by his tight-lipped expression.

Her smile gave him a strange feeling in his chest that shoved him off center. And that wasn't good. He didn't want to be vulnerable to a woman. He knew for a fact that romance would ultimately lead to disaster—one way or the other.

He forced himself to eat because he hadn't had time to since that morning and his body must be starved. But he didn't really have an appetite. In fact, the food tasted like cardboard. Thankfully Lizzie seemed impressed with it.

When she'd cleaned her plate, she pushed it aside. "Thank you. I can't wait for you to teach me how to make it."

Dante still had a couple of bites left on his plate when he set his fork down and moved the plate aside. "That isn't going to happen."

"Maybe you should at least consider it."

Her gaze strayed to the contract that was still sitting in the middle of the table and then back to him. What was she implying? That she'd drag him through the courts?

That was the last thing he needed. He already had enough important issues on his mind, including fixing his relationship with his family. And the closer it got to putting his signature on the sale papers, the more unsettled he'd become about his decision.

"You can't expect me to fulfill my grandfather's agreement."

"Why not?" She smiled as though it would melt his resistance. Maybe under different circumstances it would have worked, but not now.

"Because I don't want to be on television. I didn't like it when those camera people were here before. All they did was get in the way and create a circus of onlookers wanting to get their faces on television."

He didn't bother to mention that he was just days away from closing a deal to sell Ristorante Massimo. But it all hinged on those family recipes. And somehow parting with those felt treasonous. His grandfather had signed the entire business over to him to do as he pleased, but still he couldn't make this caliber of decision on his own.

But how did he approach his grandfather? How did he tell him that he felt restless again and without Massimo in the kitchen, it just wasn't the same? It was time he moved on to find something that pacified the uneasiness in him.

He'd been toying with the thought of returning to the vineyard and working alongside his father and brother. After all of this time, perhaps he and his father could call a truce—perhaps Dante could in some small way try to make up for the loss and unhappiness his father had endured in the years since Dante's mother had died. But was that even possible considering their strained relationship?

"It isn't me you have to worry about." Lizzie's voice drew him back to the here and now. She toyed with the cloth napkin. "The television people will want to enforce the contract. They're already advertising the segment on their station. I saw it before I left New York. Granted, we won't have a show of our own. But we will have a daily spot on the most popular show on their station."

He'd forgotten that there was a third party to this agreement. A television conglomerate would not be easily deterred from enforcing their rights. "But what makes you think that they would want me instead of my grandfather?"

"I take it your grandfather truly didn't mention any of this to you?"

Dante shook his head. A sick feeling churned in the pit of his stomach.

"That's strange. When he brought your name up to the television people, I thought for sure he'd discussed it with you." She shrugged. "Anyway, they are eager to have you included in the segments. They think you'll appeal to the younger viewers."

Dante leaned his head back and expelled a weary sigh. Why hadn't his grandfather mentioned any of this to him? Maybe Massimo just never got the chance. Regardless, this situation was going from bad to worse. What was next?

When Dante didn't say anything, Lizzie continued, "I'm sure when I explain to them about your grandfather no longer being able to fulfill his role, they will welcome a young, handsome replacement."

She thought he was handsome? He sat up a little straighter. "And if I don't agree—"

"From what I read, there are monetary penalties for not fulfilling the contract. I'm not an attorney but you might want to have someone take a look at it."

A court battle would only extend the time it would take to sell the *ristorante*. Not to mention scare off his potential buyer—the one with deep pockets and an interest in keeping Ristorante Massimo as is.

Dante's gaze moved to the document. "Do you mind if I keep these papers for a little while?"

"That's fine. It's a copy."

"I'll get back to you on this." He got to his feet. He had a lot to think over. It was time to call it a night.

"You'll have to decide soon, as the film crew will be here in a couple of days."

His back teeth ground together. Talk about finding everything out at the last minute. No matter his decision, resolving this issue would take some time. Agreeing to the filming would be much quicker than a court suit. And in the end, would he win the lawsuit?

But then again, could he work with Lizzie for two months and ignore the way her smile made his pulse race? Or the way her eyes drew him in? What could he say? He was a red-hot Italian man who appreciated women. But nothing about Lizzie hinted at her being open to a casual, gratifying experience. And he was not about to get tangled up in something that involved his heart. Nothing could convince him to risk it—not after the carnage he'd witnessed. No way.

He was attracted to her.

Lizzie secretly reveled in the knowledge. Not that either of them would act on it. She'd noticed how he kept his distance, but his eyes betrayed him. She wondered if his demeanor had cooled because of the television show. Or was there something more? Her gaze slipped to his hands, not spying any rings. Still, that didn't mean there wasn't a significant other.

Realizing the implication of what she was doing, she jerked her gaze upward. But that wasn't any better as she ended up staring into his bottomless eyes. Her heart thudded against her ribs. This was not good. Not good at all.

She glanced down at the gleaming black-and-white floor tiles. She could still feel him staring at her. With great effort, she ignored him. Her trip to Rome was meant to be a learning experience, not to partake in a holiday romance.

Putting herself out there and getting involved with Dante was foolish. She had the scars on her heart to prove that romance could come with a high price tag. Besides, she was certain she wouldn't live up to his expectations—she never did.

It was much easier to wear a smile and keep people at arm's length. It was safer. And that was exactly how she planned to handle this situation.

Dante cleared his throat. "Well, since you're a couple of days early, I'm sure you'll want to tour the city. There's lots to see and experience." He led her to the front door. "Make sure you visit the Colosseum and the catacombs."

"I'm looking forward to sightseeing. This is my first trip to Italy. Actually, it's my first trip anywhere." She pressed her lips together to keep from spilling details of her pitiful life. She didn't want his sympathy. She was just so excited about this once-in-a-lifetime experience. Years ago in those foster homes, she never would have imagined that a trip like this would be a possibility—let alone a reality.

"I'd start with the Vatican Museums."

"Thanks. I will."

He smiled as he pulled open the door. The tired lines on his face smoothed and his eyes warmed. She was struck by how truly handsome he was when he let his guard down. She'd have to be careful and not fall for this mysterious Italian.

She glanced out into the dark night. "Is this the way to the apartment?"

His brow puckered. "Excuse me."

"The apartment. Massimo told me that he had a place for me to stay?"

"He did?" Dante uttered the words as though they were part of his thought process and not a question for her.

She nodded and reached into her purse. She fumbled around until her fingers stumbled across some folded papers. Her fingers clasped them and pulled them out.

"I have the email correspondence." She held out the evidence. "It's all right here."

Dante waved away the pages. "Are you this prepared for everything?"

She nodded. She'd learned a long time ago that people rarely keep their word. Just like her mother, who'd promised she'd do whatever it took to get Lizzie back from social services. In the beginning, Lizzie had gone to bed each night crying for the only parent she'd ever known—the mother who was big on neglect and sparing on kindness. At the time, Lizzie hadn't known any other way. In the end, that mother-daughter reunion was not to be. Her mother had been all talk and no follow-through, unable to move past the drugs and alcohol. Lizzie languished in the system.

She'd grown up knowing one simple truth: people rarely lived up to their word. There was only one person to count on—herself.

However, in Massimo's case, breaking his word was totally understandable. It was beyond his control. Her heart squeezed when she thought of that outgoing man being forced into retirement. She truly hoped while she was here that she'd get the opportunity to meet him and thank him for having such faith in her. It was as though he could see through her brave front to her quivering insides. During moments of doubt, he'd calmed her and assured her that all would be fine with the television segments.

She glanced at Dante. He definitely wasn't a calming force like his grandfather. If anything, Dante's presence filled her with nervous energy.

He leaned against the door. "There's no apartment available."

Her eyes narrowed on him. "Does everything with you have to be a struggle?"

"I'm not trying to be difficult. I simply don't have any place for you to stay."

"Why is it your grandfather seemed confident that I would be comfortable here?"

"Probably because there was a remodeled apartment available, but since I wasn't privy to your arrangement with my grandfather, I just leased it. But I'm sure you won't have a problem finding a hotel room nearby."

Oh, yes, there would be a big problem. She didn't have money to rent a hotel room. She could only imagine how expensive that would be and she needed every penny to pay down her debts and to pay tuition for Jules's grad school. Every penny from the contract was already accounted for. There was nothing to spare.

"It was agreed that I would have free room and board." Pride dictated that she keep it to herself that she didn't have the money to get a hotel room.

He crossed his arms and stared at her as though debating his options. "What do you want me to do? Give you my bed?"

The words sparked a rush of tempting images to dance through her mind. Dante leaning in and pressing his very tempting lips to hers. His long, lean fingers grazing her cheek before resting against the beating pulse in her throat. Her leaning into him as he swept her up in his arms.

"Lizzie, are you okay?" Dante's eyes filled with concern.

She swallowed hard, realizing that she'd let her imagination get the best of her. "Umm, yes. I'm just a little jet-lagged. And things were busy tonight, keeping me on my toes."

His eyes probed her. "Are you sure that's all it is?"

She nodded.

Where in the world had those distracting images of Dante come from? It wasn't as though she was looking for a boyfriend. The last man in her life had believed they should each have their own space until one day he dropped by to let her know that he was moving to California to chase his dream of acting. No *I'll miss you*. Or *Will you come with me?*

He'd tossed her aside like the old worn-out couch and the back issues of his rocker magazines. He hadn't wanted her except for a little fun here and there. She'd foolishly let herself believe that they were building something special. In the end, she hadn't been enough for him—she always came up lacking.

"I'd really like to get some rest." And some distance from Dante so she could think clearly. "It's been a long evening and my feet are killing me."

Was that a hint of color rising in his cheeks? Did he feel bad about putting her to work? Maybe he should, but she honestly didn't mind. She liked meeting some of the people she'd hopefully be cooking for in the near future. That was if she ever convinced Dante that this arrangement could work.

"Putting you to work was a total mix-up. My apologies." He glanced down at the floor. "I owe you."

"Apology accepted." She loved that he had manners. "Now, does this mean you'll find me a bed?"

CHAPTER FOUR

THE QUESTION CONJURED up all sorts of scintillating scenarios.

Dante squelched his overactive, overeager imagination. Something told him that there was a whole lot more to this beautiful woman than her desire to be on television and to brush up on her skills in the kitchen. He saw in her eyes a guardedness. He recognized the look because it was something he'd witnessed with his older brother after his young wife had tragically died. It was a look one got when life had double-crossed them.

Lizzie had traveled to the other side of the globe from her home without knowing a single soul, and from the determined set of her mouth, she wasn't about to turn tail and run. She was willing to stand her ground. And he couldn't help but admire her strength.

He just hoped his gut feeling about this woman wasn't off target. What he had in mind was a bold move. But his grandfather, who'd always been a good judge of character, liked her. He surely wouldn't have gone out of his way for her if he hadn't. But that didn't mean Dante should trust her completely, especially when it came to his grandfather.

Nonno had enough on his plate. Since he'd been struck down by a stroke, he'd been lost in a sea of self-pity. Dante was getting desperate to snap his grandfather back into the world of the living. And plying the man with problems when Nonno was already down wouldn't help anyone.

"Have you told me everything now? About your agreement with my grandfather."

She nodded.

"You promise? No more surprises?"

"Cross my heart." Her finger slowly crossed her chest.

Dante cleared his throat as he forced his gaze upward to meet her eyes. "I suppose I do have a place for you to stay."

"Lead the way."

With the main doors locked, he moved next to her on the sidewalk. "It's right over here."

He led the way to a plain red door alongside the restaurant. With a key card, the door buzzed and he pulled it open for her. Inside was a small but lush lobby with an elevator and a door leading to steps. He'd made sure to give the building a face-lift when his grandfather handed over the reins to him. That was all it took to draw in eager candidates to rent the one available unit that he'd been occupying until he'd moved into his grandfather's much larger apartment.

"Where are we going?" She glanced around at the new furnishings adorning the lobby.

"There are apartments over the *ristorante*."

A look of dawning glinted in her eyes. "Your grandfather mentioned those. It's where he intended for me to stay while I am here. Are they nice?"

"Quite nice." In fact the renovations on his apartment had just been completed.

As the elevator doors slid open, she paused and turned to him. "But I thought you said that you leased the last one."

"Do you want to see what I have in mind or not?"

She nodded before stepping inside the elevator.

Good. Because he certainly wasn't going to bend over backward to make her happy. In fact, if she walked away now of her own accord, so much the better. As it was, this arrangement would be only temporary. He'd pacify her until he spoke to his solicitor.

In the cozy confines of the elevator, the faint scent of her floral perfume wrapped around him and teased his senses. If she were anyone else, he'd comment on its intoxicating scent. It was so tempting to lean closer and draw the perfume deeper into his lungs. But he resisted. Something about her led him to believe that she'd want more than one night—more than he was capable of offering her.

The thought of letting go and falling in love made his gut tighten and his palms grow damp. He'd witnessed firsthand the power of love and it wasn't all sappy ballads and roses. Love had the strength to crush a person, leaving them broken and angry at the world.

He placed a key in the pad, turned it and pressed the penthouse button. The hum of the elevator was the only sound. In no time at all the door swished open, revealing a red-carpeted hallway. He led her to his door, adorned with gold emblems that read PH-1.

Dante unlocked the door and waved for her to go ahead of him. He couldn't help but watch her face. She definitely wouldn't make much of a poker player as her emotions filtered across her face. Her blue eyes opened wide as she took in the pillar posts that supported the open floor plan for the living room and kitchen area.

He'd had walls torn down in order to create this spacious area. He may enjoy city life but the country boy in him didn't like to feel completely hemmed in. He'd paid the men bonuses to turn the renovations around quickly. Though it didn't come close in size to his family's home at the vineyard, the apartment was still large—large enough for two people to coexist without stepping on each other's toes. At least for one night.

She walked farther into the room. She paused next to the black leather couch and turned to him. "Do you live here alone?"

"I do. My grandfather used to live here. When he got

sick, he turned it over to me. I made some changes and had everything updated."

"It certainly is spacious. I think I'd get lost in a place this size." Her stiff posture said that she was as uncomfortable as he felt.

He wasn't used to having company. He'd been so busy since his grandfather's sudden exit from the *ristorante*— from his life—that he didn't have time for a social life. In fact, now that he thought about it, Lizzie was the first woman he'd had in here. He wasn't sure how he felt about that fact.

"Can I get you anything?" he asked, trying to ease the mounting discomfort.

"Yes—you can tell me what I'm doing here."

Oh, yes. He thought it was obvious but apparently it wasn't to her. "You can stay here tonight until we can get this whole situation cleared up."

"You mean when you consent to the contents of this contract."

His jaw tightened, holding back a string of heated words.

"Don't look like it's the end of the world." Lizzie stepped up to him. "With your good looks, the camera is going to love you. And that's not to mention the thousands of women watching the segment. Who knows, maybe you'll become a star."

Dante laughed. Him a star. Never. Her lush lips lifted. The simple expression made her eyes sparkle like blue topaz. Her pale face filled with color. And her lips, they were plump and just right to lean in and snag a sweet taste. His head started to lower when she pulled back as though reading his errant thoughts.

He cleared his throat and moved to the kitchenette to retrieve a glass. "Are you sure you don't want anything to drink?"

"I'm fine. Have you lived here long?"

He ran the water until it was cold—real cold. What he

really needed to do was dump it over his head and shock some sense back into himself.

"I've lived in this building since I moved to Rome. I had a smaller apartment on another floor before moving to this one. You're my first guest here." He turned, waiting to hear more about what she thought of the place. "What do you think of it?"

He was genuinely curious about her take on the place. It was modeled in black-and-white decor. With the two colors, it made decorating easier for him. He sensed that it still needed something, but he couldn't put his finger on what exactly was missing.

"It's…it's nice." Her tone was hesitant.

Nice? The muscles in his neck tightened. Who said "nice"? Someone who was trying to be polite when they really didn't like something but they didn't want to hurt the other person's feelings.

She leaned back on the couch and straightened her legs. She lifted her arms over her head and stretched. He tried to ignore how her blouse rode up and exposed a hint of her creamy skin. But it was too late. His thoughts strayed in the wrong direction again. At this rate, he'd need a very cold shower.

He turned his attention back to the apartment and glanced around, trying to see it from her perspective. Everything was new. There wasn't a speck of dust—his cleaning lady had just been there. And he made sure to always pick up after himself. There wasn't a stray sock to be had anywhere.

"Is it the black-and-white decor you don't like?" He really wanted to know. Maybe her answer would shed some light on why he felt something was off about the place.

"I told you, I like it."

"But describing it as *nice* is what people say to be polite. I want to know what's missing." There, he'd said it.

There was something missing and it was going to drive him crazy until he figured it out.

He looked around at the white walls. The modern artwork. The two pieces of sculpture. One of a stallion rearing up. The other of a gentle mare. They reminded him of home. When he turned around, he noticed Lizzie unzipping her boots and easing them off. Her pink-painted toes stretched and then pointed as though she were a ballerina as she worked out all of the muscles. When she murmured her pleasure at being free of the boots, he thought he was going to lose it. It took every bit of willpower to remain in his spot and not go to her.

He turned his back. He tried to think of something to do. Something to keep him from going to her. But there was nothing that needed straightening up. No dirty dishes in the sink. In fact, he spent very little time here. For the most part, he slept here and that was it. The rest of his time was spent either downstairs in the *ristorante* or at the vineyard, checking on his grandfather.

"You know what's missing?" Her voice drew his attention.

He turned around and tried to ignore the way her short black skirt had ridden even higher on her thighs. "What would that be?"

"There are no pictures. I thought there'd be one of you with your grandfather."

Dante glanced around, realizing she was right. He didn't have a single picture of anyone. "I'm sorry. I don't have any pictures here. They are all at my family's home."

"Do they live far from here?"

He shrugged. "It's a bit of a drive. But not that far. I like to go home on the weekends."

"But isn't the restaurant open?"

"It's open Saturday. But then we're closed Sunday and Monday. So my weekend is not the traditional weekend."

"I see. And your grandfather, is he with your family?"

Dante nodded. "He lives with my father and older brother."

Her brows drew together but she didn't say anything. He couldn't help but be curious about her thoughts. Everything about this woman poked at his curiosity.

"What are you wondering?"

She shook her head. "Nothing."

"Go ahead. Say what's on your mind."

"You mentioned a lot of men. Are there no women?"

"Afraid not. Unless you count my aunts, but they don't live there even though they are around so much that it feels like they do." He didn't want to offer a detailed explanation of why there were no women living at the vineyard. He tried to avoid that subject at all costs. He took it for granted that the DeFiore men were to grow old alone. But that was a subject best left for another day.

"Sounds like you have a big family."

"That's the understatement of the century." Anxious to end this line of conversation, he said, "We should get some sleep. Tomorrow will be here before we know it."

"You're sure you want me to stay here?" She stared directly at him.

Their gazes connected and held. Beyond the beauty of her eyes, there was something more that drew him to her—a vulnerability. In that moment, he longed to ride to her rescue and sweep her into his arms. He'd hold her close and kiss away her worries.

Lizzie glanced away, breaking the special moment.

Was she thinking the same thing as him? Did she feel the pull of attraction, too? Not that he was going to act on his thoughts. It wasn't as though he couldn't keep himself in check. He could and would be a gentleman.

"I'll deal with it. After all, you said this is what my grandfather agreed to. There are a couple of guest rooms down the hallway." He pointed to the right. And then for good measure he added, "And the master suite is in that direction." His hand gestured to the left. "Plenty of room for both of us."

"My luggage hasn't arrived yet. I have nothing to sleep in."

"I can loan you something."

Just as he said that, there was a buzz from the intercom. He went to answer it. In seconds, he returned to her. "Well, you don't have to worry. Your luggage has arrived."

She smiled. "That's great."

A moment of disappointment coursed through him. What in the world was the matter with him? Why should he care one way or the other if she slept in one of his shirts or not? Obviously he was more tired than he'd thought.

CHAPTER FIVE

LIZZIE GRINNED AND STRETCHED, like a cat that had spent the afternoon napping in the sunshine. She glanced around the unfamiliar surroundings, noticing the sun's rays creeping past the white sheers over the window. She rubbed her eyes and then fumbled for her cell phone. She was shocked to find that she'd slept away half of the morning. It was going to take her a bit to get her internal alarm clock reset.

Last night, she'd been so tired that she'd barely gotten off a text message to Jules to assure her that she'd arrived safely before sleep claimed her. This was the first time in their lives that they'd been separated for an extended period and Lizzie already missed her foster sister, who was also her best friend. She had promised to call today to fill her in on her trip. But after converting the time, Lizzie realized it was too early in New York to call.

She glanced around, not surprised to find the room done up in black and white. The man may be drop-dead gorgeous but when it came to decorating, he definitely lacked imaginative skills. What this place needed was some warmth—a woman's touch.

She thought back to his comment about her being his first guest here. She found that surprising. For some reason, she imagined someone as sexy and charming as him having a woman on each arm. Perhaps there was more to this man than his smooth talk and devastating smile. What was the real Dante like? Laid-back and flirtatious? Serious and a workaholic?

She paused and listened for any sounds from him. But then again, with an apartment this big, she doubted she'd hear him in the kitchen. She'd be willing to bet that her entire New York apartment could fit in this bedroom. She'd never been in such a spacious home before. Not that she'd have time to get used to it. She was pretty certain that Dante was only mollifying her. Today he would have a plan to get her out of his life and his restaurant.

With that thought in mind, Lizzie sprang out of bed and rushed into the glass block shower enclosure with more water jets than she'd ever imagined were possible. But instead of enjoying the shower, she wondered what Dante's next move would be concerning the agreement.

Almost thirty minutes later, her straight blond hair was smoothed back into the normal ponytail that she wore due to its ease at pinning it up in the kitchen. She slipped on a dark pair of designer jeans. Lizzie didn't recognize the name, but the lady at the secondhand store had assured her that they were the in thing right now.

Lizzie pulled on a white tiny tee with sparkly silver bling on the front in the shape of a smiley face. It was fun, and today she figured she just might need something uplifting. There were decisions to be made.

After she stepped into a pair of black cotton shoes, she soundlessly made her way to the living room, finding it deserted. Where could Dante be? She recalled their conversation last night and she was certain that he'd said the restaurant was closed today.

"Dante?" Nothing. "Dante?" she called out, louder this time.

Suddenly he was standing in the hallway that led to the master suite. "Sorry, I didn't hear you. Have you been up long?"

She shook her head. "I'm afraid that my body is still on New York time."

"I've spoken to my grandfather."

Lizzie's chest tightened. "What did he say?"

Dante paused, making her anxiety even worse. She wanted to yell at him to spit it out. Did Massimo say something that was going to change how this whole scenario played out?

"He didn't say much. I'm getting ready to go see him."

She waited, hoping Dante would extend an invitation. When he didn't, she added, "How far did you say the vineyard is from here?"

He shrugged. "An hour or so out of the city."

She glanced toward the elongated window. "It's a beautiful day for a drive."

He said nothing.

Why wasn't he taking the hint? If she laid it on any thicker, she'd have to invite herself along. She resisted the urge to stamp her feet in frustration. Why wouldn't he give in and offer her a ride? She'd already mentioned how much she enjoyed talking to his grandfather on the phone.

Maybe Dante just wasn't good with hints, no matter how bold they were. Perhaps she should try another approach—a direct one.

"I'd like to meet your grandfather."

Dante shook his head. "That isn't going to happen."

Oh, no. She wasn't giving up that easily. "Why not? When we talked on the phone, he was very excited about my arrival."

"Things have changed since then." Dante walked over and grabbed his keys from the edge of the kitchen counter. "It just wouldn't be a good idea."

"Did you even tell him that I was here?"

Dante's gaze lowered. "In passing."

He was leaving something out but what? "And did you discuss the contract?"

"No. He had a bad night and he was agitated this morning. I didn't think him hearing about what has transpired since your arrival would help things." He cursed under his breath and strode over to the door and grabbed his overnight bag.

He was leaving without her.

Disappointment washed over her. She just couldn't shake her desire to meet the man who reminded her of what she imagined her grandfathers would have been like, if she'd ever met either of her own. But she couldn't tell Dante that. He'd think she was a sentimental dreamer—and she couldn't blame him.

How could she ever explain to someone who grew up in a big, caring family with parents and grandparents about the gaping hole in her heart? She'd forever been on the outside looking in. She knew all too well that families weren't perfect. Her friends in school had dealt with a whole host of family dynamics, but they had a common element—love to bind them together, no matter what. And to have her very own family was what Lizzie had prayed for each night. And at Christmastime it had been the only thing she had ever asked for from Santa.

Instead of a mom and dad and grandparents, she was given Jules—her foster sister. And she loved her with all of her heart. She would do anything for her, including keeping her promise to help Jules reach for her dreams—no matter the price. Because of their dismal finances, Jules had to put off college for a couple of years until Lizzie got her degree. Jules always talked of helping other kids like them. This was Jules's chance to become a social worker and make a difference, but in order to do that she had to get through grad school first.

Massimo had been insistent that her plan would work. He'd been so certain. And she couldn't shake her desire to meet him and thank him for his encouragement. "Take me with you. I promise I won't say or do anything to upset your grandfather."

Dante eyed her up as though attempting to gauge her sincerity. She sent him a pleading look. Under the intensity of his stare, her insides quivered. But she refused to turn away.

"Even though he insists on meeting you, I will leave you behind if I feel I can't trust you."

"So he does want to meet me." This time she did smile.

"Don't go getting all excited. I still haven't made up my mind about taking you with me. You know it's a bit of a ride."

Meaning Dante didn't like the thought of spending yet more time alone with her. To be honest, she couldn't blame him. She'd basically dropped into his life out of nowhere with absolutely no warning. How could she possibly expect him to react any different?

But then again, she had noticed the way he'd looked at her last night. As if she were an ice cream cone on a sweltering hot day and he couldn't wait to lick her up. To be fair, she'd had similar thoughts about him. No one had ever turned her on with just a look.

She halted her thoughts. It wasn't worth it to go down this path. It'd only lead to heartbreak—her heartbreak. In her experience, men only wanted an uncomplicated good time. And she couldn't separate her heart and her mind. It was so much easier to remain detached. If she was smart, she'd turn and leave now. But she couldn't. Not yet.

"You can trust me," she pleaded. "I won't upset Massimo."

"I don't know—"

"If you won't take me to him, then give me his address. I'll find my own way there."

Not that she had any clue how she'd get from point A to point B without a vehicle, but she was certain that Italy had public transportation. That was one of the things she'd discovered when she'd researched coming here. So now Dante wouldn't stand between her and meeting Massimo.

Dante hated being put in this position.

All he wanted to do was protect his grandfather—well, that wasn't quite the whole truth. He didn't relish the car ride with Lizzie. He was certain she'd keep at him, trying to convince him to change his mind about the television spot. His jaw tightened. He had other priorities with the sale of the *ristorante* to negotiate.

Then this morning when he'd phoned his grandfather to verify that he'd agreed to this television segment, his grandfather had come to life at the mention of Lizzie's name. After weeks of Nonno being in a black mood, this was the first time he'd sounded even remotely like himself. Dante made every excuse to get out of taking Lizzie to meet him. His grandfather would have none of it.

Unwilling to disappoint his grandfather, he said, "You can come with me on one stipulation."

Hope glinted in her eyes. "Name it."

"There will be no talking about the contract or the cooking show this weekend."

"But the camera crew will be here Tuesday morning expecting to begin filming before the restaurant opens. What will we do? We haven't even decided how to proceed."

"Let me deal with them." He'd already called his solicitor that morning. Even though it was the weekend, this couldn't wait. He'd pay the exorbitant fees. Whatever it took to find a way out of this mess.

She narrowed her gaze. "You're going to break the contract, aren't you?"

"Why wouldn't I? I never agreed to give up two months of my life."

"But I…I can't repay the money."

"What money?"

She glanced away and moved to the window that looked

out over the street. "They paid me a portion of the fee up front. And it's already been spent. I can't repay them."

That wasn't his problem. But his conscience niggled at him. All in all, Lizzie wasn't bad. In fact, she was smokin' hot. And when she smiled it was as though a thousand-watt lightbulb had been switched on. But when she opened her mouth—well, that was a different story. She knew instinctively which buttons of his to push.

He wanted to think that she was lying to him just to gain his sympathy, but his gut was telling him that she was being truthful. Those unshed tears in her eyes—those were genuine. There had to be a compromise but he didn't know what that would be at this point.

Until he figured out what that was, he had to say something to ease her worry. "I can't promise you this will work out for you. But if you quit worrying while we're away, I give you my word that I'll share what my solicitor uncovers before I make any moves."

She hitched a slender hip and tilted her head to the side. He couldn't help but smile at the way she was eyeing him, trying to decide if she should trust him. He supposed he deserved it. He had just done the same thing to her.

The strained silence stretched on, making him uncomfortable. "Okay, you've made your point. I'll trust you not to pull the *poor pitiful me* card around my grandfather, if you'll trust me not to take any action without consulting you."

Why did he feel as if he'd just struck up a losing deal? For a man used to getting his way, this was a very unsettling feeling.

CHAPTER SIX

THIS WOULD IMPRESS HER.

Dante maneuvered his low-slung, freshly waxed, candy-apple-red sports car around the street corner and slowed to a crawl as he approached the front of the *ristorante*. Lizzie stood on the sidewalk with an overnight bag slung over her shoulder and her face lifted toward the sun. She didn't appear to notice him. The sun's rays gave her golden mane a shimmery glow. He wondered if she had any clue how her beauty commanded attention. Something told him she didn't. There was an unassuming air about her.

Without taking time to consider his actions, he tramped the brakes and reached for his smartphone to snap her picture. It wasn't until he returned it to the dash that he realized how foolish he was acting. Like some schoolkid with a crush on the most popular girl in school.

Back then he'd been so unsure of himself—not knowing how to act smooth around the girls. That all changed after he moved to Rome. Away from his father and brother, he'd grown more confident—more at ease with the ladies.

His older brother, though, always had a way with the women…but Stefano had eyes for only one girl, even back in school. They'd been childhood sweethearts until it came to a devastating end. The jarring memory brought Dante up short.

He eased the car forward and parked next to Lizzie.

He jumped out and offered to take her bag, but she didn't release her hold. In fact, her grip tightened on the straps. What in the world?

"I just want to put it in the boot. There's no room inside the car. As you can see, it's rather compact."

She cast him a hesitant look before handing over the bag. He opened the door for her. Once she was seated, he stowed her bag with his. He was surprised how light she packed. He'd never met a woman who didn't need everything including the kitchen sink just to go away for the night. Lizzie was different in so many ways.

And now it was his chance to impress her with his pride and joy. Anytime he wanted to make a surefire impression on a woman, he pulled out Red. He'd bestowed the name upon the luxury sports car, not just because of its color but because the name implied an attitude, a fieriness, and that was how he felt when he was in the driver's seat.

"Ready?" He glanced at her as she perched a pair of dark sunglasses on her face, hiding her expressive eyes.

"Yes. I'm surprised you'd choose to drive."

"Why wouldn't I drive?" He revved the engine just because he could, and he loved how the motor roared with power.

Who complained about riding in a fine machine like this one? He'd dreamed about a powerful car like this all of his life, but his father made him wait—made him earn it on his own without dipping into his trust fund. At the time Dante had resented his father for standing in his way. Now Dante found himself grateful for the challenge. He'd learned an important lesson—he could accomplish whatever he set his mind to. Even his father had been impressed with the car, not that he'd said much, but Dante had seen it in his eyes the first time he'd driven up to the villa.

Lizzie adjusted her seat belt. "I thought I read somewhere that people utilize public transportation here."

He glanced at her as he slowed for a stop sign. Was she

serious? She'd prefer the train to his car? Impossible. "I thought the car would be more convenient. We can come and go as we need."

"Oh. Right. And do you always run stop signs?"

"What?"

"There was a stop sign back there. Didn't you see it?"

"Of course I did. Didn't you notice how I slowed down and checked that there was no cross traffic?"

"But you didn't stop."

His jaw tightened as he adjusted his grip on the steering wheel. "Are you always such a stickler for rules?"

"Yes. Is that a problem?"

"It depends."

Silence settled over them as Dante navigated them out of the city. Every now and then he sneaked a glance at Lizzie. She kept her face turned to the side. The tires clicked over the brick roadway as Rome passed by the window. The cars, the buildings and the people. He'd never been to New York City and he couldn't help but wonder if it was as beautiful as Rome. The lush green trees planted along stretches of roadway softened the view of block-and-mortar buildings. Thankfully it was Sunday, so the roadway wasn't congested with standstill traffic.

They quickly exited the city. Now was his chance to find out a little bit more about her before she met his grandfather. His gut told him there was a lot she was holding back. It was his duty to make sure there weren't any unpleasant surprises that might upset his grandfather. Dante assured himself that his interest was legitimate. It had absolutely nothing to do with unraveling the story behind the sad look in her eyes when she thought no one was watching her.

"Where in New York do you come from?"

Out of the corner of his eye he noticed how her head swung around quickly. "The Bronx. Why?"

"Just curious. I figured if we're going to be spending

some time together, we might as well get to know a little about each other."

There was a poignant moment of silence as though she were deciding if this was a good idea or not. "And were you raised at this vineyard we're going to visit?"

Fair was fair. "Yes, I was. It's been in my family for generations. But it has grown over the years. And now our vino is a household name."

"That's an impressive legacy. So how did you end up in Rome helping your grandfather run a restaurant?"

How in the world did this conversation get totally turned around? They were supposed to be talking about her—not him. "It's a long story. But I really enjoyed the time I spent working with my grandfather. I'll never forget my time at Ristorante Massimo."

"You make it sound like you're leaving."

Dante's fingers tightened on the steering wheel. He had to be more careful with what he said. He could feel her puzzled gaze as she waited for him to affirm or deny her suspicions. That he couldn't do. He hadn't even told his family yet that he was planning to sell the place. There was always one excuse or another to put off the announcement.

But now that the negotiations were winding down, he was out of time. He needed to get his grandfather's blessing to include the family's recipes as part of the sale. Dante's gut tightened.

And the other reason he hesitated to bring it up was that he knew his father would use it as one more thing against him. His father always blamed him for Dante's mother's death during childbirth. Though logically Dante knew he wasn't responsible, he still felt the guilt of playing a part in his father's unhappiness. The man he'd known as a child wore a permanent scowl and he couldn't recall ever seeing his father smile. Not once.

When they communicated it was only because Dante

hadn't done a chore or hadn't done it "correctly." Who could blame him for moving away to the city?

But over the years, his father seemed to have changed— mellowed. He wasn't so critical of Dante. But was it enough to rebuild their relationship?

"Dante, are you planning to leave the restaurant? Is that why you're hesitant to help me?"

What was it about this woman that she could read him so well? Too well. "Why would you say that?"

Before she could respond, the strums of music filled the car. He hadn't turned on the stereo and that certainly wasn't his phone's ringtone.

"Oh, no!" Lizzie went diving for her oversize black purse that was on the floor beneath the dash.

"Something wrong?"

"I told my sister to only call me if there was an emergency." She scrambled through her purse. With the phone pressed to her ear, she sounded breathless when she spoke. "Jules, what's the matter?"

Dante glanced at Lizzie, noticing how the color had drained from her face. He wasn't the sort to eavesdrop, but it wasn't as if he could go anywhere. Besides, if she was anything like his younger cousins, it was most likely nothing more than a romantic crisis or a hair emergency—at least he hoped so for Lizzie's sake.

Most of the time when he was out in public, he grew frustrated with people who had their phones turned up so loud that you could hear both sides of the conversation. Lizzie obviously felt the same way as him, as hers was turned down so low that he couldn't hear the caller's voice. Lizzie wasn't much help as she only uttered things like: "Okay."

"Yes."

"Mmm…hmm…"

When her hand started waving around as she talked, Dante didn't know if he should pull over or keep driving.

"He can't do that!"

Who couldn't do what? Was it a boyfriend? Had he done something to her sister? The fact that Lizzie might have a man waiting for her in New York gave him an uneasy sensation.

At last, Lizzie disconnected the call and sank back against the leather upholstery. He wasn't sure what to say because he didn't have a clue what the problem might be. That, and he wasn't very good with upset women. He didn't have much experience in that department as he preferred to keep things light and casual.

Unable to stand the suspense, he asked, "Problems with your boyfriend?"

"Not a chance. I don't have one."

He breathed a little easier. "But I take it there's an emergency?"

"That depends on if you call getting tossed out of your apartment a problem."

"That serious, huh?"

"That man is so greedy, he'd sell his own mother if it'd make him an easy dollar."

"Who's greedy?"

"The landlord. He says he's converting the building into condos."

Dante was truly sorry for Lizzie's plight. He couldn't imagine what it'd be like to get kicked out of your home. Even though he and his father had a tenuous relationship, leaving the vineyard had been completely Dante's idea.

He pulled the car off the road. "Do I need to turn the car around?"

She glanced at him, her brows scrunched up in puzzlement. "Why would you do that?"

"So that you can catch a flight back to New York."

"That's not necessary."

Not necessary. If he was getting evicted, he'd be hightailing it home to find a new place to live. He must be missing something. But what?

"Don't you want to go back and figure out where you're going to live? I can't imagine in such a populated city that it'll be easy to find another place to your liking."

She clucked her tongue. "Are you trying to get rid of me?"

"What?" His tone filled with indignation, but a sliver of guilt sliced through him. "I'm just concerned."

"Well, you don't have to be concerned because the landlord gave us plenty of notice."

"He did?" Lizzie's gaze narrowed on him as he stammered to correct himself. "I…I mean, that's great. Are you sure you'll have time to find another place?"

"My, aren't you worried about my welfare. What could have brought on this bit of concern? Wait, could it be that you thought this might be your out with the contract?"

"No." The word came out far too fast. He wished he were anywhere but in this much-too-small car. There was nowhere to go. No way to avoid her expectant look. "Okay, it might have crossed my mind. But I still wouldn't wish someone to get kicked out of their home just to save me grief."

She laughed.

The sound grated on his nerves. "What's so funny?"

"The guilty look on your face. You're cute. Like a little boy caught with his hand in the proverbial cookie jar."

Great. Now he'd just been reduced to the level of a cute little kid. Talk about taking direct aim at a guy's ego. He eased the car back onto the road. If he'd ever entertained striking up a more personal relationship with Lizzie, it just came to a screeching halt right there. How did one make a comeback from being "cute"?

"So you aren't mad at me now?" He chanced a quick glance her way as she shook her head.

"I can't blame you for wanting an easy solution to our

problem. And after watching how much you worry about your grandfather, I realized that you aren't the sort to revel in others' misfortune."

Wow, she'd read all of that into him not wanting her to drag his grandfather into the middle of their situation? He was truly impressed. But that still didn't erase the *cute little boy* comment. His pride still stung.

After a few moments of silence passed, he turned to the right onto a private lane. "We're here. Are you up for this?"

CHAPTER SEVEN

SHE WAS MOST definitely ready for this adventure.

Lizzie gazed out the car window at the rolling green hills and lines of grapevines. This place was a beauty to behold. Did a more picturesque place exist? She didn't think so.

Of course, it didn't hurt that she was in the most amazing sports car, being escorted by the sexiest man on the planet. But she refused to let Dante know how truly captivated she was by him. She couldn't let him have any more leverage. They still had a contract to iron out.

And whereas he appeared to have plenty of money to hire his own legal dream team, she didn't have two pennies to rub together. She had to play her cards carefully, and by letting him know that she was vulnerable to his gorgeous smile and drawn in by his mesmerizing gaze, she would have lost before she even started.

They pulled to a stop in front of a spacious villa situated atop a hill overlooking the sprawling vineyard and olive grove. The home's lemon-yellow exterior was offset by a red tile roof and pale blue shutters lining the windows and doors. The three-story structure gave off a cheerful appeal that called to Lizzie.

Her gaze came to rest on a sweeping veranda with blue-and-white lawn furniture, which added an inviting quality. What a perfect place to kick back while enjoying a gentle breeze over her sun-warmed skin and sipping an icy lemonade.

"This is where you live?"

Dante cut the engine. "This is where my family lives."

"It's so big."

"It has to be to accommodate so many generations. It seems like every generation expands or adds something."

She especially liked the private balconies. She could easily imagine having her morning coffee there while Dante read the newspaper. "I couldn't even imagine what it would be like to call this my home."

"A little smothering."

"Smothering? You can't be serious." She turned, taking in the endless fields.

He shrugged. "When you have so many people keeping an eye on you constantly, it can be."

"But there's just your grandfather, father and brother, isn't it?"

"You're forgetting about all of my aunts, uncles and cousins. They stop over daily. There's never a lack of relatives. In fact, the dinner table seats twelve and never has an empty chair. They disapproved of my father not remarrying. So they made a point of ensuring my brother and I had a woman's influence."

"And did it work?"

"What? Oh, you mean the woman's-influence thing. I guess it helped. I just know that it was annoying always tripping over family members."

She frowned at him. "You should be grateful that they cared enough!"

His eyes grew round at her agitated tone. "I…I am."

She didn't believe him.

She couldn't even imagine how wonderful it would be to have so much family. He took it all for granted, not having sense enough to count his blessings. She'd have done anything to have a big, loving family.

"Not everyone is as lucky as you." With that, she got

out of the car, no longer wanting to hear how hard Dante had it putting up with his relatives.

He was the luckiest person she knew. He wasn't much older than herself and he already owned his very own restaurant—a successful one at that. Not to mention his jaw-dropping apartment. And she couldn't forget his flashy sports car. And on top of all that, he had a family that cared about him. Stacked up against her life, she was left lacking. She was up to her eyeballs in debt. And without the money from this television spot, she didn't know how she'd survive.

But how did she explain any of that to him? How would he ever understand when he couldn't even appreciate what he had? She'd met people like him before—specifically a guy in college. He was an only child—and spoiled. He thought he understood what hardship was when he had to buy a used car to replace the brand-new one his parents had bought him—a car he'd wrecked while out partying with the guys. She stifled the groan of frustration that rose in her throat. Hardship was choosing between paying the rent or buying groceries.

A gentle breeze brushed over her cheeks and whipped her hair into her face. She tucked the loose strands behind her ear. The air felt good. It eased her tense muscles, sweeping up her frustration and carrying it away.

In this particular case, she'd overreacted. Big-time. She had better keep a firmer grip on her emotions or soon Dante would learn about her past. She didn't want him to look down on her like she was less than everyone else since her mother hadn't loved her enough to straighten out her life and her father was someone without a name—a face. The breath caught in her throat.

She hated that being around Dante was bringing all of these old feelings of inadequacy to the surface. She'd buried them long ago. Coming here was a mistake. Nursing her dream of finding out what it would be like to have a grandfather—a family—was opening Pandora's box and her past was spilling out.

What had set her off?

Dante darted out of the car, but then froze. Lizzie's back was to him. Her shoulders were rigid. Her head was held high. He didn't want to do battle with her. Especially not here, where his family could happen upon them at any moment.

But more than that, he didn't have a clue what he'd done wrong. Did she have that strong an opinion about families? And if so, why?

His questions about her only multiplied. And as much as he'd set out to learn more about his flatmate on the ride here, he truly believed he had gained more questions than answers. Sure, he'd learned that she appeared to be very close with her sister and that she was about to get evicted. Oh, and she was a stickler for following the rules—especially the rules of the road. But there was so much more she was holding back. Things he wanted to know. But that would have to wait.

He could only hope that he could smooth things over with her before his father descended upon them. He didn't need her giving his family the impression that he didn't know how to treat a lady. His father already held enough things against him without adding to the list.

He rounded the car and stopped in front of her. "Hey, I don't know what I said back there, but I'm sorry. You must miss your family."

Her head lowered and her shoulders drooped. "It's me that should apologize. I guess it was just hearing Jules's voice made me realize it's going to be a long time before I will see her again. We've never been apart for an extended period like this."

So that was it. She was homesick. That was totally understandable. Maybe his family could help fill that gap. They certainly were a chatty, friendly bunch—even if they could be a bit overbearing at times.

"Why don't we go inside? I'm sure my father and brother are out in the fields. They keep a close eye on the vines and soil. But my grandfather will be around. Not to mention an aunt or two."

She smiled. "Thanks for including me. I'm really excited to meet your family."

"They're looking forward to meeting you, too."

"They know I'm coming?" When he nodded, she said, "But you made it sound like you'd planned to come without me."

"I had, but my grandfather had other ideas. He insisted I bring you to meet him. He told the family while I was on the phone."

"Would you have really left me behind if I hadn't promised to keep quiet about the contract?"

Dante shrugged. "I guess we'll never know. Just remember our agreement. Don't say or do anything to upset my grandfather."

Her eyes flared with indignation. But before she could say a word, there were footsteps on the gravel.

"Dante, who's your guest?"

He didn't even have to turn around to recognize his older brother's voice. Stefano was the eldest. The son who did no wrong. He'd stayed on at the villa and helped their father run the vineyard as was expected of the DeFiore men. But what no one took into consideration was that Stefano always got along with their father. He wasn't the one their father held responsible for their mother's death.

Dante turned on his heels. "Stefano, this is Lizzie."

Stefano stepped up, and when she extended her hand, he accepted it and kissed the back of it. Dante's blood pressure spiked. What was his brother doing? Wasn't he the forlorn widower?

Not that Dante wished for his brother to be miserable the rest of his life. In fact, he wished that Stefano would be able to move past the nightmare and get on with his life, but Stefano seemed certain that he would remain a bachelor…which seemed to be the destiny of the DeFiore men.

Dante had learned much from his family, especially to keep his guard up around women. He had zero intention of getting caught up in the tangled web of love. It only led to pain. Something he could live without.

While Stefano made idle chitchat with Lizzie, Dante noticed how her face lit up. He swallowed down his agitation. "Is Nonno in the house?"

Stefano turned to him. His whole demeanor changed into something more stoic—more like the brother he knew. "Of course. Where else would you expect him to be?"

Dante rolled his eyes and started for the house. When he realized that Lizzie had remained behind with his brother, he turned and signaled for her to follow him. She smiled at Stefano—a great big, ear-to-ear, genuine smile that lit up the world like a starburst. Dante's jaw tightened.

Why couldn't she be that happy around him? Why did she have to act so reserved—so on guard? After all, he was a nice guy, too. Or so he'd been told by some lady friends. Surely he hadn't lost his touch with the women. Maybe he'd have to try a little harder.

When Lizzie joined him, he said, "My grandfather is probably getting impatient. We should go see him."

Lizzie kept her smile in place and he couldn't help but wonder if it was part of their agreement to keep the mood light and happy. Or perhaps it was lingering happiness from meeting his older brother—Mr. Tall, Dark and Persuasive.

Not that it mattered if Lizzie had a thing for Stefano. It wasn't as if Dante was interested in the woman who was threatening the deal he'd been working for weeks to finalize. And it rankled him that he now felt some sort of responsibility toward Lizzie. Not only did he have to take into consideration what was best for the business, but also he felt compelled to take into account how it impacted her.

Dante stepped into the sunroom. "Nonno."

His grandfather's silver head lifted from reading a newspaper. He removed his reading glasses, focused on Dante and then his gaze moved to Lizzie. A lopsided smile pulled at his lips. Dante inwardly sighed at the effect Lizzie had over the men in his family. They stared at her as if she were a movie star. Well...she was pretty enough. Still, they didn't have to act as though they'd never seen a beautiful female before. Then again, it had been a very long time since a woman that wasn't a relative had visited the DeFiore villa. Okay, so maybe they had a reason to sit up and take notice. He just wished they didn't make it so noticeable.

"Come here." Nonno's deep voice was a bit slurred from the stroke.

His grandfather's gaze clung to Lizzie. She moved forward without hesitation and came to a stop in front of his chair. Then something happened that totally surprised Dante. She bent over and hugged his grandfather. It was as though they'd known each other forever. How did that happen?

The two of them chatted while Dante sat on the couch. He really wasn't needed as neither of them even noticed that he was in the room. And he could plainly see that Lizzie's presence had an uplifting effect on his grandfather. In fact, this was the happiest he'd seen his grandfather since he'd been forced into retirement.

"So that's why you changed your mind about visiting this weekend?" Dante's father entered the room and came to a stop by the couch before nodding in Lizzie's direction.

Dante instinctively followed his father's gaze back to the woman who'd thrown his life into turmoil. "She knows Nonno. He asked me to bring her here."

His father nodded. "If I had that sort of distraction, I might stay in the city, too. After all, it's a lot easier to have a good time with a beautiful woman than it is to do the hard work needed to keep the family vineyard running."

Dante's jaw ratcheted tight. It didn't matter what he said; it never seemed to be the right thing where his father was concerned. Some things never changed.

"At least you have good taste." That was the closest his father had ever come to giving him a compliment.

"Lizzie and I are working together, nothing more."

His father sent him a *you are crazy* look. Dante wasn't going to argue with the man—it wouldn't change things. He never lived up to his father's expectations—not like his brother, Stefano, always did. Just once, he'd like his father to clap him on the back and tell him he'd done something right—something good.

Dante sat rigidly on the couch. Not even his father's jabs were enough to make him leave the room. He assured himself that it was just to keep an eye on what Lizzie said to his grandfather. Because there couldn't be any other reason. Unlike the rest of his family, he was immune to her charms.

Sure, he knew how to enjoy a woman's company. Her smiles. Her laugh. Her touch. But that was as far as it went. He refused to let himself become vulnerable. He'd seen too much pain in his life. It wouldn't happen to him. The *L* word wasn't worth the staggering risks.

CHAPTER EIGHT

"THIS PLACE IS AMAZING."

Lizzie didn't bother to hide her enthusiasm as she glanced around the spacious living room with a high ceiling and two sets of double doors that let the afternoon sun stream in. She'd trade her Bronx apartment in a heartbeat for this peaceful retreat.

"I love it here." She spoke the words to no one in particular. "Very different from city life."

"It is different." Massimo's words took her full attention between the accent and the slight slur from his stroke. "I'm glad you're here. Is my grandson treating you well?"

Her thoughts flashed back to their first meeting. But she wasn't so sure that Massimo would find it amusing that Dante mistook her presence at the restaurant and put her to work as a hostess. She opted to save that story for a later date.

She glanced across to where Dante was pretending to read a cooking magazine. "Yes. He...he's been a gentleman."

Massimo gave her a quizzical look. "My grandson is a good man. He knows a lot. Make him teach you."

His choice of words struck her as a bit odd. Either the man was eager to shorten his sentences or he sensed that things between her and Dante weren't going smoothly.

"I will. I just wish you could be there. I was really looking forward to working next to such a legend."

Massimo attempted to smile but the one side of his

mouth would not cooperate. Her heart pinched. She had no idea how frustrating it must be for your body not to cooperate. But beyond that, the man's face spoke of exhaustion. Dante had warned her not to overtax him. And she wouldn't do anything to harm Massimo. The place in her heart for him had only grown exponentially since meeting him in person.

"I'll let you get some rest." Lizzie went to stand when Massimo reached for her hand.

His grip was strong but not painful. But it was the look in his eyes that dug at her heart. "Promise me you won't give up. Promise me you'll see through our deal."

"But—" She'd almost uttered the fact that Dante was opposed to the whole idea. "I'll do my best." It was all she could offer the man.

"My grandson needs someone like you."

The following morning Lizzie hit the ground running.

She wasn't about to waste a minute of her time at the villa. The big, brilliant ball of orange was still low in the distant horizon. She stood just outside the kitchen door with a cup of steamy black coffee in hand.

She wandered across to an old wooden fence and gazed out at the endless acres of grapes. The golden rays gave the rows and rows of vines a beauty all of their own. She'd never been someplace so wide open. She reveled in the peacefulness that surrounded her. And that was something she truly found amazing. Normally her nights were full of restless dreams and her days full of running here and there, doing this and that. But here she could take a moment to breathe—just to be.

Her thoughts trailed back to her unusual conversation with Massimo. Was the man some sort of matchmaker? But why? He hardly knew her. How would she know if she would be good for Dante? And why would Dante need her?

The questions followed one after the other. The most

frustrating part was that she didn't have an answer for any of them. Dante was even more of a mystery to her now than he was before.

She'd noticed from the moment they'd arrived here that everything wasn't so perfect in Dante's life. Though she hadn't been able to hear the conversation between father and son, she'd clearly seen the dark look that had come over Dante's handsome face while talking with his father. There was a definite distance between him and his family. Was that what Massimo thought she could help Dante with? But how? She was here for only a matter of weeks, certainly not long enough to change someone's life. And what did she know about the inner workings of families?

Still, she couldn't get her mind to stop replaying the events from the prior evening. When his family grew boisterous talking of the vineyard, she noticed how Dante had become withdrawn as if he didn't feel as though he fit in—or was it that he didn't want to fit in? Either way, she couldn't imagine Dante willingly walking away from such an amazing place.

There had to be something more to his story—something he wasn't willing to share. But what could drive him from the peacefulness of the countryside and the bosom of his family to the city? Unless… Was it possible? Her mind raced. Could he have a passion for cooking that rivaled hers? Was it possible that they at last had something in common?

The thunk of the kitchen door swinging shut startled her. She spun around and there stood the man who'd filled her every thought since arriving here. The heat crept up her neck and settled in her cheeks. She realized that she was being silly. It wasn't as if he could read her mind.

Their gazes met and held. His stare was deep and probing. Unease inched up her spine. There was no way that he could know that just moments ago, she'd been daydreaming about his grandfather's suggestion that she and Dante might be a perfect fit.

"I didn't know if you'd be up yet." His voice was deep and gravelly.

"I set my phone alarm. I didn't want to miss the sunrise."

"And was it worth the effort?"

She nodded vigorously. "Definitely. I'm in love." When his eyes widened in surprise, she added, "With the villa and the vineyard. With all of it."

"I'm glad you like it here."

"I was considering going for a walk."

"Would you care for some company?"

Her gaze jerked back around to his to see if he was serious. "You really want to escort me around? I mean, it isn't like I'll be running into any of your family. You don't have to babysit me."

"I didn't offer so I could play babysitter. I thought maybe you'd want some company, but obviously I was wrong." He turned back to the house.

"Wait." He paused, but he didn't turn around. She swallowed down a chunk of pride. "I would like your company."

He turned to her but his lips were pressed together in a firm line. He crossed his arms and looked at her expectantly. He had a right to expect more. She'd been snippy and he hadn't deserved it. But it wasn't easy for her. For some reason, she had the hardest time dealing with him. His mere presence put her on edge. And he always scattered her thoughts with his good looks and charming smile.

"Okay, I'm sorry. Is that what you want to hear?"

"Yes, it is." He stepped up to her. "Shall we go?"

She glanced down at the almost empty cup. "I need to put this in the house."

He took it from her, jogged back to the kitchen and returned in no time. He extended his arm like a total gentleman, which sent her heart tumbling in her chest. Without hesitation, she slipped her hand into the crook of his arm.

When her fingers tightened around his biceps, she noticed his rock-hard strength.

This wasn't right. She had no business letting her guard down around him. Nothing good would come of it. She considered pulling away, but part of her refused to let go. With a quick glance at his relaxed features, she realized she was making too much of the situation.

He led her away from the house and down a dirt path. "You made quite an impression on my family."

"Is that a good thing?"

"Most definitely. They're all quite taken with you. It was the most excitement they've had around here in quite a while."

Normally she kept up her walls and held everyone at bay, but being here, being around Massimo, she'd let down her defenses a bit. "I noticed you were quiet last night. Was there something wrong?"

"No, not at all. And you were amazing, especially with Nonno. He's been really down in the dumps, but you cheered him up. So I owe you a big thank-you."

She noticed how he didn't explain his quietness. She wondered if he was always so reserved around his family. Granted, she didn't understand how traditional families worked as her life had consisted of foster homes where kids came and went and there wasn't that deep, abiding love that came naturally. But she had Jules and they were as close as any blood relatives.

"Your brother, he's older than you, isn't he?" She wanted to get Dante to open up about his family. She couldn't help it. She was curious.

"Yes. He's a couple of years older."

Well, that certainly didn't strike up the hoped-for conversation. "Are you two very close?"

Dante slanted a gaze her way but she pretended not to notice. "I don't know. We're brothers."

She knew none of this was any of her business but ev-

erything about Dante intrigued her. He was like an arti-
choke and she'd barely begun to pull at the tough outer
layer. There was so much to learn before she got to the
tender center that he protected from everyone.

"They care a lot about you."

He stopped and pulled her around to look at him. "Why
all of this curiosity about my family? What's going on in
that beautiful mind of yours?"

Did he just say she was beautiful? Her gaze met his
and her breath became shallow. No, he'd said her mind
was beautiful. But was that the same thing as saying she
was beautiful?

"I was just making small talk." She tried to act innocent.
"Why do I have to have ulterior motives?"

"I didn't say you did. But sometimes you make me wonder." He peered into her eyes and for a moment she wondered if he could read her thoughts.

Heat filled her cheeks and she glanced away. "Wonder
about what?"

"You. There's more to you than meets the eye. Something tells me that you have an interesting past."

She couldn't hold back a laugh. "You make me sound
very mysterious. Like Mata Hari or something." She leaned
closer to him and whispered in his ear. "I'm here to find
out your secrets."

He grabbed her upper arms and moved her back, allowing her the opportunity to see the worry lines ingrained on
his face. "What secrets?"

His hard, sharp tone startled her. "Your secrets in the
kitchen, of course. What else did you think I meant?"

His frown eased. "You're having far too much fun at
my expense."

So the man was keeping secrets. From her? Or from the
whole world? She didn't think it was possible but she was
even more intrigued by him.

She gazed into his bottomless brown eyes. "You need

to let your hair down and have some fun. It won't hurt. I promise."

"Is that what all of the smiling and laughing was about last night? Or are you trying to sway my family over to your side so they'll pressure me into agreeing to follow through with the contract?"

She pulled back her shoulders. She knew she shouldn't but she just couldn't help herself. His gaze dipped as her fingers once again made an X over her chest. "I promised not to do that."

The vein in his neck pulsated and when his eyes met hers again, there was a need, a passion in his gaze. Her line of vision dipped to his lips.

"You do know that you're driving me crazy, don't you?"

"Who, me?" This was the most fun she'd ever had. She'd never flirted with a guy before. Sure, they'd flirted with her but she never felt the desire to return the flirtations.

Until now.

His hands encircled her waist. "Yes, you. Do you have any idea what I'd like to do to you right now?"

A few scintillating thoughts danced and teased her mind. She placed her hands on his chest and felt the pounding of his heart. She was certain that hers could easily keep time with his. It was pumping so fast that it felt as if she'd just finished a long run on a hot, muggy day. In that moment she was overcome by the urge to find out if his kiss was as moving in real life as it had been in her dreams last night.

"You know, we really shouldn't do this." His voice was carried like a whisper in the breeze.

"When have you ever done what was expected of you?"

"Not very often." His gaze bored deep into her, making her stomach quiver with need.

"Then why start now? I won't tell, if you won't."

That was all it took. His head dipped and then his lips were there. He stopped just a breath away from hers. She could practically feel the turbulent vibes coming off him.

It was as though he was fighting an inner battle between what was right and what he wanted. She needed to put him out of his misery—out of her misery.

Acting on total instinct and desire, she leaned up on her tiptoes and pressed her mouth to his. His lips were smooth and warm. He didn't move. He wanted it. She knew that as well as she knew that the sun would set that evening. Perhaps he needed just a touch more enticement.

She let her body lean into his as her hands slipped up over his broad shoulders. Her fingertips raked through his dark hair as her lips gently moved over his. And then she heard a hungry moan swell in his throat as he pulled her snug against him.

Perhaps it was the knowledge that this kiss should be forbidden that made it the most enticing kiss she'd ever experienced. Then again, it could be that she was lonely and missing her sister, and being in Dante's arms made her feel connected to someone. Or maybe it was simply the fact that he was the dreamiest hunk she'd ever laid her eyes on, and she just wanted to see what she'd be missing by holding herself back.

He stroked and prodded, sending her heart pounding against her ribs with pure desire. His hard planes fit perfectly against her soft curves. And for the moment, she felt like the most beautiful—most desired—woman in the world.

Dante moved, placing his hands on each side of her face. When he pulled his lips from hers, she felt bereft. She wanted more. Needed more.

He rested his forehead against hers. His breathing was deep and uneven. He'd been just as caught up in the moment as she'd been, so why had he stopped? What had happened?

His thumb gently stroked her cheek. "Lizzie, we can't do this. You know that it's wrong."

"But it felt so right."

She couldn't help it. She wasn't ready for the harsh light of reality. She lived every single day with the sharp edges of reality slicing into her dreams. Just once, she wanted to know what it was like not to have to worry about meeting the monthly bills. She just wanted this one blissful memory.

"Lizzie, this can't happen. You and I…it's impossible."

His words pricked her bubble of happiness. Once again she was being rejected. And the worst part was he was right. And that thought made the backs of her eyes sting.

When was it going to be her turn for just a little bit of happiness without the rug being pulled out from under her? This trip to Rome should be the trip of a lifetime, but now the entire arrangement was in jeopardy and she had no job to return to.

She blinked repeatedly, keeping the moisture in her eyes in check. If she was good at one thing in life, it was being a trooper. When life dropped lemons on her, she whipped up a lemon meringue pie with the fluffiest, tallest peaks. She could do it again.

She pulled back until her spine was straight and his hands fell away. "You're right. I don't know what I was thinking." Her voice wobbled. She swallowed down the lump of emotion. "It won't happen again."

Without meeting his gaze, she moved past him and started for the villa. The tip of her tongue ran over her lower lip, where she found the slightest minty taste of toothpaste he'd left behind. She stifled a frustrated moan, knowing that he was only a few steps behind her.

CHAPTER NINE

HE'D TOTALLY BLOWN IT.

Dante stowed their bags in the car's boot and then glanced back at the villa. Lizzie smiled at his grandfather before hugging him goodbye. A stab of jealousy tore into Dante. She'd barely spoken to him after they'd kissed, and even then, it'd only been one-word answers. Why in the world had he let his hormones do the thinking for him?

He had absolutely no desire to toy with her feelings. Hurting Lizzie was the last thing in the world he wanted to do. And though she appeared to have it all together, he knew that she had a vulnerable side, too. He'd witnessed the hurt that had flashed in her eyes when she realized that he didn't trust her with his grandfather. She wanted him to think she was tough, but he knew lurking beneath the beautiful surface lay a vulnerable woman—a woman that he was coming to like a bit more than he should.

When she at last joined him in the car, she stared straight ahead. The unease between them was palpable. Dante didn't like it one bit, but he had no one to blame but himself. There was no way he could go back in time and undo the kiss. And if he could, he wasn't so sure he would. Their kiss had been something special—something he'd never experienced before.

He cut his thoughts off short. He realized that it was thoughts like this that had gotten him into trouble in the first place. But he couldn't ignore the fact that this silent treatment was doing him in.

"Are you ever going to speak to me again?" He struggled to keep the frustration out of his voice.

"Yes."

More of the one-syllable answers. "Did you enjoy your visit to the vineyard?"

"Yes."

"Enough with the yeses and nos." His hands tightened on the steering wheel, trying to get a grip on his rising frustration. Worst of all was the fact he had no clue how to fix things between them. And whether it was wise or not, he wanted Lizzie to like him. "My grandfather seemed quite taken with you. In fact, the whole family did."

Nothing.

She crossed her arms and huffed. What did that mean? Was she about to let him have it? His muscles tensed as he waited for a tongue-lashing. Not that he could blame her. He deserved it, but it wouldn't make it any less uncomfortable.

Her voice was soft and he strained to hear her. "How do you do it?"

Well, it was more than one syllable, but he didn't have a clue what she meant. And he was hesitant to ask, but what choice did he have?

"How do I do what?" The breath caught in his throat as he waited for what came next.

"How do you drive away from that little piece of heaven at the end of each weekend and return to the city?"

This wasn't the direction he'd expected the conversation to take. His family wasn't a subject he talked about beyond the generalities. *How's your father? Is your brother still working at the vineyard? Did they have a good harvest?* But no one ever probed into his choice to move away—to distance himself from his family.

"I prefer Rome." It wasn't necessarily a lie.

"Don't get me wrong. I love the city life. But I was born and bred in a city that never sleeps. I think it's in my bones to appreciate the chatter of voices and the hum of vehicles. But you, you were raised in the peace and tranquillity."

"It isn't the perfect slice of heaven like you're thinking." He tried not to think about his childhood. He didn't want to remember.

"What wasn't perfect about it?"

He glanced her way, giving her a warning stare to leave the subject alone.

"Hey, you're the one who wanted me to talk. I'm talking. Now it's your turn."

He could see that she wasn't going to leave this subject alone. Not unless he let her know that she was stepping on a very tender subject.

"Life at the DeFiore Vineyard wasn't idyllic when I was a kid. Far from it."

"Why?"

She really was going to push this. And for some unknown reason, he wanted to make her understand his side. "I'm the reason my mother died."

"What?" She swung around in her seat, fighting with the seat belt so that she was able to look directly at him. "But I don't understand. How?"

"She died after she gave birth to me."

"Oh. How horrible." There was an awkward pause. "But it wasn't your fault."

"No, not directly. But my father blamed me. He told me that I took away the best part of his life."

"He didn't mean it. That…those words, they were part of his grief."

Dante shoved his fingers through his hair. "He meant it. I can't help but feel that I bring sadness and misery to those closest to me—"

"Nonsense. Listen, I'm so sorry for your loss. I know

how tough that can be, but you're not to blame for her death or how your father handled his grief. We all handle the death of family members differently."

That caught his attention. A chance to turn the tables away from himself and back to her. "Have you lost a parent?"

Silence enveloped the car. Only the hum of the engine and the tires rolling over the blacktop could be heard. Lizzie turned away to stare out the side window as Dante drove on, waiting and wondering.

"Lizzie, you can talk to me. Whatever you say won't go any further."

He took his focus off the road for just a moment to glance her way. She cast him a hesitant look. He had a feeling she had something important to say—something she didn't normally share. He really hoped she'd let down her guard and let him in. He wanted so badly to understand more about her.

"My mother died." Her voice was so soft.

"I'm sorry. I guess we've both had some hard knocks in life."

"Yes, but at least you have a loving family. And you can always go home when you want to…" It seemed as though she wanted to say more but stopped.

This conversation was much deeper—much more serious than he'd ever expected. He wanted to press for more information, but he sensed now wasn't the time. Spotting a small village up ahead with a trattoria, he slowed down.

"You know, we left without eating. Would you care for a bite of food? And they have the best *caffè* around. I noticed that you have quite a fondness for cappuccino."

"I do. And I'd love to get some."

He eased off the road and maneuvered the car into the lot. Before he got out, he knew there was something more he had to say. "I'm sorry about what happened back at the vineyard. The kiss was a mistake. I didn't mean to cross the line. The last thing I want to do is hurt you."

She turned to him and smiled, but the gesture never quite reached her eyes. "Don't worry. You'd have to do a lot more than that kiss to hurt me. Now let's get that coffee."

Without giving him a chance to say anything else, she alighted from the car. Her words might have been what he wanted to hear, but he didn't believe her. His gut told him that he'd hurt her more deeply than her stubborn pride would let on.

He didn't know what it was about Ms. Lizzie Addler from New York, but she was getting to him. He longed to be a good guy in her eyes, but he was torn between his desire to help her and his need to sell the *ristorante* in order to return to the vineyard and help his family. How was he supposed to make everyone happy? Was it even possible?

How had that happened?

Lizzie had entered the quaint restaurant with no appetite at all. And now as they exited the small family establishment, her stomach was full up with the most delicious sampling of pastas, meats and cheeses.

It had all started when they'd been greeted by the sweetest older woman. She'd insisted that they have a seat while she called to her husband, who was in the kitchen. Apparently they'd known Dante all of his life and were thrilled to see that he'd brought his lady friend to meet them. When Lizzie tried to correct the very chatty woman, her words got lost in the conversation.

"Are they always so outgoing?" Lizzie asked Dante as they approached the car.

"Guido and Luiso Caruso have known my family for years, and yes, they are always that friendly. Did you get enough to eat?"

Lizzie gently patted her rounded stomach. "I'm stuffed."

Dante snapped his fingers. "I forgot to give them a message from my grandfather. I'll be right back."

While Dante rushed back inside, Lizzie leaned against the car's fender and lifted her face to the sun. Perhaps she was hungrier than she thought because now that she'd eaten, her mood was much lighter. And it'd helped that Dante had opened up to her about his family. No matter how little he cracked open the door to his past, every bit he shared meant a lot to her.

But nothing could dislodge the memory of that earth-shattering kiss. It was always there, lurking around the edges of her mind. But the part that stung was how Dante had rejected her. And his reasoning did nothing to soothe her.

Somehow she'd get past this crazy infatuation. Because in the end, he was right. They did have to work together over the next eight weeks. Not to mention that they shared an apartment—anything else, no matter how casual, would just complicate matters.

"Ready to go?" Dante frowned as he noticed her leaning against the flawless paint job.

"Yes, I am."

As he got closer, she noticed how he inspected where she'd been leaning, as if she'd dented the car or something. His hand smoothed across the paint.

"Are you serious?" she asked incredulously.

He turned to her, his face perfectly serious. "What?"

He really didn't get it. She smiled and shook her head. Men and their cars. "Nothing."

"If we get going we should be home in no time. There's not much traffic. And the weather is perfect." He repeatedly tossed the keys in the air.

Lizzie moved in to catch them. "Let me drive."

"What? You're joking, right?" He reached out to take the keys from her.

She pulled her hand behind her back, which drew her

blouse tight across her chest. His gaze dipped and lingered just a moment. When his gaze met hers again, she smiled.

"Come on. You said yourself there is hardly any traffic."

And she'd love to drive an honest-to-goodness exclusive sports car, the kind that turned heads—both men and women, young and old. She may not be a car junkie, but that didn't mean she couldn't appreciate a fine vehicle. And this car was quite fine. Jules would never believe she'd gotten to drive such an amazing sports car.

"I don't think so." The smile slipped from his face. "Can I have the keys so we can get going?"

Enjoying having him at a disadvantage, she felt her smile broaden. She backed up a few steps. She was in the mood to have a little fun, hoping it'd get them back on track. "If you want them, you'll have to come and get them."

He didn't move. "This isn't funny." His tone grew quite insistent. "Hand over the keys."

Her good mood screeched to a halt. He wouldn't even consider letting her behind the steering wheel. Did he really think so little of her that she couldn't drive a car in a straight line?

Hurt balled up in her gut. She dropped the keys in his outstretched hand and strode around the car. "I assume I'm still allowed to sit in the passenger seat."

"Hey, you don't have to be like that. After all, I don't let anyone drive Red."

Her head snapped around to face him. "You named your car?"

"Of course. Why wouldn't I?"

She shook her head, having no words to describe her amazement.

"Besides, I'm sure that you'll enjoy riding in the passenger seat more. You can take a nap or check out the passing scenery."

It hurt her how easily he brushed off her request as though she couldn't possibly be serious about wanting to drive such a fine machine. All of her life people had never seen past her foster-kid status and used clothes. Even now as she sat on the butter-soft upholstery of a car that she would never be able to afford in her entire life, she was wearing hand-me-downs. But at least these clothes fit her and they didn't look as though they'd seen a better day.

She was tired of people underestimating her. She refused to sit by and take it. She would show Dante that she was just as capable as him.

CHAPTER TEN

"I KEPT MY WORD."

The sound of Lizzie's voice startled Dante.

She'd resumed her quiet mode after he'd asked for the keys. He had no idea she was so intent on driving his car—his gem. She obviously didn't know how precious it was to him and he didn't know how to describe it to her. The fact that his father liked this car almost as much as Dante did meant the world to him. And the fact that he'd bought it all on his own had earned him some of his father's respect. He couldn't afford to lose that one small step.

Dante unlocked the penthouse door. "You kept your word about what?"

"The contract. I didn't say a word while we were at the villa. But now that we're back and the film crew will be here tomorrow at 6:00 a.m., I need to know if you're on board with the whole thing." Lizzie strode into the living room. She fished around in her purse, eventually producing her cell phone. Her gaze met his as her finger hovered over the touch screen.

His curiosity was piqued. "Who are you planning to call?"

"My contact at the studio."

"Did you already tell them about my grandfather not being able to fulfill his obligation?"

She nodded. "I told them right away."

He kind of figured she would. "And what did they say?"

He wasn't so sure he wanted to hear the answer because Lizzie looked far too confident. What did she know that he didn't?

Lizzie perched on the arm of the couch. "They were sorry to hear about your grandfather."

"And?"

"And when I mentioned that you'd taken over the restaurant, they were intrigued. They pulled up some old footage of you with your grandfather and they're convinced transitioning the spotlight from your grandfather to you will work."

He should have known that eventually being on television even for a few seconds would come back to bite him. He just never expected this. Who would want him on television? He knew nothing of acting. And he wasn't inclined to learn.

"Lizzie, I haven't agreed to this. Any of it." And he didn't want to either.

"But what choice do you have at this point? If your attorney was going to uncover an easy out, he'd have told you by now."

Dante's hands pressed down on the granite countertop. He wanted to argue with her. He wanted to point out that this idea didn't have a chance to be a success. But even his solicitor wasn't rushing in, promising that all would be fine. In fact, his solicitor had said quite the opposite. That trying to break the contract would cost him money and time.

The television exposure would definitely give the *ristorante* added publicity and the asking price could easily be inflated. As it was, he'd been forced to lower the price to unload it quickly, but now there wouldn't be a rush. He could ask for a more realistic price and perhaps someone else would step forward that would want the *ristorante* without buying the family recipes.

Lizzie tossed her oversize purse on the couch. "Besides, if you help me out, I'll help you out."

"What do you have in mind?"

"If you agree to do the filming each morning before the restaurant opens, I can help you around Ristorante Massimo."

His brows rose. "You're offering to work for me?"

"Sure. What else do I have to do with my time?"

There had to be a catch. There always was. Everybody wanted something. "And what are you expecting me to pay you?"

She shrugged. "Nothing."

"Nothing?"

"I'd just like a chance to do what I would have done with your grandfather."

"And that was?"

"To learn from him. He was planning to teach me as much as he could while I was in town. I came to Italy with the sole intent to work my butt off."

Dante eyed her up. "You really don't want anything else but to learn?"

"Why do you sound so skeptical?"

He shrugged. "I'm not used to people offering me free help."

"I wouldn't get used to it. Not everyone can afford to do it. But the studio is paying me to be here, and with you providing free room and board, it should all work out."

At last he found the rub. "You intend to continue to live here? With me?"

"Is this your way of saying that you plan to kick me out?"

"You have to admit that after what happened in the vineyard the idea of us living and working together isn't a good one."

"Why? Are you saying that you want to repeat that kiss?" She moved forward, only stopping when she stood on the other side of the counter. "Are you wishing that you hadn't stopped it?"

His gaze dipped to her pink frosted lips. Oh, yes, he

definitely wanted to continue that kiss. He wanted it to go on and on. "No. That's not what I'm saying. Quit putting words in my mouth."

Her eyes flashed her disbelief. "I only call 'em like I see 'em."

"It has nothing to do with the kiss. I'd already forgotten about it." No, he hadn't. Not in the least. "It's just..."

"Just what?" Lines bracketed her icy blue eyes as she waited for his answer.

"I just don't know if you understand what will be expected from you."

"You mean you think I'm just another pretty face without anything between my ears."

"Hey, I didn't say that. There you go again, making assumptions."

"Then what did you mean?"

"I have my way of doing things. And I expect you to pay attention to the details—no matter how small or meaningless you might find them." He needed time alone to get his head on straight. There was a lot here to consider. "I'm going to my office. We'll talk more later."

"Do you mind if I go downstairs and have a look around. I want to know what I'm getting myself into."

"Be my guest. Here's the key." He tossed her a key card and rattled off the security pass code.

Her lips pressed into a firm line as she clutched the key card and turned for the door. He stood there in the kitchenette. He couldn't turn away as his gaze was latched on the gentle sway of her hips as she strode away. His pulse raced and memories of holding her and tasting her sweet kisses clouded his mind. How had he ever found the willpower to let her go?

The snick of the door closing snapped Dante back to the here and now. What was so different about her? He'd dated his share of women and none of them had gotten to him like her. But if there was any possibility of them working together and sharing this apartment, he needed to see her as just another coworker. Someone who couldn't get under his skin and give him that overwhelming urge to scratch his itch. Because that would only lead them both into trouble as had already happened back at the vineyard.

He should just show Lizzie the door and forget trying to fulfill his grandfather's wishes. If he was logical, that was what he'd do. But when it came to family, nothing was logical.

Combine that with the desperation he'd witnessed in Lizzie's gaze, and he felt an overwhelming urge to find a way to make this work for both of them. But could he keep his hormones in check around her? Suddenly his apartment wasn't looking so big after all.

She'd prove him wrong.

Lizzie strode into the impressive kitchen of Ristorante Massimo. It was more spacious than it had appeared on television. And she immediately felt at home surrounded by the stainless-steel appliances. She just wished that Massimo would be there instead of his stubborn grandson.

But she had a plan. She was going to prove to Dante that she was talented—that she could hold up her end of the agreement. She looked over the ingredients in the fridge and the freezer. Slowly a dinner menu took shape in her mind. She didn't want it to be pasta as she didn't want to compete in his arena. No, she would whip up something else.

She set to work, anxious to prove to Dante that she belonged here in Massimo's kitchen. She had the ability; she just needed to broaden her horizons with new culinary skills.

She didn't know how much time had passed when she heard a sound behind her. She turned and jumped when she saw Dante propping himself up in the doorway.

"What are you doing there?" She set aside the masher she'd used to whip up the cauliflower.

"I think I'm the one who should be asking you that question."

She glanced around at the mess she'd created. Okay, so she wasn't the neatest person in the kitchen. But to be honest, she had seen worse. And she was in a hurry. She'd wanted it all to be completed before he arrived. So much for her plan.

"I thought I'd put together dinner."

He walked closer. "And what's on the menu?"

She ran over and pressed a hand to his chest to stop him. The warmth from his body and the rhythm of his heart sent tingles shooting up her arm. Big mistake. But her heart wasn't listening to her head. A bolt of awareness struck her and all she could think about was stepping a little closer. The breath caught in her throat as she looked up at his tempting lips.

Memories of his caresses dominated her thoughts. She'd never been kissed like that before. It had meaning. It had depth. And it had left her longing for more. But this wasn't the time or the place. She had to make a point with him. And caving in to her desires would not help her cause.

She pulled her hand back. "I have a table all set in the dining room. Why don't you go make yourself comfortable? The food will be in shortly."

He strained his neck, looking around. "Are you sure I shouldn't stay and help?"

She pressed her hands to her hips. "I'm positive. Go."

He hesitated and she started to wonder if he was going to trust her. But then he relented. And turned. When he exited the kitchen, she rushed to finish up with the things on the stove. She placed them in the oven to keep them warm.

At last, it was time to start serving up the most important meal of her life. Since when had impressing Dante become more about what he thought of her and less about gaining the job? She consoled herself with the thought that it was just nerves. It wasn't as if he was the first man to kiss her. Nor would he be the last.

She pushed aside the jumbled thoughts as she moved to the refrigerator and removed the crab-and-avocado salad. She placed the dish on the tray, took off her apron and smoothed a hand over her hair, worrying that she must look a mess. Oh, well, it was too late to worry about it now.

Then, realizing that she'd forgotten something for him to drink, she grabbed both a glass of chilled water and a bottle of DeFiore white wine she'd picked out to complement the meal.

She carried the tray into the dining room and came to a stop when she noticed the lights had been dimmed and candles had been added to the table as well as some fresh greens and dahlias with hearty yellow centers and deep pink tips. The breath caught in her throat.

The table was perfect. It looked as though it was ready for a romantic interlude. And then her gaze came to rest on Dante. He'd changed clothes. What? But why?

She glanced down at the same clothes she'd worn all day that were now smudged with flour and sauce. She resisted the urge to race out of the room to grab a shower and to change into something that would make her feel sexy and alluring.

She turned her attention to Dante, taking in his creased black slacks, a matching jacket and a gray button-up shirt. Wow. With his tanned features and his dark hair, he looked like a Hollywood star. She swallowed hard. She wondered if he'd remembered to put on a touch of cologne, too. The thought of moving close enough to check was oh, so tempting.

She gave herself a mental jerk. She wasn't here for a date. This was business. She couldn't blow her chance to show him that she was quite competent in the kitchen. She would impress him this evening, but it would be through her culinary prowess and not through flirting or any of the other tempting thoughts that came readily to mind.

"If you'll have a seat, I'll serve you." She tried to act as though her heart wasn't thumping against her ribs.

He frowned. "But I want to get your chair for you."

"You don't need to do that."

"Aren't you joining me?"

She shook her head.

"But you've got to be hungry, too."

She was but it wasn't the food she'd slaved over for the past couple of hours that had her salivating. "I'm fine."

"Oh, come on. You surely don't think that I'll enjoy this meal with you rushing around waiting on me. Now sit."

What was up with him? She eyed him up as she sat in the chair he'd pulled out for her. Was he having a change of heart about teaching her what he knew—in the kitchen, that was?

"I only brought out enough food for one."

"Not a problem." Before she could utter a word, he moved to the kitchen.

This wasn't right. This was not how she'd planned to prove to Dante that she was up to the task of working in Ristorante Massimo. Frustration collided with the girlie part of her that was thrilled to be pampered. It was a totally new experience for her. But it also left her feeling off-kilter. Was she supposed to read something into his actions? The clothes? The flowers and candles? Did any of it have anything to do with their kiss?

When he returned, she gazed at him in the glow of the candle. The words caught in her throat as she realized this was her first candlelit dinner. Romance had never been part of her other relationships. She could definitely get used to this and to Dante—

No. No. She couldn't get distracted again. This was not a date. It was business. So why was Dante acting so strange? So kind and thoughtful?

"Is there something I should know?" she asked, bracing herself for bad news.

A dark brow arched. "Know about what?"

She didn't want to put words in his mouth, especially if they were not what she wanted to hear. "I don't know. I just wondered about your effort to be so nice."

He frowned. "So now you think that I'm not nice."

She groaned. "That isn't what I meant. You're taking my words out of context."

"I am?" He placed a plate and glass in front of her. "Perhaps we should talk about something else, then."

"No. I want to know why you're in such a good mood. Have you made up your mind about the television show?"

Please let him say that he had a change of heart.

His gaze lowered to the table as he took his seat. "Are you sure you know what you're asking?"

"Of course I do. All you have to do is fill in for your grandfather. And teach me everything you know." Did this mean he was truly considering the idea? Were her dreams about to come true?

"You really want to learn from me?"

She nodded.

The silence dragged on. Her stomach knotted and her palms grew damp. Why wasn't he saying anything?

"Well?" She couldn't bear the unknown any longer. "Where does that leave us?"

"It leaves us with a meal that's going to get cold if we don't get through this first course soon."

"But I need to know."

"And you will. Soon."

Was that a promise? It sounded like one. But what was soon in his book? She glanced down at her salad. How in the world was she supposed to eat now?

CHAPTER ELEVEN

HE MUST HAVE lost his mind.

That had to be it. Otherwise why would he even consider going along with this arrangement?

Dante stared across the candlelit table at Lizzie. He noticed how she'd moved the food around on her plate, but she'd barely eaten a bite. She had to be hungry because it'd been hours since they'd stopped at the trattoria on their way back to Rome.

And this food was really good. In fact, he had to admit that he was impressed. Maybe taking her under his wing wouldn't be such a hardship after all. His solicitor definitely thought it was the least painless course of action. Easy for him to say.

But the deciding factor was when the potential buyer of the *ristorante* had been willing to wait the two months. His solicitor said that they'd actually been quite enthusiastic about the *ristorante* getting international coverage.

But what no one took into consideration was the fact that Dante was totally drawn to Lizzie. And that was a serious complication. How in the world were they to work together when all he could think about was kissing her again? He longed to wrap his arms around her and pull her close. He remembered vividly how the morning sun had glowed behind her, giving her whole appearance a golden glow. It had been an experience unlike any other. And when their lips had met—

"Is something wrong with the food?"

Dante blinked before meeting Lizzie's worried gaze. He had to start thinking of her in professional terms. He supposed that if he were going to take her on as his protégée, he might as well get started. He'd teach her as much as possible within their time limit.

"Now that you'll be working here, there'll be no special treatment. You'll be expected to work just like everyone else."

"Understood."

"As for the food, the chicken is a little overcooked. You'll need to be careful of that going forward."

A whole host of expressions flitted across her face. "Is there anything else?"

It wasn't the reaction he'd been expecting. He thought she'd be ecstatic to learn that she'd be working there. And that she'd get her television spot. Women. He'd never figure them out. In his experience, they never reacted predictably.

"And use less salt. The guest can always add more according to their taste and diet."

Her face filled with color. Without a word, she threw her linen napkin on the table and rushed to the kitchen.

He groaned. He hadn't meant to upset her. Still, how was he supposed to teach her anything if he couldn't provide constructive criticism? His grandfather should be here. He would know what to say and how to say it.

Dante raked his fingers through his hair. He'd agreed to this arrangement far too quickly. He should have gone with his gut that said this was going to be a monumental mistake. Now he had to fix things before the camera crew showed up. The last thing either of them needed was to start their television appearances on a bad note—with all of the world watching.

He strode toward the kitchen and paused by the door. What did he say to her? Did he apologize even though he hadn't said anything derogatory? Did he set a precedent that she would expect him to apologize every time she got upset when he pointed out something that she could improve on? An exasperated sigh passed his lips. He obviously wasn't meant to be a teacher.

He pushed the door open, prepared to find Lizzie in tears. Instead he found her scraping leftovers into the garbage and piling the dishes in the sink.

"What are you doing?"

She didn't face him. "I'm cleaning up. What does it look like?"

"But we weren't done eating. Why don't you come back to the table?"

She grabbed the main dish and dumped it in the garbage. "I don't want anything else."

"Would you stop?"

"There's no point in keeping leftovers." With that, she grabbed the dessert.

He knew where she was headed and stepped in her way. What in the world had gotten into her? Why was she acting this way?

"Lizzie, put down the dessert and tell me what's bothering you."

She tilted her chin to gaze up at him. "Why should something be bothering me? You tore to shreds the dinner I painstakingly prepared for you."

"But isn't that what you want me to do? Teach you?"

Her icy gaze bored into him. The temperature took an immediate dive. "Move."

"No. We need to finish talking."

"So you can continue to insult me. No, thank you." She moved to go around him but he moved to block her.

"Lizzie, I don't know what it is you want from me. I thought you wanted me to teach you, but obviously that isn't the case. So what is it you want? Or do you just want to call this whole thing off?"

"I didn't know we were starting the lessons right away.

Or did you just say those things in hopes of me calling off the arrangement?"

"No, that isn't what I had in mind." How the heck had he ended up on the defensive? He'd only meant to be helpful.

"So you truly think I'm terrible in the kitchen?"

He took the tray from her and set it on the counter. Then he stepped up to her, hating the emotional turmoil he saw in her eyes. He found himself longing to soothe her. But he didn't have a clue how to accomplish such a thing. He seemed to keep making one mistake after the other where she was concerned.

"I think that you're very talented." It was the truth. And he'd have said it even if he didn't find her amazingly attractive.

Her bewildered gaze met his. "But you said—"

"That there were things for you to take into consideration while working here. I didn't mean to hurt your feelings."

Disbelief shimmered in her eyes.

He didn't think. He just acted, reaching out to her. His thumb stroked her cheek, enjoying its velvety softness. She stepped away from his touch and his hand lowered to his side.

"Lizzie, you have to believe me. If you're going to be this sensitive, how do you think we'll be able to work together?"

This was all wrong.

Lizzie crossed her arms to keep from reaching out to him. The whole evening had gone off the rails and she had no idea how to fix things. And the worst part was that she'd overreacted. Big-time.

She'd always prided herself on being able to contain her feelings behind a wall of indifference. And Dante wasn't the first to criticize her skills. But he was the first whose opinion truly mattered to her on a deeply personal level. He was the first person she wanted to thoroughly impress.

The thought brought her up short. Since when had his thoughts and feelings come to mean so much to her? Was it the kiss? Had it changed everything? Or was it opening up to him in the car? Had their heart-to-heart made her vulnerable to him?

Panic clawed at her. She knew what happened when she let people too close and she opened up about her background. She'd been shunned most of her life. She couldn't let Dante do that to her. She couldn't stand the thought of him looking at her with pity while thinking that she was less than everyone else—after all, if her own parents couldn't love her, how was anyone else supposed to?

Not that she wanted Dante to fall in love with her. Did she? No. That was the craziest idea to cross her mind in a long time—probably her craziest idea ever.

The walls started to close in on her. She needed space. Away from Dante. Away from his curious stare. "I need… need to make a phone call. I…I'll clean this all up later."

And with that, she raced for the door. She didn't have to call Jules, but she did need the excuse to get away from him. It was as if he had some sort of magnetic field around him and it drew out her deepest feelings. She needed to stuff them back in the little box in her heart.

Being alone in a strange city in a country practically halfway around the world from her home made her choices quite limited. She thought of escaping back to the vineyard and visiting some more with Massimo. He was so easy to talk to. He was her friend. But he was also Dante's grandfather. And the vineyard was Dante's home.

Her shoulders slumped as she headed for the apartment. What she needed now was to talk to Jules. It would be good to hear a familiar voice. She made a beeline for her room and pulled out her phone. She knew the call would cost her a small fortune but this was an emergency.

She dialed the familiar number. The phone rang and

rang. Just when she thought that it was going to switch to voice mail, she heard a familiar voice.

"Lizzie, is that you? What's wrong?"

The concern in Jules's voice had her rushing to reassure her. "I just wanted to check in."

"But you said that we needed to watch how much we spend on the phone. You said we should only call when something was wrong. So what happened?"

"Nothing. I just wanted to hear your voice and make sure you are doing okay."

There was a slight pause. "Lizzie, this is me. You can't lie to me. Something is bothering you. So spill it."

Calling Jules had been a mistake. She knew her far too well. And now Jules wasn't going to let her off the hook. "It's Dante. I think I just blew my chance to work with him."

"Why? What did you do?"

"I…I overreacted. Instead of taking his feedback on my cooking like a professional, I acted like an oversensitive female." Her thoughts drifted over the evening. "All I wanted to do was impress him and…and I failed."

"Don't worry about him. Just come home."

"I can't do that. Remember, I quit my job. And your tuition is due soon."

"You don't have to worry about that. I don't have to go to grad school."

"You do if you want to be a social worker and help other kids like us." The remembrance of her promise to her foster sister put things in perspective. She couldn't let her bruised ego get the best of her. She couldn't walk away. "Just ignore what I said. I'm tired. Everything will work out."

"But, Lizzie, if he's making things impossible for you, what are you going to do?"

There was a knock at her bedroom door.

"Jules, I have to go. I'll call you later."

With a quick goodbye, she disconnected the call. She

worried her bottom lip and waited. Maybe Dante would go away. She wasn't ready to talk to him. Not yet.

Again the tap at the door. "I'm not going away until we talk."

"I don't have anything to say to you."

"But I have plenty to say to you."

That sparked her curiosity, but her bruised ego wasn't ready to give in. She wanted to tell herself that his words and his opinions meant nothing. But that trip to the vineyard and that kiss in the morning sunshine had cast some sort of spell over her—over her heart.

"Lizzie, open the door."

She ran a hand over her hair, finding it to be a flyaway mess. What was she doing hiding away? She was a foster kid. She knew how to take care of herself. Running and hiding wasn't her style. She straightened her shoulders. And with a resigned sigh, she moved to the door and opened it.

Dante stood there, slouched against the doorjamb. Much too close. Her heart thumped. Her gaze dipped to his lips. She recalled how his mouth did the most exquisite things to her and made her insides melt into a puddle. If she were to lean a little forward, they'd be nose to nose, lip to lip, breath to breath. But that couldn't happen again. It played with her mind and her heart too much.

With effort she drew her gaze to his eyes, which seemed to be filled with amusement.

"See something you like?" A smile pulled at his lips and made him even sexier than the serious expression he normally wore like armor.

"I see a man who insists he has to talk to me. What do you want?"

He shook his head. "Not like this. Join me in the living room."

"I have things to do."

"I think this is more important. Trust me." With that, he walked away.

She stood there fighting off the urge to rush to catch up with him. After all, he was the one who'd ruined a perfectly amazing dinner, nitpicking over her cooking. The reminder had her straightening her spine.

Refusing to continue to let him have the upper hand, she closed the door and rushed over to the walk-in closet to retrieve some fresh clothes that didn't smell as if she'd been working in the kitchen for hours. She wished she had time for a shower, but she didn't want to press her luck.

With a fresh pair of snug black jean capris and a black sheer blouse that she knotted at her belly button, she entered the en suite bathroom that was almost as big as her bedroom. She splashed some water on her heated face. Then she took a moment to run a brush through her hair. Not satisfied with it, she grabbed a ponytail holder and pulled her hair back out of her face. With a touch of powder and a little lip gloss to add a touch of color to her face, she decided that she wasn't going to go out of her way for him.

Satisfied that she'd taken enough time that it didn't seem as though she was rushing after him, she exited her room. She didn't hear anything. Had he given up and disappeared to his office?

Disappointment coursed through her. The fact that she was so eager to hear what he had to say should have been warning enough, but curiosity kept her moving forward. When she entered the wide open living area, she was surprised to find Dante kicked back on the couch with his smartphone in his hand. He glanced up at her with an unidentifiable expression.

"What?" she asked, feeling self-conscious about her appearance.

He shook his head, dismissing her worry. "Nothing. It's just that when I think I've figured you out, you go and surprise me."

"And how did I do that?"

He shook his head. "It doesn't matter."

"Yes, it does. Otherwise you wouldn't have mentioned it."

"It's just that as tough as you act, on the inside you're such a girl." His gaze drifted over her change of clothes down to her strappy black sandals. "And a beautiful one at that."

She crossed her arms and shrugged. "I…I'm sorry for being sensitive. I'm not normally like that. I swear. It won't happen again."

But the one subject she didn't dare delve into was that her appearance was an illusion. Unlike his other women friends, her clothes didn't come from some Rome boutique. Her clothes were hand-me-downs. For a moment, she wondered what he'd say if he knew she was a fraud. Her insides tightened as she thought of him rejecting her.

"Apology accepted." He patted a spot on the black leather couch next to him. "Now come sit down."

It was then that she noticed the candles on the glass coffee table. And there were the dishes of berries and fresh whipped cream and a sprig of mint. Why in the world had he brought it up here?

When she sat down, it was in the overstuffed chair. "I don't understand."

He leaned forward. His elbows rested on his knees. Her instinct was to sit back out of his reach, but steely resistance kept her from moving. She wasn't going to let him think that he had any power over her.

"Dante, what's this all about? Are you trying to soften the blow? Are you calling off the television spot?"

CHAPTER TWELVE

LIZZIE'S HARD GAZE challenged him.

Dante wondered if she truly wanted him to step away from this project. Had she gotten a taste of his mentoring skills and changed her mind? Not that it mattered. It was too late for either of them to back out.

Somehow he had to smooth things out with her. And he wasn't well versed with apologies. This was going to be harder than he'd imagined.

"It's my turn to apologize." There. He'd said it. Now he just hoped that she'd believe him.

"For what?"

This was where things got sticky. He didn't want to talk about feelings and emotions. He swallowed hard as he sorted his thoughts.

"I didn't mean to make you feel bad about dinner." Her gaze narrowed in on him, letting him know that he now had her full attention. "See, that's the thing. I'm not a teacher. I have no experience. My grandfather always prided himself on being the one to show people how to do things. He has a way about him that makes people want to learn. If he hadn't been a chef, he should have been a teacher."

The stiffness in her shoulders eased. "But I didn't make you dinner so that you could teach me. I...I wanted... Oh, never mind."

She clammed up quickly. What had she been about to say? He really wanted to know. Was she going to say that she'd made him dinner because she liked him? Did she want to continue what they'd started earlier that day?

No. She wouldn't want that...would she? He had to resolve the uncertainty. The not knowing would taunt him to utter distraction. And if they were going to work together, he had to know where they stood.

He cleared his throat. "What is it you wanted?"

"I just wanted to prepare you a nice dinner as a thank-you for what you did by introducing me to your family. And...and I wanted to show you that you wouldn't be making a mistake by taking me on to work here. But obviously I was wrong."

"No, you weren't."

"Yes, I was. You made it clear you don't care for my cooking."

He shook his head. "That's not it. I think you're a good cook."

"So then why did you say those things?"

"Because good is fine for most people, but you aren't most people."

Her fine brows drew together. "What does that mean? Do you know about my past? Did your grandfather tell you?"

Whoa! That had him sitting up straight. "Nonno didn't tell me anything." But Dante couldn't let it end there. He wanted to believe that he was being cautious because of the business but it was more than that. He wanted to know everything there was about her. "I'm willing to listen, if you're willing to tell me."

Her blue eyes were a turbulent sea of emotions. "You don't want to hear about me."

"Yes, I do." The conviction in his voice took him by surprise.

She worried her lip as though considering what to tell him. "I don't know. I've already told you enough. I don't need to give you more reason to look at me differently."

Now he had to know. "I promise I won't do that."

"You might try, but it'll definitely color the way you see me." She leaned back in the chair and crossed her arms.

He wanted her to trust him although he knew that he hadn't given her any reason to do so. But this was important. On top of it all, if he understood her better, maybe he'd have an easier time communicating with her when they were working together. He knew he was kidding himself. His interest in her went much deeper than employer and employee.

"Trust me, Lizzie."

He could see the conflicted look in her eyes. She obviously wasn't used to opening up to people—except his grandfather. Nonno had a way with people that put them at ease. Dante was more like his father when it came to personal relationships—he had to work to find the right words. Sure, he could flirt with the women, but when it came down to meaningful talks, the DeFiore men failed.

But this was about Lizzie, not himself. And he didn't want to fail her. More than anything, he wanted her to let him in.

Should she trust him?

Lizzie studied Dante's handsome face. Her brain said that she'd already told him more than enough, but her heart pleaded with her to trust him. But to what end? It wasn't as if she was going to build a life here in Rome. Her life— her home—was thousands of miles away in New York.

But maybe she'd stumbled across something.

Whatever she told him would stay here in Rome. So what did it matter if she told him more about her past? It wasn't as if it was a secret anyway. Plenty of people knew her story—and plenty of those people had used it as a yardstick to judge her. Would Dante be different?

With every fiber of her being she wanted to believe that he would be. But she'd never know unless she said the words—words that made her feel as though she was less than everyone else. Admitting to her past made her feel as though she wasn't worthy of love.

She took a deep breath. "Before my mother died, I was placed in foster care."

Dante sat there looking at her as though he were still waiting for her big revelation.

"Did you hear me?"

"I heard that you grew up in a foster home, but I don't know why you would think that would make me look at you differently."

Seriously? This was so not the reaction she was expecting. Growing up, she'd learned to keep this information to herself. When the parents of her school friends had learned that she came from a foster home, they'd clucked their tongues and shaken their heads. Then suddenly her friends had no time for her. And once she'd overheard a parent say to another, *"You can never be too careful. Who knows about those foster kids. I don't want her having a bad influence on my kid."*

The memory made the backs of Lizzie's eyes sting. She'd already felt unwanted by her mother, who'd tossed her away as though she hadn't mattered. And then to know that people looked down on her, it hurt—a lot. But Lizzie refused to let it destroy her. Instead, she insisted on showing them that they were wrong—that she would make something of herself.

"You don't understand what it's like to grow up as a foster kid. Trust me. You had it so good."

Dante glanced away. "You don't know that."

"Are you serious? You have an amazing family. You know where you come from and who your parents are."

"It may look good from the outside, but you have no idea what it's like to live in that house and never be able to measure up." He got to his feet and strode over to the window.

"Maybe your family expected things from you because

they knew you were capable of great things. In my case, no one expected anything from me but trouble."

"Why would they think that?"

"Don't you get it? My parents tossed me away like yesterday's news. If the two people in the world who were supposed to love me the most didn't want me, it could only mean there's something wrong with me—something unworthy." Her voice cracked with emotion. "You don't know what it was like to be looked at like you are less than a person."

In three long, quick strides Dante was beside her. He sat down next to her and draped his arm around her. Needing to feel his strength and comfort, she lowered her head to his broad shoulder. The lid creaked open on the box of memories that she'd kept locked away for so many years.

Once again she was that little girl with the hand-me-down jeans with patches on the knees and the pant legs that were two inches too short. And the socks that rarely matched—she'd never forget those. She'd been incessantly taunted and teased about them.

But no longer.

Her clothes may not come from high-class shops, but they were of designer quality and gently worn so that no one knew that they were used—no one but Jules. But her foster sister was never one to judge. Probably because Jules never went for the sophisticated styles—Jules marched to a different drummer in fashion and makeup.

"I…I never had any friendships that lasted, except Jules. We had similar backgrounds and we leaned on each other through thick and thin."

"I'm so glad she was there for you. If I had been there I'd have told those people what was up."

Lizzie gave a little smile. "I can imagine you doing that, too."

"I don't understand why people have to be so mean."

She swallowed down the lump in her throat. "You can't

imagine how awful it was. At least when I was little, I didn't know what the looks and snide little comments by the mothers were about, but as I got older, I learned."

Dante's jaw tightened and a muscle in his cheek twitched. "Unbelievable."

"The kids were even meaner. If you didn't have the right clothes, and I never did, you'd be picked on and called names. And the right hairstyle, you had to have the latest trend. And my poker-straight hair would never cooperate. It seemed one way or another I constantly failed to fit in."

"I think they were all just jealous. How could they not be? You're gorgeous."

His compliment was like a balm on her old wounds. Did he really mean it? She gazed deep into his eyes and saw sincerity, which stole her breath away. Dante thought she was gorgeous. A warmth started in her chest and worked its way up her neck and settled in her cheeks.

"It's a shame they missed getting to know what a great person you are. And how caring you are."

She lifted her head and looked at him squarely in the eyes. "You're just saying that to make me feel better."

"No, I'm not." His breath brushed against her cheek, tickling it. "You're special."

She moved just a little so that she was face-to-face with him. She wanted to look into his eyes once more. She wanted to know without a doubt that he believed what he was saying. But what she found in his dark gaze sent her heart racing. Sincerity and desire reflected in his eyes.

He pulled her closer until her curves were pressed up against his hard planes. She knew this place. Logic said she should pull away. But the pounding of her heart drowned out any common sense. The only recognizable thought in her head was that she wanted him—all of him, and it didn't matter at that moment what happened tomorrow.

His gaze dipped to her lips. The breath caught in his throat. Her eyelids fluttered closed and then he was there pressing his mouth to hers. Her hands crept over his sturdy shoulders. Her fingertips raked through his short strands.

She followed his gently probing kisses until her mounting desire drove her to become more assertive. As she deepened their kiss, a moan sounded from him. She reveled in the ability to rouse his interest. Sure, she'd attracted a few men in the past, but none had gotten her heart to pound like it was doing now. She wondered if Dante could hear it. Did he know what amazing things he was doing to her body?

Did he know how much she wanted him?

The knowledge that she was willing to give herself to him just for the asking startled her back to reality. She pulled back. She wanted Dante too much. It was too dangerous. And after being a foster kid, she liked to play things safe—at least where her heart was concerned. She'd been burned far too many times.

"What's wrong?" Dante tried to pull her back to him.

She'd been here before, putting her heart on the line. Only then, she'd been a kid wanting to have a best friend and thinking that all would be fine. Then the parents had stepped in and she was rejected.

She remembered the agonizing pain of losing friend after friend. She'd promised herself that she'd never let herself be that vulnerable again. Not for anyone. Not even for this most remarkable man.

She struggled to slow her breathing and then uttered, "We can't do this. It isn't right."

"It sure felt right to me." He sent her a dreamy smile that made her heart flip-flop.

"Dante, don't. I'm being serious."

"And so am I. What's wrong with having a little fun?"

"It's more than that. It's… Oh, I don't know." Her insides were a ball of conflicting emotions.

"Relax. I won't push you for something you don't want to do."

The problem was that she did want him. She wanted him

more than she'd wanted anyone in her life. But it couldn't happen. She wouldn't let it. It would end in heartbreak— her heartbreak.

Dante placed a thumb beneath her chin and tilted it up until their gazes met. "Don't look so sad."

"I'm not." Then feeling a moment of panic over how easy it'd be to give in to these new feelings, she backed away from him. "You don't even know me. Why are you being so nice?"

"Seriously. Are you really going to play that card?" He smiled and shook his head in disbelief. "You aren't that much of a mystery."

She crossed her arms, not sure how comfortable she was with him thinking that he knew so much about her. "And what do you think you know about me?"

"I know that you like to put on a tough exterior to keep people at arm's length, but deep down you are sweet and thoughtful. I saw you with my family and especially Massimo. You listened to him and you didn't rush him when he had problems pronouncing some words. You made him feel like he had something important to say—like he was still a contributing member of the family."

"I'm glad to hear that my visit helped. I wish I could go back."

"You can…if you stay here."

What? Had she heard him correctly? He wanted her to stay? She didn't understand what was happening here. Not too long ago she'd been the one pushing for this arrangement to work and he was the one resisting the arrangement. Now suddenly he wanted her to stay. What was she missing?

"Why?" She searched his face, trying to gain a glimmer of insight.

"Why not?"

"That's not an answer. Why did you suddenly have this change of heart?"

He shifted his weight from one foot to the other. "I've had a chance to think it over. And I think that we can help each other."

"Are you saying this because I told you about my background? Is this some sort of sympathy?"

"No." The response came quickly—too quickly. "Why would you say that?"

She shrugged. "Why not? It's the only reason I can see for you to want this arrangement to work. Or is there something I don't know?"

There was a look in his eyes. Was it surprise? Had she stumbled across something?

"Tell me, Dante. Otherwise, I'm outta here. If you can't be honest with me, we can't work together." And she meant it. Somehow, someway she'd scrape together the money for Jules to go to grad school, to reach her dreams and to be able to help other unfortunate children.

He exhaled a frustrated sigh. "I talked with my solicitor before dinner."

When he paused, she prompted him. "And."

"He said that we could break the contract but it wouldn't be quick or cheap."

Her gut was telling her that there was more to this than he was telling her. "What else?"

Dante rubbed the back of his neck. "Did anyone ever tell you that you're pushy?"

"I am when I have to be—when I can tell that I'm not being given the whole truth."

"Well, that's it. My solicitor advised me that it would be easier to go through with your project. And he mentioned that in the end it would benefit the *ristorante* and bring in more tourist traffic."

So that was it. He was looking at his bottom line. She couldn't fault him for that because technically she was doing the same thing. She was looking forward to the money she earned to help her foster sister. But she just couldn't shake the memories of the past.

"And you're sure this has nothing to do with what I told you about my past."

"I swear. Now will you stay?"

She didn't know what to say. She wasn't sure how this would work now that they'd kissed twice and were sharing an apartment, regardless of its spaciousness. When she glanced into Dante's eyes, the fluttering feeling churned in her stomach. And when her gaze slipped down to his lips, she was tempted to steal another kiss.

"What's the matter?" Dante asked, arching his brow. "Are you worried about us being roommates?"

"How did you know?"

The corner of his tempting mouth lifted in a knowing smile. "Because you aren't the only one wondering about that question. But before you let that chase you off, remember the reason you came here—to learn. To hone your cooking skills."

"But I can't do that if you and I are…you know…"

"How about I make you a promise that I won't kiss you again…until you ask me. I will be the perfect host and teacher— Well, okay, the teaching might be a bit rough at first but I will try my best."

She looked deep into his eyes, finding sincerity. Her gut said to trust him. But it was these new feelings that she didn't trust. Still, this was her only viable option to hold up her promise to Jules, who'd helped her through school and pushed her to reach for her dreams. How could she do any less in return?

With a bit of hesitancy, she stuck out her hand. "You have a deal."

CHAPTER THIRTEEN

WHAT EXACTLY HAD he gotten himself into?

The sun was flirting with the horizon as Dante yawned and entered the kitchen of Ristorante Massimo. The film crew was quite timely. Dante stood off to the side, watching the bustle of activity as a large pot of *caffè* brewed. The large kitchen instantly shrank as the camera crew, makeup artist and director took over the area. In no time, spotless countertops were covered with equipment, cases and papers. The place no longer looked like the kitchen his grandfather had taught him to cook in—the large room that held some of his happiest memories.

Dante inwardly groaned and stepped out of the way of a young assistant wheeling in another camera. So much for the peace and tranquillity that he always enjoyed at this time of the day. He slipped into the office to enjoy his coffee.

"Hey, what are you doing in here?" Lizzie's voice called out from behind him.

He turned to find her lingering in the doorway. The smile on her face lit up her eyes. She practically glowed. Was it the television cameras that brought out this side of her? The thought saddened him. He wished that he could evoke such happiness in her. But it was best that they'd settled things and agreed that from now on she was hands off for him.

"I'm just staying out of the way. Is all of that stuff necessary?"

"There's not much. You should see what they have in the studio."

"I don't remember all of those things when they filmed here before."

She shrugged. "Are you ready for this?"

He wasn't. He really didn't want to be a television star, but he'd given his word and he wouldn't go back on that—he wouldn't disappoint Lizzie. She'd been disappointed too many times in her life.

"Yes, I am. We need to get this done before the employees show up to get everything started for the lunch crowd. What do we need to do first?"

"You need makeup."

"What?" He shook his head and waved off the idea. "I don't think so."

His thoughts filled with images of some lady applying black eyeliner and lipstick to him. His nose turned up at the idea. No way. Wasn't happening. Not in his lifetime.

"Is it really that bad?" Lizzie's sweet laugh grated on his taut nerves.

"I agreed to teach you to cook in front of the cameras, but I never agreed to eyeliner."

Lizzie stepped closer. "What? You don't think you need a little cover stick and maybe a little blush."

His gaze narrowed on her as she stopped right in front of him. The amusement danced in her eyes. He truly believed, next to her visit with his grandfather, this was the happiest he'd seen her. He didn't want it to end, but he had to draw a line when it came to makeup.

"I'm not doing it. And you can keep smiling at me, but it isn't going to change my mind."

Her fingertip stroked along his jaw. "Mmm, nice. Someone just shaved."

Yes, he had. Twice. "That doesn't have anything to do with makeup."

Her light touch did the craziest things to his pulse. And was that the sweet scent of her perfume? Or was it the lingering trace of her shampoo? He inhaled deeper. Whatever it was, he could definitely get used to it.

Her fingertip moved to his bottom lip, which triggered nerve endings that shot straight through to his core. Her every touch was agonizing as he struggled not to pull her close and replace her finger with her lips. But he'd once again given his word to be on his best behavior.

He caught her arm and pulled it away from his mouth. "You might want to stop doing that or I won't be responsible for what happens next."

Her baby blues opened wide and her pink frosty lips formed an O.

She withdrew her arm and stepped back. He regretted putting an end to her fun as she seemed to regress back into her shell. He wished she'd let that side of her personality out more often. But obviously he'd have to get a better grip on himself so that next time he didn't chase her away.

She was so beautiful. So amazing. So very tempting. And he'd been the biggest fool in the world to promise to be a gentleman. But he had no one to blame for this agonizing torture except himself.

"You need to loosen up. Act natural."

Lizzie glanced up at the director, thinking he was talking to Dante. After all, she'd done this sort of thing before—acting in front of the cameras. But instead of the young guy giving Dante a pointed look, the man was staring directly at her. Her chest tightened.

"I…I am."

The man shook his head and turned to his cameraman to say something.

Dante moved to her side. "What's the matter, Lizzie? Where's the woman who just a little bit ago was teasing me about makeup?"

She refused to let him get the best of her. "Speaking of which, I see that you're wearing some. Looks good. Except you might want a little more eyeliner."

"What?" He grabbed a stainless-steel pot and held it up so he could see his reflection. His dark brows drew together. "I'm not wearing eyeliner."

She smiled.

"That's what I want." The director's voice drew her attention. "I want that spark and easy interaction on the camera."

Lizzie inwardly groaned. The man didn't know what he was asking of her. She chanced a glance at Dante as he returned the pot to a shelf. She wasn't the only one who'd reverted back behind a wall. He had been keeping his distance around her, too. She wondered if he regretted their kissing? Or was it something deeper? Did it have something to do with the reason Dante lived all alone in that spacious apartment that was far too big for just one person?

"Okay, let's try this shot again."

Lizzie took her position at the counter, trying her best to act relaxed and forget about the camera facing her. But as Dante began his lines and moved around her, showing her how to prepare the *pasta alla gricia*, she could smell his spicy aftershave. It'd be so easy to give in to her desires. But where would that leave her? Brokenhearted and alone. Her muscles stiffened.

"Cut." The director walked up to her. "I don't understand. We've worked together before and you did wonderfully. What's the problem now?"

The problem was Dante looked irresistibly sexy in his pressed white jacket. She swallowed hard. As she took a deep calming breath, she recalled his fresh, soapy scent.

Mmm…he smelled divine. What was she supposed to do? When he got close enough to assist her with the food prep, she panicked—worried she'd end up caring about him. That she'd end up falling for him. And that just couldn't happen. She wouldn't let it.

"Nothing is wrong." She hoped her voice sounded more assured than she felt at the moment. "I'll do better."

The director frowned at her. "Maybe you should take a break. We'll shoot the next segment with just Dante."

Lizzie felt like a kid in school that had just gotten a stern warning from the principal before being dismissed to go contemplate her actions. Keeping her gaze straight ahead and well away from Dante, she headed for the coffeepot, where she filled up a cup. After a couple of dashes of sugar and topping it off with cream, she headed for the office. It was her only refuge from prying eyes.

She resisted the urge to close the door. She didn't need them speculating that she'd dissolved into a puddle of tears. It would take a lot more than messing up a shot to start the waterworks.

More than anything, she was frustrated. She grabbed for her cell phone, wanting to hear Jules's voice. Her foster sister always had a way of talking her off ledges. But just as she was about to press the last digit, she realized that with the time difference, Jules would still be sound asleep.

Lizzie slid the phone back in her pocket. What was she going to do now? Dante was totally showing her up in there. The thought did not sit well with her at all.

Since when did she let a man get to her? She could be a professional. She wasn't some teenager with a crush. She was a grown woman with responsibilities. It was time she started acting that way before this whole spotlight series went up in flames.

"Are you all right?" Dante's voice came from behind her.

"I'm fine. Why does everyone keep asking me that?"

"Because you haven't been acting like yourself." Concern reflected in his eyes. "Tell me what's bothering you. I'll help if I can."

"Don't do that."

His forehead wrinkled. "What?"

"Act like we're something we're not." If he continued to treat her this way, her resolve would crack. And she didn't want to rely on him. She knew what would happen then. He'd pull back just like her ex had done. Men were only into women for an uncomplicated good time.

And she was anything but uncomplicated.

"I don't know what you're talking about." Dante's voice took on a deeper tone. "All I wanted to do was help." He held up his hands innocently. "But I can tell when I'm not wanted."

He stormed back out the door.

Good. Not that she was happy that he was upset. But she could deal with his agitation much easier than she could his niceness. Each kind word he spoke to her was one more chip at the wall she'd carefully built over the years to protect herself. And she wasn't ready to take it down for him or anyone.

At last, feeling as though she had her head screwed on straight, she returned to the kitchen. The director looked at her as though studying her. "You ready?"

She nodded. "Yes, I am."

The director had them take their places as Lizzie sensed Dante's agitation and distance. She was sorry that it had to be this way, but she could at last think straight. And when the director called a halt to the filming, it was Dante who fouled up the shot. They redid it a few times until the director was satisfied.

This arrangement may have been her idea, but at the time she hadn't a clue how hard it was going to be to work so closely with Dante. Still, she had to do this. She didn't have a choice. There were bills to meet and grad school to pay.

She just had to pretend that Dante was no one special. But was that possible in the long run? How was she supposed to ignore these growing feelings when she found Dante fascinating in every way?

She was in trouble. Deep trouble.

CHAPTER FOURTEEN

NOT TOO BAD.

Lizzie stifled a yawn as she poured herself a cup of coffee. Thankfully it was late Friday night and the restaurant was at last closed. She was relieved that there was no filming in the morning. Those early wake-up calls were wearing her down. The next morning the crew was off to shoot some footage of Rome to pad their spotlights. And she couldn't be happier.

Lizzie pressed a cup of stale coffee to her lips.

"You might not want to drink that."

She turned at the sound of Dante's voice. "Why not?"

"That stuff is strong enough to strip paint off Red. You'll never get to sleep if you drink it."

She held back a laugh. "Don't worry. I'll be fine."

Dante raised a questioning brow before he turned back to finish cleaning the grill. He really was a hands-on kinda guy. She didn't know why that should surprise her. He'd never once sloughed off his work onto his staff. Everyone had their assigned duties and they all seemed to work in harmony.

Dante had been remarkable when it came to the filming, too. He may grump and growl like an old bear about things like makeup, but when the cameras started to roll, he really came through for her—for them. Maybe he hadn't nailed every scene but he'd been trying and that was what counted. And if she didn't know better, she'd swear he'd been enjoying himself in front of the cameras.

It was amazing how long it took to shoot a short segment to splice into the station's number-one-rated cooking show. But it was so worth it. What a plum spot they'd been given. It'd definitely make her credentials stand out from the competition when she returned to New York and searched for a chef position at one of the upscale restaurants in Manhattan.

She took the cup of coffee to the office and cleared off a spot at the end of the couch. No sooner had she gotten comfortable than Dante sauntered into the room.

"See, you should have taken me up on my offer to take the afternoon off." He sent her an *I told you so* look.

She shrugged. "I wanted to get a feel for how everything works around here."

"And now you're exhausted."

"Listen to who's talking. You worked just as many hours as I did."

"But I'm used to it."

Now, that did surprise her. What was a young, incredibly sexy man doing spending all of his time at the restaurant? Surely he must have an active social life away from this place. The image of him dressed in a sharp suit filled her mind. And then a beautiful slip of a woman infiltrated her thoughts. The mystery woman sauntered over and draped herself on his arm. Lizzie's body tensed.

"Is something the matter?"

She glanced up at Dante. "What?"

"You were frowning. Is it the *caffè*? I told you not to drink it."

Not about to tell him her true thoughts, she said, "Yes, it's cold. I'll just dump it out and head upstairs. Are you coming?"

He glanced around at the messy office. "I should probably do a little work in here."

She stifled a laugh. This place needed a lot more than a "little" help. "Have you ever thought of hiring someone to sort through all of these old papers?"

"I don't think there's a person alive that would willingly take on this challenge. My grandfather was not much of a businessman. He did the bare minimum. And I'm afraid that I'm not much better. I'd rather be in the kitchen or talking with the patrons."

She could easily believe that of him and his grandfather. They were both very social people, unlike her. She could hold her own in social scenes but her preference was the anonymity of a kitchen or office.

"Well, don't stay up too late." She headed for the door. "We wouldn't want you having bags under your eyes for the camera."

"Is there an in-between with you?"

She turned. "What do you mean?"

"You are either very serious or joking around. Is there ever a middle ground?"

She'd never really thought that much about it. "Of course. See, I'm not making any jokes now."

"And you're also being serious. You're wondering if I'm right."

Her lips pursed together. Did Dante see something that she'd been missing all along? And was he right?

He stepped closer. "If you control the conversation then nothing slips out—those little pieces of your life that let a person really know you. You can then keep everyone at a safe distance."

Her gaze narrowed in on him. "Since when have you become such an expert on me?"

"I'm good at reading people. And you intrigue me."

Any other time she might have enjoyed the fact that she intrigued a man but not now. Not when he could see aspects of her that made her uncomfortable.

"Are you trying to tell me that you're a mind reader—

no, wait, maybe a fortune-teller? I can see you now with a colorful turban, staring into a glass ball." She forced a smile, hoping to lighten the conversation.

"And there you go with the jokes. My point is proven."

He was right. Drat. She'd never thought about how she'd learned to shield herself from other people. When conversations got too close, too personal, she turned them around with a joke. Anything to get the spotlight off herself.

After all this time of putting up defensive postures, she didn't know if she could let down those protective walls and just be—especially around a man who could make her heart race with just a look. But something within her wanted things to be different with Dante. It was lonely always pushing people away.

"I'm just me." She didn't know how to be anyone else. "I'm sorry if that doesn't live up to your idea of the perfect woman."

He stepped closer to her. It'd be so easy to reach out to him—to lean into his arms and forget about the world for just a moment. Every fiber of her body wanted to throw herself into his arms and feel his lips against hers.

"Lizzie, you don't have to be perfect." His voice was soft and comforting. "You just have to be honest with yourself and realize that not everyone is out to hurt you. I won't hurt you."

Hearing those last four words was like having a bucket of ice water dumped over her head. Her ex had said the same thing to her to get her into bed. But when opportunity came knocking on his door, she was relegated to nothing more than an afterthought. He couldn't wait to leave New York—to leave her. The realization of how little he'd cared for her cut deep.

She wasn't going to fall for those words again.

She stepped back out of Dante's reach.

His dark gaze stared straight at her as though searching for answers to his unspoken questions.

When his gaze dipped to her lips, the breath hitched in her throat. What was he going to do? He'd promised not to kiss her until she asked him to. Would he keep that promise?

Factions warred within her. One wanted to remain safe. The other part wanted to sweep caution aside and lean into his arms. Was it possible that being safe wasn't always the best choice? Was a chance at happiness worth the inherent risks?

Dante cleared his throat. "You better go upstairs now." His voice was deeper than normal and rumbled with emotion. "If you don't, I might end up breaking my word. And a DeFiore never goes back on his word."

She turned on legs that felt like rubber and headed for the door. The warm night air did nothing to soothe her heated emotions. She needed a shower to relax her or she'd never get any sleep tonight. And Dante was worried the coffee would be stimulating. It was nothing compared to his presence.

It was on the elevator ride upstairs that she realized if he had reached out to her, she wouldn't have resisted. She wanted him as much as he wanted her. He didn't have to say the words. It was all there in his eyes. The need. The want. The desire.

Sleep was not something that was going to come easily that night.

What was wrong with him?

Dante got up from the desk in his study and strode to the window. The lights from the city obscured the stars, but he knew they were there, just like he knew there was something growing between him and Lizzie. He couldn't touch it. He couldn't see it. But there was definitely something real growing between them.

She'd appeared in his life out of nowhere. At every turn, she challenged everything he believed he wanted in life.

But above and beyond all of that, she brought the "fun factor" back to his life. He enjoyed sharing the kitchen with her. He even went to bed each night anticipating the next morning. What was it about Lizzie that had him feeling things that he'd never experienced before?

Images of her curled up in bed just down the hall from him had him prowling around his study instead of sleeping. The only good news was that there was no filming tomorrow. But it wasn't as if they had the next day off. It was Saturday, the busiest day of the week for the *ristorante*. The responsible side of him told him to go to bed this second or he'd pay for it in the morning. But he didn't relish the idea of lying there in the dark while images of the alluring woman who now shared his apartment teased and danced through his mind.

He clenched his hands as a groan rose in his throat. Pacing around his study was not doing him a bit of good. At least if he went and lay down, his body would get some much-needed rest. If he was lucky, maybe sleep would finally claim him. But first he needed a drink.

In nothing but his boxers, he quietly padded to the darkened kitchen. When he rounded the corner, the door of the fridge swung open and he stopped in his tracks, thoroughly captivated with the sight before him.

Lizzie bent over to rummage through the contents of the fridge. A pair of peach lacy shorts rode up over her shapely thighs and backside. He swallowed hard, unable to pry his eyes away from her.

Then, realizing he was spying on her, he cleared his throat. His mouth suddenly went dry. He hoped when he spoke that his voice would come out clearly. "Something you need?"

Lizzie jumped and turned around. "I didn't mean to wake you."

"You didn't."

She closed the fridge, shrouding them in darkness.

Dante moved to switch on the light over the stove. He couldn't get enough of her beauty.

She turned, casting him a questioning stare. "You couldn't sleep either?"

"Too much on my mind." He wasn't about to admit that she was on his mind. Her image had been taunting him. But those images had been nothing compared to the real thing that was standing in front of him.

The spaghetti straps of her top rested on her ivory shoulders as her straight flaxen hair flowed down her back. He didn't know that she could look even more beautiful, but he'd never be able to erase this enchanting image from his mind. He stifled a frustrated sigh and turned to the fridge. He pulled it open but nothing appealed to him. When he turned back around, her intent gaze met his.

Her fingers toyed with the lace edging of her top. "What are you worried about?"

"Nothing in particular." He really didn't want to discuss what was on his mind. "I just came out to get a snack."

He was hungry but it wasn't food he craved. When his gaze returned to her face, he noticed how she crossed her arms over her breasts. It was far too late for modesty.

"You know, you don't have to be so uncomfortable around me." He stepped forward. "I promise I just want to be your friend."

"I think it's more than that." She arched a brow. "More like friends with benefits?"

"Hey, now, that's not fair. I've kept my word. I haven't touched you." His voice grew deep as his imagination kicked into high gear. "I haven't wrapped my arms around you and pulled you close." He took another step toward her. "I haven't run my fingers up your neck and over your cheeks or trailed my thumb over your pouty lips."

Her gaze bored deep into his. The desire flared in her baby blues. He knew she wanted this moment as much as he did. He also knew that opening this door in their relationship would change things between them dramatically. But that didn't stop him. He'd gotten a glimpse of life with Lizzie in it and he wanted more of her—no matter the cost.

Damn. Why had he given his word to keep his hands to himself? Now all he had to work with were his words. He wasn't a poet, but suddenly he felt inspired.

"I…I thought you said you were going to be a gentleman?" Her gaze never left his.

"I said that I wouldn't touch you—wouldn't kiss you—not until you asked me to. But I never said anything about telling you how I feel."

She took a step toward him until their bodies were almost touching. "And how do you feel?"

His heart slammed into his ribs. He swallowed hard. "I want you so much that it's all I can think about. I can't eat. I can't sleep. All I can think about is you. Do you have any idea how much I want to wrap my arms around you and pull you close? Then I'd press my mouth to yours. I'd leave no doubt in your mind about how good we can be. Together."

She looked deep into his eyes as though she could see clear through to his soul. No one had ever looked at him that way before. The breath caught in his throat as he waited, hoping she'd cave. He wasn't so sure how long his willpower would hold out.

Her head tilted to the left and her hair swished around her shoulder. "Do you really mean it?"

"Yes, I mean it." Second by second he was losing his steadfast control. "You are driving me to distraction. It's a miracle I haven't accidentally burned the *ristorante* down."

Her lips lifted. "You're too much of a professional to do something like that."

"We'll have to wait and see. After tonight, I don't know if I'll ever get the image of you in that barely-there outfit out of my mind." He groaned in frustration. "Talk about a major distraction."

A sexy smile tugged at her lips as desire sparkled in her

eyes. Her hands reached out to him, pressing against his bare chest. He sucked in an even breath as her touch sent tremors of excitement throughout his body. Did she have any idea what she was doing to him?

This was the sweetest torture he'd ever endured. It'd take every bit of willpower to walk away from her. But he had to keep his promise to her—he couldn't be like those other people in her life who'd let her down. But he didn't want it to end—not yet.

She tilted her chin and their gazes locked. All he could think about was pressing his mouth to hers. He desperately wanted to show her exactly how she made him feel.

He was in trouble—up to his neck in it. And as much as he savored having Lizzie this close and looking at him as if he was the only man in the world for her, his resolve was rapidly deteriorating. Was this what it was like to fall in love?

Not that he was going there. Was he?

He gazed deep into her eyes, and in that moment, he saw a flash of his future—a future with Lizzie. He wanted her to look at him with that heated desire for the rest of their lives. The revelation shook him, rattling his very foundation and jarring him back to reality.

He shackled his fingers around her wrists and pushed her away from him, hoping he'd be able to think more clearly.

"You're really as good as your word, aren't you?" There was a note of marvel in her voice.

"I'm trying. But if you keep this up, I'm going to lose the battle."

"Maybe I want you to lose."

What? His gaze studied her face. A smile tugged at her lips and delight danced in her eyes. He honestly didn't know if this was another of her tests. Or was it an invitation. With a frustrated groan, he let go of her wrists and backed up until the stove pressed into his backside. He slouched against it. Defeat and frustration weighed heavy on his shoulders.

"Don't look so miserable." She stepped toward him.

When she went to touch him again, he said, "Don't, Lizzie. You've had your fun but now let me be... Please go."

"I don't want to leave you alone. Maybe I want you to pull me into your arms and do those things you mentioned."

His back straightened. "Is that an invitation?"

She nodded. "Dante, I want you just as much—"

That was all he needed to hear. In a heartbeat, he had her in his arms and his mouth claimed hers. She tasted of mint and chocolate like the after-dinner treats they handed out with the checks. He'd never taste another of those little chocolates without thinking of her.

And though the thought of letting her slip through his fingers was agonizing, he had to be absolutely sure that she wanted this, too. With every last bit of willpower, he moved his mouth from hers. "Are you sure about this? About us?"

Her big round eyes shimmered with desire. "Yes, I'm positive."

In the next instant, he swung her up into his arms and carried her back down the hallway to his master bedroom—a room he'd never shared with another woman.

But Lizzie was different. Everything about her felt so right. It was as though he'd been waiting for her to step into his life. Things would never be the same.

But exactly where they went from here, he wasn't quite certain.

He'd think about it later.

Much later.

CHAPTER FIFTEEN

DROP BY DROP...

The icy walls around her heart had melted.

Lizzie felt exposed. Vulnerable. A position she'd promised herself she'd never put herself in again. She rushed downstairs to the restaurant. When she got there she couldn't fathom how she'd found the willpower to leave Dante's side—where she longed to be right now. But she couldn't stay there. She couldn't afford to get in even deeper.

Her time in Italy was limited. In just a few weeks, she'd be preparing to return to the States—back where her responsibilities were awaiting her. And then what? She'd leave her heart in Italy. No, thank you. She had no intention of being some kind of martyr to love.

What she and Dante had was...was a one-night stand. This acknowledgment startled her. She'd never thought of herself as the type to have a fling. And now that the scratch had been itched, they'd be fine. They could go back to being coworkers.

With a fresh pot of coffee, she filled a mug and headed to the office. She had no idea how Dante could stand such a mess. It was the exact opposite of the immaculate study in his apartment, which probably explained why almost everything in here dated back years. And she couldn't find any current invoices or orders. He probably did his work upstairs and left this place as a reminder of his grandfather. Dante must miss him terribly. Her heart went out to both of them.

She knew what it was like to miss someone terribly. Her thoughts strayed to Jules. She wondered if she was still awake. She glanced at the big clock on the wall. It should be close to midnight now. Jules wasn't a partyer, but she was a night owl who had a thing for watching old movies until she fell asleep.

Needing to hear her foster sister's voice to remind her of why she should be down here instead of snug in bed with Dante, she reached for her phone. It rang once, twice, three times—

"Hey, Lizzie, what's going on?" Jules's voice was a bit groggy. "Is what's-his-face still giving you a hard time?"

"I…I just wanted to touch base and make sure things are okay with you." Her voice wobbled. Usually she told Jules everything, but suddenly she felt herself clamming up.

A groan came through the phone, the sound Jules made when she was stretching after waking up. Lizzie smiled. She could just imagine Jules stretched out on the couch. She really did miss her. They were like two peas in a pod. She couldn't imagine they'd ever move far from each other— no matter what happened in life.

"Lizzie, I can hear it in your voice. Talk to me." Her concern rang through the phone, crystal clear and totally undeniable.

This call had been a mistake. How could she tell Jules— that she'd slept with the dreamiest man on earth? She didn't want Jules adding one plus one and ending up with five.

Because there was no way she was in love with Dante. He liked fast cars and beautiful women draped on his arm. She recalled the photos of him with various stunning women hanging in the dining room. The strange thing was she hadn't found any evidence that he was anything more than a caring, compassionate man who appeared to be as commitment-phobic as herself.

"Stop worrying. I'm fine. Dante and I worked things out." Lizzie ran her thumb over the edge of a tall stack of papers. "What's new with you?"

There was a moment of strained silence.

"I had an interview for grad school. Actually, it was an all-day event. They even took the candidates out for a fancy dinner."

"I hope you didn't scare them off with all of your makeup and your black-and-white ensemble," she said in a teasing tone.

Jules sighed. "You ought to give me more credit. Actually, I borrowed some of your clothes. I even received a couple of compliments."

Excitement swirled in Lizzie's chest and had her smiling. "Does that mean you're ready for a wardrobe makeover?"

"Not a chance. I'm good the way I am."

"Yes, you are."

Jules used the makeup and clothes as camouflage—so people couldn't see the real her. But someday she hoped Jules would feel secure enough to move beyond the walls she hid behind. Whereas Lizzie's scars were all on the inside, Jules wasn't so lucky—she had them both inside and out, and she took great care to hide them.

"Anyway, it went really well and I was told unofficially that I got in. But it'll take a bit of paperwork before I get my official notification." There was a distinct lack of excitement in Jules's voice. "Lizzie? Are you still there?"

"Uh, yes. That's great! I knew you could do it. And don't worry about anything but getting through your final exams. I've got everything else under control."

"I can tell you have something on your mind. If you aren't happy there, come home."

"It's not that." And it wasn't even a lie. "I'm just tired. I didn't sleep much. That's all it is."

"Are you sure that Dante guy doesn't have anything to do with it?"

"I promise he's been great." Lizzie blinked repeatedly, keeping her emotions at bay. "If you must know, I'm a bit homesick. I miss my sidekick."

"I miss you, too. But you'll be home soon."

"I know. I'm looking forward to it."

"And here I thought Rome would be your trip of a lifetime. I was worried that you'd fall in love and I'd never see you again."

Jules was so close to the truth. Perhaps she really could use someone else's thoughts. "The truth is, Dante and I... we...umm..."

"You slept together?" The awe in Jules's voice echoed through the phone.

"Yes. But it was a one-time thing. It didn't mean anything." In her heart she knew it was a lie, but it was the reassurance Jules needed to hear to keep her calm before her finals. "Don't worry. I'll be home soon."

And the truth was it wouldn't happen again. They'd gotten away with making love once, but to have a full-blown affair with him would run the real risk of breaking her heart. Already she felt closer to him than any other man she'd ever known.

It didn't mean anything.

Those words smacked Dante across the face.

When he'd woken up, he'd reached out and found a cold, empty spot next to him. He'd begun to wonder if he'd just dreamed the incredible night. If it hadn't been for the impression of Lizzie's head in the pillow next to his and the lingering floral scent, he might have written it off as a very vivid dream. Maybe that would have been best for both of them.

By the time he'd searched the whole apartment, he'd started to panic. Where could she have gone? Why had she left? Did she regret their moment of lovemaking?

And now as he stood in the doorway with the doorjamb

propping him up, his worst fears were confirmed. Lizzie regretted last night. While he was thinking that this could possibly be the start of something, she was thinking that it would never happen again. His gut twisted into a painful knot.

Gone were the illusions that last night meant something special—for both of them. He'd been so wrong about so many things. He knew that Lizzie wouldn't intentionally hurt him. She had a good heart even though she kept it guarded.

Hearing those painful words was his own fault. He shouldn't be eavesdropping. Still, not even Red could drag him away from the spot on the white tiled floor. It was better to hear the truth than to misread things and get lost in some fantasy that wasn't real.

How could he have been such a fool? He couldn't believe he'd given in to his desires. He never lost control like that. But when he'd thought she'd finally let down her guard and let him in, he'd gotten carried away. In the end, it had all been in his imagination.

She had only one goal. To finish her job here and return to New York. Well, that was fine with him. She didn't have to worry about him clinging to her. That wasn't about to happen. No way.

Finding this out now was for the best. In the end, committed relationships didn't work out for DeFiore men. One way or another, when one of them got too close, they ended up getting burned. Luckily he'd only gotten singed, unlike his father and brother, who'd had their hearts and lives utterly decimated.

Dante stepped into the office. "So this is where you're hiding."

Lizzie jumped and pressed a hand to her chest. "I'm not hiding. And how long have you been standing there?"

"Long enough. A more important question is why did

you disappear without a word?" He should leave the subject alone but he couldn't.

His pride had been pricked and it demanded to be soothed. Because his bruised ego had to be what was causing him such discomfort. It couldn't be anything else. He refused to accept that he'd fallen for a woman who had used him for a one-night stand.

Lizzie's gaze moved to the papers on the desk. "I couldn't sleep."

Because she was horrified by what she'd let happen between them. He stifled a groan of frustration. "Something on your mind?"

Her gaze avoided his. "Uhh…no. I…ah, you must have been right. I had too much caffeine last night."

He cleared his throat, refusing to let his voice carry tones of agitation. "And you thought you'd come down here and what? Clean up the office?"

Her slender shoulders, the ones he'd rained kisses down on just hours ago, rose and fell. "I thought maybe I could organize it for you."

"And you were so excited to sort papers that it had you jumping out of bed before sunrise?"

Her gaze didn't meet his. "I like office work."

"You must."

She nodded. "I have a business degree."

He struggled to keep the surprise from showing on his face. Just one more thing to prove how little he knew about her…and yet he couldn't ignore the nagging thought that he still wanted to learn more about the beautiful blonde with the blue eyes that he could lose himself in.

He crossed his arms as his gaze followed her around the office as she moved stacks of papers to the desk. "You know, office work isn't part of the contract."

"I didn't know that we were being formal about things."

"I think it would be for the best. We don't want to forget the reason you're here."

Her forehead crinkled. "If it's about last night—"

"It's not. That was a fun night, but I'm sure neither of us plans to repeat it." *Liar. Liar.*

"So we're okay?" Hope reflected in her eyes.

"Sure." He was as far from "sure" about this as he could get, but he'd tough it out. After all, he'd given his word. A DeFiore wasn't a quitter. "You still want to complete the filming, don't you?"

There was a determined set of her jaw as she nodded. He didn't want to admit it, but he admired the way she stuck by her commitments, even if she didn't want to be around him. But there was something more. He peered closer at her, noticing the shadows beneath her eyes.

"You don't need to waste your time in here." He didn't want her wearing herself out on his behalf. "You should get some sleep since you…you were up most of the night. I don't need you walking around here in a sleep-filled haze."

"I'll be fine. I…I don't sleep much."

He wasn't going to argue with her. If she found some sort of comfort in sorting through this mound of paperwork that stretched back more years than he wanted to know, why should he stop her?

"Fine. Sort through as many papers as you like."

Her brows lifted as her eyes widened. "You mean it?"

"Sure. But I do have one question. How do you plan to sort everything when it's in Italian?"

She shrugged. "I'll muddle through. I took Italian in school."

And yet another surprise. They just kept coming, and without the aid of caffeine, he had problems keeping the surprise from filtering onto his face. He scrubbed his hand over his head, not caring that he was making a mess of his hair.

He noticed the eager look on her face. "Whatever. It has to be done soon anyway if I plan to…"

"Plan to what?"

He couldn't believe that he'd almost blurted out his plans to sell the *ristorante*. He hadn't even discussed it with Nonno. There was just something about Lizzie that put him at ease and had him feeling as though he could discuss anything. But obviously the feeling didn't go both ways.

"Once there's room, I was planning to move the business files I have upstairs in my study down here."

"Understood." She gave him a pointed look. "Before you go, we really should talk about last night—"

"It was late. Neither of us were thinking clearly. It's best if we forget about it. We still have to work together."

Her mouth gaped but no words came out. The look in her eyes said there were plenty of thoughts racing round in her mind, but that wasn't his problem. By admitting it'd been a mistake, he'd beaten her to the punch. That was fine with him.

He refused to think about how she'd discarded him and his lovemaking so readily. Soon she'd be gone. He'd just have to figure out how they could avoid each other as much as possible between now and then.

CHAPTER SIXTEEN

PRETEND IT HADN'T HAPPENED?

Was he kidding? The thought ricocheted through Lizzie's mind for about the thousandth time since Dante had spoken the words. His solution was paramount to pretending there wasn't a thousand-pound pink polka-dot elephant in the room. Impossible.

How could he just forget their lovemaking?

As the days rolled into weeks, he acted as though that earth-moving night had never happened. And he didn't leave her any room to explain or make amends. He only interacted with her on a minimal basis. The easy friendship they'd developed had crashed upon rocky shores. She missed her newfound friend more than she thought possible.

And worse yet, their chilly rapport was now apparent on the filmed segments. The director appeared to be at a loss as to how to regain their easy camaraderie. Their television segment was in jeopardy. And Lizzie couldn't let things end like this—too much was riding on their success.

While spending yet another sleepless night staring into the darkness, she'd stumbled across an idea. A chance to smooth things out with Dante.

Instead of spending another lonely weekend sightseeing while Dante visited the vineyard, she'd invited herself to accompany him to the country. Armed with an old family recipe she'd found while straightening the office and with

Massimo by her side, she'd commandeered the kitchen. She would cook the family a feast and in the process hopefully she'd mend a fence with Dante.

"Do you really think they'll like it?" She glanced at Massimo as he sat at the large kitchen table near the picture window.

"Don't you mean will Dante like it?"

The more time she spent with Massimo, the less she noticed his slurred speech and the more he could read her mind. "Yes, I want Dante to like it, too."

A knowing gleam glinted in the older man's eyes. "Something is wrong between you two."

It wasn't a question. It was a statement of fact. She glanced away and gave the sauce a stir. She didn't want Massimo to read too much in her eyes. Some things were meant to stay between her and Dante.

"We'll be fine."

Massimo got to his feet and, with the aid of his walker, moved next to her. "Look at me."

She hesitated before doing as he'd asked. She didn't know what he was going to say, but her gut told her that it would be important.

"My grandson has witnessed a lot of loss in his life. He's also been at the wrong end of his father's grief over losing my daughter. I know all about grief. When I lost my dear, sweet Isabelle, it nearly killed me. It can make a good man say things he shouldn't. It can cause a person to grow a tough skin to keep from getting hurt again."

The impact of his words answered so many questions and affirmed her suspicions. "But why are you telling me all of this? It's none of my business."

"I see how my grandson looks at you. It's the same way I looked at his grandmother. But he's afraid—afraid of being hurt like his father and brother. If you care about my grandson like I think you do, you'll fight for him."

"But I can't. Even if there was something between Dante and me, my life—it's in New York."

"Love will always find a way—"

"Mmm… What smells so good?"

Stefano strode into the kitchen, followed closely by Dante and his father. Their hungry gazes roamed over the counter and stove. She shooed them all away to get washed up while she set the dining room table.

Soon all four men were cleaned up in dress shirts and slacks. Thankfully, she'd had a couple of minutes to run to her room and put on a dress. Still, next to these smartly dressed men, she felt underdressed.

"I hope you all like tonight's dinner. Thanks to Massimo, I was able to cook some old family recipes."

"I'm sure it will be fantastic," Dante's father said as he took a seat at the head of the table.

She wished she was as confident as he sounded. It felt like a swarm of butterflies had now inhabited her stomach as she removed the ceramic lids from the serving dishes. This just had to work. She had to impress them—impress Dante.

She sat back, eagerly watching as the men filled their plates. It seemed to take forever. She didn't bother filling hers yet. She already knew what everything tasted like as she'd sampled everything numerous times in the kitchen. In fact, she wasn't even hungry at this point.

But as they started to eat, a silence came over the table. The men started exchanging puzzled looks among themselves. Lizzie's stomach tightened. What was wrong?

She glanced Dante's way but his attention was on the food. She turned to Massimo for some sort of sign that all would be well, but before he could say a word, Dante's father's chair scraped across the tiles. In the silent room, the sound was like a crescendo.

The man threw down his linen napkin and strode out

of the room. Lizzie watched in horror. She pressed a hand to her mouth, holding back a horrified gasp.

Dante called out, "Papa."

The man didn't turn back or even acknowledge him.

"Let him go." Stefano sent Dante a pointed look.

As more forks clattered to their plates, the weight of disappointment weighed heavy on Lizzie. Her chest tightened, holding back a sob. This was absolutely horrific. Instead of the dinner bringing everyone together and mending fences, it'd only upset them.

Unable to sit there and keep her emotions under wraps, Lizzie pushed back her chair. She jumped to her feet, and as fast as her feet would carry her, she headed for the kitchen.

Her eyes stung and she blinked repeatedly. She'd done something wrong. How could she have messed up the recipe? She'd double-checked everything. But her Italian was a bit rusty. Was that it? Had she misread something?

Not finding any solace in the room where she'd created the dinner—the disaster—she kept going out the back door. She had no destination in mind. Her feet just kept moving.

The what-ifs and maybes clanged about in her head. But the one thought that rose above the others was how this dinner was supposed to be her peace offering to Dante. This was what she'd hoped would be a chance for them to smooth over their differences. But that obviously wasn't going to happen when no one even wanted to eat her food.

She kept walking. She didn't even know how much time had passed when she stopped and looked around. The setting sun's rays gave the grape leaves a magical glow. Any other time she'd have been caught up in the romantic setting, but right now romance was the last thing on her mind.

She should turn back, but she wasn't ready to face anyone. Oh, who was she kidding—she wasn't willing to look into Dante's eyes and to find that once again in her life, she didn't quite measure up.

When others looked at her as though she were less than

everyone else, she could choke it down and keep going. After all, those people hadn't meant anything to her. It'd hurt—it'd hurt deeply, but it hadn't destroyed her. And she'd clung to the belief that whatever didn't destroy you made you stronger.

But Dante was a different story. A sob caught in her throat. She couldn't stand the thought of him thinking that she was inept at cooking—the one ability that she'd always excelled in—her one hope to gain his respect.

And now she'd failed. Miserably.

"Are you serious?"

Dante sent Stefano a hard stare. The main dish Lizzie had prepared was his mother's trademark dish. She only prepared it on the most special occasions.

"Of course I'm serious. Did you see how all of the color drained from Papa's face? It was like he'd seen a ghost or something."

Dante raked his fingers through his hair. "I guess I was too busy watching the horrified look on Lizzie's face. She worked all day on that meal. She wouldn't say it but I know that she was so anxious to please everyone—"

"You mean anxious to please you, little brother."

"Me? Why would she do that?" He wasn't about to let on to his older brother that anything had gone on between him and Lizzie. No way! He'd never hear the end of it. "We're working together. That's all."

Stefano elbowed him. "Whatever you say."

Dante leaned forward on the porch rail and stared off into the distance, but there was no sign of Lizzie.

"I just have one question."

Dante stifled a groan. "You always have a question and most of the time it's none of your business."

"Ah, but see, this does have to do with me. Because while you're standing there insisting that you don't care about Lizzie, she's gotten who knows how far away. So is it going to be me or you that goes after her?"

Dante hated when his brother was right. She had been gone a long time. Soon it'd be dark out. He'd attempted to follow her right after the incident, but Massimo had insisted she needed some time alone. But the thing was she didn't understand what had happened to her special dinner and he needed to explain that it had nothing to do with her. Still, he figured that after her walk she'd be more apt to listen to him.

"Dante, did you hear me?"

He turned and glared at Stefano. "How could I help but hear you when you're talking in my ear?"

"You're ignoring the question. Are you going? Or should I?"

"I'm going."

"You might want to take your car. Hard to tell how far she's gotten by now."

"Thanks so much for your expert advice."

Stefano sent him a knowing smile. "You always did need a little guidance."

They'd probably have ended up in a sparring match like they used to do as kids, but Dante had more important matters than showing his big brother that he was all grown up now. Dante jumped in Red and fired up the engine. He headed down the lane to the main road, not sure he was even headed in the right direction. No one had watched Lizzie leave, but he couldn't imagine that she'd go hiking through the fields in a dress and sandals.

He slowly eased the car along the lane, doing his best to search the fields while trying to keep the car from drifting off the road. Thankfully it was a private lane as he was doing a good deal of weaving back and forth.

Where was she?

As he reached the main road, his worries multiplied. Had he missed her? Had she wandered into the fields and somehow gotten lost? He pulled to a stop at the intersection and pounded his palm against the steering wheel. Why had he listened to his grandfather? He should have gone after her immediately.

A car passed by and his gut churned. Was it possible she was so upset that she hitched a ride from a passing motorist? A stranger?

His whole body stiffened. This was his fault. He'd been so upset by her rejection that he'd built up an impenetrable wall between them. Maybe if he hadn't been so worried about letting her hurt him again, she wouldn't have been trying so hard to impress him and his family—his dysfunctional family. If he couldn't please his father—his own flesh and blood—how was she supposed to succeed?

Dante's gaze took in the right side of the main road, but there was no sign of Lizzie. And then he proceeded to the left, the direction they'd come from the city. That had to be the way she'd gone. He could only hope that she was wise enough to keep to herself and not trust any strangers. If anything happened to her—

He cut off the thought. Nothing would happen to her. She would be fine. She had to be.

And then he spotted the back of her red dress. He let out a breath that had been pent up in his chest. He sent up a silent thank-you to the big man upstairs.

He pulled up next to her and put down the window. "Lizzie, get in the car."

She didn't stop walking. She didn't even look at him. He was in a big mess here. He picked up speed and pulled off the road. He cut the engine and jumped out of the car.

By this point, Lizzie was just passing the car. She was still walking and he had no choice but to fall in step next to her. It was either that or toss her over his shoulder. He didn't think she'd appreciate the latter option. And he didn't need any passing motorists calling the *polizia*.

"Lizzie, would you stop so we can talk?"

Still nothing. Her strides were long and quick. His car was fading into the background. He should have locked it up, but he never imagined she'd keep walking.

"What are you going to do? Walk the whole way back to Rome?"

She came to an abrupt halt and turned to him with a pained look. "It's better than going back and facing your family."

"Lizzie, they didn't mean to hurt you. It's just…just that your food surprised them."

"I know. I saw the looks on their faces. Your father couldn't get away from the table fast enough. It was as if he was going to be sick." A pained look swept over her face. "Oh, no. He didn't get sick, did he?"

"Not like you're thinking." Dante really didn't want to discuss his family's problems here on the side of the road. "Come back to the car with me. We can talk there."

She crossed her arms. "We can talk here."

"Fine. The truth is your cooking was fantastic."

She rolled her eyes. "Like I'm going to fall for that line."

She turned to start walking again when he reached out, grabbing her arm. "Wait. The least you can do is hear me out."

Her gaze moved to his hand. He released his hold, hoping she wouldn't walk away.

"I'm listening. But don't feed me a bunch of lies."

"It wasn't a lie," he ground out. "The honest-to-goodness truth is your dinner tasted exactly like my mother's cooking. At least that's what I'm told since I never had the opportunity to taste anything she prepared."

Lizzie pressed a hand to her mouth.

"It seems that particular dish was her favorite. She made it for special occasions—most notably my father's birthday. He hasn't had it since she was alive. So you can see how it would unearth a lot of unexpected memories."

She blinked repeatedly. "I'm so sorry. I never thought—"

"And you shouldn't have to know these things. It's just that my family doesn't move on with life very well. They have a tendency to stick with old stories and relish memories. If you hadn't noticed, my mother's memory is quite alive. And Massimo had no clue that the dish was special to my mother and father."

"I feel so awful for upsetting everyone."

"You have nothing to worry about. In fact, you might be the best thing that has happened to my family in a very long time."

Her beautiful blue eyes widened. "How do you get that?"

"My family has been in a rut for many years. And you're like a breath of fresh air. Instead of them going through the same routine day in and day out, now they have something to look forward to."

"Look forward to what?"

"To you."

"Really?" When he nodded, she added, "But the dinner was supposed to be special—for you."

"For me?" He pressed a hand to his chest. "But why?"

"Because ever since that night when we…uhh…you know…"

"Made love." It had been very special for him—for both of them. There was no way he could cheapen it by calling it sex. No matter what happened afterward.

"Uh, yes…well, after that you grew cold and distant. I was hoping that this dinner would change that."

"But isn't that what you wanted? Distance?"

Her fine brows rose. "Why would you think that?"

Now he had to admit what he'd done and he wasn't any too proud of it. "I heard you."

"Heard me say what?"

He kicked at a stone on the side of the desolate road. It skidded into the field. "When I found you gone that morning, I went searching for you. I knew that the night wasn't anything either one of us planned and I was worried that maybe you'd regretted it."

"But I didn't…not like you're thinking."

He pressed a finger to her lips. "Let me finish before I lose my nerve." He took a deep breath. "I'm not proud of what I have to say."

Her eyes implored him to get to the point.

"After I'd searched the whole apartment including your bedroom and found it empty, I panicked. I'd thought you'd left for good. But then I saw your suitcase. So I went down to the *ristorante* and that's when I heard your voice. When I moved toward the office, I heard you on the phone. And when you said that what we had was a one-time thing— that it didn't mean anything—I knew you regretted our lovemaking."

"Oh, Dante. I'm so sorry you overheard that."

Hope swelled in his chest. "Are you saying that all of this time I misunderstood?"

Her gaze dipped. "I wish I could tell you that, but I can't."

Piercing pain arrowed into his chest. His jaw tightened as he took a step back. He was standing here making a fool of himself for a lady who wanted nothing but to put thousands of miles between them.

"We should get back to the house and get your things." He turned for the car feeling lower than he'd ever felt in his life.

"Wait! Please." The pleading tone in her voice caused him to pause. She rushed to his side. "When I said those words, I was in the midst of a panic attack. That night had been so special. It had me reconsidering my future. I didn't know what I was feeling for you. I just knew that I didn't want to get hurt."

"And then I turned around and hurt you by putting so much distance between us."

She bit down on her lower lip and nodded.

Damn. What he knew about dealing with women and relationships couldn't even fill up the thimble his father kept on his dresser as a reminder of his mother. "I'm sorry. I didn't mean to hurt you. That's the last thing in the world I wanted to do."

"I never wanted to hurt you either. Is there any way we can go back to being friends?"

"I think we can do better than that." His head dipped and caught her lips.

Not sure that he'd made the right move and not wanting to scare her off, he restrained himself, making the kiss brief. It was with great regret that he pulled away. But when she looked up at him and smiled, he knew that he'd made the right move. There was still something there. Something very special.

"See. Your dinner was very successful. It brought us back together. Thank you for not giving up on me and for going to all of the trouble to get through my thick skull."

She lifted up on her tiptoes and pressed her lips to his. No way was he letting her get away twice. His arms quickly wrapped around her waist and pulled her close. It seemed like forever since he'd tasted her and held her. He didn't ever want this moment to end. When she was in his arms, the world felt as if it had righted itself.

The blare of a horn from a passing motorist had Lizzie jumping out of his arms. Color filled her face. "I don't think we should put on a show for everyone."

"Why not?" He didn't feel like being proper at the moment. He had more important things on his mind, like getting her back in his arms. "Who doesn't enjoy a couple—" he'd almost said "in love" but he'd caught himself in time "—a couple enjoying themselves on a summer evening."

"Is that what we were doing?"

Not comfortable exploring the eruption of emotions that plagued him when they'd kissed, he didn't answer her question. Instead he slipped his arm over her shoulders and pulled her close. "How about you and I head back to the villa?"

"I don't know. Couldn't we just go back to the city?"

"But your things are still there."

She didn't move. Then he noticed her gaze searching out his car that was a ways back the road. In that moment he knew how to get her back to the vineyard.

He jangled the car keys in front of her. "I'll let you drive Red."

Her surprised gaze searched his face. "Are you serious?"

"I'd never joke about driving Red."

She snatched the keys from his hand and started for the car.

"That's it?" He started after her. "You just take the keys and don't say a word. You know I never let anyone drive Red, right?"

"I know. But you owe me."

"And how do you get that?"

"I put up with your moodiness lately." She smiled up at him, letting him know that her sense of humor had returned. "And I didn't complain."

He stopped in his tracks and planted his hands on his sides. "I wasn't moody!"

"Oh, yes, you were," she called over her shoulder. "Worse than an old bear awakened during a snowstorm. You better hurry or you'll miss your ride."

"You wouldn't…"

Then again, she just might, depending on her mood. He smiled and shook his head. Then, realizing that she hadn't slowed down for him, he took long, quick strides to catch up with her.

CHAPTER SEVENTEEN

LIZZIE CHECKED HER tattered pride at the door. With her shoulders pulled back, she entered the DeFiore home once again. She didn't know what she expected but it certainly wasn't everyone relaxing. Massimo was reading the newspaper. Stefano was in another room watching a soccer game on a large-screen television. She'd been corrected numerous times that on this side of the pond, it was referred to as football. Not that it mattered one way or the other to her. She'd never been a sports fan.

"See. Nothing to worry about." The whisper of Dante's voice in her ear sent a wave of goose bumps down her arms.

She moved to the kitchen. Everything had been cleaned and put away. "I still haven't seen your father anywhere."

Dante shrugged. "He isn't one for sitting around. He's always complaining that there aren't enough hours in the day."

"I'd really like a chance to talk to him—to apologize."

Dante moved in front of her. "You have nothing to apologize about."

"Yes, I do. I made him unhappy and that's the last thing I meant to do."

"He should be the one apologizing to you. That man always has to have things his way—even if it makes the rest of us miserable."

She studied Dante's furrowed brow and darkened eyes. He wasn't talking about her or the disastrous dinner. There was something else eating at the relationship he had with his father.

Maybe she could do something to help. "Have you tried talking to him? Telling him how you feel?"

"Don't go there." Dante's brusque tone caught her off guard.

She took a second to suck down her emotional response. "Listen, I know there's something wrong between you and your father. When he enters the room, you leave. Your contact is bare minimum."

Dante shrugged. "It's nothing."

"No. It's definitely something. And take it from someone who never knew their father and would have moved heaven and earth to get to know him—you need to fix this thing before it's too late."

"But it's not me. It's him. There's nothing about me that he approves of."

"Aren't you exaggerating just a bit?"

"Not really." Dante raked his fingers through his hair. "But you don't want to hear any of this. Compared to you, I have nothing to complain about."

She worried her bottom lip. In her effort to make him realize how lucky he was to have a family, she'd made him feel worse. "My background has nothing to do with yours. But I would like to hear more about you and your father, if you'll tell me."

Dante stared at her as though trying to decide if she was being on the level or not. The silence grew oppressive. And just when she thought he was going to brush her off, he started to talk.

"We didn't exactly get off to a good start as he got stuck with a newborn baby in exchange for losing his wife. Not exactly a fair trade."

"Still, it's nothing that you can be held responsible for."

"I resemble my mother in more than just my looks. Instead of being drawn into the vineyard like my brother, I got restless. My father didn't understand why I wasn't interested in the family business. We fought about it continually until I moved to Rome."

"And that's where you found your passion for cooking."

He nodded. "I thought I had found my calling until Massimo left. It hasn't been the same since." Dante turned to her and looked her straight in the eyes. "If I tell you something, will you promise it'll go no further?"

She crossed her heart just like she used to do as a kid with Jules. "I promise."

"I'm in negotiations to sell the *ristorante*—"

"What? But why?"

"I figured that it's time I moved home. Make amends. And do my part."

"And you think that'll make you happy?"

He shrugged and looked away from her. "I think it's the best thing I can do for my family. Maybe at last it'll make my father happy."

Lizzie bit back her opinion. She'd have to think long and hard about what to say to him because she didn't have much experience when it came to families. With it just being her and Jules, they'd been able to work things out pretty easily. But this bigger family dynamic had her feeling like a fish out of water.

"Why don't you talk to your father? Tell him your plan."

He shrugged. "Every time I try, we end up arguing. Usually over the choices I've made in my life."

She heard the defeated tone in his voice and it dug at the old scars on her heart. "Don't give up. Promise me. It's too important."

Dante's eyes widened at her plea. "I'll do my best."

That was all she could ask of him. And she believed him. Though she didn't think that selling the restaurant and moving back here was the answer to his problems. But that was for Dante to figure out on his own.

"Now, where did you say I could find your father?"

* * *

Was she right?

Dante rolled around everything they'd talked about in his mind as he led Lizzie to the barrel cellar. When his father wasn't out in the fields checking the grapes or the soil, he was in the cellar—avoiding his family. As a young child, Dante resented anything and everything that had to do with the vineyard. He blamed the grapes for his father's notable absence.

But as Dante grew up, he realized it wasn't the vineyard he should blame—it was his father. It was his choice to avoid his children. And though his father wasn't as remote as he used to be, some habits were hard to change.

Dante glanced over at Lizzie. "Are you sure you want to do this?"

She threaded her fingers with his. With a squeeze, she smiled up at him. "I'm positive. Lead the way."

He wanted to lean over and press his mouth to hers—to feel the rightness of holding her in his arms. But with his father close by, Dante would settle for the comfort of her touch. He tightened his grip on her much smaller hand and led her down the steps.

As they walked, Lizzie asked about the wooden barrels containing the vineyard's bounty. The fact that she was truly interested in his family's heritage impressed him. He and his father may not hit it off, but he still had pride in his family's hard work. It was why he showcased DeFiore vino exclusively at the *ristorante*.

"This is so impressive." Lizzie looked all around at the walls of barrels. "And they're all full of wine?"

He nodded. "This place has grown a lot since I was a kid."

"Dante, is that you?"

They both turned to find his father holding a sample of vino. "Hey, Papa. I thought we'd find you down here."

"I was doing some testing." His father glanced at Lizzie.

"We do a periodic analysis of the contents and top off the barrels to keep down the exposure to oxygen due to evaporation."

"With all of these barrels, I'd say you have a lot of work to stay on top of things."

"It keeps me busy." His father smiled, something he didn't do often. "Is there something you needed?"

Lizzie glanced at Dante, but if she thought he was going anywhere, she was mistaken. He wasn't budging. He crossed his arms and leaned against a post. His father could be gruff and tactless at times. Dante wasn't about to let him hurt Lizzie's feelings any more than had already been done.

Lizzie turned to his father. "Mr. DeFiore, I owe you an apology for tonight. I'm so sorry I ruined your dinner and…and brought up painful memories. I had absolutely no idea that the recipe held such special meaning for you. If I had, I never would have cooked that meal."

There was an awkward pause. Dante's body tensed. Please don't let his father brush her off as though her apology meant nothing. Lizzie didn't say it, but she wanted his father's approval. And Dante wanted it for her. He didn't want her to feel the pain of once again being rejected.

Dante turned his gaze on his father, planning to send him a warning look, but his father was staring down at the vino in his hand.

The breath caught in Dante's chest as tension filled the room. When his father spoke, his voice was softer than normal and Dante strained to hear every word.

"I am the one who owes you an apology. I reacted badly. And I'm sorry. The meal, it…it caught me off guard. It tasted exactly like my wife's."

The pent-up breath released from Dante's lungs like a punctured balloon. He didn't know what was up with his father, but Dante was thankful he'd paid Lizzie such a high compliment. As far as Dante knew, there was no higher compliment than for his father to compare Lizzie's cooking to that of his mother. Was it possible his father truly was changing for the better?

"I'll try not to cook any of your wife's favorites in the future—"

"No. I mean I'd like you to. I know this meal caught me off guard, but it brought back some of the best memories." His father set aside the vino and reached for Lizzie's hand. "I hope I haven't scared you off. I'd really like you to come back and cook for us. That is, if you'd still like to."

"I would…like to cook for you, that is."

"Maybe next weekend?"

Dante at last found his voice. "Papa, we can't be here next weekend. There's been a change in the filming schedule and they're pushing to wrap up the series, so we'll be working all next weekend."

"Oh, I see." His father turned to Lizzie. "So what do you think of my son? Is he good in the kitchen?"

Lizzie's eyes opened wide. "You don't know?"

His father shook his head. "He never cooks for us. Always says it's too much like work."

Lizzie turned an astonished look to Dante. Guilt consumed him. He shrugged his shoulders innocently.

The truth was that cooking was an area where he'd excelled and he didn't want his father's ill-timed, stinging comments to rob him of that special feeling. But witnessing this different side of his father had him rethinking his stance.

"We'll have to change that." Lizzie turned back to his father. "Your son is an excellent cook and he's turning out to be an excellent teacher."

"I have an idea." There was a gleam in his father's eyes. "I'm sure Dante has told you that Massimo hasn't had an easy time moving away from the city and leaving the *ristorante* behind."

Lizzie nodded. "He mentioned it. What can I do to help?"

"That's the spirit." Papa smiled. "I was thinking that we should celebrate his birthday."

"You mean like a party."

He nodded. "Something special to show him that...well, you know."

"To let him know that everybody loves him."

Papa nodded. "I'll hire the musicians."

Lizzie's face lit up and she turned to Dante. "What do you think? Would you be willing to bring me back here?"

He couldn't think of anything he'd like more. "I think it can be arranged."

She smiled at him and a spot in his chest warmed. The warmth spread throughout his body. And he realized that for the first time he was at total ease around his father. Lizzie was a miracle worker.

"Don't worry about a thing." She patted his father's arm. "Dante and I will take care of all the food. Although your son might have to get a bigger vehicle to haul everything."

That was not a problem. Her wish was his command. He had a feeling that this party was going to be a huge deal and not just for his grandfather. He had a feeling his own life would never be the same again.

CHAPTER EIGHTEEN

AND THAT WAS a wrap!

Two weeks ahead of schedule, the filming was over. Lizzie was exhausted. They'd worked every available minute to get enough footage for the studio to splice together for the upcoming season.

And so far Dante hadn't said a word about everything they'd shared at the vineyard. Every time she'd worked up the courage to ask him about it, there was no opportunity for them to talk privately. And it was driving her crazy wondering where they went from here. Technically, she still had another two weeks in Rome to learn as much as she could from him. But her biggest lessons hadn't been taught in the kitchen.

Somewhere along the way, she'd fallen in love with Dante. Oh, she'd been in love with him for longer than she'd been willing to admit. And she accepted that was the reason she'd been so freaked out after they'd made love. She just couldn't bear to have him reject her, so she did the rejecting first. Not her best move.

"Something on your mind?" Dante asked as he strolled into the living room Saturday morning.

"I was thinking about you." She watched as surprise filtered across his handsome features.

"You were?" In a navy suit, white dress shirt and maroon tie, he looked quite dashing. "Only good thoughts, I hope."

"Definitely." Her gaze skimmed down over him again, enjoying the view. "You look a bit overdressed to be heading downstairs to help with the lunch crowd."

"That's because I'm not. I made arrangements so the kitchen is covered today. You, my pretty lady, have the day off." His smile sent her heart tumbling.

To spend with him! She grinned back at him.

She shouldn't have worried. It'd been the rush of the filming and keeping up with the increasing crush of patrons that had kept him from following up on those kisses at the vineyard. She was certain of it now.

"I like the sounds of that. What shall we do with the day?"

"I don't know about you, but I have a meeting."

"A meeting?" The words slipped past her lips.

A questioning brow lifted. "Is that a problem?"

"Umm...no. I just thought we could do something, you know, together." Did she really have to spell it out for him?

The intercom buzzed. Who in the world could that be? From what she'd gathered living here for the past several weeks, Dante didn't entertain much, and when he did, it was down in the restaurant.

"That'll be for me. They sent a car."

"Who did?"

His face creased with stress lines. "The people interested in buying the *ristorante*."

His words knocked her off-kilter. She sat down on the arm of the couch. And here she'd been daydreaming about them one day running the restaurant together. She didn't have a clue how she'd work things out with Jules being so far away, but Massimo's words came back to her: *Love will always find a way.* Now all of her daydreams were about to be dashed.

"You're really going through with it?" Her voice was barely more than a whisper.

"Why do you seem so surprised? I told you I was considering it. And thanks to you, things between me and my father are looking up. It's time I do what's expected of me."

He was trying to be noble and earn his father's respect and love. That she could admire. But at what cost?

"Dante, do you really think that you'll be happy working at the vineyard? After all, you couldn't wait to leave when you were younger. Do you really think it'll have changed?"

His gaze darkened. "Maybe I've changed."

"And you aren't going to miss the restaurant—your grandfather's legacy? Have you even told Massimo?"

Dante's brows gathered. "When I took over the *ristorante*, he gave me his blessing to do what I thought was appropriate with it. And that's what I'm doing."

She knew the decision was ultimately up to him, but if she didn't say something now, she'd regret it—they both might regret it. "Don't do it. Don't sell the restaurant."

Dante grabbed his briefcase and headed for the door. "I've got to go."

"Wait." She rushed over to him. "I'm sorry. I'm butting in where I don't belong, but I don't want you to have any regrets."

"I won't. I know what I want."

And it wasn't working here side by side with her. Her heart sank.

"We'll do something when I get back." The buzzer sounded again. "I really do have to go."

He rushed out the door. She willed him to come back, but he didn't. Deep down she had a bad feeling that Dante was about to make a decision that he would come to regret. But there was nothing else she could do to stop him.

Not quite an hour later, as Lizzie was trying to find a television show to distract her from thinking of Dante, the phone rang. Maybe it was him. Maybe he had come to his senses and couldn't wait to tell her.

"Hello."

"Lizzie, is that you?" Definitely not Dante's voice, but still it was familiar.

"Yes."

"This is Dante's father."

"Oh, hi. Dante isn't here. But I can give him a message."

"Actually, you're the one I wanted to speak to. I wanted to know if you needed any help with the food for the party tomorrow. My sisters have been pestering me to know how they can help."

How in the world had she let Massimo's party slip her mind? Of course, with the crazy filming schedule and the vibes of attraction zinging back and forth between her and Dante, it culminated into a surge, short-circuiting her mind.

"Don't worry about a thing. I have everything under control." No way was she telling him the truth. Not after that disastrous dinner.

"I knew I could count on you." His confidence in her only compounded her guilt. "This party is going to be just what Massimo needs. A houseful of family and friends with great food, music and the best vino."

They talked for a few more minutes before she gave in and said that his sisters could do the appetizers, but the entrées were her and Dante's responsibility.

As she hung up the phone, her mind was racing. That was when she realized they hadn't picked up the collage of photos of the restaurant through the years to hang in Massimo's room at the vineyard. A quick call assured her that the order was complete, but she'd have to get there right away. In twenty minutes, they closed for the weekend. She tried calling Dante's cell phone but it went straight to voice mail.

A glance at the clock told her that she didn't have time to wait. She needed to go right now. She wouldn't let Dante down in front of his family. Not when he was so anxious to fix things with his father. This gift was from the both of them, but it was more Dante's idea than hers.

Spotting the keys to Red on the counter, she wondered

if Dante would mind if she borrowed the car. After all, this was an emergency and he had let her drive it when they were in the country. What could it hurt? The shop wasn't too far away.

Before she could change her mind, she grabbed the keys and headed out the door. Her stomach quivered with nerves as she fired up the engine. As she maneuvered Red down the street, heads turned. She could only ever dream of having a luxury sports car for herself. Without even checking, she knew that the price tag on this gem was not even in her realm of possibilities…ever.

In no time, she placed the large framed collage in the passenger seat. Being cautious, she used the seat belt to hold it in place. She didn't want anything to happen to the gift. It was perfect. And she was certain that Massimo would treasure it.

Mentally she was listing everything she needed to start preparing as soon as she got home. The fact that there would be a hundred-plus people at this "small" gathering totally boggled her mind. When she and Jules had a birthday party, it usually ended up being them and a handful of friends—less than ten people total. The DeFiore clan was more like a small village.

She would need at least four trays of lasagna alone. Thankfully the restaurant was kept well stocked. When they'd talked about the party previously, Dante had told her to take whatever she needed and just to leave him a list of what she used. That was a big relief—

The blur of a speeding car caught her attention. Lizzie slammed on the brakes. Red immediately responded. Her body tensed. The air became trapped in her lungs.

The blue compact car cut in front of her, narrowly missing her.

Lizzie slowed to a stop. She blew out the pent-up breath. Thank goodness nothing had happened to Red. Dante would have freaked out if she'd damaged his precious car. The man truly loved this fine vehicle—

Squeal!

Thunk!

Lizzie's body lurched forward. Her body jerked hard against the seat belt. The air was knocked out of her lungs.

CHAPTER NINETEEN

"THAT'S NOT POSSIBLE. Lizzie wouldn't be out in Red." Dante gripped the phone tighter. "You're sure it was her?" He listened intently as though his very life depended on it. "What do you mean you don't know if she's okay?" His gut twisted into a painful knot. "I'm on my way."

Was it possible his newly hired busboy was mistaken? Lizzie had been in a car accident with Red? The kid didn't know Lizzie very well. He had to have her mixed up with someone else.

Dante strode toward the elevator of the corporate offices after his meeting. He could only hope the hired car would be waiting for him. When the elevator didn't come fast enough, he headed for the stairwell. Lizzie just had to be okay. His feet barely touched the steps as he flew down the two flights of stairs.

After nearly running into a half-dozen people, he made it to the street. The black car was waiting for him. When the driver went to get out to open his door for him, Dante waved him off. There wasn't time for niceties. He had to know if Lizzie was okay.

It seemed to take forever for the car to get across the city. He tried calling her. She didn't answer at the apartment and she didn't pick up her cell phone. Dante's body tensed. Was the kid right? Had she been in an accident? Was she hurt?

Then feeling utterly helpless, Dante did something he

hadn't done since he was a kid. He sent a prayer to the big guy upstairs, pleading for Lizzie's safety.

What had she been doing? Where had she gone? And what was she doing with Red? He couldn't come up with any plausible answers. All he could do was stare helplessly out the window as they slowly inched closer to the accident site.

"This is as close as I can get, sir. Looks like they have the road shut down up ahead." The driver sent him an apologetic look in the rearview mirror.

"Thank you."

Dante sprang out of the car and weaved his way through the throng of people on the sidewalk, sidestepping a cyclist and a few strollers. He inwardly groaned. Just his luck. Everyone seemed to be out and about on such a sunny day.

And then he saw the familiar candy-apple-red paint, but his gaze kept moving, searching for Lizzie's blond hair. She wasn't by the car. And she wasn't standing on the sidewalk.

And then he spotted the ambulance. His heart tightened. *Please. Please. Don't let her be hurt.*

He ran to the ambulance and moved to the back. Lizzie was sitting there with a stunned look on her face. His gaze scanned her from head to foot. No blood. No bandages.

Thank goodness.

"Lizzie."

It was all he got out before she was rushing into his arms and he nearly dropped to the roadway with relief. As his arms wrapped around her, he realized that he'd never been so scared in his entire life. If he had lost her— No, he couldn't go there. Losing her was unimaginable.

As he held her close and felt her shake, he realized that he loved her. Not just a little. But a whole lot. In that moment, he understood the depth of love his father had felt for his mother. He'd never before been able to comprehend why his father never remarried—why his father kept all of the memories of his mother around the house. Now he understood.

Lizzie pulled back. "Dante, I'm so sorry. I...I—"

"Are you okay?" When she didn't answer right away, his gaze moved to the paramedic. "Is she okay? Does she need to go to the hospital?"

"She refused to go to the hospital."

Dante turned to her. "You've got to go. What if something is wrong?"

"It looks like she's going to be bruised from the seat belt and a bit sore in the morning, but she should be okay."

Lizzie patted Dante's arm to get his attention. "He's right. I'm fine. But..."

"But what?" If she so much as had a pain in her little finger, he was going to carry her into that ambulance himself.

"But Red isn't in such good condition. Oh, Dante, I'm sorry..." She burst out in tears.

What did he do now? He didn't know a thing about women and tears. He let his instincts take over as he pulled her against his chest and gently rubbed her back. "It's okay. I'm just glad you're okay."

He truly meant it.

While she let her emotions flow, he realized how close he'd come to losing her in a car accident. He knew this scene. He'd lived through it with his brother. Stefano's wife had died so tragically—so unexpectedly.

The memory sent a new cold knife of fear into Dante's heart. He'd watched the agony his brother had endured when he'd joined the ranks of the DeFiore widowers' club. Dante had sworn then and there that wouldn't be him. He'd never let someone close enough to make him vulnerable. And that was exactly what was happening with Lizzie. Every moment he was with her. Every time he touched her, she got further under his skin and deeper in his heart.

He had to stop it.

He couldn't go through this again. Because next time they both might not be so lucky.

As though sensing the change in him, Lizzie pulled back and swiped quickly at her cheeks. "Dante, I'm so sorry."

"It's not your fault."

"Of course it is. I didn't ask you…I tried. But your phone was off. And I had to hurry."

"I had my phone switched off for the meeting."

"I'd forgotten. Then your dad called. And there wasn't time to wait. Then this car cut me off—"

"Slow down. Take a breath." In her excitement she wasn't making much sense and he was worried she might hyperventilate.

"The car—Red—it's not drivable. They called for a flat-bed."

This was the first time he truly looked at Red. Any other time that would have been his priority. Warning bells went off in his head. He loved Lizzie more than anything in the world. When his gaze landed on the crumpled rear corner panel, he didn't feel anything. Maybe he was numb with shock and worry after seeing Lizzie in the back of the ambulance.

She sniffled. "I can't believe it happened. I was on my way home when this little car cut me off. I braked just in time. Before I could get moving again, I was hit from behind by that delivery truck."

Dante's gaze moved to the nearby white truck. The size of it was much, much larger than he'd been anticipating. The damage could have been so much worse. The thought that Lizzie could have been seriously injured…or worse hit him in the gut with a sharp jab.

"I don't know if they can repair the car but…but I'll pay the bill or replace it. Whatever it takes."

She didn't have that kind of money. Not that he'd accept it even if she did. The only important part was that she was safe. He'd be lost without her. The words teetered on his tongue, but he couldn't vocalize them. Telling her that would just be cruel. He refused to get her hopes up and have her think they were going to have a happily-ever-after ending. That simply couldn't happen.

Stifling his emotions, he said, "I still don't understand why you took the car without asking."

She turned and stared directly at him. "I told you. I tried to call you but it went straight to voice mail. And I couldn't be late. Otherwise they would have closed."

"Who would have closed? What was so damn important that you almost got yourself killed?"

Pain flashed in her eyes. "Listen, I know you're worked up about your car, but I was trying to do you a favor."

"A favor? You call totaling my car and scaring me *doing me a favor*?" He rubbed the back of his neck. His words were coming out all wrong. His gut continued to churn with a ball of conflicting emotions.

Lizzie glared at him. "I told you I'm sorry."

"But that won't fix anything." And it wouldn't ease the scare she'd given him.

The groan of the motor hauling his car up onto the back of the tow drew his attention. The bent, broken and cracked car was slowly rolled onto a flatbed. It was a miracle Lizzie had escaped serious injury.

If this worry and agony was what loving someone was about, he didn't want it. He didn't want to have to care so deeply—to depend on someone. The price of loving and losing was too steep. He didn't care if that made him a wimp or worse. He wasn't going to end up a miserable old man like the rest of his family—with only memories to keep him company on those long lonely nights. No way.

"Stay here." He wanted to keep her in sight just in case she started to feel ill. "I need to speak to the *polizia* and the tow driver."

In truth, he needed some distance. A chance to think

clearly. He had to break things off with Lizzie. It was the only logical thing to do. But why did it feel so wrong?

What was his problem?

Lizzie had never seen Dante in such a black mood. Did he really care about his car that much? She glanced over to see broken bits of the car being cleaned up. Okay. So she had totally messed up today. She knew it was her fault, but did he have to be so gruff? This wasn't the man—dare she say it—the man she loved.

After he spoke with the tow driver and the *polizia*, he returned to Lizzie. His face creased into a frown. "I'll call us a taxi."

There was no way she wanted to spend any more time around him. She already felt bad enough and had offered to pay for the damages. There was nothing else she could do to make things better. "I'd rather walk."

"You aren't up for walking." His gaze wouldn't even meet hers. "You were just in an accident."

His body was rigid. A vein pulsated in his neck. He was doing his best to bottle up his anger but she could feel it. And she couldn't stand it. He hated her for wrecking his car. "Just say it."

"I don't know what you're talking about, but I'm calling a taxi." He placed the call, ignoring her protests. "The taxi will be here shortly."

She wished he'd get it off his chest. If they couldn't even talk to each other, how in the world did she think they were going to have an ongoing relationship? Her mind was racing. She had to calm down. Everything was under control… except Massimo's birthday party.

And that was when she realized that the gift—the whole reason for this illuminating calamity—was about to be hauled away inside Red. Her gaze swung around to the damaged car atop the tow. Anxious to get to the truck before it pulled out, she took off at a brisk pace. Her heeled black boots kept her from moving quicker.

"Lizzie!" Dante called out behind her. "What's wrong? Would you talk to me?"

She kept moving until she was next to the truck. She reached up and knocked on the window. When the driver rolled down his window, she explained that she needed a package out of the vehicle.

"Couldn't this have waited?" Dante sighed.

"No. It couldn't." Lizzie stood there ramrod-straight, staring straight ahead. She refused to let Dante get to her. Instead she watched as the driver climbed up to the car and retrieved the large package.

When the man went to hand it down, Dante intercepted it. "Let me guess. This is the reason you couldn't wait for me."

She nodded. "It's the gift for your grandfather."

The tension on his face eased. It was though at last he realized she'd been trying to do something for him and she hadn't taken his car for a joyride.

When the taxi pulled up and they climbed inside, exhaustion coursed through Lizzie's veins. It was so tempting to lean her head against Dante's shoulder. They'd both been worked up. They'd both said things that they regretted. Everything would be all right when they got back to the apartment.

Satisfied that everything would work itself out, she leaned her head against him. She enjoyed the firmness of his muscles against her cheek and the gentle scent of his fresh cologne. She closed her eyes, noticing the beginning of the predicted aches setting in. But if that was all she ended up with, she'd be grateful. It could have been so much worse.

But she noticed how Dante didn't move. He didn't attempt to put his arm around her and draw her closer. He sat there stiffly and stared out the window. Maybe he was embarrassed about his heated reaction. That was understandable. She was horrified that she'd wrecked his car. Once they were home and alone, they could sort this all out.

CHAPTER TWENTY

IF THERE WAS another way to do this, he didn't know what it was.

Guilt ate at Dante. Though the ride back to the apartment was only a few minutes, it felt more like an eternity. And having Lizzie nestled against him only made him feel worse about his decision to end things. But he just couldn't live like this—always wondering when the good times would come to a crashing halt. And now that he'd had a small sample of what the pain and agony would be like—he just couldn't commit himself to a relationship.

The sooner he did this—laid everything on the table with Lizzie—the less pain they'd both experience. It was what he kept telling himself on the elevator ride to the penthouse. But somehow he was having trouble believing his own words.

It was nerves. That was it. He didn't want to hurt Lizzie any more than he had to. But in the end, this was what was best for both of them. After all, her life was in New York.

Once they stepped inside the apartment, Lizzie moved to the kitchen area. "I'll need to make a list of what we need from downstairs."

"For what?"

"The party. Remember, we're in charge of the food. Your father wants to taste your cooking."

The party where she would be introduced to his extended family—the party where people would start hint-ing about a wedding. His aunts were notorious for playing the part of matchmakers. That was why he ducked them as much as possible.

Dante sighed. This was all getting so complicated now. "Lizzie, can you come in here so we can talk?"

She rummaged through a drawer, pulling out a pen and paper. "It's already getting late. We really need to get to work on the food prep. You never did say how we're going to get all of this to the vineyard. You know, it might be easier if we'd take the supplies there and prepare it—"

He'd heard her ramble on a few occasions and each time she'd been nervous. "Lizzie, stop!"

She jumped and turned wide eyes in his direction. He felt even worse now that he'd scared her than he did before. He was making a mess of this.

"I'm sorry. I didn't mean to startle you. I just wanted your attention." He walked toward the black leather couch. "Come here. There's something I need to say."

Lizzie placed the pen and paper on the kitchen counter and hesitantly walked toward him. She knew what was coming, didn't she? It was obvious this wasn't going to work. He just wasn't cut out to be anyone's better half. He'd laugh at the thought if he wasn't so miserable.

She perched on the edge of the couch with her spine straight. "Is this about the restaurant? About your meeting today. Did you go through with the sale?"

That was what she thought he wanted to talk about? He scrubbed his hand over his face. "No, this isn't about that."

"Oh. But did you sell it? Not that it's any of my business. But I was just curious because of Massimo—"

"You don't have to remind me. I know that my grandfather put his whole life into that business." And this was just one more reason why he needed to end this relationship. She was already influencing his decisions—decisions that only a couple of months ago he hadn't needed or wanted anyone's input. "No, I didn't sell the place."

"I didn't think you could part with it. It's in your blood. You'd be lost without the restaurant." A hesitant smile pulled at the edges of her lips. "Massimo will be so pleased to know the restaurant is in safe hands. It will make his birthday gift even more special."

The collage. She'd been hurt because of him—because he'd forgotten to pick up the present. Guilt ate at him. An apology teetered on the tip of his tongue, but at the last second he bit it back. Comforting her would only muddy things. He had to end things as cleanly as possible—it would hurt her less that way.

"There's something else we need to talk about." There, he'd gotten the conversation started.

Lizzie sent him a puzzled look. "But we have so much to do for the party—"

"Don't you see, we can't do this? I can't do this." He turned his back to her, unable to bear the weight of seeing the inevitable disillusionment on her face. "We were kidding ourselves to think that we could ever have something real."

"What's going on, Dante? I thought that we were getting closer. I thought—"

"You thought wrong," he ground out. He hated himself for the pain and confusion he was causing her.

"You...you're ending things because I screwed up and wrecked your car?" The horror came across in the rising tones of her voice.

"It's not that."

He turned around then and saw the shimmer of unshed tears in her eyes. It was almost his undoing. But then he recalled the paralyzing fear of thinking that something serious had happened to her. He just couldn't cave in. It would mean risking his heart and waiting for the day that his whole world would come crashing down around him.

"Then it's my past." She looked at him with disbelief

reflected in her eyes. "I should have never told you. Now you think that I'm damaged goods."

"I never thought that. Ever." He stepped closer to her. No matter what it cost him, he was unwilling to let her think such a horrible thing. "You're amazing." His fingers caressed her cheek. "Any man who is fortunate to have you in his life will be the luckiest man in the world."

She stepped back out of his reach. "You expect me to believe that when you're standing there saying you don't want to see me again."

He groaned. "I'm doing this all wrong. I'm sorry. I never wanted you to think this had anything to do with you. You're the most beautiful woman I've ever known." He stepped toward her. "You have your whole future ahead of you."

She moved back. "Save the pep talk. I've heard lines like yours before. I don't need to hear it again. I was so wrong about you."

"What's that supposed to mean?"

"It means I thought you were different from the other guys I've known. I thought that I could trust you, but obviously I was wrong."

Her words were like spears that slammed into his chest. He didn't know it was possible to feel this low. He deserved every painful word she spewed at him. And more...

To keep from reaching out to her, he stuffed his hands in his pockets. "Don't you get it? I don't do well with long-term commitments."

She waved off his words. "Save it. I don't need to hear this. I have packing to do."

There was still the surprise party to deal with and Lizzie was in charge. But after the accident, he couldn't imagine that she'd be up for any part of it. Still, he couldn't just disinvite her. "What about Massimo's party?"

Her gaze lifted to meet his. "Are you serious? You really expect me to go and pretend that everything is okay between you and me?" She shook her head, her long blond hair swishing over her shoulder. "That party is for your family—something I'll never be."

His gaze dropped to the black plush rug with a white swirl pattern. He choked down the lump in his throat. "What should I tell everyone?"

She gave him a hard, cold stare. "This one is all on you. I'm sure you'll figure something out." She strode off down the hallway. Without even bothering to turn around, she called out, "Don't worry. I'll be gone before you return to the city."

Her back was ramrod-stiff and her shoulders were rigid. He tried to console himself with the knowledge that she'd be better off without him. The fate of women who fell in love with a DeFiore was not good. Not good at all.

CHAPTER TWENTY-ONE

HE COULDN'T BRING himself to celebrate.

Dante worked his way to a corner on the patio. There was no quiet place to hide. The musicians his father hired didn't know how to keep the volume down. And the cacophony of voices and laughter grated on Dante's taut nerves.

It didn't matter who he ran into, they asked about Lizzie. It was as though he and Lizzie were expected to head for the nearest altar as soon as possible. When he explained that Lizzie was returning to the States, they all sent him an accusing look.

He should be relieved. He had his utter freedom back. No chance that he could get hurt and grow old, miserable and alone like his grandfather, father and Stefano. No taking part in the DeFiore legacy. So why did he feel so miserable?

Dante could barely hear his own thoughts. There was nothing quiet about the DeFiore family. Everyone spoke over everyone else, hands gestured for emphasis and laughter reigned supreme. Lizzie would have loved being part of such a big gathering. And she'd have fit right in.

"How's the *ristorante*?"

Dante turned to find his father standing behind him, puffing on a cigar. Dante hadn't even heard him approach.

"It's good." Now that the decision had been made, he decided to let his father in on it. "There was an offer to buy the *ristorante*. It was made by some outfit looking to expand their portfolio."

"Are you going to accept?"

It was good to talk with someone about something other than Lizzie and his failed relationship. "I thought about it. I considered selling and moving home to help with the vineyard."

His father's bushy brows rose. "You'd want to come back after you fought so hard to get out of here?"

Dante shrugged. "I thought it'd make things easier for you."

"I don't need you to make things easier for me." His father's tone was resilient. "I take it you came to your senses and turned down the offer."

Dante considered telling him that they wanted the family recipes as part of the deal but that he just couldn't go through with it. No amount of money could compensate for giving away those family secrets. Some things weren't meant to be shared. But that wasn't the real reason he'd ended up turning down the offer.

Dante nodded his head. "I almost went through with it. But in the end, I couldn't do it."

"What changed your mind?"

"Lizzie." Her name slipped quietly over his lips as the pain of loss overwhelmed him.

"You were planning to run the place with her by your side? Like your grandparents had done?"

Dante didn't trust his voice at that moment. He merely nodded.

"Then why are you here alone? Why did you let her get away?"

His father always thought he failed at things. Well, this time his father was wrong. "I didn't let her get away. I pushed her away."

"What? But why would you do that?" His father put out

his cigar in a nearby ashtray before approaching Dante. "Let's walk."

Dante really didn't want a lecture from his father, but what did it matter? He couldn't be more miserable. His father led him off toward the vines. When people wanted to be alone, the vines always offered solace.

"Son, I know you never had a chance to know your mother, but she was an amazing woman. You remind me a lot of her. I know if she were here she'd insist that I give you some advice—"

"Papa, I don't need advice. I know what I'm doing. I won't end up like you." He realized too late that he'd said too much.

"You sent Lizzie away so you wouldn't end up miserable and alone like your old man, is that it?"

Dante couldn't deny it, so he didn't say anything. He kept his head low and concentrated on the path between the vines, which was barely wide enough for them to walk side by side.

"I'll admit it," his father said. "I didn't handle your mother's death well. I never expected to be alone with two young boys to raise. I...I was scared. And...I took my anger and frustration out on you. I'm sorry. You didn't deserve it. Not at all."

What did Dante say to that? *You're right* didn't seem appropriate. *No big deal* wouldn't work either because it was a big deal—a huge deal.

"If you had to do it over again—falling in love with Mama—would you?"

"Even knowing how things would end, I'd still have pursued your mother. She was amazing. When she smiled the whole world glowed. Loving your mother was one of the best parts of my life."

"But you...you always look so sad when anyone mentions her."

"And that's where I messed up. I closed myself off

from life. I dwelled so much on my loss—my pain—that I couldn't see clearly. I missed seeing what I was doing to my family."

"Is that why you never married again?"

Papa nodded. "I was too consumed with what I'd lost to see anything in front of me." He ran a hand over his face. "I can't go back and change any of it. My only hope is that you boys don't make the same mistakes. Love is like life—it's a gift not to be squandered."

Dante studied his father's face, trying to decide if his father was being on the level with him. "Are you serious? You'd be willing to give love another try?"

"If the right woman came along. What about you? Do you love Lizzie?"

Dante's heart pounded out the answer before he could find the words. He nodded. "But how do I live knowing that something might happen to her? That someday I might be alone?"

His father gripped his shoulder. "You don't. You just have to cherish the time you have together. No one knows the future. But by running from love, you're going to end up old and alone anyway."

Dante hadn't thought of it that way. In fact, if it weren't for Lizzie, he wouldn't be having this conversation with his father. Somehow Lizzie had worked her magic and reconnected him with his family.

His father cleared his throat. "Here's something else for you to consider. You've always known you're different from me and your brother. It's your mother's genes coming out in you. I know sometimes that drove a wedge between us. But that doesn't mean that I love you any less. Sometimes being different is a good thing."

Really? And here he'd been punishing himself for being so different from his father and brother. But if he differed from them in his choice of professions, why couldn't he be different when it came to love? Maybe there was a chance his story would end differently than theirs.

"Now, what are you doing standing here talking to me?" His father gave him a pointed stare, like when he was a boy and had forgotten to do his chores. "Go after the woman you love."

Dante turned to the villa when he realized that he didn't have his car. And the next train was hours away. He didn't have time to waste if he was going to catch Lizzie and beg her forgiveness.

"Hey, Papa, can I borrow the truck?"

His father reached into his pants pocket and pulled out a key ring. "You know it's not fancy like that sports car of yours."

"That's okay. I've learned that sort of stuff isn't what makes a person happy."

Lizzie had taught him that lesson.

Now he had to track her down, even if it meant flying to New York. He'd beg her forgiveness. Whatever it took, he'd do it.

Maybe he and his father weren't all that different after all.

CHAPTER TWENTY-TWO

How could she have let herself get caught up in a dream?

That was what this whole trip had been—one amazing dream. And now Lizzie had awakened to the harsh glare of reality. The truth was no matter how much she wanted to believe that Dante was changing, he was never going to be willing to let his guard down enough to let her in—even if she'd foolishly let him into her heart.

After Dante had left, she'd spent the night lying in the dark reliving her memories of Dante—memories that she'd treasure for a lifetime. Because no matter how the fairy tale ended, it'd still been a dream come true—falling in love under the Italian sky and kissing the man of her dreams in a breathtaking vineyard.

Tears streamed down her cheeks as she called the taxi service to take her to the airport. She took one last look around the apartment, but she couldn't bring herself to walk down the hallway to the master suite. Some memories were still too raw for her to delve into.

With the front door secure, she made her way down to the restaurant. With it being Sunday, it was closed. Maybe she had time to slip inside and—what? Remember the time she'd spent there with Dante? No, that wasn't a good idea. There was only so much pain she could take.

Would that taxi ever show up?

At the sound of an approaching vehicle, she turned. She frowned when all she saw was an old truck ambling down the road. Needing something to distract her, she reached into her purse and pulled out her cell phone. She'd been putting off calling Jules for as long as possible. Her foster sister would be full of questions as soon as she learned that Lizzie was catching an earlier flight than was planned.

Her fingers hovered over the keypad. How was she going to explain this?

"Hey, are you here for the hostess position?" came a familiar voice from behind her.

Lizzie spun around to find Dante leaning against an old truck. "What are you doing here? I mean, what are you doing back so soon? Is the party over already? You did have the party, didn't you?"

She was nervously rambling and he was smiling. Smiling? Why was he smiling? The last time she saw him, he'd looked miserable.

"The party is probably still in full swing. Once my family gets started, it goes on and on."

"That's good." She didn't want to think that anything she did would ruin this special day for Massimo. "I…I'll be out of your way in just a minute."

"Don't go."

"What?" Surely she hadn't heard him correctly.

Before Dante could repeat himself, a taxi pulled over to the curb. She should feel relieved, but she didn't. Whatever Dante's reason was for returning early, it was none of her business. He'd made that abundantly clear before he left yesterday.

Lizzie turned and slung her purse over one shoulder and her carry-on over the other shoulder. She grabbed the handle of suitcase and turned in time to see Dante leaning in the window of the taxi, handing over a wad of cash. What in the world?

As she approached them, Dante straightened and the taxi pulled out.

"Hey! Wait!" She was going to miss her flight. The last

one for the day. She turned on Dante. "What did you go and do that for?"

"We need to talk."

She frowned. She wasn't up for another battle of words. She was bruised and wounded from their last go-round. All she wanted was to be alone to lick her wounds. "There's nothing left to say."

"I'm sorry."

His words caused the breath to catch in her throat. This time she was certain about what she heard. But whether he was talking about how he'd dumped her or whether he was referring to dismissing the taxi, she wasn't sure.

"About what?"

"Let's go inside and talk." He moved to the restaurant door and unlocked it. When he held it open for her, she didn't move. "I promise that if you hear me out and you don't like what I have to say that I'll drive you to the airport myself."

She glanced at her wristwatch. "You've got five minutes."

"Fair enough."

She must be losing her grip on reality. What other reason would there be for her to agree to put herself through more heartache and pain?

Her feet felt as though they were weighed down as she walked inside the oh-so-familiar restaurant. She really was going to miss this place and the amazing people that she'd gotten to know here—most of all, she'd miss Dante.

She stopped by the hostess desk and turned to him. "What is it you want?"

"You."

"What?" Her lack of sleep was not helping her make sense of what he was telling her.

"I want you, Lizzie. I love you."

Her heart tripped over itself. She'd been waiting for so long to hear those words, but before she went flying into his arms, she needed to understand. "But what about yesterday?"

"I panicked. When I got a phone call telling me that you'd been in an accident, I overreacted. It seems like the DeFiore men are destined to grow old alone and I thought— Well, it doesn't matter. All I could think about is that if I lost you I'd be devastated and unable to go on."

Really? No one had ever cared about her that much.

"But if you felt that way, how were you able to just dump me?"

"I thought that by protecting myself that I wouldn't be hurt. But my father pointed out the fallacy of my logic—"

"Your father? You two were discussing me?" She wasn't so sure how she felt about that detail.

"Thanks to you, we had a talk that was long overdue." He looked around at the restaurant and then back at her. "You opened my eyes to a lot of things including how much I love this place...especially with you by my side."

Her heart tap-danced in her chest. "Do you really mean that?"

He peered deep into her eyes. "I love you with all my heart. And I would be honored if you'd consider staying here and running Massimo's with me."

"I couldn't think of anything I'd like more."

He stepped closer and wrapped his arms around her. "I promise no more panic attacks as long as you promise not to take up skydiving."

"Now that's a promise I can readily make." She smiled up at him as she slipped her arms up over his shoulders. "I'm scared of heights."

"So we're partners?"

She nodded. "But I think we should kiss to make it official."

"I think you're right."

His head dipped. Their lips met and the rest of the world slipped away.

At last Lizzie was home.

EPILOGUE

A month later

THE CLINK OF champagne flutes sounded in the empty dining room.

"To the most amazing man." Lizzie stared into the eyes of the only man she'd ever loved. "I love you."

"I love you, too." Dante pressed a kiss to her lips that promised more to follow. And soon.

"Can you believe we were on television? Our grand premiere." Lizzie couldn't keep a silly grin from her face.

"And you were amazing."

She waved off his over-the-top compliment. "I think those bubbles are going to your head."

"Nope. It's just you."

"Can you be serious for just a minute?"

The truth was that she had never been this deliriously happy in her entire life. Even the evenings she'd spent sitting next to Dante on the couch watching soccer…erm, football made her smile. And she never thought she'd ever appreciate sports, but Dante was opening her eyes to football and so much more.

"I can be serious. As long as it doesn't take too long." His gaze dipped to her lips.

When he started to lean forward, Lizzie held out her hands. "Dante, do you think of anything else?"

A lazy smile pulled at his lips. "Not if I can help it."

"Well, try for just a second."

His tempting lips pursed together. "What's on your mind?"

"What do you think about the television studio's offer to give us our own show?" They'd just received the call and Lizzie was too excited to trust her own reactions.

"I can think of something I'd like better."

She searched his face to see if his mind was still in the bedroom, but his expression was totally serious. "What is it?"

"How about you become my partner?"

"Well, of course I'll be your partner. That's what the studio is interested in. You and me working together—"

"No, I don't mean that." He took her hand in his and looked deep into her eyes, making her heart skip a beat. Then he dropped to his knee. "I mean I want you to be my family."

The breath hitched in her throat as tears of joy obscured the view of the man she loved with all of her heart. She blinked and the tears splashed onto her cheeks. With effort she swallowed the lump of giddy emotion in her throat.

"I can't think of anything I'd like better."

He got to his feet and encased her face in his palms. "I'm sorry I'm unprepared but I hadn't been planning to propose tonight. I've been playing it over and over in my mind. And I just couldn't wait any longer."

She stood up on her tiptoes and pressed her lips to his. Her heart thumped with excitement. She didn't know how it was possible but she'd swear with every kiss it just kept getting better and better.

When Dante pulled away, she pouted. He smiled and shook his head. "I take it that was a yes?"

"Most definitely."

"I have one more serious question."

"Well, ask it so we can get back to the good stuff."

He laughed and she grinned.

"I have an idea and I don't know how you'll feel about it, but what about having the wedding at the vineyard?"

She couldn't think of a more romantic spot on the entire earth. "I love it but…"

"But what?"

"What about Jules?" The thought of being permanently separated from her foster sister dimmed her excitement. "She's my only family—"

"Not anymore—I'll be your family, too. And Jules is always welcome here."

"But she has grad school. I won't let her give up. She's worked too hard for this. I want her to reach for her dreams."

"And she will. We'll make sure of it."

"But how?"

Dante pressed a finger to her lips. "Shh… Nonno always says, *Where there's a will, there's a way.*"

Lizzie's mind and heart were racing. The two people she loved most in this world were divided by an ocean. "I don't know."

"Look at me." Dante's gaze caught and held hers. "Do you love me?"

Without any hesitation she uttered, "With all of my heart."

"Then believe in us—in the power of our love. Believe that the future will work out for all of us. Maybe not in the way we'd expect, but sometimes the unexpected is just what people need. There's a way to make this work with Jules and we'll find it. Do you believe me?"

"I do."

He pressed his lips to hers and the worries faded away. Together, they could do anything.

* * * * *

TUSCAN HEAT

DEBORAH FLETCHER MELLO

To my Muse
for keeping me dreaming.
You make my heart sing!

Chapter 1

She and her sister were identical twins, and most people were never able to tell the two women apart. But Gianna Martelli had taken a pair of scissors to her sibling Carina's dark locks, cutting the young woman's waist-length tresses to pixie short. Carina's natural curls were suddenly less abundant as she stood in the center of the room, her head waving slowly from side to side to show off her new hairdo to their family.

"Wow!" Graham Porter exclaimed, his dark eyes shifting back and forth between the two women. "Wow!"

"What's that mean?" Carina questioned, her eyebrows lifted as she tossed her husband a look. "Why do you keep saying wow like that?" A wave of panic flashed across her face. "You don't like it!"

He met the look his wife was giving him, holding

his hands up defensively. "No... I mean yes... I do! It's just unexpected," he said, turning to his father-in-law for assistance. "What do you think, Franco?"

Franco Martelli grinned. "It's lovely, daughter. But it's a definite change. And like Graham said, it's unexpected! I think what your husband is trying to say is that you've surprised us, is all."

"I told you to trust me," Gianna said as Carina smiled, pulling her hands through the new short length of her hair. "It really does look great!"

"Are you going to cut yours, too?" Franco asked, turning in his seat to stare at Gianna.

The young woman shrugged. "I was thinking about it, but Carina doesn't want me to."

"I want us to look different," Carina said. "Just for a little while. No one will mix us up now."

Gianna rolled her eyes skyward, tossing the extensive length of her own dark waves over her shoulder. "It's been forever since anyone last got us confused."

"Last week at the market, Mrs. Falco thought I was you."

"Mrs. Falco is half-blind," Gianna said with an eye roll. "She gets *papà* and Graham mixed up!"

Graham chuckled as he rose to his feet, moving to his wife's side. He leaned down to kiss her cheek. "It's a very flattering style on you, sweetheart. I really like it," he said softly. "You look beautiful!" He trailed a finger across Carina's cheek, and she smiled brightly as he leaned in to kiss her lips.

Gianna threw the two a look, the faintest hint of jealousy furrowing her brow. She blew a low sigh. "You two need to get a room," she quipped. She rose from her seat and moved toward the door. "I'll be in my office. Some of us have work to do."

"Speaking of," Carina said, "I sorted your mail and typed up your notes. And your agent called. She needs to speak with you about the changes in your next contract."

"I don't have a next contract. I told you to tell her I'm not interested in what they're offering."

"I did, which is why she wants to speak with you."

Gianna nodded. "I'll call her," she said, trying to ignore the gentle caresses passing between her sister and brother-in-law. The couple's very public displays of affection were often distracting and unsettling, the love the two shared enviable. Gianna couldn't help but wish that she had what they had. With one last wave of her hand she turned and disappeared from the room.

Behind the closed door of her office, Gianna ran her fingers through her own thick tresses, pulling the wealth of her hair up into a high bun. She found herself wishing that she'd cut her own hair first, motivated by the effort it took to maintain the lengthy locks. That, and she found herself in want of a change. One that might bring a man into her life with a slow hand that glided like silk across her bare skin. She blew a low sigh as she turned to stare out the window to the landscape outside.

The sun was shining brightly, and she had full view of the family's vineyards. Their family home was situated in the Ombrone Valley, one of the most beautiful stretches of countryside in Italy. She stared out to the Chianti vines, the cornfields and the lengthy rows of cypress trees. In the distance the expanse of chestnut forests reached up to kiss the bright blue sky. The view paid homage to unparalleled art, the land a masterpiece of blessings. For a brief moment Gianna sat staring at the beauty, lost in her thoughts as the morning's bright rays peeked through the window to kiss the round of her high cheekbones.

She blew one last sigh as she spun around in her leather executive's chair toward her computer. Powering up the device, she waited for the unit to engage then typed in her password. Minutes later she stared at a blank screen, unable to decide in what direction she planned to take her next story. Writer's block had suddenly crept in with a vengeance. When nothing came, she swung her chair around to stare back outside.

Donovan Boudreaux found the pomp and circumstance of the Catholic ceremony somewhat sobering. He was standing at the altar of Saint Patrick's Church in New Orleans holding his niece, Cecily Boudreaux, in his arms. The infant was being christened, she and her twin brother, Sydney, both receiving the sacrament of spiritual cleansing and rebirth. Light shimmered through the stained glass that enclosed the building's front turret.

He fought the urge to yawn as Father Charles Dussouy made the sign of the cross in front of one baby and then the other. He stared down into the infant's sweet face as the priest announced her Christian name, sprinkled holy water over the child's head and welcomed her into the congregation. She never once opened her eyes, barely shifting her small body when the water saturated her curls. Her brother, on the other hand, screamed at the top of his small lungs.

Donovan grinned as he and his brother Kendrick exchanged a look. Kendrick was rocking young Sydney vigorously, trying his very best to calm the baby down. But Sydney wasn't having any of it, no ounce of consolation from his uncle and godfather bringing him any comfort. It wasn't until the matriarch of the family, Katherine Boudreaux, lifted her grandchild from her son's arms did the little guy finally settle down as she snuggled him against her chest. There was something about their mother's touch that put them all at ease, and as each of her children watched, it made them all smile.

The private ceremony was over almost as quickly as it had begun. After the priest wished them well and disappeared from the sanctuary, the family stood in a protective circle around the twins, who'd been returned to their parents' arms.

Mason "Senior" Boudreaux, the family patriarch, cleared his throat, swiping at a tear that lingered in the corners of his dark eyes. "Your mama and I are glad that all you kids could make it home to celebrate these babies," he said, his tone low. The man's gaze swept around the circle.

The eldest Boudreaux child patted his namesake's broad shoulder. "Where else would we be, Senior? You know once you and Mama give the command we follow orders!" Mason Boudreaux III said.

His siblings laughed, their heads nodding in agreement. Donovan leaned to kiss his mother's cheek, his arms wrapped around her shoulders as he hugged her close. His own eyes roved from one face to the other. There was no escaping the Boudreaux lineage. Their distinctive features hinted of an African-Asian ancestry, with their slight angular eyes, thin noses, high cheek lines and full, pouty lips. Side by side they were a kaleidoscope of colorations that ranged from burnt umber to milk chocolate.

His brother Mason, who could have passed for his twin, stood at his side. The low lines of their closely cropped haircuts complemented their distinctive facial features. Mason's wife, Phaedra, clutched his elbow on his other side. Then there was his very pregnant sister, Maitlyn, and her husband, Zakaria Sayed. Maitlyn was the second child and oldest girl in the Boudreaux family. Standing beside them was his sister Katrina, who was a year younger than Donovan, with her husband, Matthew Stallion, and their two sons, Collin and Jacoby, or Baby Jake, as he was affectionately called. On his right side stood his younger brother Darryl, and Darryl's wife, Camryn, who held their newborn baby, Alexa Michelle, in her arms. The twins, Kendrick and Kamaya were next, Kamaya linked arm in arm with their baby sister, Tarah, and Kendrick's wife, Vanessa. His brother Guy, and Guy's wife, Dahlia, the twins' parents, closed their family circle. In that moment, the love between them all billowed like the sweetest breeze all around.

"Can we please go eat now?" Tarah suddenly whined. "This lovefest has made me hungry."

Katherine shook her head. "I declare, child! You are always hungry."

"I would really like to know how you stay so thin!" Kamaya exclaimed, her head waving.

"Good genes," Tarah said with a soft giggle.

Maitlyn rolled her eyes, slapping a hand against her hips. "We have those same genes, so I don't think that's it," she said with a warm chuckle.

They all headed in the direction of the exit and home. Minutes later the joy and laughter continued at the Boudreaux family's Broadway Street house. The food was abundant, plates overflowing as the family all caught up, conversation sweeping from one room to the other.

"I like the name Rose. Rose Lynne Sayed," Maitlyn was saying, her hand gliding in a tight circle across her abdomen. "Although Zak is still insisting we're having a boy!" she said, leaning in to whisper with her sisters. "He even told the technician that did the ultrasound that she didn't know what she was talking about."

Kamaya laughed. "At least it's not twins!"

"I wouldn't mind having twins," Tarah said. "A boy and a girl. You get it all done in one shot. Dahlia never has to be pregnant again. How perfect is that? You, on the other hand, might have to do it again to get a boy. Maybe even twice."

"If I had thought that way after Kendrick and Kamaya were born, you wouldn't be here," their mother interjected as she joined in the conversation. She took the seat beside Tarah, giving her daughter's ponytail a playful tug.

Kamaya laughed. "I know!"

Katherine turned her attention to Donovan, who was leaning against the home's brick fireplace, a glass of red wine in his hand. "So, Donovan, what's going on with you? What's the big news you wanted to share?"

"Yeah, Don Juan! Are you engaged? Pregnant? What?" Tarah said teasingly.

"You have to date first," Kamaya said with a deep chuckle. "Are you finally dating, big brother?"

Donovan shook his head, amused by his sisters' teasing. "Don't call me Don Juan," he said, cutting an eye at Tarah.

"What's going on?" Kendrick asked, moving into the room. "Who's calling who names?"

"Tarah," Mason said, sauntering in on his brother's heels. "You don't even need to ask."

Tarah threw her brother a look. "Why do you assume I did something? How come it can't be Maitlyn or Kamaya who's doing something?"

"Because it's always you," her brothers all answered in unison.

The women laughed, Maitlyn and Kamaya nodding their heads in agreement.

Tarah rolled her eyes skyward, her arms crossing over her chest. Her lips were pushed out in a full pout as she tossed her body back against the sofa cushions.

Katherine smiled. "Y'all stop now. Donovan was just about to tell us his news."

The family all turned in Donovan's direction, eyeing him curiously. He shook his head, the attention suddenly unnerving. His brow furrowed.

"Well?" Katherine prodded. "What is it, baby?"

"I'm moving to Italy," he pronounced, his gaze sweeping around the room. "I leave at the end of the semester. I've been invited by the University of Siena in Tuscany, Italy, to come teach there. I'll be a visiting professor for one year teaching the structure of associative algebras relative to their radicals."

Tarah jumped up excitedly. "Hot dog! I get to visit Italy! Yes, yes, yes!" she exclaimed as she rushed to Donovan's side. She threw her arms around her big brother's shoulders.

"I didn't hear anyone in the room say anything about you going to Italy," their mother noted. "Sit your tail down, Tarah, and give your brother some space."

Tarah tossed her hands up as she moved back to her seat, plopping her body back down against the sofa.

Everyone in the room laughed.

Donovan laughed with them. "I hope that once I get settled, you'll all come visit me at some point," he said.

"You couldn't find a college in Texas or Florida or someplace closer? You're a mathematician, after all. Everyone needs a good numbers man," Katherine said, her bright smile dropping into a deep frown.

He shook his head, meeting his mother's gaze. His smile was consoling. "This is a great opportunity that I can't pass up. It's a definite résumé builder."

Congratulations rang warmly through the room as his siblings moved to shake his hand and give him hugs.

His mother moved to his side, her hands clasping his shoulders. There were tears in her eyes. "Why must all of you move so far away? Italy is halfway around the world, for heaven's sake!"

Senior joined them, wrapping his own arms around his wife's shoulders. "Leave that boy be. Your son's almost forty years old! Cut them apron strings already, woman!" The man's smile filled his dark face as he kissed her cheek.

She rolled her eyes, fighting the smile that pulled at her own lips and the tears that burned hot behind her eyelids. "He's only thirty-seven. He's nowhere near close to forty yet. And I'll cut the apron strings when I darn well please, Senior Boudreaux!"

Donovan smiled, the pad of his thumb swiping at a tear that had rolled down his mother's cheek. "It's not like I won't come back, Mama. I'm not planning to be there forever. And I hope you'll definitely come visit me."

Tarah suddenly waved her hands for attention. "Can I live in your apartment while you're gone?"

Senior eased his body into the queen-size bed beside his wife. Katherine sat upright against the pillows, her electronic reader open on her lap, her reading glasses perched low on her nose. She cut her eye at her husband as he snuggled his body close against hers. He leaned up on one elbow, his head resting against an open palm as he stared at her.

"What?"

"What do you mean what?"

"I mean, why are you staring at me?"

"I'm staring," he said softly, his hand trailing a heated line across her leg, "because you're so beautiful."

Katherine shifted her glasses from her face, resting them easily in her lap. She met the look the man was giving her. "What do you want, Senior Boudreaux?"

"Why do I have to want something, woman?"

"Because when you start tossing out compliments, you're up to something. So what is it?"

Senior rolled his eyes skyward as he dropped onto his side, then moved onto his back. He pulled one arm up over his head as the other clutched the covers around his body.

"I tell you how beautiful you are all the time. That doesn't mean I want something."

Katherine pulled her glasses back against her face. She threw one last gaze in his direction. "Mmm-hmm!" she muttered under her breath.

Senior laughed. "Okay, so maybe I want something," he said as he rolled back toward her.

"You're working my nerves right now, Senior," she quipped, a smile pulling at her thin lips. "You see me reading. You know I don't like to be interrupted when I'm in the middle of a good book!"

Senior shrugged his shoulders. "I was thinking that we probably need to update our wills," he said, ignoring her comment.

She pulled at her eyeglasses a second time, closing the cover on her electronic device. "What brought that up?"

"Our babies. With all of our new grandbabies we need to make sure they're going to be taken care of. We don't have much, but I want to make sure they each get a little something from us when the time comes."

Katherine nodded. "Do you remember when it was just Collin? Back then I used to think he was going to be the only grandbaby we would ever have!"

Senior laughed. "And you spoiled him like it, too!"

The matriarch nodded. "Katrina was going through so much back then, raising Collin by herself after his daddy died."

Senior fell into his thoughts, thinking about the army helicopter pilot who'd married his daughter and fathered his eldest grandson. He'd been a good man, and his untimely death during the Gulf War had been devastating. Both he and Katherine had been thrilled when Katrina had found love a second time with Matthew Stallion. Matthew loved their daughter immensely and had stepped in to parent Collin without a moment's hesitation. The couple had been blessed again when their second son, Matthew Jacoby Stallion Junior, had been born. Everyone in the family called the youngster Jake. Only his beloved grandmother called him Jacoby.

Senior tossed his wife an endearing smile. "Katrina's happy, and them boys is doing good. She and Matthew are doing a fine job raising Collin and Jake."

"My sweet little Jacoby is a handful. But he's got a great big brother!"

"Collin takes after his granddaddy," Senior said with a chuckle.

Katherine laughed with him. "That's not a bad thing! Not a bad thing at all!" She trailed a warm finger against the side of her husband's face.

"Now we've got the twins, and little Alexa, and Maitlyn will be having her little munchkin soon. Before you know it, Tarah will be married and having babies. I just think we need to make sure we're prepared."

"It used to drive me crazy worrying about our kids

getting married and having families of their own. I wanted them all to know the kind of love you and I have, but your sons were determined to do things their own way."

"And look at them now. I think my sons are doing a fine job. You were worrying for nothing."

She smiled. "I guess I was," she said as she thought about her children and the people who'd come to share their lives. Her eldest son, Mason, had married Matthew Stallion's sister, Phaedra. Mason wanted children, but Phaedra wasn't ready to rush into the responsibility. She imagined it would be another year, maybe even two before the young woman would be ready. Katherine had told her son that waiting wasn't a bad thing. It would happen when God was ready for it to happen.

Then there was Maitlyn. Her oldest daughter had been heartbroken over the demise of her first marriage despite both her parents having warned her that her ex had been no good for her. Meeting her brother's best friend, Zak Sayed, had shown Maitlyn how a woman was supposed to be treated. And now Maitlyn and Zak were expecting their first child.

With Guy and Dahlia settling in nicely with their twins, and Darryl and his wife, Camryn, loving on their new baby, only three of their children had yet to find happiness in a committed relationship. Donovan was the only son still an eligible bachelor. Their daughter Kamaya's happily-ever-after was right in front of her face, but she was the only one who couldn't see it, and their youngest, Tarah, was still looking for Mr. Right, although Tarah was often quick to settle for Mr. Right Now. Katherine blew out a low sigh.

She suddenly felt her husband eyeing her intently, and she met his stare. "I think you're worrying for nothing," she said. "Every one of our kids is doing well, and their babies will want for absolutely nothing."

Senior reached his arms around his wife's waist and hugged her close. "Maybe, but I'd rather be safe than sorry."

She nodded, gently caressing his shoulders as she hugged him back. "We've done good with our children, Senior Boudreaux," she whispered softly. "We've done really good, old man! It's time you and I both stop worrying."

"So, does that mean you're happy about Donovan going to Italy?"

"I like having my children close to home, you know that, Senior. I will never be happy about Donovan going so far away, but I'm happy that he's been blessed with this opportunity."

He gave her a quick squeeze. "Donovan needs a change of scenery. This trip will be good for him. He's been focused on school and work and nothing else for too long now."

Katherine blew a soft sigh. "Maybe, but I'm still gonna miss my baby!"

Senior laughed heartily. "Your babies are grown!" he said as he reached to swipe a tear from her eye.

She leaned her cheek into the palm of his hand. "They will always be my babies!"

Senior reached up to kiss her mouth, allowing his lips

to linger against hers for a good long while. Katherine broke the connection, suddenly laughing as she turned off her reader and rested it against the nightstand. She reached to turn off the light that decorated the tabletop.

Her husband eyed the wide grin across her face. "What's so funny?"

"I think we should make a baby!" she said, still giggling as she nestled herself beneath him.

Senior laughed with her. "You're hoping for a miracle, aren't you?"

"Not really. I just thought we could have a whole lot of fun practicing," she answered as she slid her lips back to his.

Chapter 2

Donovan moved from his kitchen into his family room, hanging up the telephone he carried in his hand. He'd been on a conference call with Maitlyn and his brothers, acquiring help for his impending trip. His Lafayette Street loft had been his single greatest investment, and he needed to ensure that someone in the family stayed on top of things while he was gone, lest Tarah turn his home into a sorority party house.

Making sure the doors were locked and the security system engaged, he headed to his office. He sat down in the leather executive's chair, pulling it up to the large oak desk as he turned on his computer. As he waited for it to power on, Donovan folded his hands in his lap, dropping into deep thought.

Donovan was the third child and the second son in

the family of nine. With a doctorate in mathematics, he was a tenured professor at Tulane University. The most conservative of all his siblings, he was an intellectual challenge to most. His staid demeanor made his sister Katrina, a district court judge, and his brother Mason, a billionaire entrepreneur and business executive, look wild in comparison. His younger siblings frequently professed that he defied all logic with them having careers in the arts and him having no artistic inclinations whatsoever. Even his brother Kendrick, who had often kept much of his life a deep, dark secret until meeting Vanessa, was more outspoken and outgoing than Donovan tended to be.

But Donovan had secrets, too, the likes of which would make his whole family sit up and take notice. His very conservative, very organized lifestyle had always been an open book, and now he was keeping details close to the vest. His interest in Italy was just the tip of the cache of secrets he'd been keeping from his family. A full grin pulled wide across his face.

He focused on the lengthy list of email messages that filled his inbox folder. He was searching for one in particular, and when he found the familiar email address his smile widened.

For months now he'd been pen pals with a woman who lived in Italy. A woman he had yet to meet or speak to in person. He only knew her from the award-winning books she was renowned for, her promotional photo gracing the back cover of each. But he'd become obsessed with the email messages from her that came daily, the engaging exchanges brightening his otherwise

dull existence. And now he was being afforded an opportunity to visit Italy and meet her in person. Never
much of a risk taker, Donovan rarely found himself
out of his comfort zone. He could only begin to imagine what his siblings would have to say if any of them
were to find out.

He didn't have to imagine what his parents would
say. He could already hear their admonishments and
concerns, both asking questions he didn't necessarily
have answers for. He had never heard of any online relationship turning out well. For all any of them knew,
he could have just as easily been chatting with Bubba in
the state penitentiary. He no more knew who was on the
other end of that computer than she did. He only knew
what he was being told, and any of it could have been
a bold-faced lie. The anonymity of the internet made
embellishing and stretching the truth an easy thing to
do. But something about the eloquence of her words had
Donovan trusting that he did indeed have a connection
with the illustrious author.

He read the message that had come hours earlier.

I live a charmed life. I get to live in a beautiful villa in
the Tuscan Maremma, eat pasta prepared by an amazing Italian chef and travel to charming cities whenever I
want. What's not to love? I imagine that finally meeting
you will be the icing on some very sweet, sweet cake!
So, please, come. I can't wait to show you everything
exquisite about Italy.

A shiver of excitement surged up Donovan's spine.
He reached for the four-hundred-page mystery novel

that rested on the corner of the desk. *Mayhem and Madness* by Gianna Martelli had landed on the *New York Times* bestseller list three weeks earlier and didn't seem to be going anyplace anytime soon. He flipped the book in his hand to stare at the photograph on the back jacket.

Gianna Martelli was a stunning beauty, and he imagined that the professionally shot black-and-white image didn't begin to do her justice. Her dark eyes were focused on the camera, and he felt as if she were staring directly at him. The look she was giving was searing, her gaze intense. But there was something about her expression that gave him pause, made him wish he could reach through the pages to draw her into his arms and hold her tight. He sighed.

Two books ago he'd reached out to email her, wanting to offer his opinion of her current novel at the time. He'd been excited to share his opinions about her characters, the protagonist a math professor at a historically black college. He'd been eager to tell her where she'd gotten it wrong and what had been wholeheartedly right. He had only half expected a polite but scripted response. Instead, he'd gotten an intriguingly worded reply that had challenged his sensibilities. Curiosity had gotten the best of him and he'd written back, receiving another reply that had him suddenly wanting more. Before he knew it, they were exchanging lengthy emails and a delightful friendship was born.

He typed a quick message back.

You've convinced me and now I'm counting the days. I can't wait to see that sunset you are always bragging about.

After adding his travel details, he pushed the send button. Moving from his office to his bedroom, he pulled an oversize suitcase from a closet shelf and began to pack.

Rushing into the large kitchen, Carina looked from her husband to her father and back. Both men paused, concern washing over their expressions.

"What's wrong?" Graham questioned.

"Are you okay?" Franco asked, resting the knife in his hand on the butcher-block counter.

She shook her head vehemently. "Gianna's going to kill me!"

The two men cut eyes at each other.

"What did you do, Carina?" Franco asked, eyeing his daughter with a narrowed gaze.

She raised both hands. "It's really not that bad, but Gianna isn't going to like it!" she exclaimed.

"What isn't she going to like?" Graham asked.

Carina crossed the room to stare out a window. She moved from one to the other, and then to the door, to ensure that her twin was nowhere near.

Franco shook his head. "Gianna went into town for me. She's not here."

"He's coming to Italy," Carina blurted. "He'll be here next week."

"Who's coming to Italy?"

"Donovan Boudreaux, the math professor from the United States."

Both men seemed confused, tossing each other another look.

Carina sighed. "The man she's been communicating with, except she doesn't know she's been communicating with him because I've been sending the messages."

Both men snapped in unison. "You've been doing what?"

The young woman nodded. "I've been pretending to be Gianna. He's been writing to her, and I've been answering."

"Carina, why would you do something like that?" Graham snapped.

"Because I knew she wouldn't, and I think they would make a really great couple. He's just as nerdy as she is."

"But he hasn't been building a relationship with your sister, Carina—he's been building one with you," Franco said, crossing his arms over his chest.

Carina shook her head. "That's not true. Every word I sent, she wrote. I copied them out of her journals."

"You read your sister's journals?" Her father's look was disapproving.

"I've been reading her journals since we were twelve. Besides, I am her personal assistant. I'm supposed to answer her mail."

"I don't think that's what your sister intended, daughter." Franco shook his head from side to side. He went back to chopping the bulb of garlic that rested on the wooden chopping board. "Gianna is going to kill you!"

Graham laughed. "She is definitely going to kill you," he said.

Carina rolled her eyes at her husband. "Thanks for the support."

"So, what do you know about this guy?" Graham asked. "How do you know he's not a psycho?"

"He teaches at Tulane University in New Orleans. He comes from a big family, and he reads the same boring stuff Gianna reads."

"So he is a psycho!"

"He's very sweet and a bit of a romantic. He's exactly what Gianna needs."

"So, tell me," Graham said, turning to stare at his wife, a wooden spoon waving in his hand, "exactly when were you going to tell Gianna about this guy?"

"I hadn't figured that out. I thought I had a little more time until he decided to come to Italy to meet me... I mean her."

Graham continued to eyeball her. "I'm having some issues with this," he said. "You've been having a relationship with another man for weeks..."

"Months actually," Carina interrupted, her tone casual.

Graham paused, his eyebrows raised. "Months?"

His wife nodded as she gave him a quick shrug. "I was building a friendship between them. That takes time. And I was going to tell her. I think."

He shook his head. "You've been building this relationship for months now, but I'm supposed to believe that you did it for your sister, when you didn't even know if you were going to tell her?"

"You're making it sound worse than it is!"

"It sounds the way it sounds, Carina, and it's not kosher! It's not kosher at all!"

Her father moved from the tomato sauce he'd put on

the stove toward the door. "I'll let you two have a minute," he said. "Watch my pot while I'm gone, please."

Carina blew out a soft sigh. She locked gazes with her husband, noting the disappointment and confusion that gleamed from his eyes. She didn't have the words to explain how she'd rationalized what she'd done. All she knew was that in the beginning, it had made all the sense in the world to her. And that even in that moment she knew beyond any doubt that she'd done the right thing.

Since the publication of Gianna's first book, Carina had stepped in to do those things Gianna neglected to do for herself. From managing her fan page to answering reader questions, Carina had been her sister's personal assistant and marketing guru, maintaining her Twitter, Facebook and Instagram accounts. When Donovan's first email message had come, there had been something in the tone of his words that had caught her attention. His comments had been thoughtful and provoking, his words laden with emotion. She instinctively knew he was exactly what her best friend in the whole wide world needed.

Her response had been all Gianna, the wisecracking, tongue-in-cheek retorts her sister was known for. As their emails had gotten lengthier, she'd pulled lines and paragraphs from Gianna's personal writings to respond, wanting him to know her twin the way she knew her, in her sister's own words. And it had worked because now he wanted to meet the woman he'd befriended. Admittedly, Carina hadn't thought her plan through to the end. She'd imagined that once she'd vetted the man, she could have told Gianna and passed on the reins. Despite hoping that her twin would be happy to step in and take over, Carina knew that happy was probably going to be the last thing Gianna would feel about the situation.

She felt her husband still staring at her, and she lifted her eyes back to his. "Donovan likes Gianna. Everything he knows, he knows about Gianna. He doesn't know me or anything about me! And when she finds out and gets to know him, she's going to like him, too. I'd bet my last dollar on it. I just wanted her to be as happy as you and I are, and you know she wouldn't have done anything like this on her own."

Graham shook his head from side to side. "So when do you plan to tell Gianna?"

"Tell Gianna what?" Gianna asked as she moved into the room. She looked from one to the other. "What's going on?"

Carina moved too quickly to her husband's side, leaning against him for support. The two exchanged a quick look, a wave of nervous energy palpable around them.

Moving to the counter, Gianna dropped her bags against the wooden top. Her eyes were still locked on her sister and brother-in-law. The bubbling pot on the stove interrupted the moment as tomato sauce suddenly spewed over the sides and down to the stove top.

"Oh, hell!" Carina exclaimed, moving to lower the heat on their father's meal.

Gianna watched with one hand on her hip as she waited for the duo to clean the mess. When the last dishrag had been rinsed, the pot back on simmer, she asked a second time, "So what is it that you have to tell me?"

Mumbling, Graham leaned over to kiss his wife's cheek, then moved toward the door. Without another word, he disappeared through the entrance, leaving the two women alone. Gianna moved to stand in front of her sister, her arms crossed over her chest.

"What's going on, Sissy?"

"Why don't we sit down? Did you find everything you needed at the market?"

Gianna shook her head, her index finger waving in front of her sister's face. "Oh, no, you don't! You are not changing the subject, and don't you move until you answer my question!"

Carina took a deep breath and then another. "I found you a boyfriend," she said, and then she spewed out the story, not bothering to take another inhale of air until the last word had spilled past her lips.

"Open the door, Gianna," Franco commanded. "You can't hide in there forever."

"I'm not hiding!" Gianna yelled back. "I just don't want to talk to anyone."

"Now, daughter! And don't make me say it again."

Gianna sighed deeply as she moved onto her feet toward her office door. She undid the lock and pulled it open just enough to peer out into the hallway. Standing on the other side, her father gave her that look, his mouth pursed tightly, his eyes narrowed. Sighing again, she stepped aside to let the man enter.

Franco moved to the upholstered sofa and sat down,

turning his gaze to stare at his daughter. Neither spoke, Gianna still pouting in anger. As she sat down beside him, she couldn't help but marvel at her father. His calm demeanor was soothing, and his dashing good looks made her smile.

The older she and her sister got, the more Gianna thought they were starting to look like their beloved father. His complexion was warm, his loose curls more silver than black. They had his nose and jawline, but neither had inherited his chilling blue eyes. He swore that both his girls resembled their mother, but Gianna didn't necessarily agree, thinking they were a nice mesh of the two. She suddenly thought about her mother.

The beautiful black woman from New York City had been the love of her father's life. A chance meeting while Angela Wilson had been an exchange student in Tuscany had solidified their future. Franco had always believed that they would have grown old together, but his beloved Angela had suffered a brain aneurysm when the twins were twelve years old. The loss had been devastating. Franco had thrown himself into running his family winery and loving his children. He still mourned the loss.

As long as Gianna could remember, she and her sister's antics had been enough to keep him on his toes, and keep his head gray. And despite their love for one another, they spent more time angry with each other than not angry, with Gianna, the elder by ten minutes, always pouting because of something Carina had done.

"So when do you plan to speak to your sister?" her father asked.

Gianna rolled her eyes skyward. "Never! I cannot believe she would do this to me."

"It was a little extreme, but her heart was in the right place."

"This man is coming to visit, and he thinks there's something between us and there isn't. I don't know anything about him."

Her father nodded. "I imagine he's going to be disappointed."

"And his disappointment falls on me. She used my name. That's unforgiveable."

"Everything is forgivable."

"Not this."

Franco chuckled softly. "Even this. You just need to figure out how to make it right."

"Why do I need to make it right? I didn't do anything!"

"That may be true, but just like you pointed out, your sister used your name and now a man who doesn't deserve it is going to be disappointed."

Gianna screamed as she shook two fists in the air. "Aargh! I swear I could kill her!" She began to rant in her native Italian.

Franco chuckled softly. "That's an option," he said with a nod, "but I'm sure you can come up with something more creative. Something that will make everybody happy." He tapped a warm palm against her knee.

Gianna shook her head as her father stood back on his feet.

"Carina loves you, Gianna. And you love her. What

she did, she did out of love. Don't you forget that, *mia cara.*" He leaned down to kiss her cheek.

She nodded slowly, meeting his gaze. *"Va bene, papà,"* she said, her expression unmoved.

As the patriarch made his way out of the room, Gianna rose to lock the door behind him. She wasn't yet ready to face her twin, and she knew it would only take a quick minute for Carina to come busting her way inside if she found an opportunity.

She moved back to her desk and the oversize manila folder that rested on its surface. After her admission Carina had given it to Gianna, insisting she read the contents. Gianna still hadn't bothered to break the cover to see just how deep Carina's deception ran.

There was a soft knock at the office door. Carina called her name but Gianna ignored her sister, still staring at the stack of documents. Despite her anger she was intrigued, the curiosity pulling at her. Of all the stunts her sister had pulled over the years, this one had to be her most devious by far. And she was scared to death, fearful that there might be something she liked hidden in those pages that would draw her into her twin sister's madness.

Outside Gianna's window, a plethora of bright stars and a full moon illuminated the dark sky. She'd been reading for hours, the home on the other side of the office door having gone quiet for the night. Carina had tried more than once to get her attention until she'd finally given up, her tear-filled tone apologizing again and again for what she'd done.

Gianna picked up the very first message from the man named Donovan, rereading the words she'd already read a few dozen times.

Dear Ms. Martelli,
My name is Donovan Boudreaux. I'm a math professor at Tulane University in New Orleans, Louisiana. I have been a fan of yours since your first book, *Bruised and Battered*. Despite my previous intentions to write and tell you how much I've enjoyed your writing, I've always stopped myself, feeling that you probably would not want to be inundated with more fan mail. But I was so enthralled with your last story, and the character Dr. Hanover, that I could not let the opportunity to tell you what I think pass by. Your artistry is rare and your words are epic. I was captivated from the first sentence to the last. However, I'm curious to know if you intentionally wanted your readers to empathize with the protagonist despite his being so unlikable. Your disdain for this man was obvious, but as I found myself rooting for him I had to question your intent and wondered if the reflection of him as a man mirrored my own projections. Or are they reflections you masterfully and purposely elicited from us? I'd love to discuss him in further detail. I do hope you'll respond.
Yours truly,
Donovan Boudreaux

Carina's response had been brilliant, her sister pulling excerpts from two news interviews she'd done and quoting one of her favorite proverbs.

Mr. Boudreaux,

Thank you for your kind words. Your support of my work is appreciated, and I found your question interesting. I think what you deemed disdain was anything but. Dr. Hanover was one of my favorite characters to write, and I'm pleased that the dynamics of his personality did not get lost in the details of the mystery. Dr. Hanover's character was drawn to invoke a whirlwind of emotion from the reader, that connection both thought-provoking and substantive. To quote one of my favorite Scriptures: "As iron sharpens iron, so one person sharpens another." Proverbs 27:17. Dr. Hanover served his purpose if you were rooting for him, his advice and wisdom intended to sharpen yours. Thank you for reaching out and please do keep in touch.

Happy reading,

Gianna

And Donovan had kept in touch, continuing to write. His brief paragraphs had expanded to lengthier messages, and Carina had kept up nicely, pulling her responses right from Gianna's private writings. Gianna was surprised by how her twin had pieced the responses together, some of the replies so spot-on that she would never have believed Carina had anything at all to do with them if she hadn't known better. It was almost as if her twin had been stowed away in her head, privy to her thoughts and possessing an understanding of her worldview. It was a cosmic connection like no other, and Gianna didn't know if she could have done the same so successfully.

She pulled one of his last messages from the folder, the literary connection having evolved into something she couldn't even begin to define.

Dearest Gianna,

I marvel at how you're able to articulate what I'm feeling, when I can't even find the words. You are correct. I would be disappointed if I'm not selected for this teaching fellowship. But I'm a man, and my disappointment should not be telling. There are some issues I should not be sensitive about, and because I'm a man that sensitivity should definitely not show. If it does, it would be seen as a sign of weakness. What woman would want a weak man?

Gianna marveled, too. Her sister's crafted reply had been award-worthy.

Donovan, Donovan, Donovan!

Every woman wants a man who owns his feelings! Sensitivity can never be seen as weakness if it walks hand in hand with honesty. Owning our emotions is empowering. Of course you'll be disappointed! You worked hard to qualify for the opportunity. You want it! You are deserving of it! So claim it and think of the day you land in Italy, when you can stand beneath the brightest blue sky and watch the sunset that I watch daily. No woman should want a man who would do any less than that!

And now this stranger, who was connected with Gianna in a way that she found outrageously absurd, was on his way to the Italian coast, expecting that she would be as excited to see him as he was to see her. It was crazy and overwhelming, and despite every ounce of reservation she was feeling, she was intrigued and curious in the same breath.

Chapter 3

Donovan stood with his brother Kendrick, the two men waiting in the flight hangar for the preflight maintenance check on their brother Mason's private plane to be completed. Membership having its privileges surely applied as Donovan eyed the luxury aircraft, one of a dozen planes that Mason had at his disposal. The opportunity to fly private planes had been a gift, the gesture humbling, and Donovan couldn't begin to know how he'd ever be able to repay the favor.

"I promise, baby! I will call you the minute I land," Kendrick was saying while rolling his eyes. He exchanged a look with his brother as he continued his conversation. "Vanessa! It's only three days. I'll be back before you know it. I promise!"

There was a pause, Vanessa's raised voice echoing

out of the receiver in Kendrick's hand. The man blew a heavy sigh. "I swear, honey! This is not a covert mission. I am not disappearing underground on any assignment. I ride a desk now, remember?"

Donovan smiled. Kendrick settling down with his new wife had come with a host of challenges for his younger brother. The couple had met when the FBI agent had been assigned to Vanessa's protective detail, whisking her away to one of the world's most romantic honeymoon spots to protect their cover. Despite Kendrick's assurances that his secret agent days were over, Vanessa remained unconvinced, crippled by anxiety every time he disappeared from town.

Kendrick shook his head as he disconnected. "She's going to kill me."

Donovan laughed. "You tagging along with me isn't what she thinks it is, is it?"

Kendrick shook his head. "I have some work to take care of once we drop you off and send Mason's plane back his way. I'll be meeting up with my unit in Florence and going on to Greece. I just didn't give Vanessa *all* the details of this little venture. I just told her you were scared and wanted me to check things out for you."

"Why would I be scared?"

His brother shrugged. "Your sisters have her convinced that you're a little soft. I just rolled with it."

Donovan's eyes widened as he stared his brother down.

"What?" Kendrick asked, tossing him a look. "Even you know the girls think you're a little easy. They're always afraid someone's going to take advantage of you because you're so trusting."

Donovan shook his head.

Kendrick chuckled. "Hey, it's no big deal. It gives me an excuse to go do what I need to do."

"Do I even want to ask?" Donovan said.

"Nope! Because if I tell you I'll have to shoot you, and we don't want to ruin your trip." Kendrick laughed as he changed the subject. "So, are you excited?"

"I'm nervous. *Not* scared," he emphasized, "but nervous."

"About teaching? That's your thing, bro! Why would you be nervous?"

Donovan met his brother's curious stare. "I just... well..." he stammered, his eyes skating back and forth as he tried to choose his words carefully. "There's someone...a woman... She..."

Kendrick eyed him with a raised brow. "Okay, spill it. What aren't you telling me?"

There was a moment of pause before Donovan answered, lost in his thoughts about Gianna as he reflected on what he knew about the woman.

From her bio, he'd discovered that she held two advanced degrees in science and mathematics. From their communications, he knew that she abhorred traditional intellectual attitudes. So much so that she'd been initially reluctant to communicate with him when she discovered he was a professor.

From reading her novels, he knew that she was proficient at spinning a good thriller and murder mystery. Gianna had a talent for creating male protagonists who appealed to male readers. Despite her literary accolades, she was famously reclusive and purposely avoided the public eye, preferring to spend her time at her family's Tuscan estate working in their winery.

From their exchanges, he took her to be something of a free spirit who practiced yoga religiously, followed an organic diet and was a self-professed nudist. She was passionate about the family's Tuscan estate and winery, and had once stated that she would readily give up her pursuit of the next great novel to work the vineyards.

He took a deep breath. "I have a friend there, and I'm nervous about meeting her," he said finally. "We've only communicated by email."

Kendrick grinned, his smile full and bright. "A friend? When did you get a friend? Who's a girl? In Italy?" he questioned, crossing his arms over his chest.

Donovan felt his own grin spread full and wide across his face. "We've been acquainted for a while now."

"And she's Italian?"

Donovan nodded.

"Is she in education, too?"

"She's a writer. Her name is Gianna."

Kendrick paused for a moment. "Gianna Martelli? The author of *Mayhem and Madness*?"

"You know her?"

"I know her writing. Vanessa bought me a copy of her book to read. It's really good."

"She's extremely talented," Donovan stated.

"She's also quite the looker, if I remember correctly," Kendrick noted with a nod.

Donovan shrugged. "She's all right," he said, trying to keep his tone in check.

Kendrick gave him a swift punch to his upper arm. "Look at you, big brother! I think you're actually blushing! Wait until I tell the family!"

Donovan laughed, lifting his hands up as if in surrender. "You wouldn't. You cannot tell the girls! I would never live it down." He mocked his sisters, imitating Tarah's shrill tone. "Don Juan has a girlfriend? Don Juan is actually speaking to a woman? Let's give Don Juan some advice!"

Kendrick laughed heartily. "You're right. I can't do that to you!"

"Thank you!" He changed the subject. "So have you and Vanessa decided on a honeymoon spot yet?"

As the two men continued their conversation, the flight attendant gestured for their attention. "Gentlemen, we're ready for you to board now," the woman said politely. She gave them both a smile, her gaze shifting between them.

Donovan reached for his carry-on bag and led the way. Minutes later the two men sat comfortably, secured in the plush leather seats as the plane taxied down the runway. He relished the camaraderie he shared with his siblings. He could laugh easily with his brothers, and since it wasn't often that the two were able to spend time together, he was grateful that Kendrick was taking the trip with him, whatever the other man's reasons.

Donovan also didn't mind the teasing from any of his family. He knew that no matter what, he had their support, and the tight bond they all shared was unconditional. But as he thought about Gianna and what might be waiting for him when they finally landed, he was only willing to share so much about the exquisite woman and what he felt about their unique situation. As he stared out the window, watching as the plane lifted easily into the cloud-filled sky, Donovan took a deep breath and then another, hoping that the fear he felt in his heart didn't show on his face.

Sophie Mugabe and Alessandra Donati stood at the arrival gate of Pisa International Airport waiting for the American professor to gather his luggage and exit the travel center. Both were excited as they stood with handmade signs, Donovan's name printed in bold black letters across both sides.

Sophie was Donovan's host and the department chair at the University of Siena. She'd been following him since they'd first met three years earlier at the International Conference on Mathematics and Statistics. That year the conference had been held in London, and Donovan had been presenting the theories he'd published in his book, *The Deconstruction of Associative Algebras of Prime Characteristic.*

Sophie had been enamored from day one, her enthusiasm for the professor and his work almost compulsive. Her regular emails had been just shy of stalking, but he'd been exceptionally kind in his responses. The prospect of getting to know him personally through the next year had her excited in a way she would have never imagined. She was fighting to contain the emotion bubbling through her midsection, desperate to maintain her decorum in front of her student.

Alessandra Donati stood with indifference, her gaze sweeping around the airport lobby. Since the girl's freshman year, Professor Mugabe had mistaken her proficiency with mathematics for interest, singling her out for attention that Alessandra had neither needed nor wanted. But the perks of being the teacher's pet outweighed the disadvantages. So despite wanting to be in Venice with her friends who'd driven up for the day, she'd agreed to come with her mentor to welcome some visiting professor from the United States. She sighed heavily as she looked down at the thin gold watch on her wrist.

"He's landed," Sophie said, excitement ringing in her tone. "It should not be too much longer now."

Alessandra forced a smile onto her face. She was about to comment when she caught sight of the college professor, the man eyeing them both curiously. The distinguished black man smiled sweetly, and the gesture took her breath away. Tall, dark and handsome to the nth degree, he actually had her heartbeat fluttering. She threw her teacher a quick look, not missing the other woman's glazed stare. Her professor was likewise moved.

"He's quite handsome, isn't he?" Sophie muttered as she waved excitedly.

Alessandra chuckled beneath her breath. "Oh, yes, he is!" she exclaimed.

"Professor Mugabe! What a surprise!" Donovan said,

moving to their side. He leaned in to give his benefactor a warm embrace.

"Dr. Boudreaux, welcome to Italy! I could not let you arrive and not be here personally to welcome you. I hope that your trip was pleasant?"

Donovan nodded. "The flight was great. My brother flew with me, and it gave us an opportunity to catch up."

Sophie tossed a look over his shoulder, her eyes skating back and forth. "Your brother is with you?"

Donovan smiled again. "He's actually headed on to Greece as soon as they refuel his plane."

Alessandra cleared her throat, stepping forward for attention. Her eyes swept from one to the other, settling on the beautiful black man.

Sophie tapped her hand to her forehead. "Forgive me. Where are my manners! Dr. Boudreaux, allow me to introduce you to one of our prized students. This is Alessandra Donati. Alessandra is a senior mathematics major. She's quite gifted and looking forward to being in your class this semester."

Alessandra smiled, her gaze narrowing ever so slightly. "Dr. Boudreaux, it's very nice to meet you," she said as she tossed the length of her blond hair over her shoulder. She extended a manicured hand in his direction as she batted her false eyelashes.

"The pleasure is mine, Ms. Donati," he said, shaking her hand.

"I was very excited to hear that you would be coming to the university. Your paper on Lie algebras was quite engaging."

Donovan laughed. "It really wasn't, but I appreciate you saying so."

The young woman's smile was bright, the glint in her eye even brighter.

Sophie interrupted the moment. "I thought we'd get you settled into your cottage, then take you by the school and out for your first meal here in Italy. Unless you have other plans?"

Donovan took a deep breath. "I'd actually love to visit the school, but I'm having dinner with friends. I apologize, I didn't know…"

She shook her head swiftly, interrupting his comment. "Oh, please, no apology necessary. I just thought I'd make the offer."

"You have friends here in Tuscany?" Alessandra asked.

Donovan smiled. "Yes, Gianna Martelli and the Martelli family. They have a vineyard in the heart of the Tuscan Maremma, not far from the province of Grosseto."

Both women shrugged indifferently. "Martelli is a very common name here in Italy," Sophie said, disappointment shimmering in her tone.

Donovan nodded. "Perhaps we can have breakfast in the morning and you can show me around? I'm very excited to see the campus and get acquainted with the faculty."

The older woman grinned. "Definitely! That is definitely doable."

Gianna was as nervous as her sister, the two women scurrying about trying to ensure everything was perfect before Donovan Boudreaux arrived for dinner. Freshly cut flowers decorated the home, resting atop the tables and counters. All the windows had been opened, and a warm breeze blew like a whisper through the space. A roasted chicken scented the air, and handmade pasta waited on the wooden countertop to be dropped into lightly salted water.

Franco and Graham exchanged a look as both women came to an abrupt halt, eyeing each other from across the room. A silent conversation passed between them, something unique that only they understood. The brevity of it could have filled a thimble, but in that brief moment there was something magnanimous that happened between them.

Gianna sighed softly, and as if she'd caught the warm breath, Carina folded her hand into a tight fist, pulling it to the spot between her breasts. Both women smiled, and then just as abruptly resumed their frantic fussing about.

Franco broke the silence. "Have you spoken to this man, Gianna?" he asked curiously.

She paused to meet her father's stare. "I sent him a text message. His flight should have landed by now, and once he gets settled he's going to find his way here."

"Did you want me to go get him?" Graham asked.

"No!" both women answered in unison.

"It's just a ride!" Graham replied, bristling slightly.

"You would tell him. I know you," Carina said.

Gianna nodded in agreement. "It has to come from us. From Carina."

"Why from me?" her sister asked, turning to stare at Gianna.

"Because this is all your fault. You're the one who allowed this lie to snowball."

"You could have told him already," Carina said. "You've been emailing back and forth for the last two weeks. So you've been playing in that snow, too!"

"I could have," Gianna said matter-of-factly. "But then he might not have come." She cut an eye in Carina's direction.

Her sister laughed. "I knew you would like him!"

"I find him interesting. So, yes, I'm curious."

Carina jumped up and down excitedly. "You *really* like him!" she exclaimed.

Franco laughed as he rose from his seat, peering out the front window. "That's a good thing because your new friend just pulled up outside!"

Chapter 4

Donovan stood nervously outside the luxury villa. After settling into the one bedroom cottage the university had rented for him for the next year, he'd asked the property owner for directions to the winery. The rotund woman looked like soft biscuit dough and spoke little if any English. She had stared at him, chattering away in Italian, and despite the obvious communication issues, he'd felt right at home. It had taken a moment, but she'd eventually pointed him in the direction of the groundskeeper, who spoke perfect English and had been happy to give him a ride.

Donovan had read the winery's promotional brochures, scouring their website for anything he could learn. Cantina Moderna was a restored country farmhouse situated on a luxurious hilltop. It was surrounded by vineyards and olive groves, and the views were breathtaking. He knew from his readings that the entire wine estate included the vineyards, a state-of-the-art wine cellar and the private villa.

The *bottaia*, or wine cellar, was modern, yet sat in perfect harmony with the surrounding landscape. It showcased massive, hand-hewn oak barrels that held aged and refined wine. There was a meeting room that looked out to the Ombrone Valley and could host up to sixty people, and a tasting room with panoramic views equipped with one hundred indoor seats and a professional, gourmet kitchen. There were also rooms for the actual wine-making and a warehouse that had been designed to carry out the production needs of the winery from wine-making to bottling.

Now, standing at the edge of the floral beds that bordered the stunning home and wine facility, Donovan found himself feeling like a teen on his first date, anxiety flooding every muscle in his body. In one hand, he held a stunning bouquet of orange and pink roses, lisianthus, orchids and vibrant green ruscus tied with a simple yellow ribbon. In the other, he clutched a bottle of homemade strawberry vinaigrette, courtesy of his landlady, because how could you bring wine to a family with their own winery? He took a deep breath, and then a second one before moving slowly toward the entrance to knock on the front door.

Donovan was just about to knock a second time when Franco Martelli swung open the door, greeting him cheerily. The man pumped his arm enthusiastically as the two shook hands. "*Benvenuto*, Dr. Boudreaux!" he said as he pulled him inside the home, the door closing easily behind them.

Donovan smiled. "*Buonasera*, Signor Martelli. Thank you for having me in your home."

"Please, call me Franco." The patriarch gestured around the room. "Let me introduce you," he said as he pointed to a man sitting on a stool at an oversize counter. "This is my son-in-law, Graham Porter. Graham is married to my daughter Carina."

Graham came to his feet, extending his hand in greeting. "It's nice to meet you," he said, eyeing Donovan with reservation.

Donovan nodded. "The pleasure is mine. Gianna has told me a lot about you. She holds you in very high regard."

Graham smiled ever so slightly as he and Franco exchanged a look. "The girls should be out in a moment," he said. "You know how women do. It takes forever to make sure their faces are just right."

Donovan nodded his understanding. "I have four sisters. I understand perfectly."

"If you are like my husband and my father, then I'm sure you exaggerate," a warm voice chimed from the other side of the room. "We really are not that bad."

Donovan turned, his eyes skipping anxiously in the direction of the voice. He was greeted by a bright smile, the young woman moving quickly to his side. "Donovan, hello. I'm Carina Martelli-Porter. Gianna's sister. Welcome!"

"Carina, hello!"

"How was your trip?"

His head continued to bob up and down. "It was good. Very good. Thank you for asking."

Carina moved to her husband's side. An awkward silence suddenly filled the space, the family watching Donovan anxiously. They all seemed to take a collective breath, heavy sighs blowing around the room.

Carina pressed a palm to her husband's chest. "Darling, pour Dr. Boudreaux a glass of wine!" she said, her voice quivering ever so slightly. She shifted her gaze in Donovan's direction.

"Dr. Boudreaux, please, have a seat!" she said as she gestured toward the couch with her hand.

"Thank you, and please, call me Donovan."

He suddenly remembered the bottle in his hand. "This is for the family. It's…"

Carina interrupted. "Strawberry vinaigrette! You must be staying with Signora Rossi."

He smiled. "I am. How did you know?"

Carina held up the bottle he'd passed to her. "This stuff is pure gold and hard to come by. I'd recognize it anywhere. We are always trying to copy her recipe, and no one in the village has ever been able to get it right!"

Graham handed Donovan a full goblet of red wine as he took a seat in an upholstered chair, the floral bouquet resting in his lap. Carina moved to the chair across from him.

"I guess there really is no easy way to say this," she started.

Donovan eyed her curiously. "To say what?"

Her eyes flitted between the men in the room, pausing momentarily over each one of them. "There's something I need to tell you."

"Are you boring my company with one of your stories about me, Sissy?" another female voice interjected.

Everyone in the room turned at the same time. Gianna Martelli stood in the doorway, a bright smile painting her expression. Donovan pushed himself up from his seat, a wave of anxiety washing over him. Gianna met his stare, a nervous twitch pulsing at the edge of her lip. Light danced in her eyes as her gaze shifted from the top of his head to the floor beneath his feet and back, finally setting on his face.

Donovan Boudreaux was neatly attired, wearing a casual summer suit in tan-colored linen with a white dress shirt open at the collar. Brown leather loafers completed his look. His dark hair was cropped low and close, and he sported just the faintest hint of a goatee. His features were chiseled, and at first glance she could have easily mistaken him for a high-fashion model. Nothing about him screamed teacher. The man was drop-dead gorgeous, and as she stared, he took her breath away.

The moment was suddenly surreal, as though everything was moving in slow motion. As she glided to his side, Donovan was awed by the sheer magnitude of the moment, feeling as if he was lost somewhere deep in the sweetest dream. And then she touched him, her slender arms reaching around to give him a warm hug.

"It's nice to finally meet you," Gianna said softly. "Welcome to Italy."

Donovan's smile spread full across his face, his gaze dancing over her features. Although she and her sister were identical, he would have easily proclaimed Gianna the most beautiful woman he'd ever laid eyes on. The photo on the dust jacket of her books didn't begin to do her justice. Her complexion was dark honey, a sun-kissed glow emanating from unblemished skin. Her eyes were large saucers, blue-black in color and reminded him of vast expanses of black ice. Her features were delicate, a button nose and thin lips framed by lush, thick waves of jet-black hair that fell to midwaist on a petite frame. She was tiny, almost fragile, but carried herself as though she stood inches taller. She wore a floral-print, ankle-length skirt and a simple white shirt that stopped just below her small bustline, exposing a washboard stomach. Gianna Martelli was stunning!

Starstruck, Donovan suddenly realized he hadn't spoken, standing with his mouth open in awe. He swallowed hard as he took a deep inhale of air.

"Gianna, hello!" he finally exclaimed, unable to contain the excitement in his voice. He suddenly remembered the flowers he was still clutching, and thrusted them at her. "These are for you," he said.

She grinned as she pressed her nose into the bouquet, taking a deep inhale of their sweet aroma. "They're beautiful. Thank you," she said politely.

The two stood face-to-face, nervous energy like a match and lighter fluid igniting the space between them. Their gazes danced back and forth together, both taking in the moment.

"I hope everyone's hungry," Franco interrupted as he lifted the lid on a pot bubbling with salted water.

Everyone turned to watch as he added in a bowlful of homemade ravioli. "These won't take any time at all."

Gianna reached for Donovan's hand. "Help me put these in water while we chat," she said.

She suddenly peppered him with questions about himself and his family. In the blink of an eye everyone's anxiety dissipated, the five of them chatting and laughing easily together.

"So, tell us about your work," Franco said as he reached for the large wooden bowl filled with tossed salad.

"There's really not much to tell," Donovan said as he pressed a cloth napkin to his full lips and rested it back in his lap. "I teach and I love it. I'm excited to have this particular opportunity. This year I'll be teaching advanced mathematics at the university."

Gianna waved her hand. "Donovan is being modest. He's quite accomplished in his field. He's held membership in several professional organizations, served on a number of science and technology boards, and he's received numerous awards not only for his work and knowledge in the field of mathematics, but for his community service, as well."

She tossed him a bright smile and he smiled back, impressed that she remembered so much about him.

"Where did you get your degree?" Graham asked, just before taking a bite of his ravioli.

"I did my graduate work at MIT."

Graham nodded. "Very impressive. I attended Oxford. That's where I met Carina and Gianna."

"I always hated math when I was in school," Carina interjected. "Numbers are always so boring."

"Not really," Donovan said. "Numbers are extremely complex, and there are a myriad of ways to get them from point A to point B. The excitement lies in discovering new formulas or deciphering an old one. It's like Gianna's writing," he said as he cut his eye in her direction. "There are only twenty-six letters in the alphabet, but look at what she's been able to accomplish with just twenty-six letters!"

"Don't let my daughters fool you, Donovan. They may have hated their courses, but that was only because they were bored! Too smart for their own good, both of them!"

Franco pointed to Gianna. "This one, she has two advanced degrees in science and mathematics. She also speaks five languages. Brilliant, my girls are! Like their mother. My Angela, she was a genius, too!" he exclaimed. There was no missing the pride that filled the man's spirit.

Donovan tossed Gianna a look. "Five languages? You never told me that."

She laughed. "*Papà* is the only one who brags about me being a child prodigy!"

"I was no slacker now!" Carina said, moving them all to laugh again.

"Me," Franco concluded, "I'm glad I make wine. What you all do hurts my head!"

The laughter continued to be abundant, filling the room.

Donovan took a sip of the robust Cabernet in his

glass. The wine had been picked especially for the meal, a delightful complement to the dumpling-like pasta that had been filled with butternut squash, sage and goat cheese, served in a hazelnut brown-butter sauce with thick slices of freshly baked bread. "It's very good wine, by the way!"

Franco lifted his own glass in salute. "To new friends," he chanted as everyone joined him.

"New friends!"

"Donovan, would you like a tour of the winery?" Gianna asked as she pushed her chair from the table.

"I'd like that," he said with a nod of his head. He reached to clear his plate off the table.

"Don't you do that," Carina said, fanning her hands in his direction. "Graham and I will take care of the dishes."

"I'm always on dish duty," Graham said teasingly.

His wife leaned in to kiss his mouth. "Do good, honey, and I'll give you a treat later!"

Franco shook his head at the couple. "I think I'll take a walk through the gardens and enjoy a cigar. Donovan, I hope to see you again."

Donovan shook the man's outstretched hand. "Thank you again, sir," he said.

Gianna crooked her index finger and gestured for him to follow. Not needing a second invitation, Donovan went willingly.

For almost an hour, Gianna was the consummate professional as she gave him a guided tour of the grounds and winery. It was easy to see how passionate she was about her family's business and her role in its operations. Donovan was duly impressed.

The winery was substantial in size, and minutes into the tour he realized he knew very little about wine or its history. He was transfixed as Gianna schooled him.

"Many have called the Maremma the 'Wild West,' because of its landscapes and its wine-making. The Etruscans started making wine thousands of years before us in Northern Tuscany. They introduced viticulture to the Maremma in the nineteenth century."

"What is viticulture?" Donovan asked.

"Viticulture is the study of grapes and wine-making."

Donovan nodded as she continued.

"The wines here in Maremma didn't become popular until the 1980s, and credit for putting us on the map goes to Marquis Mario Incisa della Rocchetta. Because of his efforts, we've created Bordeaux-style wines that are considered noble and refined. My father idolized him."

"Is he still in this area?"

"Sadly, he passed away in the 1980s. His son runs his winery now."

They moved to another area of the winery, stepping into a massive room that housed huge wooden barrels of wine that were resting to age. Gianna continued, explaining the process and even including a geography lesson.

"The Maremma is very different from other areas of Italy. Regions in the north, like northern Tuscany, Florence, Siena and Lucca, are always overrun with tourists. Their wineries cater to the tourism, and most of their cellars are always open to the general public. Not so much here. We are more exclusive, and the area is less populated with tourists.

"Serious wine lovers find us to be a very attractive region to visit. There's the town of Castiglione della Pescaia with its charming fishing port and castle, and Pitigliano, an amazing village completely carved out of the rocky outcrop below an ancient Jewish village. And one of my favorite places is Massa Marittima with its quaint cobblestoned streets. They're all fabulous little gems that you must explore while you're here in Tuscany."

Donovan stood in reflection, taking it all in. His arms were crossed over his chest, and he seemed as though he were lost deep in thought. Gianna found herself unable to take her eyes off him. His chiseled features were perfection, and she was suddenly imagining what it might be like to trace his profile with her finger. She stood in pause until he seemed ready to move on, tossing her a quick look and that dimpled smile.

"So, when do you find time to write?" he asked as the private tour came to a close.

Gianna chuckled warmly as they moved back outside, dropping to a wooden bench that decorated the gardens. She twisted her body around to face him.

"At night mostly, when I'm alone."

Donovan nodded as the two shared a gaze. They held it for a brief moment, the intensity almost combustible. As quickly as they connected, they both looked away. An awkward silence filled the space between them. He looked past her shoulder, staring off into the distance. Her eyes were cast down to the ground, and the blades of grass flattened beneath her leather sandals. They both cut their eyes back at each other at the same time. Then laughed to ease the tension.

"I didn't expect to be so nervous around you," Donovan said. "I feel like I'm fifteen all over again."

Gianna laughed. "I know, right!" She smiled. "I figured since we knew so much about each other that this would be easy."

He nodded, smiling back. He stared at her, taking in her delicate features as if casting each pore to memory. "You are so beautiful!" he exclaimed softly.

She laughed again, the gentle timbre a soft flutter that left him thinking of champagne bubbles and the gentle trickle of a waterfall.

"You're very sweet, Donovan Boudreaux."

He shifted forward in his seat. "Can I see you again tomorrow?"

"Don't you have classes tomorrow?"

"I have a commitment at the school in the morning, but I won't actually start teaching for another week. I'm free after the lunch hour tomorrow. And I really want to see you again!"

She grinned. "I know we have an inspection tomorrow, but once that's done I'll be free. Why don't you call me when you're done and we can make plans then?"

"Great!" Donovan exclaimed.

There was a pause before he finally stood. "I should be going. I don't want to overstay my welcome, and I'm sure you have things you need to get back to."

She shrugged. "You don't have to rush off on my account."

His full lips lifted up into a deep smile. "I wish I could stay, but I need to unpack and get settled in. Plus, I don't get the impression that Signora Rossi is going to tolerate me coming and going at all hours of the night." He extended his hand to help her up.

The touch was electric as her fingers gently glided against his. Both felt it, pulling away as if they'd been burned. Gianna's eyes were wide, and she inhaled swiftly. Donovan was suddenly aware of heat raging in his southern parts. He broke out into a cold sweat, perspiration beading against his brow.

"I'm glad you came to Tuscany, Donovan," Gianna said, her voice a soft whisper.

He nodded. "Me, too!"

The questions and comments came before Gianna could get the door closed behind Donovan's exit.

"Do you like him?"

"I think he was nice!"

"Why didn't you tell him the truth?"

"You really need to tell him the truth!"

"Are you going to see him again?"

"You really should see him again!"

Gianna laughed heartily as her family assaulted her with commentary. She held up her hand, amusement shimmering in her eyes.

"Donovan asked me to extend his gratitude to you all for a lovely evening. He said to tell you that he had a very nice time."

"Did you have a nice time, Sissy?" Carina leaned across the kitchen island, meeting her sister's stare.

Gianna shrugged slightly, her shoulders pushing toward the ceiling. "It was okay."

"Just okay?" Graham asked.

Franco laughed. "It was better than okay. Look at that grin on her face."

Gianna felt herself blush, color warming her cheeks a brilliant shade of crimson. She moved toward the door, tossing them all a slight wave of her hand, their laughter echoing behind her as she headed to her room.

Inside, with the door closed and locked, Gianna fell back against the bed, staring up toward the ceiling. Joy painted her expression. It had been a great day, and she'd had an exceptional time with Donovan Boudreaux. He hadn't been at all what she'd expected. Even after committing every word he'd written to her to memory, thinking that she had some sense of who the man was, she'd actually been surprised.

Donovan was a refreshing breath of air. His intelligence was complemented by a compassionate spirit and wicked sense of humor. And he didn't take himself seriously. She liked that he could laugh at himself, all the while bringing a smile to everyone else's face. His exuberance as they'd walked through the winery was almost childlike, and his enthusiasm had fueled her own. Donovan was multilayered, and she had only begun to scratch the surface to discover everything she could about him. Throw in his dashing good looks, and there was much to like about the math professor from the United States.

The decision to not tell him about Carina's little prank had come at the last minute. The moment she'd laid eyes on him, Gianna knew she didn't want to mar their first encounter with bad news. She could come clean in due time, she thought with a sigh. For now, all she wanted was to enjoy the magic that had her feeling giddy with happiness.

He was so excited by the afternoon's events that Donovan hadn't given any thought to how he planned to get back to his cottage. Luckily for him, the walk down the hillside was manageable. The sky was just beginning to darken. The cool evening air was comfortably warm with the gentlest of breezes pushing him forward. And as he headed downhill, he had a beautiful view of the Tuscan coast, the sun beginning to set over the bright blue water.

As he sauntered back to the village, he passed a spattering of homes that dotted the landscape. The area of Maremma was a host of everything that was extraordinary about Tuscany. There was blue sea, long beaches, black rock, hills covered with woods, marshes and flatlands, green hills, natural thermal baths and, most exquisite of them all, Gianna Martelli.

He felt lovestruck as he thought about the delightful woman who'd been everything he imagined and more. Beautiful didn't begin to describe her, inside or out. She had the purest spirit of any woman he'd ever known. There was something both delightful and decadent about her. Just the nearness of her had him giggling like an adolescent, and he couldn't remember any woman ever making him feel so frivolous.

To say that he was enamored with Gianna was putting it mildly. The woman left him breathless, and in that moment he was hard and wanting as thoughts of their time together frolicked through his memory. Gianna made his heart sing, and he was excited to see where their time together might take them.

As he passed a home that sat close to the roadside, there was a couple standing outside in deep conversation. Both looked up and eyed him warily as he moved in their direction. Donovan accepted that most in the community weren't used to seeing a large black man in their midst when it wasn't tourist season, and maybe not even then. He also imagined that seeing a large black man practically skipping with joy was a sight to behold, as well.

He raised a hand and waved excitedly, his bright smile warm and endearing. The husband gestured back with a nod of his head, the two suddenly talking rapidly in Italian. *"Buonasera!"* Donovan exclaimed as he got closer to the front gate of their property.

The wife greeted him cheerily, gesturing with both hands for him to come closer. As she spoke, he comprehended one, two, maybe three words of what she was saying, welcoming him to their village. Pausing in front of her, he was surprised when she reached up to grab his cheeks in her hands, squeezing his face as if he were six years old. His eyes widened with surprise as she pulled him close, kissing one side of his face and then the other.

Seconds later, her husband, who'd gone into the home, had come back through the door, a plate wrapped in a kitchen towel perched in the palms of his hands.

"Welcome!" the husband said as he extended the gift toward Donovan.

Donovan nodded. "Thank you!"

"You are the teacher, no?" the man questioned.

He bobbed his head a second time. "Yes, sir, I am."

"From my wife," the man gestured. "To say hello and welcome."

His wife said something in Italian, clearly passing on instructions to her spouse. He nodded and waved his hand for her to let him speak.

"My name is Fabrizio D'Ascenzi, and this is my wife, Pia."

"It's a pleasure to meet you, Signor D'Ascenzi! Signora D'Ascenzi, *ciao, mi chiamo* Donovan Boudreaux."

Signora D'Ascenzi grabbed his cheeks a second time. *"Piacere di conoscerti."*

Donovan nodded. "It's a pleasure to meet you, too, ma'am!"

"Pia has made her famous ricotta cheesecake to welcome you. It's the best cheesecake you will ever eat! All the women in the village have heard that you were coming to town, so I imagine you will eat well while you are here. All of them trying to marry off their daughters!"

Donovan laughed. "Do you and Signora D'Ascenzi have a daughter?"

The man shook his head. "No. If we did, you wouldn't be getting this cheesecake," he said with a hearty chuckle. "I would have had her make you a five-course meal!"

His wife punched him playfully, and Donovan realized that she understood English better than she spoke it.

"Well, thank you," Donovan said.

"Where are you headed?" Signor D'Ascenzi asked, looking up the road one way and then the other.

As Donovan explained his predicament, the couple nodded in understanding.

"Now, those are two beautiful women!" the other man exclaimed. "Franco's daughters are very easy on a man's eyes! But only one is unmarried, no?"

He nodded. "Yes, sir."

He said something to his wife in Italian that Donovan didn't understand. She responded with a wave of her head, her hands tossed in the air in frustration.

Donovan looked at one and then another, suddenly feeling like the ball in a tennis match.

Signor D'Ascenzi flipped his hand at the woman as she suddenly turned, muttering under her breath as she stomped into her home.

Donovan looked on, confused, as her husband gestured for him to follow him to his truck, offering him a ride for the rest of his journey. Once they were headed down the road, his new acquaintance explained the conversation.

"My wife says you need to watch that Martelli girl. That one is too wild for such a distinguished professor as yourself. And she has a tongue like a viper! You might want to walk to the vineyards on the other side and introduce yourself to the Carusos' daughter. She's round like a barrel and has the face of an old cow, but she's quite the cook and she doesn't talk a lot."

Donovan laughed heartily. As Signor D'Ascenzi continued, his assessments of the women in the community sometimes moving him to tears, he knew beyond any doubt that moving to Italy had been the best decision he could have ever made.

Chapter 5

The following morning Donovan rose bright and early. Signora Rossi was knocking on the door minutes after he'd stepped out of the shower, chattering a mile a minute. She'd pushed her way inside, armed with a plate of warm baked pastries, a pot of hot coffee and a basket of fresh fruit.

The conversation was very one-sided, although she chatted as if they were old friends. Every so often she would pause to look at him as if she expected an answer to something she'd said. A simple nod of his head and a smile with an occasional yes sent her back to talking without skipping a beat. Donovan found himself hoping that by the end of the year, he'd understand enough to hold a full conversation in Italian, or at least enough to know if he were promising the old woman his first-born child.

After his stomach was full and his head clear, he watched as his new house mother commenced cleaning and sweeping behind him. With a wave of his hand, he wished her a good day and headed outside to meet the groundskeeper. His new friend handed him an old road map, a functioning GPS and the keys to an older model Fiat 500 parked in the driveway, a perk to his residency.

The drive to Siena and the university had been breathtaking. Donovan was quickly discovering that he loved everything about Italy. He was eager to play tourist and visit Rome. To see the Colosseum and the ruins, the Spanish Steps, the Vatican and the Sistine Chapel. Florence was also on his must-see list, and he wanted to lose himself in the stunning architecture.

As the GPS barked out a turn, guiding him closer to his destination, he suddenly found himself hopeful that Gianna might want to share in those experiences with him.

For a few brief moments Donovan stood outside the university, taking it all in. The building was massive, the old-world architecture like nothing he'd seen before. The magnitude of all his accomplishments that had brought him to this place suddenly rang through to his core as he understood the significance of the blessing that had been bestowed on him. He whispered a quick prayer, snapped a photo with his cell phone and texted a message to his mother.

Sophie was standing at the campus entrance, waiting to greet him. The head of the mathematics department, she was tall and lean like a racehorse with skin the color of dark mahogany. Her hair was shaved close, accentuating her chiseled features. She reminded him of the model Alek Wek, her exotic look distinct to her African lineage. She was an attractive woman who carried herself with refined grace. Her pleasant personality was endearing, and since their very first meeting, she'd been eager to learn from him and he'd found that flattering. More than anything, he considered her a friend and looked forward to the opportunity to work with her.

Sophie welcomed him warmly, eagerly wrapping him in a tight hug. She grabbed both his hands between her own. "*Buongiorno!* This is so exciting!" she exclaimed.

"Good morning, Sophie! How are you this morning?"

"I'm fantastic. How about yourself? Did you settle in comfortably?"

"I did. Everything is perfect."

"That's so good to hear. I was concerned. When you requested to be housed in Maremma, I had my doubts. Plus, I worried that the commute might be problematic."

"Actually, the drive was delightful. I'm about an hour away, but it will give me a chance to prepare myself in the mornings and unwind in the evenings. But I like Maremma. It's quiet where I am, and I like being away from the hustle and bustle of city life."

She nodded. "Well, let me get you settled in and show you to your office."

Leading the way, Sophie began by introducing him

to the school's director, Dr. Alistair Northway. He was a small man who spoke English as if he were spitting bullets after each word. At first glance, he reminded Donovan of a white Kevin Hart with flaming red hair and a toothy grin. As they shook hands, Donovan noticed that the man's grip was Herculean. He felt as though he were trying to break his fingers. But his words were kind as he welcomed Donovan to his staff, lauding his many accomplishments and acknowledging the faith he had in what they'd all be able to accomplish for the good of his students.

In the school's administrative offices, he'd been assigned a parking space, taken a photo for his identification badge and filled out more employment papers than he cared to count. After an hour, the names and faces had become a blur. He met most of the department chairs, a number of instructors and probably twice as many students.

Finally, he stood at the head of his lecture room, taking it all in. The space felt more like an old movie theater auditorium with upholstered velvet seats and antique finishes. His oversize desk and the chalkboard on the front wall kept the reality of the moment intact. As he leaned back against his desk, Donovan fought back hot tears that burned behind his eyelids. Loving to teach as much as he did made the experience all the sweeter. It was going to be a very good year.

Gianna's cell phone rang just as she was packing an assortment of items into a large wicker basket. She answered on the third ring, propping the device between her ear and shoulder. *"Ciao!"*

"Gianna, hello! It's Donovan."

"Donovan, hello," she answered, her tone rising. "How are you?"

"I'm really good, but I'll be even better if you say you can still spend some time with me this afternoon."

She laughed. "I think that can be arranged. What did you have in mind?"

"I wasn't sure, to be honest with you. I thought maybe we could grab something to eat and you could give me a tour of the city?"

There was a pause as Gianna seemed to be reflecting on his proposition. "Are you still at the university?" she asked suddenly.

"Yes. I should be leaving here in about an hour, then it's a good hour commute. I'll just need to stop home and change."

"Good. I'll meet you when you get there," she said. Then before he could respond, she disconnected the call, leaving Donovan hanging on the other end.

Carina laughed. "So, are you playing hard to get with Donovan, or easy breezy?"

Gianna tossed her sister a look. "I'm not playing anything with the man. Not yet anyway!"

Carina giggled again. "Oh, you're up to something. I don't know what it is, but I know you."

Gianna grinned. "Maybe I am, and maybe I'm not. We'll just have to see."

"Poor Donovan," Carina said, shaking her head. "He doesn't have a clue what's about to hit him!"

Gianna laughed with her sister, not bothering to respond to the comment. "I have someplace to be," she said as she grabbed the handles of her picnic basket and headed toward the door.

Carina waved goodbye. "Tell Donovan I said hello!"

As Donovan moved to the door of his new home, his landlady poked her head out of her own entrance. Her gaze was narrowed, her jaw tight as she gnashed her teeth together. He instinctively knew she wasn't happy about something.

"*Ciao!* Signora Rossi!" He raised a hand in greeting.

He was suddenly reminded of a bird cackling nonstop as she berated him about something, her index finger wagging as frantically as her tongue. Before he could think to respond, his own door flew open and Gianna stepped outside. Both women were suddenly in heated conversation, hands waving excitedly to make a point.

Gianna suddenly said something that gave Signora Rossi reason to pause. The older woman stood staring for just a brief moment, and then she burst out laughing. When Gianna laughed with her, Donovan sighed with relief, thankful that whatever had been amiss between the two women hadn't brought them to blows.

He looked from one to the other as their conversation continued, tones lowered and amusement dancing in their words. "Do I even want to know?" Donovan asked after Signora Rossi waved her finger at him one last time before going back into her home, leaving the two of them alone.

Gianna smiled. "She's worried about your virtue. Afraid that I may take advantage and sully your upstanding reputation."

He laughed with her. "Is there something about *you* I need to know?" he asked.

She laughed with him. "I guess that depends on who you ask!"

"Should I be scared?"

Ignoring his question, Gianna turned an about-face and moved back into his home.

Donovan followed behind her. As he moved through the door he came to an abrupt halt, his eyes skating back and forth over the space inside. "When did you...? How did this...?" he stammered, fighting to focus and find the words to ask the thoughts suddenly racing through his head.

When he'd left that morning, the sun had been on the other side of the small unit, yet to stream brightly through his windows. Signora Rossi had been sweeping the tile floors with one hand and dusting the wood furniture with the other. His suitcases had rested on the pullout sofa in the room, waiting to be unpacked. And the whole space lacked the personal touches that would eventually make it feel like a home.

But since he'd been gone, the entire room had been transformed. The windows were all open, a warm breeze billowing through the space. Light was abundant, bright and sweeping from one wall to the other. Fresh flowers had been strategically placed, and a potted cactus rested on the kitchen counter. There was a tablecloth on the kitchen table and appliances on the counter in the small kitchenette. Beautifully woven throws decorated the sofa and chairs, with complementary pillows adorning the corners. And the framed photos that had been in his luggage were placed strategically around the room, with the photo of him and his parents sitting front and center on a bookcase.

"Wow!" he exclaimed as he moved farther into the room. "Wow!" He tossed her a quick look as he spun around in a circle, taking it all in.

"All your clothes are unpacked, and there are extra linens in the closet. I know you like to eat clean so there's a blender *and* a juicer, and the icebox is fully stocked with fresh fruit and vegetables. I told Signora Rossi that she needs to replace the lightbulbs in the bathroom. They really do need to be brighter, and she said she'd have someone take care of it while we're gone." Gianna paused to take a breath. "Now, I hope you haven't had anything to eat because I packed us a picnic lunch."

Donovan rested his gaze on her face. She wore no makeup, her warm complexion crystal clear, her hair pulled back into a loose bun. She was glowing, looking like a freshly minted penny. She stood in denim shorts and a Bob Marley T-shirt, and if Donovan were a betting man, he would have bet his last dollar that she wasn't wearing a bra, her breasts at full attention beneath her top. He struggled not to stare at her chest.

Gianna broke the trance he'd fallen into. "You should change. Something casual. I left your jeans and a black T-shirt on the bed for you."

He smiled. "Are you always so…?"

"Controlling?"

"Efficient."

She smiled back. "Efficient...no. Controlling...yes!"

He nodded, still eyeing her as she pointed him in the direction of his bedroom.

Stepping into the room, he closed the door behind him. The bedding was new, an assortment of pillows leaning against the wicker headboard. A stack of books rested on the nightstand. The titles made him smile. There was an advanced reading copy of Gianna's next book, a Fodor's travel guide for Italy, a children's book by Shel Silverstein and an official King James Bible. But the single greatest surprise was the framed photograph of Gianna, an image of her standing between rows of olive trees. She wore a white dress that complemented her warm complexion, and her smile was sweet, a hint of mischief dancing in her eyes.

As Donovan rested the frame back on the nightstand, he couldn't help but think that Gianna had officially laid claim to her territory. A huge grin filled his dark face—he was happy to have been claimed. He was overwhelmed with everything she'd done, amazed by the effort she'd put forth on his behalf. No woman had ever done anything like that for him before. Ever.

Minutes later the two were headed inland to Mount Amiata, the largest of the lava domes in the area. Their conversation was easy, a comfortable exchange that felt like they'd been conversing forever. Donovan told her about his day and his excitement over his teaching job. She explained the inspection process that allowed the winery to remain operational and how the periodic scrutiny always gave her anxiety. They talked about books, hers, topping bestseller lists worldwide, and his, the mathematical publications preeminent only in educational circles. And they laughed, abundantly, the richness of it like the sweetest balm in the afternoon air.

He asked questions about where they were and where they were going, and Gianna infused the geography lesson with history and anecdotes. She described the area as one of the regions most unmarred by its inhabitants. The beaches were pristine, the umbrella-shaped maritime pines unique and the cork-oak woodlands abundant. As they passed another wine estate near Orbetello, he was in awe of the spotted pink flamingos that grazed in a lagoon.

In Amiata they moved from the car to the trails, hiking through the luxuriant trees. Donovan was dazzled by the wealth of color that decorated the landscape. He suddenly wished he could paint, that he was able to capture the striking images in an organic manner. Speaking his wish aloud had Gianna encouraging him to step out of his comfort zone to try things he'd never tried before.

"If that's what you want to do, then you should, Donovan," she said. "People are always waiting until the perfect time, or the right moment to do things. But life is too short to put off things you want to do. No one's promised you tomorrow."

He nodded his agreement, although his expression seemed to say that he was still mulling it over.

"So do you plan to start painting while you are here in Italy?" she asked as they continued to navigate the trails.

He shrugged, his eyes wide as he stared at her. "I'll do it," he said, a wry smile pulling at his lips. "Soon."

She laughed at him. "You are too funny!"

"You know I have to analyze everything, Gianna. Weigh all the pros and cons. I need to be certain before I commit to something."

"Or miss out on opportunities because you take too long doing all that thinking!"

Donovan chuckled softly. "I really am not that bad."

"Maybe not, but you need to be more spontaneous. You and I will work on that while you are here."

He smiled as she turned off the path and headed through the trees. He trailed behind her, following where she led. Minutes later Gianna found a perfect spot for them to picnic, and set to work covering the ground with an oversize blanket. She gestured for him to take a seat, and when he did she pulled off his shoes and socks and tossed them aside. As he wiggled his toes, he watched as she stood and kicked off her own shoes before taking a seat beside him.

Inside the picnic basket she'd made him carry, she had packed a light afternoon meal. There was an assortment of cheeses, salami, olives, two loaves of fresh bread, an assortment of fresh fruit, a bottle of her father's wine and two wine goblets.

"Do you come here often?" he asked as he took a bite of a creamy Asiago cheese.

"Not nearly as often as I'd like," she answered. "I love this area, though. Next to my father's vineyards, it's one of my favorite places." She tore off a bite of bread and popped it into her mouth.

A blanket of quiet dropped around them as they sat focused on the meal. Neither spoke, both seeming to drop into their own thoughts. In the distance a voice called out, someone besieging a friend not to hurry so fast. Between the trees, they caught a glimpse of denim-covered legs and a small dog on the end of a leash. They both paused to stare at the same time, watching the small terrier race to get to someone ahead of them.

Donovan shifted his gaze to her face, noting the color that had risen to her cheeks. She smiled, and he felt his stomach do a slight flip. He cleared his throat, suddenly feeling nervous for no reason at all.

"What?" Gianna asked suddenly.

"What do you mean what?"

"What are you staring at me like that for?"

"I wasn't staring at you."

"Yes, you were!"

"Well, if I was it's only because you're so beautiful."

Gianna rolled her eyes. She reached for a grape and pulled it to her mouth, not bothering to respond.

Donovan cleared his throat. "I wrote once and asked if you were in a relationship, and you didn't respond. Was there a reason?"

She met the look he was giving her, curiosity furrowing her brow. She shook her head. "I'm sure I answered."

"No, you didn't."

"I'm sure I did."

He pursed his lips, then pulled them into a deep smile. "Stop ignoring the question, Gianna. Are you seeing someone?"

She laughed. "I wasn't ignoring the question! But to give you an answer, no, I'm not. Are you?"

He hesitated for a brief second. "Well...actually..." His gaze skated off into the distance.

Gianna bristled ever so slightly, sitting straighter as she folded her extended legs behind her. She shifted forward as if readying herself to stand and leave. "Actually what? You wrote that you weren't dating anyone," she said, an air of attitude in her tone. "I distinctly remember reading that. So was that a lie?"

A wide grin spread full across Donovan's face. "Gotcha!"

She narrowed her gaze, not at all amused.

"I was joking!" Donovan exclaimed. "You told me I needed to loosen up and stop taking things so seriously. So why are you mad?"

She shook her head. "I'm not mad. I just didn't find your little joke funny."

He laughed heartily. "Gianna Martelli has a little bit of a jealous streak," he teased.

"I do not!"

"Yes, you do." He reached for her hand, entwining her fingers between his own. His touch was electric, the current between them combustible. "And I kind of like it," he said, his voice dropping to a loud whisper. "But if I'm honest," he continued after another brief pause, "I'm really hoping that you and I are seeing each other. Or getting close to that point."

The hint of a smile danced across her face. His touch was heated, fire coursing through her palm, up the length of her arm and exploding with a vengeance through her body. A shiver ran down her spine and back up, the sensations close to orgasmic.

She suddenly pulled her hand from his, color heating her cheeks. Turning her body around, she lay back against him, resting her head in his lap. She pulled a grape from the bunch in her hands and slid it into her mouth.

Donovan felt the muscles in his lower half twitch as he watched her chew, her mouth rolling in the cutest pout. Just the hint of tongue peeked past the line of her of her lips, the gesture teasing. He closed his eyes and inhaled swiftly, fighting to stall the rise of nature.

Gianna shifted his attention away from his growing predicament by changing the subject. "Why aren't you married, Donovan? You're successful, handsome and intelligent. For all intents and purposes, most would consider you a good catch, so why hasn't some equally accomplished, beautiful and smart woman gotten you to the altar?"

Donovan pondered her question for a moment. Over the years his personal life had taken a backseat to his professional one. Even as his siblings were building relationships, finding favor with significant others, he'd been focused on his career. At best, dating had been hit or miss, no woman ever catching his full attention. Until he'd started corresponding with Gianna.

His gaze met hers as she stared up at him, still waiting for him to answer. Curiosity seeped from her stare, questions shimmering in the light that shone in the dark orbs, and he could feel himself falling headfirst into the depths of her gaze.

He finally answered. "I was waiting for you," he said softly, the early evening air carrying his words away on a warm breeze.

Chapter 6

Gianna felt giddy. Lovesick giddy, and she hated not
being able to hide it. But the emotion flooded her face.
It seeped from every pore in her body. And it wasn't
going away. It had taken every ounce of fortitude not
to giggle like a little girl when Donovan had said that
he'd been waiting for her. Instead, she'd changed the
subject again, rambling on and on about the merits of
olives and wine for one's health.

She blew a soft sigh as she rolled onto her side, a
good night's sleep promising to elude her. They'd spent
the entire afternoon together, moving from the forests
of Amiata to La Guardiola, a local bar in the area that
she often frequented. The Rossella Graziani Jazz Trio
had been performing, and the atmosphere had been
seductive. The staff there knew her by name, and her

favorite drink was delivered to their table before either had a chance to get comfortable in their seats.

There wasn't much that they hadn't talked about, although Gianna had purposely avoided any conversation that might have led them back to what was happening between them. Donovan had tried more than once to steer their talk to things more personal, but she had shut him down, not yet ready to voice what she found herself feeling. Because Gianna wasn't ready to label their relationship. It was too new to her, and even though she understood he had more time and energy invested in their connection, she was still gun-shy where Donovan Boudreaux was concerned.

But she did like him. She liked him a lot. Even his conservative nature, which was so contrary to her own, thrilled her. They balanced each other nicely, and most surprising to her was how comfortable she felt when she was with him. That level of comfort had been apparent from day one. There had only been a few moments of anxiety, and that apprehension had everything to do with her attraction to the man and the rising desire that seemed to consume her every time he was near.

Because every time Donovan was close, Gianna found herself heated with desire. The intensity of her longing was almost like an out-of-body experience. Gianna had never wanted any man like she found herself wanting Donovan, and her body reacted on its own accord each and every time.

With a deep sigh, she rolled to the other side of the bed, curling her body around an oversize pillow. An hour later she drifted off to sleep, thoughts of Donovan still trailing through her mind.

Donovan sat upright in the full-size bed, Gianna's upcoming book in his lap. It was everything he imagined it would be and more. The woman's talent and imagination awed him as he wondered where she found the inspiration that breathed life into her mysteries. Clearly she loved what she did, but Donovan knew that she was ambivalent about her achievements, wanting only to enjoy the peace and quiet of her Tuscany home. Her writing was an added perk to her resort-like lifestyle, but she would have easily given it up to work the vineyards.

Admittedly, he was starstruck, idolizing everything about her. Donovan imagined that he probably came across a tad fan-crazed, and he couldn't help but wonder if his enthusiasm might be perceived as a little creepy. He blew a heavy sigh as he closed the cover of her book. He shifted his body against the headboard and heaved another deep sigh.

He had wanted them to talk more about the two of them and their growing relationship, but Gianna had changed the subject each and every time. It felt as if he might be reading more into the connection he thought they had than she did. And maybe she wasn't feeling him the way he was feeling her. Because he was feeling her, feeling bewitched and spellbound by all things Gianna. But he had more concerns and questions than he had answers. He suddenly wondered if he should have been more open about his growing emotions before coming to Italy and potentially getting his feelings hurt.

Rising, he crossed the room to shut off the lights, then crawled back into the bed. He stole a glance at the alarm clock on the nightstand, the early morning hour shining back at him. Sleep had not been his friend; he was unable to turn off the thoughts running through his mind. He missed Gianna. The day had been exceptional. They'd had a great time together, and it had ended earlier than he would have liked. Now he was missing the woman who had him tossing and turning, unable to get her out of his head.

The ringing telephone pulled Donovan from a deep sleep. Startled, he jumped, then struggled to find his cell phone. He'd practically fallen out of the bed when he finally pulled it to his ear, shouting "hello" into the receiver.

Kendrick laughed on the other end. "Hey, big brother. What's going on?"

Donovan sat upright in the bed, blinking his eyes rapidly as he struggled to focus. The faintest hint of light shimmered through the sheer curtain that covered the one window in the space.

"Kendrick?"

"Yeah! Are you okay?"

"Nothing that another couple of hours of sleep won't fix."

"You're sleeping late? That's not like you at all."

Donovan yawned. "I didn't get a lot of sleep."

"Oh. Are you not alone? Because I can call back if you have company."

Donovan could sense his brother grinning into the phone. He shook his head. "No, I don't have company."

"You and your friend haven't hooked up yet?"

"We've spent time together." Donovan could feel himself blushing, heat warming his cheeks. "But not like that."

"But you've hung out! That's good, right? So, what's she like?"

There was a pause as Donovan found himself once again lost in thoughts of Gianna. "I like her," he said finally. "And I think Mom is really going to like her, too."

This time Kendrick paused for a quick moment before responding. "Is it that serious? I thought you were just looking to hit it and quit it, sort of like a holiday fling. But you're thinking you want to introduce her to the old people?"

"Yes," Donovan said softly. "I think Gianna's the kind of girl you definitely take home to meet your family. She's special."

"And she feels the same way about you?"

He shrugged, doubt suddenly flooding his spirit. When he didn't respond, Kendrick turned the conversation, sensing Donovan wasn't prepared yet to answer questions about his new friend and her feelings.

"I had some time before I head back to the States, so I thought I might swing by and check out your place so I can give the girls the four-one-one. They've already called me a half-dozen times to see what I know, and I might have mentioned something about you and Gianna. I figured a few cell-phone photos would get them off both our backs."

Donovan laughed. "*Might* have mentioned?"

"Yeah, it might have slipped out during a conversation or two, but that's neither here nor there. You know how nosy the girls are. We have to give them something or they might show up on your doorstep to see for themselves."

Donovan shook his head. "Those are your sisters!"

"They were your sisters before they were mine," Kendrick said, laughing with him.

Donovan suddenly realized how much he missed his family. "What time can you be here?"

When the Martelli twins pulled up in front of Donovan's cottage, he and his brother were standing outside in conversation. The two sisters shot each other a look, a wry smile pulling at Carina's thin lips. "Oh, my!" she muttered, her voice dropping to a low whisper.

"Don't you dare embarrass me," Gianna hissed under her breath.

Carina giggled softly.

"I mean it," Gianna countered, cutting an eye at her sister.

Carina giggled again, meeting the look her twin was giving her. "What?"

Gianna looked from one man to the other, immediately noting the resemblance. No one needed to tell her that they were somehow related. Like Donovan, the other man was a dark, tall drink of water. He wore his hair in a full afro, and he was dressed in low-slung, tattered jeans, a T-shirt adorned with a Duke University emblem and rugged Timberland boots. But his demeanor seemed more bad boy and deviant, not nearly as conservative as Donovan's. Side by side, the two men were like night and day, yet everything about them was similar.

As the two women approached, Donovan's smile pulled full and bright across his face. He tossed up an easy hand and gave the two women a slight wave. "Hello!" he greeted cheerily.

"Hi," Carina said, almost too enthusiastically.

Gianna shot her sister another look, grabbing her forearm in warning. She nodded in greeting. "How are you?"

Donovan gestured toward them. "Let me introduce you to my brother. Kendrick, this is Gianna Martelli and her sister, Carina Martelli-Porter. These two ladies run the winery up the hill along with their father and Carina's husband. Ladies, this is my brother, Kendrick Boudreaux."

"It's nice to meet you," Carina said as she extended a hand.

"Kendrick, hello!" Gianna greeted.

"The pleasure is all mine," Kendrick replied, a bright smile pulling at his full lips. "It's nice to meet you both."

"You didn't tell us your brother was coming to visit," Gianna said as she eased her way to Donovan's side. The two exchanged a look, their stare intense. The connection was intoxicating, and it was only when Carina faked a cough that they turned back to the conversation, self-consciously giggling.

Kendrick responded to the young woman's remark. "I'm just passing through. I finished some business in Florence earlier than anticipated and figured I'd make a quick stop here to check on Donovan before I made my way back to the States."

Donovan rolled his eyes. "So what are you two up to?" His gaze shifted back toward Gianna as his voice dropped an octave. "I didn't think I was going to see you today."

The two sisters traded a look, something secretive passing between them. Carina lifted her eyebrows, seeming to wait for Gianna to take the lead.

Gianna answered. "Carina and I were headed to the market and just wanted to see if you were interested in tagging along," she said, tossing her twin another strained look.

Kendrick tapped his brother on the back. "They want you to tag along to market, big brother! That sounds like fun! And I can take pictures!"

Neither woman missed the amusement in the man's tone as color flooded Donovan's face a deep shade of embarrassed. He shot his brother a look as the other man suddenly pulled out his cell phone and engaged the camera on the device. Before either could say cheese, he snapped the side-by-side shot of Donovan and Gianna standing just millimeters from each other.

Donovan shook his head. "It does sound like fun," he finally said. "We'd love to join you."

Hours later, joined by Graham, the five of them sat around a table at an outdoor bistro sipping on short shots of espresso from demitasse cups as they snacked on cannoli pastry shells filled with a mixture of chocolate chips and ricotta cheese and garnished with slivered almonds. Laughter rang through the air as they shared stories and anecdotes about each other.

"We never could get Donovan to jump with us," Kendrick was saying, a wide smile on his face. "All of us gave it a shot, but not him."

"I wasn't that crazy," Donovan said, amusement painting his expression. "It was all fun and games right up to when Kendrick missed the mattress and broke his arm."

Gianna laughed. "I can't imagine a bunch of little kids jumping out of a window onto a mattress."

Donovan nodded. "Well, my brothers and sisters did. The girls dared the boys so they all jumped two stories down."

"And I only missed the mattress because my twin, Kamaya, pushed me!"

They all laughed.

"Sounds like you all were a handful. And I thought our father had it hard with the two of us," Carina said as she exchanged a look with Gianna.

"Were you two a challenge?" Donovan asked, looking from one to the other.

Gianna nodded. "We weren't easy, I'll say that."

"Kamaya and I weren't too bad together," Kendrick said. "The best we could muster up was our secret language that none of the others understood. It used to drive our oldest sister crazy!"

Donovan nodded. "It never bothered us boys, but the girls hated it!"

Graham chuckled. "These two liked to play practical jokes pretending to be each other. Almost got me in serious trouble when we were in college and I was trying to get Carina's attention."

The twins laughed. Carina drew a warm palm across her husband's broad back as she wrapped herself around him. "We were only testing you, baby," she said.

Graham laughed. "Some test!"

Gianna smiled brightly at the two of them. She turned her attention toward Donovan's brother. "So, Kendrick, how long do you plan to be here? We'd love to invite you to the winery for dinner and the grand tour."

Kendrick nodded. "I appreciate that, but I have to fly out tonight. But if the invitation stands, I'd love to take you up on it the next time I'm in town. I hope to get back sometime soon and bring my wife. Vanessa and I have never seen Italy together."

"Since you two eloped, maybe you can have an official celebration here with the family?" Donovan suggested.

"We can do a fabulous reception at the winery!" Carina added. "Graham and I were actually married in the olive groves, and that's a beautiful option if you want to take your vows again."

Kendrick laughed as he held up his hands. "Slow it down! Y'all are moving way too fast. Let me talk it over with my favorite girl, and I'll get back to you. Vanessa's almost done with school, and then we'll take it from there."

"What is your wife studying?" Graham asked.

"She's a documentary film major."

"That's exciting!" Carina said.

Kendrick tossed a quick glance toward his wristwatch. "I hate to run because this has been a great time, but I need to get a taxi back to the airport."

"We can give you a ride," Graham said, looking toward his wife. "Carina and I need to head back, as well."

"Or you can ride with me and Donovan," Gianna said, looking around the table.

Donovan shook his head. "Gianna and I don't need to rush off," he said, his brow raised. "Thanks, Graham."

Kendrick laughed. "Yes, Graham, thank you. I appreciate the offer," the man replied as he stood up.

Gianna and her sister exchanged a look, a sly smile lifting Gianna's mouth.

Carina rose to her husband's side. "Well, I guess we will catch up with you two later," she said as she leaned down to kiss Donovan's cheek. "Don't let her scare you," she whispered into his ear.

He laughed as Kendrick shook his hand, tapped fists and bumped his shoulder. "I'll call you when I get home," he said.

His brother nodded. "Safe travels."

Goodbyes and well wishes rang out between them until Gianna's sister and brother-in-law and Donovan's brother had made their exit, the car pulling off in the direction of the airport.

A soft lull wafted between the couple as the two settled into the sudden quiet. Gianna reached for a cannoli that rested on Donovan's plate and took a large bite. As she chewed, she extended the decadent pastry in his direction, pausing as she reached his lips. Clasping his palm over her hand, he took his own bite of the dessert, his eyes locked on her face.

Her stare was teasing, heat flickering in the dark orbs. Their gazes danced in perfect synchronization, flitting back and forth in an easy give-and-take. Gianna was the first to break the silence.

"So why did you think we wouldn't see each other today?" she asked.

"Excuse me?"

"Earlier you said that you didn't think you were going to see me today. Why was that?" She slowly scooped a trail of chocolate from the plate with her finger, easing the decadent treat past her lips.

Donovan's eyes lifted as he shrugged. He cleared his throat before speaking. "I thought I might have been a little pushy yesterday. I was worried that you were put off by me trying to define our relationship."

Her head bobbed ever so slightly as she seemed to be reflecting on his comment. She leaned forward in her seat as she slowly licked the cream filling from her fingers. Eyeing her, Donovan felt a rush of heat course through his body, the seductive motion like a lit match igniting a low flame between them. He opened his mouth to speak, but nothing came out. The gesture was distracting, and he was suddenly at a loss for words, unable to form a coherent thought as he watched her suck her index finger slowly.

He closed his eyes and shook his head, then waved his own finger in her direction. "You're a tease!" he said, amusement dancing in his tone. "You're a tease, and you're enjoying every minute of this! You're also trying to distract me from having this conversation."

Gianna laughed as she wiped her hands on a paper napkin. "I don't know what you're talking about."

"You know exactly what I'm talking about and what you were doing." He shifted toward her, easing his body closer to hers. They were practically nose to nose as he held her gaze. "You're teasing me, and I fell for it."

There was a brief moment of silence before she nodded, her eyes wide as she eased back in her seat, needing to fill the space between them with a waft of cool air. Once again, Gianna changed the subject.

"So why do we need to define our relationship?"

Donovan sighed softly before answering. "We don't, but it would be nice to know where I stand with you." He shifted closer a second time, his leg pressing hot against hers. "Because I really care about you, Gianna. I know we just met, but what's happening between us has been building for months now. So why can't we just say it? Unless I'm reading something into our friendship that's not there?"

She shook her head, her eyes skating from side to side as she tried to think. A wave of anxiety suddenly flooded her spirit, washing over her sensibilities. She took a deep breath and then another before speaking. "Donovan, you already know where you and I stand. You and I are friends. Very *good* friends. What more do you need to know…or want me to say about us?"

Donovan sat back in his seat, still staring at her. That nervous twitch he'd noticed before was suddenly quiv-

ering, the muscle in her face dancing of its own volition. She suddenly drew her fingers to her face as if to
will it to stop. Gianna shifted her gaze from his, and he
could almost feel the wave of anxiety that had dropped
like a blanket around her shoulders. For the first time
Donovan sensed that Gianna wasn't as certain as she
wanted people to believe. The tough veneer she exuded
had cracked, exposing an air of fragility that he'd not
sensed before.

Gianna took a deep inhale of air and held it, silently
counting to ten before blowing it slowly past her parted
lips. Donovan's intense stare had her quivering with
nervous excitement. She was suddenly feeling vulnerable and transparent, as if he could see right through
her. He wanted to define them, to hear her say what was
clearly in his heart. But even in his certainty, she felt
most uncertain, something like fear clutching her heart.
And then he smiled, the beauty of it like the sweetest
balm, and all she could do was smile with him.

Donovan reached into his wallet, pulling money from
inside to leave a tip. He rested the ten euro banknote in
the center of the table. Standing, he extended his hand
toward her. As she slid her fingers between his, their
touch was electric…and comforting.

"We should go," he said softly, pulling her to her feet.

Gianna nodded, suddenly wishing she could find
the words to tell him that she really didn't want to. If
she were honest, she wasn't ready to tell him goodbye.

Chapter 7

Donovan stood at the window, looking out over the landscape. The ride back had been exceptionally quiet, neither he nor Gianna knowing what to say. For the first time since connecting with the woman, he felt as if she was a stranger, and he couldn't begin to understand why.

He turned back to the textbooks that lined his kitchen table. He needed to finalize his teaching plan for the first semester, but his mind wasn't on the curriculum. Donovan was feeling out of sorts about what had happened between him and Gianna. Or more accurately, what wasn't happening. He hadn't wanted to push, sensing that she would have felt as if she was being backed into a corner. And then it had dawned on him that what he had hoped for between them was probably not meant to be.

He sighed deeply as he moved back to the table and

took a seat. As he pored over the documents before him, he was desperate to focus his attention on anything that would take his mind off Gianna. But time seemed to drag as he tried to fix his mind on the numbers he so loved to manipulate.

The knock on his front door startled him. Donovan looked toward the clock on the wall. It was well after midnight, and he couldn't begin to imagine who'd be paying him a visit at such a late hour. The knock came a second time, the rapping abrupt and impatient. Moving from his seat to the door, he opened it just enough to peek out.

Gianna stood on the other side, eyeing him as warily as he eyed her. "I didn't think you'd be sleeping," she said matter-of-factly.

"Why not?"

"Because you're still thinking about the two of us."

He paused, wanting to tell her she was wrong. But he couldn't, as the words would prove to be a lie. Instead he shrugged his shoulders. "What are you doing here?"

"I came to talk…about us," she said as she pushed her way past him. As she turned to stare, she was taken aback, her breath catching deep in her chest. Her eyes grew big as her gaze ran the length of his body to the floor and back. Donovan was wearing a pair of cotton sleeping pants and little else. Bare-chested, he reminded her of a cover model for a men's magazine or a steamy romance novel. Clearly he took meticulous care of his body, his skin smooth like melted chocolate. He had the pecs of a body builder, and his abdominal muscles were easily a rippled eight-pack.

Before she could catch herself, Gianna reached out to trail her hand across his torso, gasping loudly as her fingertips connected with his flesh. Her eyes suddenly widened as she snatched her hand back, mortified that she'd been so brazen. Donovan took a step toward her.

"I should probably go put something on," he said, his voice a loud whisper.

"No... Yes... I mean...!" she sputtered, meeting his gaze. She clasped her hand to her chest as she turned and hurried back to the door. "I'll be waiting for you out here," she called over her shoulder.

Donovan shook his head, a smile blossoming across his face. Moving into his bedroom, he slipped his bare feet into a pair of leather sandals and pulled on a T-shirt, then he headed out the door after her.

Outside, Gianna still clutched her hand close to her chest, feeling as if it had been burned. Her fingers tingled, the quivers going all the way down to her toes. Just the briefest touch had her wanting to splay herself open to the man, to give him a taste of her sweets and treats. Donovan Boudreaux had her imagining the two of them in the most compromising positions, heated and dirty and pleasurable beyond measure.

She took a deep breath, gulping air as if her life depended on it. She suddenly found herself having a change of heart, not knowing if coming to see Donovan had been a good idea, after all. When she'd tiptoed out of the farmhouse, she'd known exactly what she'd wanted to say to Donovan. She knew she needed to clear the air, to be open and honest and tell him about

Carina's involvement in putting them together. That had been her intent when she and Carina had come earlier, meeting his brother instead. She'd known since that first day that for them to move forward, there could be no secrets between them. Donovan needed to know the truth. Now she couldn't even think clearly, unable to remember the speech she'd been practicing in her head since they'd last parted.

Donovan stepping up behind her caused her to jump, startled out of her thoughts.

"You scared me," she snapped as she turned to face him.

He held up both hands as if he were surrendering. "I'm sorry. I didn't mean to frighten you."

They both took a collective breath and held it before either spoke again.

Donovan broke the silence. "So, what did you want…" he started, before suddenly noticing the horse standing off to the side.

The massive, bay-colored animal stood majestically, looking at them both as if he were waiting for something to happen. Even in the late-night darkness, there was no mistaking how exquisite the creature was with his rich, red-toned coloration and white stripe down the center of his face. Surprised, Donovan found himself staring as he and the horse eyed each other.

"His name's Raffaello," Gianna said as she moved to stroke the horse's snout.

"He's beautiful. What breed is he?" Donovan asked, moving closer to the animal, who gave him a subtle push with his nose. He brushed his hand against the horse's neck.

"He's a Maremmano. It's a local Tuscan breed."

"You rode over?"

Gianna nodded. "It was too dark to walk, and I didn't want to drive. I needed to think."

Donovan shifted his gaze to meet hers, nodding in understanding. He took another deep breath. "So, what did you want to talk about?"

Gianna hesitated, and then she shook her head as she shrugged her shoulders. "Do you want to ride?" she suddenly asked.

Before he could respond, she swung her body up onto the horse's back, nothing between her and the animal but a soft cotton blanket. She extended her hand toward him.

Donovan paused for just a brief moment. "What's his name again?" he asked.

"Raffaello."

"After the painter?"

She laughed. "No, the turtle."

Confusion washed over Donovan's face. "The turtle?"

Gianna laughed again. "The Teenage Mutant Ninja Turtles."

Donovan was still staring at her as if she'd lost her mind.

A huge grin crossed her face. "There's Leonardo, Donatello, Michelangelo and Raphael. You really don't know your pop culture!"

He shrugged his broad shoulders. "Something you'll need to teach me."

"Carina and I named all the horses after them."

"All the horses?"

"We have six."

"And the other two are named?"

"Hermione and Ginevra—Ginny for short."

Donovan paused. "Harry Potter! I know those!" he said with a deep chuckle.

Gianna laughed with him. "That was all Carina's idea. I'm not a Harry Potter fan."

"But you like the turtle things?"

"I *love* the turtle things!" She waved her hand. "So, are you coming or not?"

Donovan took a deep breath as he clutched her arm and jumped, swinging the bulk of his body onto the horse's back behind her.

The beast beneath them neighed in response, twisting his head just enough to glare at the two of them. Gianna caressed the side of his thick neck. "Good boy!" she said. "Good boy!"

Once he was settled comfortably atop the animal, Donovan rested his hands lightly against her sides. Gianna grabbed one hand and then the other, pulling his arms closer around her waist.

"You'll need to hold on," she said, her words lost in the air as the horse started at a brisk gallop. "Hold on tight!"

Just the hint of a breeze was blowing as they rode beneath the late-night sky. Donovan's body was nestled close to Gianna's, her back leaning easily against his chest. Above their heads, stars shimmered brightly against the dark canvas, lighting their path. Everything about the moment felt surreal, and Donovan was awed by how at ease they both were.

He was completely lost as she navigated their way through the countryside, coming to a halt as they reached the coastline and the pristine Blue Flag beaches so popular with tourists. She led them to a secluded cove, then slid like a nymph from the horse's back and out of Donovan's arms. She left him sitting atop Raffaello as she skipped toward the expanse of warm, shallow water. Donovan watched as she kicked off her shoes, dipping her feet into the warm waters that lapped at the edge of the sand.

There was something exquisite about Gianna as she danced beneath the full moon, her thick waves loose and whipping over her shoulders. She was braless, wearing a simple tank top that amplified her small bustline. Her nipples had blossomed against the cotton fabric and pressed teasingly for attention. Boy-cut shorts complemented her well-rounded backside, her buttocks tight and firm like two generous-sized melons. She was lean, and despite her petite stature, her legs seemed to be a mile high. He suddenly imagined her in his arms, pressed against him, his hands trailing the lines and curves of her body. As if she were reading his mind, she suddenly turned and stared in his direction, wrapping her arms around her torso.

Donovan gently caressed the horse's side. "Easy boy," he said softly. "Easy."

Raffaello lifted his head and whinnied, the tone low

and gentle, as if he were encouraging Donovan to catch up to the woman.

The man chuckled softly as he dismounted. He gave the horse an easy hug. "Give me a break, big guy. She's a hard one to keep up with," he said out loud. The horse lifted his head again as though he were cosigning Donovan's statement.

A full moon reflected off the water, casting a glow around the landscape. As Donovan moved in Gianna's direction, she stared, turning to watch him. When he was close enough for the sea spray to kiss his face, she turned back and continued to walk, kicking up water beneath her feet. Donovan followed behind her, his arms crossed over his chest and his hands clutched tightly beneath his armpits.

"You look nervous," she said, coming to an abrupt stop as she turned again to face him.

He shook his head. "No. I'm just curious. Wondering what we're doing here in the middle of the night."

"I wanted to show you this place. It's one of my favorites. I come here and walk the sand when I need to figure something out."

"What are you trying to figure out?"

"*Our* story," she said emphasizing the word *our*. "Whether or not the hero gets the girl."

Donovan smiled ever so slightly. "The hero *always* gets the girl."

She smiled with him. "Not in my books."

"But you don't write romance."

"I don't. I've never really believed in happily-ever-after."

"Do you believe in the girl at least giving the hero a chance?"

Gianna took a breath, blowing it out slowly. "I do, but our story is different."

"Different how?"

Gianna suddenly changed the subject. "Do you smell that?" she asked, tilting her face upward as she inhaled deeply.

Donovan took his own deep inhale, noting the faintest hint of floral sweet that tinted the ocean air. He nodded.

"It's Italian jasmine," she responded. "It's still blooming, and it's late for this time of year. That's a good omen."

Donovan took a step toward her, closing the gap between them. "How is *our* story different, Gianna?"

She met the intense look he was giving her, hesitating for a split second before answering. "The heroine wasn't in it from the beginning. Only the hero."

Donovan stared at her, her comment spinning in his mind. His gaze dropped to the ground, flitting back and forth as he tried to make sense of her statement. When he lifted his eyes back to her face, she was gnawing nervously on her bottom lip.

She continued. "Carina was the one who initially reached out to you. Pretending to be me."

"Carina?"

Gianna nodded. "She wanted to fix us up. Her methods were just a little wayward."

"So it wasn't you who's been writing to me all these months?"

Gianna shook her head. "No. I only found out about you a few weeks before you arrived."

"So this whole time, all of this has been a game?" He suddenly thought back to the conversation with Kendrick and Graham and how the twins liked to play tricks on people.

"No! Not at all," she said emphatically. "Carina just wanted us to get to know each other. But everything she wrote, or rather what she sent you…those were all my words, my feelings. She took the writings from my personal journals to respond to you. And I've read every word you wrote me. I could probably recite them verbatim. Her responses would have been exactly what I would have said to you."

Donovan drew his hand over the top of his head and down his face. "No wonder you've been so…" He paused.

"I didn't want you to be hurt by this. I know you've been invested in our relationship far longer than I have, but I assure you, even though I've been playing catch up, you and I…"

He cut her words off, his tone harsh. "You and I don't have a relationship. You and your sister have been playing me for a fool," he said. "I can't believe after all this time that I didn't figure it out."

"I'm so sorry, Donovan," Gianna said, contrition in her eyes. "I really am. I needed to apologize. And I needed you to know the truth."

"Now you want me to know the truth? Why didn't you just tell me when we first met?"

Gianna eased even closer to him. She pressed her

palms to his chest, her fingers clutching the front of his shirt. "That very first day I wanted to, but once I met you... I...well... I really wanted to get to know you better. Carina and I had even planned to tell you earlier today, but when we got to your home and your brother was there, I changed my mind again."

"What difference does it make now?"

She took a deep breath and held it for a brief second. Donovan shook his head, moving to turn from her.

Gianna grabbed his arm, spinning herself back to stand in front of him. "Because when I do this," she whispered, "you need to know that it comes from me. From my heart."

Donovan's brow furrowed with confusion again. "When you do what?" he snapped.

Gianna closed what little space remained between them, pressing the warmth of her body to his. "This," she whispered softly as she stood on her tiptoes, tilting her face to his. And then she kissed him, capturing his mouth with her own.

Had he been asked, Donovan would have sworn on everything he held sacred that when Gianna kissed him, fireworks erupted in the sky and a symphony was playing blissfully in the distance. In his mind's eye he would have bet his last dollar that he'd seen the colorful striations connecting the bright stars above and that he'd heard the music that had danced with the lull of the waves that teased the sand.

He had never before been kissed as passionately as when her mouth blessed his. Her lips were soft, satin pillows. They parted slightly, her tongue playfully teasing his. It was an easy give-and-take of magnanimous proportions fueled by something too sweet to ever be believed. It was the best first kiss of all the first kisses in his small world.

As his lips danced over hers, she wrapped her thin arms around his neck, drawing him so close to her that it felt as if they were one body and not two. Her soft curves melded into every hardened line of his body, and neither could begin to decipher where one began and the other ended.

Donovan wrapped his arms around her waist, lifting her from the sandy foundation beneath her feet. As he did, she wrapped both legs around his waist, locking her ankles together at the small of his back. He clutched the round of her backside with one hand, his fingers teasing the taut flesh as the other skated up and down her torso.

The moment was surreal. Gianna was so lost in the vastness of it that when Donovan broke the connection, pushing her gently from him, the infraction felt magnanimous. They were both breathing heavily, gasping for air as he eased her back onto her feet and took a step from her, putting what she thought was far too much distance between them.

Donovan's head bobbed up and down against his neck, his mind racing with too many thoughts, but there was something in his eyes Gianna had never seen before. He reached a hand out, trailing his fingers along her profile as she closed her own eyes and leaned her cheek into his palm. When she reopened her eyes, Donovan was still staring, his gaze misted with emotion.

"I'll find my own way home," he said softly, the comment not at all what Gianna had expected.

"Donovan, please," she whispered back, clutching a hand to her chest. "Let's just talk."

He shook his head as he took two additional steps backward. "I'm sorry, Gianna, but I don't have anything else to say," he replied. And then he turned and disappeared into the darkness.

Chapter 8

Donovan stared out at the students who were taking their first exam of the semester. The surprise pop quiz was solely for his benefit, to assess the capabilities of his students and identify those mathematical areas where he needed to focus more energy and those he could dismiss. As he eyed each student, he was surprised to find Alessandra Donati staring back at him intently. The young woman slowly licked her lips just as she drew her number two pencil to her mouth, then gave him a suggestive wink. The overt gesture threw Donovan off course for a brief moment as he shifted his eye to the paperwork on his desk, pretending not to have noticed.

He took a deep breath before returning his gaze to the rows of seats and the thirty-six students sitting in them. He resumed his study of the classroom, starting his trek on the other side of the room. They were a great group, eager, inquisitive and bright. They would make the teaching experience a joy. Then there was young Ms. Donati, her flirtatious manner beginning to cause him concern.

The girl was intellectually gifted, but she had no boundaries. Her brazen antics since the semester had started went far above and beyond those of students he'd had in the past. And in the past, there had been many a student who'd hoped to know him outside of the classroom on a more intimate level, but Donovan had always been able to shut them down.

Shutting down Ms. Donati was proving to be a challenge. The first day of classes, she'd made her interest in him known in front of the whole class, the sexual innuendo making him blush a time or two. He'd pulled her aside immediately after class to express his disapproval, and she had only laughed, pretending not to know what he was talking about as she trailed her hands over her full breasts, drawing attention to the large nipples that poked through the sheer fabric. But the overt comments had since stopped, at least when there were others around to hear.

As the clock chimed through the room signaling the noon hour, Donovan moved onto his feet, collecting the exam papers as each student passed by his desk toward the exit. He wished them each a good afternoon as comments rang out about the ease or difficulty of the test.

"I wasn't prepared for that, Dr. Boudreaux!" one young man said, laughing.

"That was a breeze, sir!" another interjected. "You'll have to do better challenging us!"

Ms. Donati brought up the rear, hanging back to be the last to leave, as she did after every class. Before she could comment, her wide eyes showing her eagerness to whisper out of turn, Professor Mugabe burst through the door.

"Donovan, how was class? Oh, Alessandra, dear, how are you?"

The student shrugged her narrow shoulders, annoyance visible across her face. "I'm well, thank you," she answered.

There was a brief pause as the two instructors stood staring at the girl.

Alessandra shifted her gaze toward Donovan. "Professor Boudreaux, will you be having office hours today?" she asked as she twisted the beads around her neck between her fingers. "I'd like to speak to you, if I may? Alone."

Donovan shook his head. "I'll be in early tomorrow. In the common area until ten. You're more than welcome to come see me then," he answered, his eyebrows lifted ever so slightly.

She forced a smile. "Tomorrow then," she said as she sashayed out the door.

Professor Mugabe looked from him to Alessandra and back.

"You'll need to keep an eye on that one," she said as Alessandra disappeared from sight. "She's one of our best and brightest but..." The woman's words stalled. She pressed a hand to Donovan's forearm. "But I'm sure you've already figured that out." She gave him an all-knowing smile before she continued. "Do you have plans for lunch?"

"I was actually planning to just head home early since I don't have a class this afternoon." His brow furrowed, something else obviously on his mind.

"Nonsense!" Sophie exclaimed. "You must have lunch with me. We really haven't had an opportunity to talk since you got here." She headed for the door, calling over her shoulder, "I insist!"

Gianna entered the family home, a blank expression across her face. Carina and her father exchanged a look as she and Franco both turned to stare at the same time.

"Ciao, bambina!" the patriarch called out, gesturing for his daughter to come to his side.

Gianna crossed to the other side of the room, leaning in to kiss her father's cheek. *"Ciao, papà,"* she replied.

"Where were you?"

She shook her head. "I just went for a walk. No place special," she answered.

The old man nodded. "Have you spoken to Donovan?"

Gianna took a deep breath and sighed softly. She turned abruptly, not bothering to answer.

"You should try to call him, Sissy!" Carina called after her. "If you want I can try…"

Gianna turned to give her sister a look, cutting off the comment. "Leave it alone, Carina. You have helped more than enough," she said sarcastically.

Franco moved onto his feet, crossing to stand by her

side. "Carina is right. You two need to talk. You should try to call him."

She shook her head. "Donovan has made it quite clear that he isn't interested in talking to me, so let it go. Please."

Gianna stepped into her father's outstretched arms. Franco wrapped his daughter in a warm hug. He held her, no one saying another word. As she stood in his arms, she could feel the hurt that consumed her flooding her spirit, building yet again.

It had been a few weeks since she'd told Donovan the truth, and since then a wall of silence had stood like stone between the couple. All of the family had wanted to intervene, but Gianna had been adamant about none of them doing anything at all. It was over, no possibility of a future between them existing. Gianna had accepted such, and everyone else just needed to, as well.

Franco gave her a quick squeeze before kissing her cheek one last time and letting her go. Turning from him, Gianna moved toward her office, leaving them behind. Before she could close the door, Carina moved into the space.

"Please don't start," Gianna muttered. She swiped at a tear that burned hot behind her lashes.

"I just wanted you to know that I haven't gotten to your mail or your email messages yet. If you want me to, I can take care of them now."

Gianna shook her head. "No, I'll take care of it. I have some calls to make, too. If I need anything, I'll just let you know."

"You're pushing your deadline. How's the writing going?"

Gianna paused. Truth be told, she hadn't written a word since that last night with Donovan, her mind a complete and total blank. The writing wasn't going well at all. She forced a smile as she met her sister's stare. "Fine. The writing is going very well."

"So, you'll make your deadline? Because if you don't think you will, we should send your editor a message."

"I said it's going to be okay, Carina. I'm handling it."

Carina nodded. "Well, let me know if that changes, okay?"

"Okay, Carina!" Gianna snapped.

An awkward silence fell between them. Carina said nothing else as she backed her way out of the office, closing the door behind her.

Gianna sat down at her desk, then flung the felt-tip pen she'd been holding across the room, the device landing in front of the wooden bookcases. She shifted forward in her seat, dropping her head into her hands. Frustration creased her brow.

Nothing felt as if it was going to be okay. She felt lost and couldn't begin to explain to anyone why. Donovan turning from her had broken her heart, and she couldn't begin to know or understand when her heart had gotten caught up in the fray. And then she thought about that first kiss.

Kissing Donovan Boudreaux had been everything she'd imagined and then some. The man's touch had been searing, and in that brief moment, when their connection had been the most intimate experience of her life, Gianna had imagined her fairy-tale romance and happy ending. Nothing about how he held her, his body pressed tightly against hers, had prepared her for that being their very last kiss. Nothing. But that's where they were. Done and finished before anything had been able to start.

Shaking the thoughts from her head, Gianna turned on her computer. As she waited for the device to power up, she eased her headphones over her ears and flipped the on switch to her MP3 player. The English crooner Sam Smith was suddenly serenading her, his melodic tone instantly calming her spirit. He sang, and Gianna allowed herself to drift into the emotion of his tune.

She slid her finger across the laptop's mouse pad, opening her email folder. After entering her user name and password, she watched as a lengthy list of new messages rolled across the screen. She scanned the names beneath the list titled FROM. One name suddenly screamed for her attention. As she clicked on the message, a bright smile pulled at her lips, joy flooding her face. She read it once and then again.

Dear Ms. Martelli,

My name is Donovan Boudreaux. I'm a math professor currently teaching at the University of Siena in Tuscany. I have been a fan of yours since your first book, *Bruised and Battered*. Despite my previous intentions to write and tell you how much I've enjoyed your writing, I've always stopped myself, feeling that you probably would not want to be inundated with more fan mail. But I have been reading an ARC of your latest work,

Primed and Pursued, and have been so engaged with the characters that I could not let the opportunity to tell you what I think pass by.

I am awed by the beauty of your words. From the first sentence to the last, I was pulled in and captivated. But I was also haunted, your protagonist's pain seeming to mirror my own. So I had to write to ask if his heartbreak was intentional on your part or just a consequence of your heroine's actions. I'd be curious to know as well if you ever considered rewriting the ending to mend the hurt the infraction caused him. Clearly, you had compassion for this man, so does he not deserve a happier ending?

I'd love to discuss him and your story in further detail. I do hope that you'll respond.

Yours truly,

Donovan Boudreaux

Excitement bubbled like boiling water in a pot as Gianna grabbed an ink pen and yellow-lined notepad from the corner of her desk. As a response formed in her mind, she began jotting down notes, anxious to send a reply.

As Sophie prattled on and on about testing and student scores, Donovan found himself drifting off into his own thoughts. The woman had been talking nonstop since they'd taken a seat at the sidewalk trattoria. He'd given up trying to get in a comment and resigned himself to just listening, occasionally nodding in agreement.

The meal had been a delight—appetizers of classic

caprese salad with tomatoes and buffalo mozzarella cheese, and Tuscan prosciutto with cantaloupe melon. He'd chosen saffron risotto with veal *ossobuco* ragout for his main course, and had finished off with a scoop of mango sorbet in a bowl of raspberry soup.

Now he sat clutching his smartphone in his lap, hoping for the distinctive sound that alerted him to an incoming email message. Before leaving home, he'd sent Gianna an email, hoping against all odds to start their relationship over again. For days he'd stopped himself from climbing that hill to the winery to see her, wanting to forget that he'd left her and her horse standing alone on the beach in the dark of night. And as often as the thought of seeing her came to him, he'd talked himself out of it, able to forgive but unable to forget that she and her sister had played him for a fool.

But this morning had started differently than all the other mornings. Signora Rossi had wakened him as usual, her boisterous chatter like its own alarm clock on the other side of his bedroom door. The old woman had knocked for his attention, and when he'd finally wrapped a bathrobe around himself to greet her, she'd been in an exceptional mood.

Pushing him out of her way, he'd watched as she stripped the sheets from his bed, and then out of nowhere she'd reached into his nightstand drawer and had pulled Gianna's framed picture from where he'd hidden it inside. Propping it back onto the tabletop, Signora Rossi had given him an evil eye and had shaken her index finger at him as she'd berated him in her native tongue. He'd understood just enough to know that she thought him a bigger fool for allowing the rift between them to continue. And so he'd given in to his wanting and had gone to his computer to send Gianna a message.

Sophie interrupted his thoughts. "Maybe we can have dinner together tomorrow?"

"Excuse me?" He struggled to focus his attention back on Sophie, shaking the thoughts of Gianna from his mind.

"Dinner? Tomorrow? I was thinking that you could come to my apartment and I could cook a traditional Nigerian meal for you." Sophie smiled brightly, her porcelain white teeth a striking contrast against her dark complexion.

As Donovan stared into the woman's eyes, he realized something between them had changed, Sophie reading more into their friendship than he'd ever considered.

"I'm sorry," he said. He repeated himself a second time. "I'm really sorry, but…"

She held up her hands, her smile still bright. "No pressure. I just sense that you've been off your game lately, and I thought some downtime with a good friend might help alleviate some of your stress. So think about it, and if you change your mind or you just feel like spending some time together, I'm available."

Donovan nodded. "I appreciate that," he said, feeling extremely uncomfortable.

His phone suddenly vibrated. As he stole a quick glance to see who the incoming message was from, Sophie changed the subject, telling him about her family and the journey from Africa that had landed them on the Italian coast. Despite wanting to focus his attention on his phone, he instead leaned toward Sophie to hear the story she was so excited to share. The message from his sister could wait. He wouldn't be rude to the woman who was trying so hard to be a good friend.

An hour later, he stole a quick glance at his wristwatch. Half the afternoon had passed, and he found himself wishing he were anywhere but where he was. He moved as if to ready himself to leave.

"Don't rush off," Sophie said as she shifted in her seat. "It's still early. We could order a bottle of wine, maybe take a stroll through the piazza?"

He smiled. "I appreciate the invitation, Sophie. I really do, but I have to head back to Maremma."

She nodded. "I'm glad we could spend some time together." She reached across the table for his hand. "I'm really glad that we're getting to know each other better. You know how much I've always admired you."

"Sophie...look..."

She interrupted, batting her eyelashes at him. "Donovan, I'm really not good at this kind of thing, but I like you and you like me, and we have so much in common. I feel like we could have more with each other. I know you feel it, too!"

His palm was sweaty as she caressed his fingers, a look of longing in her dark eyes. Extricating himself from her touch, he shifted backward in his seat, dropping both of his hands into his lap. "Sophie, I'm sorry. I hope I didn't give you the wrong impression but..."

"But you're lonely and you crave companionship and a woman's touch in your life. I see it in your eyes, and the past few weeks in particular I've felt like you've been missing something."

He shook his head vehemently as he stammered. "I was… I mean… I am… I don't…" He took a deep breath, his two hands suddenly gesturing in the air as he tried to explain himself. "I have had a lot on my mind lately, but it's not what you think. I appreciate everything you've done for me, but I don't want to give you the impression that you and I are anything but friends. Good friends. And colleagues! But that's all we are."

"Aren't you attracted to me? Because I'm very attracted to you, Donovan. I think you know that. And we're so at ease with each other!"

Donovan took a deep breath. "You're a beautiful woman, Sophie! There's no doubt about that, but I'm just not…"

"Is there someone else? Because if there's someone else, you should have told me!"

Donovan felt the woman bristle with indignation. He shook his head. "It really doesn't matter! What matters is that I hope you and I can continue to be friends. I do value our friendship, and I enjoy working with you. I wouldn't want to see anything happen to that friendship because of a misunderstanding."

Sophie sat staring at him, the glare in her eyes shifting to something cold. "Well, don't I feel silly," she said. "I'm completely embarrassed. I can't believe I just threw myself at you like that, just to have you shoot me down."

"Don't be," he said, shaking his head. "And I didn't shoot you down. Don't think like that. We're just on different pages right now. Maybe some other time, some other place, things would have been different. But I'm a man. Always a day late and a dollar short when it comes to women!" Donovan tried to laugh it off to ease her discomfort. But Sophie wasn't feeling it.

Silence swelled thick between them. He suddenly felt even more awkward than he had before. He moved onto his feet, practically jumping out of his seat. "Thank you for lunch…and the company. I had a good time. And again, I'm really sorry if I gave you the wrong impression."

Sophie shrugged, fighting not to let her embarrassment flood her face. "Have a good night," she muttered as she waved a dismissive hand.

Donovan moved to the other side of the table. He dropped a heavy hand against the woman's shoulder. She turned her head, leaning to search the interior of her handbag. When she didn't bother to look at him again, he gave her shoulder a slight squeeze as he said goodbye. Heading in the direction of his car, Donovan suddenly wished he could run, not walk, from the woman's sight.

His hour-long ride home to Maremma helped ease the anxiety that had afflicted the last few minutes of his time with Sophie. He thought about her and about Alessandra—both women had put him in an awkward position. Although it wasn't the first time someone had expressed interest in him, Donovan had avoided commitment by throwing himself into his work. Not many women readily accepted taking a backseat to a man's

profession. But he instinctively knew that the few he
had dated were not the partners he was meant to spend
his life with. And then Gianna had come along.

He accelerated the car, frustrated by the limited cell
service in the area. Before pulling out of the restaurant's
parking lot he'd checked his phone, but there had been
no message from the woman. He was hoping that once
he got closer to home and a better signal that Gianna
might have finally responded to his message.

Chapter 9

Donovan caught sight of Raffaello as he pulled his car in front of the cottage. The horse was grazing out in the fields, seemingly oblivious to his surroundings. Donovan's heart began to race with excitement as he stepped out of his car. Then he heard the two women bickering. Gianna and Signora Rossi sounded like two cats trapped in a burlap bag. His heart skipped a beat, and then a second one. As he neared the front door of his home, he stopped to listen, able to understand more of the language than he'd anticipated.

Signora Rossi was fussing about pasta and how it needed to be hand-formed. Gianna said something about her father and having perfected his methods of pulling the dough through a pasta machine. One of them mentioned watching Mario Batali and how he did it on television, and then the raised voices sniped at each other again like nails against a chalkboard.

Amusement painted Donovan's face as he stepped through the entrance into the house. He looked from one woman to the other, then settled his gaze on Gianna's face. The two stood in the center of his kitchen, flour dusting Gianna's face as she took direction from Signora Rossi. Startled, both women jumped in surprise.

"Hi," Donovan said, his eyes locking with Gianna's. He stood staring, something large and magnanimous shifting between them as they eyed each other.

"Ciao!" she replied, a warm smile pulling at her thin lips.

Signora Rossi grinned as her own gaze shifted between them. "You are early!" she said, speaking English to him for the very first time.

His eyes widened in surprise, but before he could respond the old woman rushed him, fanning her hand for him to get out of their way.

He and Gianna both laughed.

"I wanted to surprise you with dinner," Gianna said. "But it seems like I don't know what I'm doing!"

He nodded. "I guess I'll go into the other room until you two are done," he said, locking gazes with her a second time.

She nodded. "Read your mail," she said as he moved toward the bedroom.

Tossing her a quick glance over his shoulder, he smiled, a huge grin filling his face as he shut the room door between them. As soon as it was closed, the back-and-forth between the two women began again, Signora Rossi admonishing Gianna for not having his meal ready when he came through the door. Donovan couldn't help but laugh.

A legal-sized envelope rested in the center of the bed. Donovan took a seat against the mattress as he pulled it into his hands and opened the seal. The letter inside was handwritten, dark ink staining two pages of bright white copy paper. Shifting his large body back against the headboard, Donovan began to read.

My dearest Donovan,

I've drafted this response more times than I care to count, and just when I thought I was ready to push the send button on my computer, I hesitated. What if you thought the response came from someone other than me? The fear of you not trusting that these words were mine was haunting! Letter writing has become a lost art, but I knew that it needed to be revived between us, and so I put pen to paper.

Your support of my writing warms my heart. And to have your friendship means the world to me. But you are more than just a friend, and I haven't even begun to show you just how much more you mean to me.

So to answer your question, no, it was never my intention to break my hero's heart. He is *my* hero! The alpha of *my* story! But he is also a man, and the circumstances of the story and the actions of those he could not control proved to be his undoing. But he is *my* hero! And I lay claim

to him because he has my heart and is everything
I could ever want in a man. Even as he fell, there
was no denying his strength, his unyielding ability to rise like the phoenix to fly again! So there
was no need to rewrite his ending, because even
in his hurt, there was hope and a heroine's love
to pull him from the ashes!

Hope! And love! The words of a romantic!
Something I knew nothing of…until you.
PS: I would give anything to have you kiss me
again like you kissed me that very first time! I
just thought I would share that with you.

Donovan reread the letter again before tucking it between the pages of his Bible and putting the book on the
nightstand. In the other room, laughter rang warmly,
even as the clatter of pots and pans vibrated through
the air.

Donovan and Gianna talked over bowls of linguine
tossed with artichokes, Roma tomatoes and fresh Par-
mesan cheese. They washed the meal down with a bottle
of white wine, then finished it off with slices of tira-
misu and cups of dark coffee topped with steamed milk.
They talked for hours, falling easily into a comfortable
rhythm with each other.

Outside, Gianna's horse slumbered on his feet. After
clearing the dirty dishes, the young woman rose to
check on the animal. Before she returned, she stopped
to call her father so that he would not worry about where
she was. She wasn't surprised to learn that the village

gossips had already carried the news, everyone whispering about her and the handsome professor. Then she'd called her sister. Carina had cried with excitement, moving Gianna to shed her own tears of joy.

Back inside, there was a lull in the conversation as both took sips of their hot beverage. Gianna rested her gaze on Donovan's face. The emotion that suddenly flooded her spirit was unexpected. Being back with him felt surreal, and she imagined that it would be devastating if she suddenly found herself waking from the sweetest dream. As if he were reading her mind, Donovan smiled.

"I'm sorry," she said, her voice a loud whisper. "I hope that you know that Carina only wanted the best for both of us. I should have told you the truth the minute I found out what she had done, and I apologize for not doing so."

"I do know that, but my feelings were hurt. I felt deceived. Hell, I was deceived! And I didn't understand why you just weren't honest with me." He leaned toward her, dropping his forearms against his thighs as he stared, his hands clasped tightly together.

A hint of a blush crossed her face. She took a deep breath, blowing it out slowly before she responded. "After I read all the messages you'd sent, I really did want to get to know you. I was curious. Then when we met...well... I thought you were the most beautiful man I'd ever laid eyes on. And one of the sweetest. Once I felt like we'd connected, I didn't think it would matter. So, no, I'm not going to apologize for how I felt, but I'm sincerely apologetic for not being transparent."

He nodded. "What made you change your mind?"

"I didn't want our relationship to be built on a lie. You wanted more from me, and when I realized that I did, too, I felt like I owed it to you to be honest."

His head continued to bob up and down as he reflected on what she had to say. "So you wanted more?"

Gianna scooted her chair against his, easing herself closer. She clasped his hands between her own and pressed a kiss against his palm. She shook her head. "No."

Donovan suddenly looked confused. "No?"

She smiled. "I *want* more. There's nothing past tense about what I feel for you, Donovan Boudreaux! Or what I hope will happen between us."

Donovan smiled. Just as he leaned forward, his face mere millimeters from hers, there was a hard rap at his front door. Before either could stand to answer, the door flew open and Signora Rossi pushed her way inside. She took one look at the two of them and tossed up her hands, her thick accent ringing in the air as she scurried to clean up the dirty dishes.

Gianna leaned forward and kissed Donovan's cheek. She brushed her own against the stubble of new growth that had sprouted across his face. Donovan blew a frustrated breath of air past her ear.

"I should be leaving," she said. "It's past your curfew."

"I was hoping you could stay," he whispered, cutting an eye at the old woman who was pretending not to notice them.

"We're not ready for that yet," Gianna answered as she stood, her smile endearing.

Donovan stood with her and slowly walked her toward the sliding glass doors to the rear patio.

Signora Rossi called out from the other side of the room. *"Dille buonanotte. È necessario il riposo."*

Donovan's eyes widened. "Did she just say that I needed my rest?" he muttered.

Gianna giggled. "And she told you to tell me good-night so you could get that rest."

"Dille buonanotte!" Signora Rossi repeated, waving a wooden spoon at the two of them.

Donovan shook his head, his smile miles wide as Gianna drew her hand along his profile in a gentle caress. There was no denying the wealth of emotion between them. Donovan suddenly imagined that they had a lifetime of loving to carry them forward. Because in that moment, he could have easily said, without an ounce of reservation, that he had fallen head over heels in love with Gianna Martelli. He knew beyond any doubt that he would spend a lifetime ensuring she and everyone else knew it. Those few weeks apart had been telling, and devastating, and he refused to be away from her that long ever again.

He pressed his forehead to hers, his eyes closed as he held her tightly. When he opened them, every ounce of emotion he was feeling was mirrored in her eyes. She smiled, joy and happiness shimmering in her stare. Donovan suddenly wanted to kiss her.

As if reading his mind, Gianna gently pressed her closed lips to his, the touch sweet and easy, like the delicate touch of butterfly wings against a blade of summer grass. Donovan felt his heart stop and then start again, and a level of calm washed over them both. Perfection didn't begin to describe the moment between them.

"Good night," she said softly.

Donovan nodded. "Good night, Gianna!"

And Signora Rossi had the last word, wishing them both a very good night. *"Buonanotte!"*

Mason, Kendrick, Guy and Darryl were all laughing into their telephones as the Boudreaux brothers caught up with Donovan via a conference call.

"That's taking blocking to a whole other level!" Guy said.

Donovan nodded, his gaze focused on the road as he talked with his earpiece in place. "I thought our sisters were bad," he said, "but they've got nothing on Signora Rossi!"

"But it sounds like things are good with you and Gianna, yes?" Kendrick asked.

"I think we're on the right path. We're talking, and things are comfortable between us."

"That's good," Kendrick said, "because the woman is beautiful. I don't think you can do any better than that."

Donovan laughed. "Excuse me?"

His brothers all laughed.

"I've seen a picture," Guy added. "Kendrick might be right."

Mason spoke. "As long as it feels right and you're happy, that's all that matters. Have you spoken to the old people?"

"Dad called the other day, and I was planning to call Mom after my morning class today."

"Make sure you do that. Mom is missing you. And she's had a lot to say about you and your new friend. The rest of us are tired of hearing it, so this will give her a chance to tell you directly."

Darryl laughed. "Mom's not missing him! She's hoping he'll be married with a child on the way by the time he gets back from Italy."

"That may be true," Mason said in agreement, "but she needs to tell him and not us."

"And he might not come back from Italy," Kendrick interjected.

There was a brief pause before Mason broke the silence. "Are you thinking about staying in Italy?" he asked.

Donovan took a deep breath. "I don't see Gianna wanting to leave."

There was a collective sigh from all the brothers.

Kendrick laughed. "Please, please, please! Have a wedding so your sisters will have something to focus on. I need them to leave me and Vanessa alone!"

"Just let them give you a damn party and get it over with!" Guy exclaimed. "That's all they want to do!"

Mason agreed. "They're all still pissed that you eloped. Since they couldn't get a wedding, and Vanessa's school schedule is keeping them from throwing you guys a reception to celebrate, they're chomping at the bit!"

The siblings all laughed as the banter between them continued. By the time Donovan pulled into his parking lot at the university, he'd laughed until tears spilled out of his eyes.

"I've got to go," he said as he shut off the car. "I'll give you a guys a call in a few days."

"Full day today?" Mason asked.

"No. I only have office hours this morning, then I'm done for the weekend."

"I have to come back for business in a few weeks," Kendrick said. "Let's plan on doing dinner."

"I think I might come with him," Mason said.

"I think we should all go. Make it a guy's trip," Guy said.

"I'm in!" Darryl chimed.

Donovan cosigned. "Sounds like a plan!"

After saying their goodbyes, he disconnected the call and headed for the entrance. Accustomed to Sophie meeting him at the door, he was only slightly surprised to not see her standing there. After grabbing his mail from the boxes in the office, he headed for the common area to fulfill his office hours and be available to his students.

Donovan favored the out-of-office environment and had discovered over the years that many of his students preferred to seek him out in an open area instead of behind closed doors. A public environment also made things easier when dealing with students like Alessandra.

She sat waiting, like a stalker, desperate to seek him out. Pacing the floors, she almost jumped with joy as he moved in her direction. "Dr. Boudreaux, I thought you forgot about me."

He smiled politely. "Why would you think something like that?"

She looked at her watch, then lifted her eyes back

to his. "I guess I am a little early," she said with a soft giggle.

Donovan nodded. "Thirty minutes early, to be exact." He gestured for her to take a seat at the table, pulling out a chair for her. "So, what can I help you with, Ms. Donati?"

Alessandra fumbled her books and bags as she twisted in her seat to face him. "I just wanted to take an opportunity to personally welcome you to our university. Everyone is so excited to have you here."

He nodded, his eyebrows raised. "I appreciate that," he said slowly. "Is that it?"

She gave him a sly smile and curled her bottom lip as she bit down against the soft flesh. "I also wanted to volunteer to help you get settled in. I imagine being in a new country can be intimidating, especially when you don't know anyone. I want you to know that I'm at your disposal, day…or night," she said with emphasis. To further punctuate her meaning, she winked at him.

Donovan sat back in his seat, staring at her. He took a deep breath before he spoke. "That's very kind of you, Ms. Donati…"

"Please, Alessandra. Ms. Donati is so formal."

"Which is why I won't call you by your given name. There is nothing casual about our relationship. I'm your instructor and you are my student, and I have no intentions of crossing that line. Neither should you."

"But, Donovan…"

"Dr. Boudreaux. Please."

She bristled, twisting her mouth as annoyance flashed across her face. "Most men would welcome my attention," she snapped, her eyes narrowing into thin slits.

Donovan smiled. "Ms. Donati, I'm not like *most* men!"

Donovan watched as Alessandra stormed out of the common room, pausing once at the door to give him one last dirty look. As she made her exit, he missed her encounter in the hallway, the young woman almost slamming into Professor Mugabe. Nor was he privy to the subsequent conversation between the two. A conversation that had the two women whispering frantically until taking their discussion behind the closed doors of Professor Mugabe's office.

Before he could reflect on what had happened, another student waved for his attention, the young man in need of actual assistance with his math work. Two hours later he was wishing he could be done for the day, anxious to get back to Maremma, and Gianna. But there was still a mountain of paperwork that he needed to get through.

"Dr. Boudreaux?"

Donovan lifted his eyes from the stack of test papers he'd been grading. A young woman with doe-like eyes and a mousy pixie cut stood staring. She clutched a stack of books in her arms, the tomes almost as big as she was.

"Yes?" He eyed her curiously.

"You have a visitor in the front office. They asked me to come tell you."

"Grazie mille," he said, expressing his gratitude.

As she turned on high heels and headed toward a table of friends watching them curiously, he began to pack his papers into his leather attaché case. Minutes later he took his exit, heading in the direction of the university's reception area.

Gianna was standing in the office, her hands clasped together in front of her. Her eyes were darting back and forth as she took in the comings and goings of the students. She wore a blue skirt that was gathered on both sides and a blue-printed bandeau top that was tied into a bow between her breasts. Low cut, brown leather boots covered her feet, complementing her casual country look. She'd straightened her hair, the luscious strands falling well past her shoulders. He could feel a wide grin pull across his face at the sight of her spying into the glass-enclosed room.

As he moved in Gianna's direction, he was surprised when Sophie entered the office ahead of him and greeted her, the two women seeming to know one another. Neither seemed pleased to see the other, and he sensed their meeting was chilly at best. There was a brief exchange of words before Sophie did an about-face, slamming the door harshly as she made an exit. Moving in the opposite direction, she didn't see him, and for that he was grateful. He made a mental note to ask Gianna about their connection once they were alone.

She greeted him with a hug and a damp kiss to his cheek. "Donovan, *ciao!*"

"*Ciao*, Gianna! What brings you here?" he asked as he hugged her back.

"I came to steal you away. You don't have any classes this afternoon, right?"

Donovan nodded and smiled. "No, I don't. In fact, you caught me just in time. I was just about to head back to Maremma."

She grinned. "Then I'm glad I caught you."

Minutes later the couple was driving in a Mini Cooper convertible with the top down.

"Cute car," Donovan said as he threw an arm over the back of her seat. "Is this yours?"

"It's Carina and Graham's," she said. "I borrowed it so we could enjoy the sunshine." She tossed him a look and giggled. "There are some cars that large black men should never be seen in." She laughed.

Donovan laughed with her. "I assume a Mini Cooper is one of them?"

"That and a Volkswagen Beetle. The original ones!" She nodded as she took a narrow curb without slowing her speed. Donovan grabbed the dashboard to steady himself. His stomach jumped slightly.

"Hey, can you slow down?" he said, his voice raised.

Gianna laughed. "You're in safe hands, Donovan!" she said. "Very safe hands."

"I'm not so sure about that," he said as she took another curve without hitting brakes. He shook his head and laughed with her. "So where are we going?"

She gave him another look out of the corner of her eye. "The hot water springs!"

Chapter 10

The environment was relaxing and harmonious. Steam wafted off the surface of the thermal waters, the sulfurous spring nicely heated. The thermal waterfalls of Gorello were renowned for their therapeutic properties, immersion seeming to give healing and relaxation.

Donovan sat waist-deep in the open pools, his bare back against a rock formation, bathing in absolute tranquillity. Gianna sat beside him, her legs extended as she poked one foot and then another up above the warm waters. His hand rested against her upper thigh, gently kneading the soft skin, while hers caressed his forearm, a slow up and down stroke as her fingertips teased his flesh. Their gentle caresses were light and easy. The sensual exchange had them both heated, desire billowing in gusts as thick as the steam.

Donovan had read everything about the Tuscan region and he knew the science behind the geothermal activity underneath its surface, but to see it and experience the luxury was something else altogether. "This is wonderful," he murmured, his eyes closed as the waters flowed like a whirlpool around him. "This place has to be heaven-sent!"

Gianna nodded, leaning her head against his shoulders. "The old people will tell you that the springs were formed by lightning bolts thrown by the mythological deity Jupiter. During a violent quarrel with Saturn, the violent bolts thrown missed, causing the formations." She sat forward, turning to stare at him. "So the gods might have had something to do with it!"

Donovan chuckled. Opening his eyes, he met her stare. "Thank you," he said softly.

"For what?" she asked curiously.

"For this," he said as he leaned forward and pressed his mouth to hers.

Kissing Gianna had become his absolute favorite thing to do. The woman always tasted of peaches and honeysuckle, like the sweet Moscato blend that had become one of his favorite wines to indulge in. Her mouth was soft, a gentle cushion against his own, and at the first touch every nerve ending in his body fired with joy.

When he pulled away, breaking the connection, he was dazzled by the light that shimmered in her eyes and across her face. In that moment, everything was right in his small world. A tear suddenly misted at the edges of her eyes. His own widened, concern wafting across his face. "Baby, what's wrong?"

She shook her head. "Nothing. I'm just happy," she answered as she kissed him again. She moved onto her feet and held out her hand.

"So, where are we going now?" he asked as Gianna pulled him along behind her.

She threw him a quick look over her shoulder, the expression across her face saying everything Donovan needed to know.

As they pulled her car into the driveway, Signora Rossi stood in conversation with Signor D'Ascenzi and his wife, Pia. The three seniors were animated, laughing heartily. Their conversation came to a halt as they watched the couple exit the vehicle and move toward the door. Donovan and Gianna both waved heartily.

The two women cut their eyes at each other, all-knowing smirks across their faces. The two called Gianna's name, their tones sounding like admonishments, and the exchange between the three was quick and tense. But it was the hand gestures that gave away the tone of the conversation, a few overt and blatant.

Gianna tossed up her own hands as she laughed. *"Mamma mia,"* she muttered beneath her breath. She turned toward Donovan. "I'll wait for you inside," she whispered.

"Arrivederci!" she said as she gave them all a wave, professing that she had work she needed to finish.

The old man grinned, and Donovan felt himself blush ever so slightly as he and Gianna traded a look.

"It is good to see you again," Signor D'Ascenzi said.

Donovan shook his outstretched hand. "And you, too, sir!"

"My wife wanted to stop by and bring you some of her cookies," he said. "Signora Rossi put them on your counter."

"*Grazie!* I appreciate that."

The man gestured toward his wife. "Well, it's getting late and these two have been cackling like hens for over an hour now. My head needs a rest so I'm going home to put my feet up."

The two men shook hands one last time. "*Grazie,* Signora D'Ascenzi!" Donovan said as he leaned down to kiss first one cheek and then the other.

She said something in response and Signora Rossi laughed, the two women resuming their conversation. Donovan looked toward the other man for translation. Signor D'Ascenzi shook his head. "Those two say *la signorina* Martelli has kissed many frogs before finding herself a prince."

Donovan laughed as the man gestured for him to walk with him toward his truck. As they moved out of earshot, he gave Donovan a tap on the back and pointed toward the door Gianna had disappeared behind.

"She is a lot of woman, that one," he said approvingly, his voice a loud whisper. "And she doesn't look anything like a cow! So don't pay those two any mind. That one is a keeper!"

Donovan stood with Signora Rossi, the two watching as her guests disappeared down the road. He was suddenly conscious of the look the older woman was giving him, and then out of the blue she tapped him on his backside. His eyes widened in surprise.

"Non tenere una signora in attesa," she said as she pointed toward his front door before turning to her own unit and disappearing inside.

With a low chuckle, Donovan did what he was told and headed into his own space. The home was quiet save for the soft music that echoed out of the back bedroom. And dark, the only hint of light coming from the rear. A wave of nervous excitement suddenly flooded his spirit, moving him to shake in his shoes.

Gianna was sitting in the only chair in the room, a plush recliner newly upholstered in a soft brown fabric. She was barefoot, her shoes kicked off in the doorway and her legs pulled up beneath her buttocks. She sat with a yellow-lined notepad and an ink pen in her lap. As he entered, she looked up from the notes she was writing, meeting his dark gaze.

Donovan grinned, twisting his hands together anxiously.

"Finally got enough of their teasing?" Gianna asked.

He laughed. "They're definitely having fun at our expense. Signora Rossi just told me not to keep my lady waiting, then she goosed my left cheek and tapped my bottom."

Gianna laughed. "She's always been a little wild! After my mother died, she was a real help to my father. We fuss with each other, but I really do adore her."

"I get the impression she's fond of you, too."

The young woman gave him a slight shrug. The two exchanged glances, eyeing each other intently.

Donovan took a deep inhale of air, blowing it out slowly. "Would you like a glass of wine?" he asked, lifting the blanket of silence that had dropped between them.

She shook her head no as she let the notepad and pen slide to the floor. She moved onto her feet, saying nothing as she headed in the direction of his bathroom. With each step, she was coming out of her clothes, kicking off her skirt first and then pulling her top up and over her head.

In the doorway she turned, standing in nothing but a black lace G-string, the look in her eyes making her the perfect temptress. Her breasts were pert, standing at full attention. Her stomach was washboard flat, and there was just enough curve to her hips to give him pause. She slowly drew her hands through her hair, pulling the thick strands into a high topknot.

Stunned, Donovan felt his knees lock, his feet like lead weights against the hardwood floors. She looked delicious, and he found himself salivating with want. Every muscle in his body had hardened, each sinewy fiber like a rubber band pulled taut and ready to pop. With her boundaries and coyness nonexistent, he could do nothing but marvel at her boldness.

She crooked her finger and gestured. "Come wash my back," she said and then she turned, disappearing into the room.

Racing behind her, Donovan's own confidence never faltered as he dropped his pants, stepping out of them in the doorway. He pulled at his T-shirt, ripping the cotton fabric as she turned on the shower, pausing as the water warmed. The air around them had changed. The room was charged with excitement and a sensuality neither had experienced before. He moved swiftly to Gianna's side, brushing his finger across her bottom lip before capturing her mouth with his own, his hands sweeping in broad passes across her body.

Donovan kissed her lips, and then her neck, and the feel of his tongue on her skin made her breathing hitch, air catching deep in her chest. He gladly followed as she pulled him into the shower, dousing them both under the misted spray.

Gianna found herself wanting Donovan more than she had ever wanted anything or anyone before, and she suddenly questioned if she'd ever be able to tame the uncontrollable urges he'd suddenly stirred within her. She couldn't stop her heart from racing, the pounding beat thunderous as he began to kiss her breasts, suckling her nipples. He nibbled and teased the chocolate protrusions, making her moan as he licked around each hardened nub in turn, intensifying the wetness between her thighs.

The sweet spot between Gianna's legs throbbed, and the moist feeling exposed the yearnings and anticipation that suddenly consumed her. She was starved for Donovan's touch, and the craving was so intense she suddenly feared never coming back from the ecstasy she'd fallen into. Her desperation for more had suddenly become unbearable.

So lost in the warmth of each other, neither knew when or how they'd made it from the shower to Donovan's bed, the bedspread snatched away and strewn to the floor, the sheets damp from the moisture of their skin. They danced in perfect sync across the bed top, moving from corner to corner as they explored each other's bodies, gentle caresses followed by soft kisses. Both licked and nipped and teased and taunted the other until they were both breathing heavily, gasps and moans resounding through the room.

Gianna clasped the back of his head as his tongue explored her mouth, grazing the line of teeth as he playfully dueled with her tongue. His mouth trailed damp kisses up and down the length of her body, and then he paused, blowing warm breath against her inner thighs. His fingers teased the line of her intimate folds, her feminine moisture coating the tips. Her hips lifted off the bed, her body moving of its own volition as she pressed herself into his palm.

And then he tossed her a sexy smirk just before pressing his face between her legs, the intimate kiss causing her to cry out with pleasure. She clutched his ears as he reached for heaven with each decadent lick. It was more than she could bear as her body convulsed with pleasure, wave after wave of hedonistic delight exploding through every vein.

As she rode each swell, her emotions surging with a vengeance, Donovan quickly sheathed himself with a condom and entered her swiftly. He clutched her hair, his fingers tangled in the thick curls as he plunged his body into hers over and over again. His pace was rapid, each thrust of his hips harder and harder until she shouted his name over and over again into his chest.

Gianna screamed and Donovan screamed with her, muffling their cries as he pressed his mouth to hers. They orgasmed together, over and over again, lost in the wealth of emotion that had taken hold of them and refused to let go. Minutes later they were snuggled tightly together, their breaths syncing on each inhale and exhale, settling into each other's heartbeats until sleep sent them both to their dreams.

It was almost noon when Donovan woke from a deep slumber. He and Gianna had spent most of the night wide-awake, making love again and again. Their loving had been sweet and gentle, then Gianna had taken their intimate connection south, her ministrations dirty and hard. He'd lost count of the number of times she'd brought him to orgasm, each one like an out-of-body experience. The last time had been back in the shower just before they'd passed out in his bed, the morning sun beginning to peek through the window.

He stretched his body lengthwise and yawned as he rolled against the mattress. Reaching for Gianna, he found the bed empty. He jumped, startled to find her gone. The barest hint of disappointment billowed through his spirit. Rising, he moved into the bathroom. When his face was washed and his teeth polished to a bright white shine, he headed for his kitchen.

Gianna was seated at the kitchen table wearing one of his dress shirts. One knee was pulled to her chest, the other leg dangling casually off the wooden stool. She sat writing in her notepad, her attention focused on the words flying out of her pen. She was so absorbed in her work, she didn't notice him until he'd eased to her side and gently planted a warm kiss against her neck.

She purred softly. "Hmm! *Buon pomeriggio, come stai?*"

He kissed her again. "Good afternoon, and I would have been better if you had been in the bed when I woke. But thank you for asking."

She giggled as she tilted her head to kiss his lips. "Sorry about that, but I sometimes have to follow my muse when it leads me."

He nodded in understanding. "Something smells really good."

She nodded. "Signora Rossi left breakfast. There's fresh pastry in the oven, muesli and yogurt in the icebox, and I can pour you a cup of cappuccino whenever you're ready."

"I can do it," he said. "You keep writing."

"I actually think I'm done," she said as she laid down her pen. "I'll type up my notes when I get back home." She took a sip of the fresh coffee he'd poured for her.

Donovan moved from the counter to join her at the dining table. He came to an abrupt halt, spying an easel and oversize blank canvas sitting in the corner of the room. He pointed with his index finger. "What's that?"

She tossed a quick glance in the direction he pointed. "I thought you could paint," she answered, her own finger pointing to the supplies that rested on the coffee table. "I bought oils, watercolors, acrylics and a ton of brushes. There's also extra canvas, canvas board and some other stuff the man at the art store said you might like."

"Wow!" he exclaimed once, and then again. "Wow!"

She smiled. "You only live once and it's something you wanted to try, so I think now is as good a time as any."

He took a seat beside her, taking a moment to sip his coffee. "Before I forget again, how do you know Sophie Mugabe? I saw you two talking yesterday."

Gianna looked up to meet his curious gaze. "What makes you think I know her?"

"I saw you two talking yesterday," he repeated facetiously.

She rolled her eyes. "Last year we dated the same man. He was an English professor there at the university."

"At the same time?"

"Unfortunately. He wasn't honest about dating the two of us. We both found out when she showed up unannounced at his apartment and walked in on him and me unexpectedly."

Donovan eyed her with a raised brow. "I'm sure that was interesting!"

"There might have been some words exchanged and a punch or two thrown. It wasn't pretty, and definitely not one of my proudest moments."

His eyes widened. "Now that sounds like a Jerry Springer fiasco."

"Jerry who?"

"I guess I'm not the only one who needs to brush up on my pop culture." He laughed.

She narrowed her gaze on him.

"It's not important," he said, meeting her stare. "So what happened to the guy?"

"After they wired his jaw, he moved to Florence. At least that's what I was told."

"You broke his jaw?"

She tossed up her hands, a smile twitching at the edge of her mouth. "Why does everyone think that I had to be the one to break his jaw? Why couldn't she have broken his jaw?"

"Did Professor Mugabe break the man's jaw?"

"No. But that's not the point."

Donovan laughed. "So, that means you have a serious right hook. You are just full of surprises!"

"I reacted in the heat of the moment."

"And Sophie?"

"She's still holding a grudge like I purposely dated a man she was interested in."

He suddenly thought back to his last conversation with the woman.

"What?" Gianna asked, eyeing him curiously.

They locked gazes. "You might be," he said with a slight shrug.

Gianna stared for a brief moment, then shook her head, understanding washing over her expression. "So that's why she got so heated when I told her I was there to see you!"

"She got heated?"

"Royally! Why didn't you tell me you and she had something going on?" She leaned back in her seat and crossed her arms over her chest. "Because I do not play second to any other woman!"

Donovan laughed. "There's nothing going on between the two of us, and you are my one and only."

"But she likes you?"

"She does."

"And she wants to be in a relationship with you?"

He nodded. "But I told her that couldn't happen because I only see her as a friend and colleague, nothing more."

She hesitated for a split second. "Don't trust her. She's one of those women who puts the *fury* in 'hell hath no fury.'"

"I don't think..." he started, before being interrupted.

"David had a stellar reputation at the university. Granted, our little incident didn't bode well for him, but me breaking his jaw was the least of his problems. I made him hurt for breaking my heart, but she set out to destroy him. By the time she was done, he wasn't able to teach. At least not anywhere here in Italy."

"It couldn't have been that bad," he said, his tone hopeful.

Gianna shook her head. "It was worse than bad. Do not, I repeat, do not trust her."

The sound of rushing water suddenly bore down against the rooftop. The weatherman's prediction of bad weather with torrential rains had finally materialized. Donovan rose and moved to the front door, staring outside. Gianna eased her body against his, her thin arms wrapping around his waist as she looked past him.

"There goes my picnic lunch down by the beach," Donovan said.

"We were picnicking today?"

"I thought it would be a nice idea."

"We can picnic here instead. While you paint my portrait."

He nodded and smiled. "We can definitely do that."

She squeezed him, tightening her arms around his torso. "We can also go back to bed," she said as she released her grip and turned, moving back toward the bedroom. As she disappeared through the doorway, she tossed him a seductive wink over her shoulder as she let that dress shirt fall to the floor, her naked backside beckoning him to follow.

Chapter 11

As Donovan moved into the room, Gianna lay sprawled out on the bed, her naked body posed seductively atop the pillows. Moving to the foot of the bed, he stood staring down at her, marveling at just how beautiful she was.

Gianna lifted her torso upward, her weight resting on her elbows and forearms. A pointed toe slowly trailed the length of her other leg as she pulled her knee to her chest and pushed her leg down again. As he eyed her, lust searing in his gaze, her nipples hardened and she couldn't suppress the shiver that quickened her breath and raced the length of her spine. Her pulse rate soared.

Donovan lifted one knee and then the other, crawling onto the mattress top. He grabbed her foot and pulled her toward him, the gesture possessive and demanding as he straddled his body above hers.

Gianna reached up to wrap her arms around his neck, pulling him against her as she kissed his lips. This time there was nothing gentle about the connection, not like the many times before. It was rough and fiercely passionate as she thrust her tongue toward the back of his throat. She could barely stifle a moan as he drew her closer to deepen the embrace.

Lips and tongues were moving rapidly, both tasting like the strawberries and grapes they'd shared over breakfast. Donovan's kisses moved from her mouth down to her neck as he nibbled at the soft flesh, leaving a love bite against her skin. He lowered his head to slowly draw his tongue across one breast as he pinched the other lightly with his thumb and forefinger.

Gianna inhaled swiftly, the sharp intake of breath moving him to lift his eyes to her face. Rapture painted her expression, her eyes closed and her head thrown back against her neck. He resumed his salacious ministrations, his hands traveling slowly across her stomach and downward. The trek was teasing, fingers kneading and massaging until he was able to slip his large hand between her thighs, two fingers dipping into her sweet spot. She parted her legs to allow him easier access, and he dragged a fingernail across her slit and the pad of his thumb tapped at her clit, the pressure against her love button moving her to moan. He repeated the action again and again until Gianna was fighting to catch her breath, her moans like the sweetest balm.

He dipped his fingers deeper, penetrating her opening. The gesture met with copious fluid that made the transition seamless. He slowly thrust one finger and then three, furiously rubbing the sensitive spot until she was close to orgasm. He felt her tense, her muscles beginning to contract around his thrusting fingers. And then she cried out, tipping off the edge of ecstasy.

The two made love for hours, over and over again, the entire weekend lost in Donovan's bed. Donovan couldn't fathom any intimate connection being sweeter. He loved her intensely, every fiber in his being needing her. Wanting her like he'd never wanted anyone else. And when the sky darkened that last night, his manhood throbbing like a piston between her legs, Gianna whispered in his ear, the words *I love you* echoing around the room.

Franco stood at the kitchen stove, the ingredients for a tomato-based sauce resting atop the counters. When Gianna entered the home, he paused to stare as he reached for a dishcloth to swipe his hands clean.

"Buongiorno, papà," she chimed as she kissed his cheek, then took a seat at the counter.

Her father nodded. "Welcome home. I was starting to think that I was going to have to send the troops out to find you."

Gianna reached for a stalk of celery, pulling the vegetable to her lips. "Please, like we don't both know that Signora Rossi was keeping you posted on my whereabouts."

Her father laughed. "She may have told me something. She knows I'm a concerned father!"

"That's why she told you *everything*! I'll never understand why you two never married."

"We never married because I have only loved one woman in my life, and that was your mother. Felice Rossi is a sweet person and a good friend, but she could never hold a candle to my Angela." His gaze shifted as he fell into the memories of the woman who was gone. He changed the subject. "So, things are good with this young man of yours?"

She nodded. "Things are very good! Donovan's..." She paused, her eyes shifting from side to side. She suddenly looked back up at her father. "I love him, *papà*," she said, voicing aloud what had been in her heart for a while.

Her father smiled. "He's a good man. I like him, and I know he'll do right by you. I look forward to our becoming friends. And I'll be even happier when I can call him son. I will be able to call him son, right? And soon?"

Gianna laughed. "I don't know about that, *papà*! We'll have to see."

"Have you talked about it? About what you want out of the relationship?"

"We're still learning each other. I'm not trying to rush things."

"You spent the weekend with that man. I think you've already rushed things."

Color flushed Gianna's cheeks a deep shade of red. This time she was the one to change the subject. "Where are Carina and Graham?"

"They went to visit his parents. They'll be back at the end of the week."

Nodding, she rose from her seat. "If you need me

I'll be in my office. I have some work I need to catch up on."

Her father turned back to his sauce. "Let's walk the vineyards later. I want to see if the rain did any damage," he called after her. "And we can finish our conversation about your new boyfriend's intentions!"

Donovan couldn't remember ever being so happy. Waking next to Gianna had spoiled him, everything about their time together confirming what he wanted for his future. Their future together. When they hadn't been making love, they'd talked, some of the conversations mindless ramblings, others intense debates. And he'd painted, testing the waters for a retirement hobby. He'd approached the task with reservation until Gianna had pushed him to just let go and let whatever came to him be. The beginnings of a few projects had him excited to try again. And painting a trail of flowers across Gianna's butt had excited him.

Once or twice they'd simply fallen into the quiet, enjoying how the other breathed. It had been easy to be with her, and even when she had him dancing naked in the middle of his kitchen, a protruding erection bouncing in time to some dance tune, his comfort level had been at an all-time high. Gianna had a way of pushing him to let go and do things he would not necessarily do if left to his own devices. Her devil-may-care attitude had transcended his conservative one, and together they meshed nicely.

He hadn't wanted to take her home, and driving her back to the winery had been heartbreaking. They'd parted with a gentle kiss, Gianna promising to catch up with him the minute his day was through. Together they were electricity and fire, and with her gone he could feel the energy that filled him waiting to be re-ignited.

The hour-long ride to the school allowed him to pull himself together, to seriously think about the two of them and where they might be headed. Gianna made his heart sing, and he was past ready to fully commit to her and the relationship. The dynamics of how they'd come together and their brief bump in the road spoke to where they both were in their lives and where they wanted to be. Both had been searching for something that was missing, something neither had any idea they'd needed. Until they found each other. They complemented each other, as both had been whole to start with. It was the perfect icing on some very sweet cake!

Pulling into the school's parking lot and exiting his car, Donovan practically skipped to the front door. He anticipated having a very good day, the excitement gleaming in his eyes. He wasn't expecting Dr. Northway, the school's director, to meet him at the door.

"Dr. Northway, *buongiorno!*"

The man nodded, a quick snap of his neck and head. "Dr. Boudreaux, if you'll join me in my office, *per favore.*" His tone was brusque, almost abrasive, his expression stone-cold. He turned abruptly and headed down the hallway, expecting Donovan to follow behind him.

As he did, Donovan suddenly got the distinct impression that his good mood was about to be shot to hell.

* * *

Gianna slammed her phone down against the desktop. She'd been trying to reach Donovan since lunchtime, and he hadn't returned any of her calls. She'd been half tempted to ride down to his cottage, but she didn't want to come across as that type of woman: obsessive, jealous and untrusting. Because she was none of those things, and never had been. And she didn't want to think he was that kind of man, done once he'd bedded her. Because she knew he was better than that, but he hadn't answered his phone or returned any of her calls since saying goodbye and wishing her a good day.

Her intuition told her something was amiss, and she was worried because she knew in her heart Donovan would have wanted to talk with her as much as she wanted to speak with him. Something or someone was keeping Donovan from at least sending her a text message. From whispering the words he'd whispered in her ear over the weekend. From wanting her to know how much he loved and desired her.

The weekend had been flawless. She'd given herself to him without hesitation, not an ounce of doubt about their commitment to each other. From day one, Donovan had said and done all the right things. He'd been sweet and caring, wooing her slowly. His actions had mirrored his words, and she'd known beyond any and all doubts that he was the one for her. Their relationship was sheer perfection!

Outside the air had cooled nicely, and the barest sliver of a moon hung in the dark sky. A gentle breeze blew through the open window behind her. Gianna jumped from her seat, feeling as if the winds had whispered to her. Something was wrong, and she had to figure out what it was. She would start at the cottage, she thought, and if he wasn't there, she would drive to the university and make someone there let her in to search for him.

Just as she reached for her coat and keys, there was a knock on her office door. Pulling it open, she was surprised to find her father standing on the other side.

"Where are you off to?" he questioned, his eyes dropping to the keys in her hand.

"I was going to go see Donovan. I haven't been able to reach him."

Her father nodded. "Probably because your young man has been in the vineyard talking with me."

"He's here?" Her eyes widened.

Franco nodded. "He's been here for a couple of hours now. I was outside when he drove up, and I could see something was on his mind, so I made him come help me check the vineyards. It gave me a chance to talk to him about his intentions."

Her eyes widened even more. "You didn't?"

Her father laughed. "I most certainly did. Now, I'm going to go grab a quick shower. Donovan is prepping the pasta. We should be ready to eat in about thirty minutes."

Gianna tossed her keys aside and dropped her coat to the floor. Her father was still laughing heartily as she pushed past him, headed for the kitchen.

Donovan stood at the counter chopping vegetables. His brow was furrowed in thought as he sliced and diced tomatoes picked from her father's gardens. Three large steaks were marinating in a glass dish, and a pot of water was just beginning to simmer for the fettuccine.

Gianna paused in the doorway, staring. He wore her father's apron, the one given to him by her mother. In all her years, she'd never known her father to let anyone else wear the treasured garment. Clearly, she thought, Donovan had made quite an impression.

"*Ciao*, Donovan," she said as she entered the room. She moved to his side to kiss his cheek.

Donovan turned to meet her lips instead, his mouth dancing easily over hers. *"Ciao, bella!"*

"I was worried about you."

"I'm sorry. I would have called you back, but your father..."

She held up a hand, stalling the rest of his comment. "Say no more. I know my father," she said with a smile.

Her eyes flitted over his face, and she could see the stress that tensed the muscles. "What's wrong?"

Donovan shook his head, fighting to pull a smile onto his face. "Let's talk about it later," he said, turning to toss minced garlic and onion in the pan with the tomatoes.

"Let's talk about it now," she said as she eased to his other side, clasping her hand over his.

He met the look she gave him as he relinquished the spoon, leaving her to stir his sauce. He took a deep inhale before answering. "Dr. Northway met me at the door this morning and called me to his office."

"The school's director?"

He nodded. "A female student has filed a formal complaint against me for inappropriate conduct. She claims I asked for a sexual favor in exchange for giving her a passing grade. She says that when she told me no, I threatened to fail her. I was given the choice to hand in my resignation and leave the school quietly or to appear before a disciplinary review committee next week and risk being terminated and having my work visa pulled permanently."

"And you told him you were going to fight the allegations, correct?"

He nodded. "I did. Either way, though, just the hint of any kind of impropriety could kill my career."

"You do know that this is all Sophie Mugabe's doing. I warned you!"

"I know that she supposedly received the complaint and passed it on to the administration. So she's had a hand in it somehow."

"We're not going to let her get away with this."

Donovan sighed and kissed Gianna one more time. "I want you to know that I didn't do this," he said.

"I know that."

"Your father wasn't so sure. He asked a lot of questions."

"He just does that. It's a father thing. He was sure."

"How do you know?"

She tapped the gray cotton fabric embroidered with the word *Chef* across the front. Donovan looked confused.

"My mother gave him this. He's never let anyone wear it. He was sure." She looped her arms around his neck and hugged him tightly.

Tears misted Donovan's eyes as he hugged her back.

When he'd come to the winery, wanting Gianna to re-assure him that everything was going to be all right, he hadn't given any thought to what he would say to her father. Franco had been in the front yard when he'd pulled in, and when the patriarch had commanded Don-ovan to join him in the vineyards, he'd gone reluctantly.

For the first half hour all they'd talked about were grapes and the best grapes for the best wines. Then the old man had asked him what was wrong, and Dono-van was suddenly giving him a detailed blow-by-blow recap of his meeting with the school's administrator and being temporarily removed from his teaching position. Franco had listened intently, allowing Donovan to spill until he didn't have anything else to say.

"So, did you do it?" the old man had asked him.

Donovan had shaken his head steadfastly. "No, sir. I didn't. I'm not that kind of man."

"Why would this young woman say such a thing?"

"I honestly don't know. I did reject her advances, so I think she's trying to get revenge. But I would never compromise my integrity like that. And I would *never* disrespect Gianna like that."

Franco had nodded, then just like that, he'd changed the subject. "Has my daughter talked to you about her mother at all?"

He'd shaken his head. "No, sir. She always changes the subject when I bring her up."

Franco gestured for him to take a seat, and the two rested on one of the wooden benches in the garden. Gi-anna's father leaned forward, resting his arms against his thighs as he thought about the history that would soon be the story he would tell. Minutes passed before he finally cleared his throat and spoke.

"Gianna was devastated when her mother died. Both girls were, but it hit Gianna harder. She and my Angela were together when that blood vessel burst in Angela's head. Gianna had gotten into trouble with Sister Mary Frances at the school. Gianna was always smarter than the average bear, and she had no problems making sure you knew it. She was bored in class and smart-mouthed the nun, and they called her mother. Angela and I had already decided that Gianna needed to be moved up a grade, and so Angela went down to the school to talk to them about doing that. They were waiting for Carina to get out of class, and then my girls were all going to go get gelato. She and her mother were sitting together, and then Angela just slumped over and was gone. For years, Gianna blamed herself. She thought that if she had just been a good girl, then Angela wouldn't have been stressed. And if she hadn't been stressed, she wouldn't have had the aneurysm. I sometimes think she still blames herself."

The man swiped a tear from his eye as he continued his story. "Angela was an exchange student doing a semester at the university when we met. I was much older and already running the winery. Mutual friends introduced us, and I thought she was the most beautiful vision I'd ever laid eyes on. Everything about her was warm. Warm brown eyes, warm brown skin and the warmest, sweetest spirit of any woman I'd ever known. My girls are just like their mother!

"Angela had a roommate at the university. A girl

named Gina Puccini. Gina's father was a government official in Nice. Gina had a crush on me, and she wasn't happy about me liking Angela. She wasn't very nice to Angela when she found out we were seeing each other. She tried everything she could think of to break us up. She lied and said that Angela was seeing other boys at the school. Wouldn't give her my messages. Would show up at group events and try to monopolize my attention. She made things very difficult for the two of us." Franco sighed heavily as the memories flooded his spirit. He paused briefly before continuing.

"One day I had planned to take Angela to dinner, and I went to pick her up. I arrived early because she hadn't gotten back from class yet, but Gina was there in the room. We exchanged words, and I told her I would never love anyone the way I loved Angela. She stormed out, and I thought it was over. Minutes later the police were there asking me questions. Gina was down the hall crying, her clothes torn, claiming that I had assaulted her. When Angela arrived, they were taking me away in handcuffs.

"Angela saved my life and my business. Had I been convicted, it would have been all over. But she did everything she could to discredit Gina's story. And Angela went up against Gina's father, who was determined to see me pay for what his daughter said I did. It was not a good time.

"Gina finally admitted that she lied, but the stigma of people thinking I might be a rapist followed me for a good long while. Some even said that my Angela couldn't do better than a man like me because she was a black woman, and only a rapist would want a woman like her. But Angela never let any of that keep us from loving each other and our girls."

"I'm so sorry that you two had to go through that."

Franco chuckled. "Me, too! And in all of our years together, my Angela never once asked me if I had done it. Her faith in me was unwavering. She loved me that much."

Donovan nodded, reflecting on the man's words.

"My Gianna, she loves you that much, Mr. Boudreaux," Franco added matter-of-factly.

Donovan shifted his eyes toward the man, the two locking gazes.

"I expect we'll be having a wedding soon, no? I won't have my daughter's good reputation sullied. These old bats in the village would love to talk badly about her."

Donovan nodded, a smile pulling at his full lips. "Yes, sir. I hope so."

"Soon, before the Carusos' daughter comes sniffing around for a husband!"

Donovan laughed. "No worries there, sir! I will never love anyone like I love my Gianna," he said.

Franco nodded his approval. "We should prepare dinner. I've worked up an appetite. Do you cook?"

As Donovan thought back to his time with his future father-in-law, he hugged Gianna close, grateful that she and her family had come into his life. Together, they were a formidable force to be reckoned with. Every ounce of worry suddenly subsided, dissipating like water on a hot pan.

Franco pulled the duo from their reverie. Moving into the room, he smiled as he eyed them wrapped comfortably around each other. He cleared his throat. "If burning the gravy is how you prove to me you can cook, you're doing a mighty fine job, son! A mighty fine job!"

Chapter 12

Gianna woke with a start, something dark chasing her in her dreams. Relief came the instant she opened her eyes and spied Donovan slumbering sweetly beside her. She eased her leg from under his and lifted herself up against the headboard to stare down at him.

He lay on his back with his legs splayed open, one hand cupping his privates. His head was rolled to the side, his face pressed between two pillows. He snored softly, the exhale ending in a low whistle. Watching him made Gianna smile.

After dining with her father, she'd followed Donovan back to his home. They'd been there ever since, only leaving once to meet with Gianna's attorney. Despite his reluctance, she'd insisted he needed legal representation. He'd argued the point, insisting that he hadn't done anything wrong. But as her lawyer had pointed out, it would come down to being his word against Alessandra's if they couldn't find any proof to refute the girl's claims.

Signora Rossi had fed them quite a few times, her maternal instincts kicking into full swing. She'd been fawning over them both, always squeezing his cheeks, and then hers, as the moment moved her. The older woman still fussed, giving Gianna a hard time, and she wouldn't have had it any other way. As she thought about them, Gianna admitted that one of her most favorite moments was Donovan and Signora Rossi practicing Italian and English together. He was learning quickly—their elderly friend not so much.

Donovan shifted his body, turning his back to her. He seemed to settle down, his breathing easy, and then he rolled back again, his arms outstretched as he reached for her. Once his hands touched her skin, his fingers warm against her thighs, he curled himself close against her. The nearness of him made Gianna smile.

He suddenly lifted his head to stare at her, his eyes thin slits as he struggled to focus. "Are you okay?" he mumbled.

She nodded, her voice a low whisper as she snuggled back down against him, wiggling her butt against his crotch. "I'm fine, *amore mio*. Go back to sleep."

And he did, closing his eyes and drifting back into his dreams.

Gianna had only been asleep for a few hours when Donovan's hands trailing across her body pulled her from her rest. His fingertips glided across her stomach to her breasts and back, dipping low to gently pull at the swirls of hair between her legs. His touch tickled, and she could feel herself smiling in her sleep.

His warm breath blew gently against the back of her neck, and a full, hammer-hard erection pressed like steel against her butt. She felt him moving slowly against her, a gentle back-and-forth gyration as he used her body to massage himself.

Donovan whispered, "Are you asleep?"

Gianna chuckled softly. "How can I sleep with you teasing me like that?" she purred.

"Sorry," he apologized. "This woke me up." He rotated his hips against her a second time, the bulge between his legs like steel.

Gianna giggled softly. "That feels like it might be a problem. I think we should do something about it," she whispered in reply.

He nodded, his head bobbing against a pile of pillows. "I think so."

Gianna suddenly pulled her body from his, spinning around to face him. His eyes opened wider as she began to kiss her way down the length of his torso, pressing her mouth to that spot beneath his chin, his broad chest and the well of his belly button, until she'd crawled down low beneath the sheets.

His erection stretched full and wide with desire. He was nicely endowed, and as she took him into the palm of her hand, his organ twitched with anticipation. Donovan sucked in a large gulp of air and held it, every muscle in his body clenched tightly.

Without hesitating, Gianna stuck out her tongue and

lightly licked the tip of his member. His whole body jumped, nerve endings firing rapidly. He blew out the breath he'd been holding and gasped out loud, his voice ringing through the early-morning air.

Gianna swirled her tongue over the head, then licked up and down his shaft, even tonguing his testicles. Donovan groaned with pure, unadulterated pleasure, her touch taking him right to the edge of ecstasy.

She sucked him in as she fisted the base, her hand and mouth moving in perfect sync. It was more than Donovan had anticipated, and he could feel himself giving in to the sensations that were sweeping through his body.

He moaned as he stroked the top of her head, his fingers tangling in the thick curls. "So…so…good!" he stammered, the words coming with a raspy breath. He started to move his hips faster and faster, pushing himself in and out of her mouth. She clutched his butt with both hands to control his ministrations, her own body becoming heated, moisture pooling in her private crevices. She squeezed and manipulated the taut flesh, bringing him close to orgasm then pulling back until he couldn't hold on. With one final shove past her lips, Donovan exploded in her mouth, wave after wave of pleasure surging with a vengeance. "Oh, sweet Jesus!" he cried. *"Mio Dio!"*

Gianna savored the taste of him. She continued to suck and lick his organ as his body spasmed over and over again. When she finally pulled him from her mouth, she tilted her head back and swallowed.

Donovan was completely spent, his entire being feel-

ing as if he'd gone through ten rounds. He pulled her
into his arms and nuzzled his face into her neck. He
could feel the hands of slumber beginning to pull him
back into its clutches. Unable to fight it, he whispered
her name, promising to return the gesture before the
new day was done.

Carina burst into Gianna's office, storming through
the door like a hurricane on steroids. Eyes wide, Gianna looked up from the chapter she was trying to finish, surprised to see her twin.

"What's wrong?" Gianna asked, a quiver of nervous
energy like a shock wave through her system.

Carina dropped into the upholstered seat in front
of her sister's desk. "What are we going to do about
Donovan?"

"Excuse me?"

"Donovan. What are we going to do?"

"What are you talking about, Sissy?" Gianna leaned
forward in her seat.

"Everyone is talking about Donovan and some girl
from the school. They're saying she claims that he tried
to take advantage of her and that he threatened her. It's
all kinds of messy!"

Gianna blew a low sigh. "I know. He's hired Dante
to represent him."

"Your attorney, Dante?"

She nodded. "Donovan has to defend himself before
a university review board next week. There was no way
I was going to let him do that on his own. His Italian's
not that good yet!"

Carina nodded, blowing out a sigh of relief. "Dante's good. That's good! But what are *we* going to do? Because we can't let this girl get away with telling these lies."

Gianna smiled. "So you do believe him? You know he didn't do it?"

Her sister's expression was incredulous. "Of course I know he didn't do it! That is definitely not the kind of man I would fix you up with."

Gianna moved around the desk to give her sister a hug. The two held tight to each other, tears misting in both their eyes.

Carina shook herself free from the embrace. "You still haven't answered my question."

Gianna shrugged. "I don't know. It's been driving me crazy trying to figure out what's going on and how I can fix it. I do know that Mugabe woman is behind it, though."

Carina's gaze narrowed. "That professor who was dating your ex-boyfriend? Or were you dating her boyfriend?" She giggled. "You're referring to that third leg in that little ménage à trois of yours last year?"

She nodded. "One and the same. She's interested in Donovan and he rejected her. I know she's going after him to get even with him, and me."

"Then we're definitely about to burst her bubble!"

There was a pause as Gianna stood staring at her sister. Her smile slid slowly across her face. "What do you have in mind, Sissy?"

Carina grinned. "I think we need to take a ride."

* * *

Donovan sighed deeply into his cell phone receiver. On the other end, his mother was talking a mile a minute, voicing her disapproval and unhappiness in one big breath. He'd given up trying to ease her concerns, figuring once she got it out of her system they'd be able to move on. But it was starting to look as if she wasn't going to get over it anytime soon.

"I knew you going to Italy wasn't going to be a good idea."

"Mom, this has nothing to do with me being here in Italy. You know how these young people are today. They have an air of entitlement, no sense of responsibility and they don't concern themselves with how their bad behavior will impact other people. Unfortunately, this young woman is just plain messy. She's told a bold-faced lie, and now I have to deal with the consequences. But you and I both know the truth will always prevail."

"Well, I'm coming," Katherine said. "As soon as your father and I can get a flight out, we'll be there."

Donovan could hear his father fussing in the background.

"We don't need to go to Italy! That boy is grown. He knows how to handle his own business, Katherine!"

"I'm not talking to you, Senior Boudreaux!" Katherine fussed back. "I just know we're not going to let our baby go through this mess by himself. Now call Mason and see how soon we can get on one of his planes, please! And then call Katrina and have her recommend a good attorney over there."

Donovan chuckled, shaking his head. "Mom, please, you don't need to worry. We've got this handled."

"Donovan James Boudreaux, don't you tell me not to worry! I'm the parent in this relationship. It's my job to worry!"

He let out a gust of air past his full lips. "Yes, ma'am."

"Besides, it'll give me a chance to meet this young lady you've been seeing. Your brothers have told me a lot about her."

"You're really going to like her. Gianna's wonderful, Mom!"

"You haven't known her that long. You don't know what she is," his mother said matter-of-factly.

"I know her, Mom, and I love her," he said softly. "And you need to trust me on this."

There was a lengthy pause, and Donovan could visualize the expression across his mother's face: her gaze narrowed, her lips pursed and her jaw tight. He waited for the sharp comment that would remind him once again of his place as the child in their relationship. He knew that he and his siblings could be eighty years old, and their parents would still be reminding them of the respect that was their due.

He took a deep breath. "I promise, Mom, you won't be disappointed," he concluded.

Katherine sniffled, then cleared her throat. "You have never been a disappointment. Your father and I have always been proud of you. We love you, son."

Donovan smiled. "Thank you," he said. "And I love you both, too."

"Senior's on the phone with Mason now. He'll send you our flight information as soon as we know."

Donovan chuckled. "I guess that means I didn't change your mind, huh?"

His mother laughed with him. "I don't know why you even wasted your time trying!"

Gianna was seated in the student quad waiting for her sister to return. Around her, college kids were enjoying the afternoon weather, lounging on the grass and benches as they discussed courses, the opposite sex, music and a host of topics that had their voices ringing with laughter through the air.

She still didn't have a clue what Carina had up her sleeve, but she knew enough about her sister to be just a teensy bit concerned. She'd lost count of all the stunts her twin would pull that had gotten them both in trouble over the years.

She caught sight of her out of the corner of her eye, her look-alike moving in her direction. She carried a tray of food and was walking with two young women Gianna didn't recognize. She stared as they approached, Carina giggling with them as if she was in her teens again. Gianna smiled brightly as the trio joined her at the picnic table where she sat.

"Ciao!" she said brightly, nodding slightly.

"Hello!" one of the other women responded as she helped Carina with the food.

Carina pointed as she took a seat beside her sister. "This is Alessandra and Simona. They are both math majors here at the university. And this is my sister, Gianna. She's a literature major."

Alessandra glanced from one to the other. "You two look like twins!" she exclaimed.

Carina laughed. "Everybody says that, but she is older than I am."

Gianna threw Carina a look, ignoring the smirk on her sibling's face. "I'm not that much older," she said with a giggle.

Alessandra nodded. "You should not cut your hair," she said to Carina before shifting her gaze to Gianna. "I love your long curls!"

Gianna smiled. "I wish it was straight like yours. Your hair is beautiful!"

Alessandra tossed her blond locks over one shoulder and then the other, smiling brightly.

Simona eyed her warily. "You actually look familiar. Where do I know you from?"

Gianna shrugged. "Maybe we had a class together?"

"Or maybe you saw her on the back of a book," Carina said facetiously. "She has that kind of face." She pursed her own lips and winked. "So do I, now that you mention it!"

Alessandra giggled. "Simona's not big on reading. I'm sure it couldn't have been a book!"

Gianna laughed, joining in the giggles.

Carina passed her sister a sandwich and a canned soda. "Alessandra says these are the best, so I had to try them," she said as she took a bite of her own sandwich, a meatball wedge laden with cheese. She nodded. "Oh, they are really good!"

Alessandra's head bobbed. "Not as good as the ones you can get in Grosseto, but very close! Grosseto has the best meatballs, I think."

The four women sat enjoying their meal, the conversation casual as Carina made nice with her new best friends. Gianna marveled at how easily her sister manipulated the truth, the other two women actually believing they, too, were students. She was giggling over the boys and making plans to join them on a weekend trip to Rome. Anyone else would have thought they'd been best friends since forever, instead of new acquaintances chatting for the very first time.

Gianna was less inclined to be so nice. Despite Carina's efforts to pull her into the conversation, wanting her to play pretend right along with her, all Gianna wanted was to smack the smug look off Alessandra's face. The moment Carina had said she was a math major, Gianna had known who she was. Knowing the allegations the young woman had made against Donovan, the lies she had told, had Gianna seeing red, and it was difficult not to just punch the girl in her mouth. Her eyes skated back and forth between Alessandra and Simona as she forced her lips into a smile.

Carina swiped a paper napkin across her mouth. She locked eyes with her sister, her brows lifted. "I was telling them before about your problem with your professor. How he led you on, and then you found out he was married."

Simona shook her head from side to side. *"Gli uomini sono tutti i cani!"* she muttered.

Carina laughed. "Yes, men are all dogs!" she said in agreement.

Gianna tried not to let her emotions show on her face. "He broke my heart," she muttered, feigning heartbreak.

"So what happened?" Alessandra asked. She shifted forward in her seat, resting her elbows against the table and her head in her hands.

Gianna took a deep breath. "We were dating for months. We traveled together, and it was perfect. Then one day I was at his apartment, and we were making love when I hear the bedroom door open and this woman is suddenly screaming at us!"

Simona slapped a hand over her mouth. "She walked in on you?"

Gianna nodded. "We were naked in his bed. It was horrible!" she exclaimed, her tone exaggerated.

Carina laughed. "He was bottom up and head down. I'm sure it was quite a sight!"

The other two women laughed heartily.

Gianna cut a look at her sister. Amusement danced in Carina's eyes. "It wasn't pretty," she said.

Simona nodded. "You should do like Alessandra. She always gets even."

"You waste too much time holding a grudge. Get even and move on. That's my motto," Alessandra noted.

"Alessandra had a boyfriend who cheated. She got him drunk, set him up with the police chief's daughter, then posted pictures of the two online. The police chief ran him out of town!"

"You really did that?" Carina exclaimed. "You are my new hero!"

Alessandra shrugged, a devious smirk across her face. "Sometimes you just have to teach a man a lesson."

Simona nodded in agreement.

"I need to be more like you." Gianna laughed.

"I'm always available for hire," Alessandra said smugly.

Carina laughed. "Do you come with references?"

"As a matter of fact, I do," the girl said. "I'm helping out someone now. One of my professors."

Gianna glanced at her sister. "Do tell!" she said, both women shifting to the edge of their seats.

Chapter 13

The two women sat in their car after waving their good-byes to Simona and Alessandra. When the other car pulled out of sight, Gianna tossed up her hands in frustration.

"Aargh!" she screamed, tight fists clenched in front of her. "Do you believe her? She was actually bragging about what she was doing!"

Carina nodded, a wide smile across her face. "Yes, she was and it's a good thing, too!"

Gianna eyed her sister, confusion furrowing her brow. "Why is that a good thing?"

"How else was I going to get it on tape?" she said, holding up a small audio recorder. She pushed the re-wind button and then pushed Play. Alessandra's voice vibrated through the space. "He'll think twice about telling me no again!" She pushed the stop button.

"You taped it all?" Gianna asked, her eyes widening.

Her sister grinned. "Everything we needed."

Gianna threw her arms around her sister's neck and hugged her tightly. Tears suddenly streamed down her face, a weight feeling as if it had been lifted off her shoulders. Carina hugged her back, swiping at the moisture that had pooled behind her own eyelids.

"We're not done yet," Carina said as she pushed Gianna away.

"What do you mean? We have her on tape."

"We do, but we have to get that Mugabe woman, too. Luckily for us, Alessandra said they were meeting at the Duomo tonight. She invited us to go along."

"How are we going to do that? Sophie Mugabe knows me! And even with your short hair, we still look alike. She'll know who you are the minute she lays eyes on you."

Carina nodded. "Which is why we're not able to go," she said as she dialed a number on her cell phone and waited for it to ring.

Curiosity shifted in Gianna's eyes as she sat waiting for her sister to complete her call. Her smile returned when the party answered on the other end.

"Graham, honey, it's me! I need you to go to Florence. Gianna and I really need your help!"

The three most important men in the Martelli women's lives sat staring at the duo, completely floored by the story they told. Franco shook his head from side to side, his arms crossed evenly over his chest. Graham sat at the counter, nothing about what he'd participated in surprising him. Donovan was the only one who was visibly stunned by what had transpired. He looked from one woman to the other, then shot a glance toward Graham and the family patriarch.

They had played the audio tapes twice, the first recording of Alessandra and the second of Alessandra and Sophie Mugabe. Both conversations left no doubt of Donovan's innocence and the twisted plot between the two women. He still didn't understand how the twins had managed to pull it off.

"So you actually befriended Alessandra?" he asked.

Gianna shook her head. "Not me. Carina. That witch was lucky I didn't smack the mess out of her because I really wanted to hit her." Disdain painted her expression.

Carina laughed. "You will never win any awards for your acting."

"I'm still confused," Donovan said.

Carina leaned across the counter. "Alessandra is narcissistic, and she craves attention. I followed her on Instagram and started commenting on her photos. When we went to the school, I pretended we'd just run into each other, and when I commented on her social media account and flattered her vanity, she couldn't wait to be my friend," Carina said with a shrug. "It was Psychology 101, and she fell for it. We just got lucky with the rest of it."

"Very lucky," Graham interjected, "and it's a good thing, too, because Carina was ready to break into her apartment and commit too many crimes to mention. At least all I had to do was sit at the table next to them, turn on the recorder and sip my drink."

"And you actually got that close that you were able to record them in the club?" Donovan questioned.

Graham nodded. "I even danced with the blonde! My wife gave me very specific orders!"

"I just want to know how they finagled you into their scheme," Franco stated.

Graham shrugged, his broad shoulders pushing toward the ceiling. "You know I can't say no to your daughter! She scares me!"

The older man laughed. "*Figlio*, you better learn before she gets you locked up behind bars one day!"

Both Donovan and Gianna had been excited to turn over copies of the audio tapes to Dante the attorney. After hearing how they'd acquired them and listening to the transmissions, he assured Donovan that he had nothing to be concerned about. "*Risolveremo il piu rapidamente possibile*," Dante had said, promising to resolve the matter promptly. It was now just a matter of time before they'd know the outcome.

The drive back to Maremma was quiet, the two enjoying the quiet and the low melody of the music playing on the car radio. The weather was near perfect—the temperature ideal, the sky a brilliant shade of blue and a bright sun shining above the treetops.

As Donovan rode shotgun, he was awed by the sheer beauty of the landscape. Minutes passed before he turned to stare at Gianna, reaching a large palm out to caress her thigh. The ease of his touch made her smile.

She shifted her gaze in his direction, her eyes wafting back and forth between him and the road. "Are you happy, Donovan?" she asked as he trailed his fingers against her profile.

He smiled "Very. Are you?"

She nodded. "You make me happy!"

"Gianna, have you ever thought about living in the United States?"

She turned her gaze on him and held it for a split second. Donovan felt the vehicle slow down significantly before she refocused her gaze.

She shook her head. "No, I haven't," she answered honestly.

"Do you think you can ever leave Tuscany?"

She answered his question with a question of her own. "Would you consider staying?"

Donovan smiled. "We really need to decide what we're going to do. I want to make an honest woman of you, and that needs to happen before your father and my mother join forces."

She laughed. "Define honest."

He smiled. "I'm hoping you'll be the next Mrs. Donovan Boudreaux."

"The next? Was there a last Mrs. Boudreaux?"

His expression was smug. "No, but you never know. There might be another in the future."

Gianna scoffed. "Not if I have anything to say about it!"

They giggled together softly.

"So, what do you want to do?" she asked.

He paused in thought before answering. "I know for certain that I can get work in the United States. I'm not so sure what's going to happen here. Not that I'm worried about supporting us because we can live quite comfortably off my savings and investments if I never teach another day in my life. But I don't want to stop teaching."

Gianna nodded but said nothing, seeming to fall into thought. It was a good few minutes before she spoke again.

"This is my home. It's all I've ever known. I never imagined not being able to work the vineyards or help my father with the winery. But…" She hesitated a second time.

Donovan prodded. "But?"

She took a deep breath. "But… I will follow you wherever you want to go. I trust that you will always do what will be in the best interest of our family. So…if we need to live in America, that's where we will live. I can write anywhere."

He kissed her cheek. "I love you, Gianna Martelli. I love you with everything in me!"

Her smile was engaging, emotion misting her bright eyes. "I love you, too, *mio caro*. I love you, too!"

"I want babies with you, Gianna. Five or six."

Gianna laughed. "Now you've lost your mind! One set of twins and we're done."

"You say that now, but I can be quite persuasive. And we might not get twins the first few times, so we'll have to keep trying," he teased.

She pulled the car into the parking area outside the

winery. Stepping out of the vehicle, she stood still, her gaze roaming the countryside. She suddenly couldn't see herself ever leaving the Tuscan heat, a wave of melancholy washing over her. And then she turned to stare at Donovan, the beauty of his smile assuring her that everything would be well no matter where they settled in the world, taking that Tuscan heat with them.

Reading her mind, Donovan moved to her side, easing his body against hers. With her back pressed against his chest and his arms wrapped around her waist, he pressed his face into her lush curls and kissed the top of her head. The scent of her perfume teased his nostrils.

In the distance, the sun was just beginning its descent, the wealth of it falling behind the trees in the distance. The sky blazed in shades of red, yellow and purple, a kaleidoscope of colors that made the view look like a priceless work of art.

"We have the most beautiful sunsets here in Maremma," she whispered.

Donovan nodded in agreement as he tightened the hold he had her wrapped in. He spun her around in his arms, his stare meeting hers. "You'll never miss one," he said. "This is our home, and here is where I want to see our children raised."

Gianna's eyes widened. "*Sei sicuro,* Donovan?"

"I am very sure. You have to be happy or I won't be."

She threw her arms around him, and the tears she'd been fighting spilled over her cheeks.

The late night ride atop the two horses was a perfect ending to the day. Gianna rode Raffaello and Donovan had saddled Michelangelo, a large black Arabian stallion with a majestic gait and a coat that was pitch-black in color.

There was a full moon in the dark sky, seeming almost like a spotlight leading their way. It was a slow stroll down to the coastal way as they rode side by side, trading easy conversation. Once on the damp sand, Gianna lowered her reins and applied pressure with her knees to transition Raffaello to a slow trot. Donovan and Michelangelo followed behind them.

Once they reached Gianna's secret cove they dismounted, the horses moving to stand in the only grassy area high up on a hill. Hand in hand, the couple walked the shoreline, savoring the cool evening air that wafted off the water.

Coming to a stop, Gianna turned into him, sliding easily into Donovan's arms. She reached up to kiss his mouth. He wrapped her in his arms and held her as he tossed a look over his shoulder and up the beach.

"I want to make love to you," he whispered loudly. "Right here, right now."

She laughed. "Then you should."

"Someone might see us."

She laughed again. "Don't let that stop you."

Fervor danced in Donovan's eyes. He watched as Gianna took a step back, slipping the T-shirt she wore over her head, exposing her bare breasts. He threw a look over his shoulder a second time, then wiped away the sweat that had beaded across his brow with the back of his hand. As Gianna pushed her sweatpants down to the sand beneath her feet, he tore at his own clothes until they were both naked.

With a wink and a giggle, Gianna skipped to the shoreline and then into the warm water.

"Are you coming?" she called out, laughter spilling past her lips.

Nervous energy sent a shiver up Donovan's spine. Without giving it a second thought, he raced behind her.

They swam and danced in the warm waters. Kissed beneath the star-filled sky. The moon caressed and teased them as they made the sweetest love, their bodies carving imprints in the damp sand. Donovan loved her easily, oblivious to their surroundings. In that moment he felt immensely blessed. The intimacy between them was a mélange of everything that was good and decent, those things they loved most, wrapped in the prettiest paper and tied with one big bow. Perfection defined the love the two felt for each other, and in that moment, beneath that full moon, life was the best it had ever been.

The call came four days later, Dr. Northway apologizing profusely and asking Donovan to report immediately back to the classroom.

"Miss Donati has been suspended for the rest of the semester, and after some discussion, Professor Mugabe felt it was in everyone's best interest that she resign. And once you're settled back in, we'd like to talk to you about possibly assuming the department chair position."

Donovan nodded into the receiver. "I'll have to think about it," he answered. "For now, I think it's important that I fulfill my contractual obligation and finish out the school year. We can talk more on Monday when I return."

Dr. Northway had apologized one last time before hanging up the phone. Donovan pumped his fist in the air, a huge grin filling his face. He'd been expecting the director's call. Dante had called earlier that morning to give him the news that he'd been completely vindicated. Donovan was grateful, but he still found himself feeling some kind of way and didn't have the words to explain it. Before the call he'd been painting, his easel and chair sitting out on the patio as he stared out to the vast green fields. Signora Rossi had fussed about earlier, leaving them a pretty salad, an antipasto tray and two ramekins of panna cotta.

Gianna looked up from the story she was working on, five hundred pages of copyedits she needed to complete and return to her editor. "Are you okay?" she asked, concern wafting between them.

"I don't know. I'm happy that it's over but I don't know if I want to go back."

"But you want to teach, right?"

He nodded. "There's nothing else I'd rather be doing. But I don't know if this position is the right one."

"Well, the secondary school is always an option if you like teenagers."

Donovan contemplated the comment for a brief moment. "I might give that some thought," he said, moving back toward the door.

She smiled. "How's the painting coming along?"

He grinned. "I think I'm about to give Picasso a run for his money!"

"Picasso?" She laughed. "That should be interesting."

"Extremely!"

Before Donovan could get out the door, his cell phone chimed against the countertop. He moved back inside to answer the call.

"It's my brother," he said as he engaged the device. "Hey, Kendrick! I have you on speaker. Say hi to Gianna!"

"Hey, there! Hi, Gianna! How are you?"

"I'm good, Kendrick. How are you?"

"I just called to warn you two. We all just landed."

"We all who?" Donovan asked as he and Gianna exchanged a look.

His brother laughed. "Everybody! The whole family is here!"

Chapter 14

Donovan's family came in like a storm wind. They were loud and forward, and in a split second after their arrival he remembered what it was about all of them that he missed most.

Even Tarah, with all her annoying ways, brought a smile to his face. "Don Juan finally has a girlfriend!" she exclaimed as she gave Gianna a warm hug.

Gianna laughed. "Don Juan?"

"Our nickname for him because he was always such a ladies' man...*not!*"

Donovan rolled his eyes. His mother still had an arm around his waist, hugging him warmly.

"Leave your brother alone, Tarah. Go outside and explore! There's a reason we left all the kids back in the States!"

Tarah rolled her eyes, pushing her lips into a feigned pout.

"Where are the kids?" Donovan asked, inquiring about his nephews and nieces.

Katrina grabbed Matthew's hand. "This is an adults-only excursion. We left all the babies in Dallas with Matthew's family."

Katherine laughed. "My grandbabies are all being spoiled rotten! You know how them Stallions do!" She gave Donovan another squeeze as she changed the subject. "I'm so glad you were able to resolve that mess with the university. But we were all prepared to be right here by your side at that hearing."

Donovan nodded. "Thank you, but now you all can just enjoy your time here."

"How long are you all staying?" Gianna asked.

"Not too long," Mason answered.

"Long enough for some of us to get into trouble, I'm sure." Maitlyn giggled. She wrapped a protective arm around her pregnant belly.

"Won't be none of that," Senior interjected. "I'm not bailing anyone out!"

"I just want to know where the boys are!" Tarah quipped.

Their mother pointed her index finger. "Outside!" she said, her eyebrows raised at her youngest child.

The chatter continued as the family inspected Donovan's small space, his artwork and the landscape outside, and interrogated Gianna.

"This is absolutely delightful!" Katherine exclaimed.

"It's small," Senior said. "And there's nothing wrong with small."

Donovan shook his head. "I wasn't expecting a family reunion anytime soon," he said.

Donovan's brother Guy laughed. "You people are going to scare Donovan's new friend away."

Gianna gave Donovan a look, her smile bright. "I'm not going anywhere," she said.

"How did you two meet?" Tarah asked. "I mean, Don Juan here hasn't been in Italy long enough to suddenly have a girlfriend."

The couple traded a look as the room quieted, everyone waiting for a response.

"We met online," Donovan said.

"My sister introduced us," Gianna said at the same time.

Confusion washed over everyone's expression. Shaking his head, Donovan told them their story from the beginning, Gianna filling in any details he missed. When they were done, there was silence, everyone exchanging amused looks.

Tarah suddenly burst out laughing. "Only you, Don Juan! Only you could make dating a textbook topic for what to do and how not to do it!"

The laughter was abundant, and it filled the space with an immense amount of joy. In the kitchen, his mother and Signora Rossi were in deep conversation. The family members marveled at how easily the two women seemed to intuitively know what the other was saying, although one was speaking English and the other Italian. Together, the antipasto and salad Signora Rossi had prepared earlier was enough for the Boudreaux army to all snack on. At one point the duo burst into laughter and Gianna blushed profusely, shaking her head.

"What?" Donovan asked, wrapping his arms around the woman.

Gianna laughed. "You really don't want to know!" she said as she moved back to join the two matriarchs.

Donovan's father pulled him aside, the two moving to a corner of the small home. The patriarch stared down at the painting Donovan had been working on, studying it intently.

"It's good," he said, impressed by his son's talents. "It's very good!"

"Thank you, Senior."

His father slapped him gently on the back. "You look happy, son."

"I am happy, Senior. I'm very happy."

"That's good. Your mother has been worried to death about you being here all alone with no family close by."

Donovan shook his head. "I don't know why."

Senior shrugged. "Donovan, you were always the quiet, studious one. You were always home while the others were all out running the streets doing what they do."

Donovan smiled. "Kendrick said Mom and the girls thought I was soft."

"Maybe not soft, but the most vulnerable. And that's only because they coddled you more than the other boys. You were always around and you let them. But I think these last few months, your mother's been able to see that your quiet strength has been a formidable resource. And I just wanted to tell you how proud I am of you, son!"

Donovan smiled as his father hugged him. "Thank you, Senior!"

"So when are you going to tell your mother that you don't plan to come back home?"

Donovan shot his father a look, and the two men locked gazes. "How...?"

"Kendrick told me."

Donovan sighed softly. "How do you think Mom's going to take it?"

Senior shrugged. "You know your mother. She wants you all home, or close to home. She hates it when you and your brothers and sisters aren't close enough for her to love on you."

Donovan nodded. "I'll tell her," he said softly.

His father nodded. "I'll help soften the blow afterward," he said. "She'll be okay as long as she knows she can come visit anytime she wants."

Donovan smiled. "Mom knows she can always come see me!"

Gianna moved to Donovan's side. "I don't mean to interrupt..."

"Not at all, pretty lady! You're not interrupting us at all!" Senior hugged her, too.

Donovan pressed a kiss to her forehead. "What's up?"

"I just spoke to my father, and he and Carina want

to prepare dinner for everyone if you all don't have other plans."

"We'd love to meet your family," Katherine said, joining the conversation.

Tarah suddenly rushed in from outside. "I love Italy!" she exclaimed, jumping up and down excitedly. "Can I stay?"

Franco greeted them at the door, his own excitement shimmering in his bright blue eyes. Donovan introduced them all one by one.

"Franco, this is my oldest brother, Mason, and Mason's wife, Phaedra. My sister Maitlyn and her husband, Zakaria. My sister Katrina and her husband, Matthew Stallion. My brother Darryl and his wife, Camryn. My brother Kendrick and his wife, Vanessa. My brother Guy and his wife, Dahlia, and my sisters Kamaya and Tarah."

Franco hugged and kissed and shook hands with them all. *"Ciao! Ciao!"* he said as he pointed everyone to Carina and Graham. "This is Gianna's twin sister and her husband."

Lastly, Donovan introduced his parents. "And this is my mother, Katherine, and my father, Senior Boudreaux. Mom, Senior, this is Franco Martelli, Gianna's father."

Franco and Senior shook hands before Franco threw his arms around the man. "What a spectacular family!" he said.

He moved to stand in front of Katherine. *"Ciao, bella!* I see where your daughters get their beauty from."

He grabbed her hand and kissed the back of it, his lips lingering. "It is a pleasure to meet you," he said, batting his baby blue eyes at her.

"Down, Giusseppi. That's my queen you're kissing," Senior said, a teasing smirk on his face.

Everyone in the room laughed.

Katherine giggled. "Pay him no mind!" she said as she looped her arm through Senior's. "He's not jealous."

Franco laughed heartily. "With such a beautiful woman by his side, I would understand him being jealous!"

Katherine giggled, a deep blush darkening her cheeks. "Gianna, your father is quite the charmer! You two should fix him up with my new friend, Felice."

Gianna and Carina both laughed. Carina moved to give Donovan's mother a welcoming hug. "We've been trying to get him and Signora Rossi together for years!"

The two fathers shook hands, cementing their new friendship.

"This is a mighty fine place you have here," Senior said.

Franco grinned. "Thank you. We are very proud of it. You must let us show you around."

"Please," Gianna said. "I'd love to give you the tour."

"There's wine involved, right?" Tarah asked.

Franco nodded. "Much, much vino!"

"I'm in!" Tarah exclaimed, clapping her hands together excitedly.

Kamaya shook her head, holding up a palm. "Don't worry, Mom. I'll keep an eye on her." She gave Tarah a slight push, and the two sisters burst into laughter.

* * *

Hours later the Boudreaux and Martelli families were still laughing and sharing, telling tall tales about Donovan and Gianna. The couple leaned against each other, overwhelmed by the love and support, and mutually embarrassed by the attention.

"I like her!" Katherine said, her husband's arms wrapped warmly around her shoulders. "I really like her a lot!"

Senior nodded. "She's a sweet, sweet girl. Donovan's done good!"

"And she loves him! Just look at her face."

"Look at his! That boy is caught up something fierce."

There was a lull in the conversation as they sat watching their children. They were all basking in the moment, their time together much needed. Both knew that it would only be days before each of their offspring would be headed off in their own directions, back to the daily responsibilities that kept them apart. Pride shone across both their faces.

"May I join you?" Franco asked, moving to Senior's side.

"Of course," Katherine said with a bright smile.

Senior gestured for him to take a seat. "Still flirting with my woman, I see."

Franco chuckled. "I can't help myself," he said as he gave Katherine a wink.

Senior kissed his wife's cheek. "I'm a lucky man, Franco. A very lucky man!"

Across the way, Donovan was watching his parents. He smiled with amusement as he eyed them teasing each other. "Senior's being quite the romantic," he noted, gesturing with his head toward the two as his father kissed his mother.

"It's Tuscany!" Gianna said with a bright smile. "Everything is romantic here!"

Donovan nodded. He shifted forward in his seat, grabbing both her hands between his own. "Are you ready to marry me, Gianna Martelli?"

She met the intense look he was giving her. "Are you proposing, Donovan Boudreaux?"

Donovan suddenly slid down onto one knee, still holding tight to her fingers. He reached into the pocket of his jeans, and as if out of nowhere he held up a diamond ring in fourteen-karat white gold. The vintage setting was stunning, pavé-set diamonds along the top half of the stunning band and around a single three-carat round-cut stone.

Gianna gasped in surprise, her eyes wide with wonder. "Donovan!"

The room suddenly fell quiet, everyone turning to stare. Smiles were wide and abundant as the two families moved in closer, not wanting to miss a moment of the proposal.

"Gianna, I love you. I can't imagine my life without you. You move me in ways no other woman will ever move me. I want to devote my life to you. To us. To the family I hope we have. Will you marry me? Will you be my wife and the mother of my children?"

Tears spilled past Gianna's lashes as she nodded her head. "Yes!" she exclaimed as Donovan slipped the ring onto her left hand.

The room erupted into cheers as their families celebrated the moment, congratulations ringing in the air. The women all pressed in to admire the new piece of jewelry that adorned Gianna's hand.

Kamaya turned toward her mother. "Is that Grandma's ring?" she asked, her smile widening.

Katherine nodded, tossing her husband a look. "It is."

Senior met his daughter's stare. "Your brother was the only one who asked me for my mother's ring."

Katherine nodded. "Maitlyn had it cleaned and a larger diamond put in the setting for him."

Senior and Franco shook hands. "Congratulations, sir!"

"And to you, sir!"

Both men hugged Katherine.

Donovan's brothers shook his hand and slapped him on his back, each offering congratulations and advice. He hugged Gianna to his side, both overwhelmed by all the excitement. Gianna suddenly leaned in to whisper in his ear.

"Are you sure?" he asked, beaming with joy.

She nodded, kissing his lips.

Donovan waved his hand for everyone's attention. "I just want to say thank you to everyone," he said, his gaze sweeping over each of them. "Thank you all for being here. For supporting me. For all the love you've shown to me and Gianna," he said, pausing for a quick moment before speaking again. "Now, we're going to challenge you."

Gianna grinned, biting down on her bottom lip. "Carina, Maitlyn, all you girls. Since everyone is here, do you think you all can help us pull off a wedding by this Sunday?"

Maitlyn and Carina both jumped with excitement. Kamaya threw her arms around Tarah, who squealed with joy. Phaedra, Camryn, Dahlia and Vanessa all chimed in with glee. Everyone was chattering with enthusiasm.

Katherine laughed. "Baby girl, you don't have to worry about a thing! You're going to get the wedding of your dreams!"

Chapter 15

Donovan woke to Gianna standing in the center of the bed jumping up and down with excitement. Her early-morning exuberance brought a smile to his face as he rubbed the sleep from his eyes with both hands.

"Good morning, sleepyhead!"

He shifted his body upward in the bed, resting his back against the headboard. "Good morning," he said with a yawn. "Why are you up? It's too early to be so happy!"

She laughed as she continued to bounce up and down. "It's not early. It's almost eight o'clock. And I'm always happy. I'm in love, didn't you hear?"

He reached for her hand and pulled her down against him. He embraced her in a deep bear hug. "I hope he's a really great guy because you, beautiful lady, deserve a really great guy."

Gianna grinned. "My guy is the greatest guy in the whole wide world," she said as she kissed his cheek.

Donovan laughed. "So, what's on your agenda today?"

"I'm going to go find my wedding dress today."

His brow suddenly furrowed in confusion. "Why did I think that's what you disappeared to do yesterday?"

Gianna shrugged, Donovan missing the look that crossed her face. "No. I had some errands to run but not for my dress."

He still looked confused. "I could have sworn that's what Carina told me you two were headed out to do."

She smiled, that nervous twitch making her eye jump as she tried to brush it off. "Maybe that's what she thought your sister had planned for us, but we had other things to do first. So we're going today and I'm nervous."

"Why?"

"I'm scared that I won't be able to find the perfect dress off the rack that will be ready by Sunday."

"Don't be scared. You'll find the perfect dress, and you'll be even more beautiful in it."

She kissed him again. "What are you going to do today?"

Donovan hesitated for a moment. "I think I'm going to go to the university this morning. I just want to show my face and get some things ready for when I go back to teaching next week."

"Do you think you should go alone?"

"I think I'll be fine. If any of my family members want to come, I'll enjoy showing them the school." He changed the subject. "How are all the wedding plans going?"

"Your sisters are amazing! I can't believe what they've done so far. Maitlyn has thought of everything!"

"Maitlyn has contacts all around the world. If you want something done, she is definitely your go-to girl."

"She and Carina have become good friends, and she's been giving her some advice about renting the winery more for private functions and increasing that revenue stream. Carina's determined to make us the wedding destination of destination weddings!"

Donovan laughed. "That sounds like my sister."

"Well, all of our paperwork is done, and my father spoke to the priest and he's on board, so we are good to go as long as I find a dress."

He kissed that sweet spot beneath her chin. "Then you need to find a dress!"

Gianna shifted against him, straddling his body. Donovan closed his eyes as she began to rock her pelvis back and forth, savoring the sensation of his member rising between her legs. She ground herself against him, over and over again. Her touch was heated and inviting, and he felt himself lengthen and swell beneath her caresses.

Reaching out both hands, he slipped them beneath the top she wore, grabbing her breasts. The soft tissue filled his hands nicely as he gently teased her nipples until they were hard like rock candy and protruded against the fabric of her shirt. Her skin was heated and perspiration suddenly dampened his palms. Gianna continued to taunt his member, the lengthy protrusion like a steel rod between them.

"Do you like this?" she whispered as she reached a hand between his legs to stroke him.

"Don't tease me, Gianna," he said as he pulled at her nightclothes. He was suddenly anxious to settle himself deep inside her. "I've got to have me some!"

She giggled softly as she reached for a condom out of the nightstand drawer. "I'm very serious about wanting some, too, so you better hurry. Your sisters will be here in an hour!"

After Gianna and the girls were gone, Donovan headed toward the school. At the last minute he'd decided against asking any of his family to join him, wanting some time to himself to think. Feeling like the stars had aligned perfectly, he sang to himself, the lyrics to a love song ringing through the air.

Gianna was going to be his wife. The reality of that made his heart skip. As he thought of the vows they would soon take, he hoped he could capture with words the wealth of emotion that had been flooding his spirit on a daily basis.

He wanted to be the best husband he could be. He'd promised Franco that his daughter would want for nothing, and Donovan had meant every word. Protecting and caring for Gianna had become a mission, and it would be a lifelong journey he couldn't wait to explore. She was his, and he felt immensely blessed.

He was so absorbed in thoughts of her and him together that he wasn't paying any attention to the other cars parked in the employee spaces at the school. Inside, he waved hello, stopping to have a quick conversation with Dr. Northway before heading to his office. Everyone was excited to welcome him back and disappointed that he wasn't going to officially be back for another few days.

His desk was stacked with papers that needed his attention, and as he flipped casually through them he couldn't begin to fathom how he was going to get them graded before his wedding. As he organized what he needed to do and how he needed to do it, there was a knock on his door.

He looked up just as the door opened. "Yes?"

One of the young men from his linear equations class poked his head in. "Dr. Boudreaux, *buongiorno!*"

"*Buongiorno*, Marco! How are you?"

"*Bene grazie*, signor. I wanted to welcome you back."

Donovan smiled. "I appreciate that, Marco."

"I will see you in class today, no?"

"Not today," Donovan said with a shake of his head. "I will be here on Monday."

The boy nodded. "Very good, signor! I will see you then."

For the next hour Donovan entertained students and instructors alike, all stopping to express their happiness with his return and their regrets for everything he'd been put through. Realizing that he was going to get little accomplished, he packed up the stacks of paperwork and dropped them into his attaché case, then headed to his car.

Sophie was leaning against his car, her arms crossed over her chest. Her car was parked beside his, the backseat loaded with boxes and books from her office. She stood upright as he approached, and it wasn't until he was standing before her that he noticed her black eye and swollen face. His eyes widened.

"Sophie, what happened to you?"

She shook her head, and when she went to speak he realized her jaw was wired shut, her teeth clenched tightly together. "I just...wanted...to apologize...to you...for my part...in what happened." The words came slowly, barely audible.

Donovan nodded. "I appreciate that."

She rolled her eyes as she took a breath. "I hear... you are...getting...married."

"I am," he said, suddenly curious that word of their wedding had traveled so quickly.

"Good...luck...with that!" she said as she tossed up a hand. She turned to get into her vehicle.

Donovan called after her.

"Yes?"

"May I ask how you broke your jaw?"

The woman paused as she thought back to her last encounter with Alessandra, her prized student turning on her. She'd dodged the first punch the young girl had thrown, but the second had caught her in just the right spot. Sophie's eyes were angry slits as she met his stare. "Yes," she said. "I...ran into...the wrong...woman."

Donovan narrowed his gaze on Gianna's face. Carina sat beside him. Both women looked as if they'd been caught red-handed. His tone was scolding as he shared the details of his encounter with Sophie Mugabe.

"That's a shame!" Carina said, her voice quivering ever so slightly.

Across the room Franco shook his head, he and Graham grinning broadly.

Donovan had to ask. "Did you break that woman's jaw, Gianna?"

Gianna tossed up her hands. "Why do you think that I had something to do with what happened to her?"

Donovan tilted his head slightly. "Did you break her jaw, Carina?"

"It wasn't me!"

"So where did you two disappear to the other day when I thought you were dress shopping?" He glanced from Gianna to Carina and back.

The two sisters exchanged a look. Neither said a word.

Donovan shook his head at Gianna. "That right hook of yours again, huh?"

Gianna scoffed. "Why are you assuming I busted that woman in her face? Not that she didn't deserve it for what she put you through, but still…"

Tarah laughed. "I'm so glad it's not me this time. I used to always get blamed for everything!"

Guy laughed. "That's because usually it's always you doing something you shouldn't be doing!"

Tarah rolled her eyes. "Well, I'm not unhappy that woman got her jaw broke. She spread lies about Donovan, and if I'd seen her I might have popped her, too!"

Katherine laughed. "So would I!" she exclaimed.

The men all shook their heads. Donovan pulled Gianna into a hug, and she allowed herself to melt into the embrace. She tilted her head to stare up at him.

"Are you mad?" she asked.

He smiled and shook his head. "Just don't do it again," he said.

She sighed in frustration. "I'm telling you, I didn't do a thing!"

Carina laughed. "Did I forget to tell you that her nickname used to be Little Mike, for Mike Tyson!"

Franco tapped his chest as he tossed Donovan a wink. "She got that from me!"

The twins were enjoying a moment of quiet where it was just the two of them, alone together. Carina had pinned her sister's hair in an updo, and was delighting in how very beautiful she looked. They glanced at each other and smiled.

"Are you still mad at me?" Carina said softly, moving to sit by Gianna's side.

Gianna laughed. "How could I ever be mad at you, Sissy?"

"I just don't want Donovan thinking you attacked that woman. We both know there's no way you could have done something like that. I mean, you do have a perfect alibi. You were with me."

"He doesn't. And even if he did, once he finds out the truth, it will all be good."

Carina smiled. She pressed a hand over her abdomen, tears filling her eyes. "I'm having a baby, Sissy! Can you believe it? Me? With a baby!"

Gianna laughed as she gave her sister a warm hug. "You're going to be a wonderful mother! And I'm blessed to have been there at the doctor with you when you found out." She squeezed Carina's hands. "Now, when are you going to tell Graham?"

"After the wedding. I didn't want my joy to overshadow your joy. This is your moment, and I want it to be the very best day of your whole life."

Gianna shook her head. "Tell your husband, Sissy. We have so much to celebrate, and with all this love around us there's no reason for both of us not to share our joys with everybody."

The two women embraced again, pulling back to wipe each other's tears.

"Don't cry," Carina admonished. "You're going to ruin your makeup."

"Donovan doesn't care if I wear makeup!"

"So do I get a pass now for the way I fixed you and Donovan up? Am I totally forgiven?"

Gianna nodded. "Completely. If it wasn't for you, I wouldn't be this happy!"

There was a sudden knock on the door. Both women turned to stare just as Maitlyn peeked her head inside the room. "I don't mean to interrupt, but it's time to go get you married. Are you ready to get into your gown?"

The two sisters connected gazes one last time. Gianna took a deep breath and held it for a quick minute as Carina squeezed her hand.

Carina waved all of the Boudreaux women into the room. "She's ready!"

Donovan was nervous as he stood at the front of the little country chapel, his brothers by his side. They were all dressed in designer, blue silk suits, white dress shirts and printed navy blue ties with thin orange and white stripes.

Flowers in every shade of the rainbow decorated the small space, their sweet scent billowing through the warm air. A trio of violins played sweetly, the soft lilt of music dancing with the breeze that blew through the open windows and doors.

Father Cesare Balducci, the Martelli family's priest, stood on Donovan's other side. He was a tall and slender man who looked regal in his robes as he held a leather-bound Bible in his hands.

Father Balducci tapped Donovan's arm. "We are ready to begin," he said softly as he tilted his head toward the back of the church.

The violin tune suddenly shifted, the prelude to the "Bridal Chorus" announcing Gianna's arrival. Family and friends and people from the village all turned at the same time to watch the procession down the aisle.

Tarah led the way, Kamaya, Katrina, Maitlyn and Carina following. They wore strapless, tea-length gowns that bore a soft floral print. Each was stunning, with French braids complementing their faces. Even Carina's short locks had been braided with extensions.

Donovan was grinning from ear to ear, clenching his fists together tightly. He took a deep breath and then a second as Carina and his sisters all greeted him with a smile.

Then, there she was! Gianna was a vision to behold, an apparition of magnanimous proportions. Donovan was in awe of just how exquisite she was. Her gown was everything she had wanted it to be. It was a strapless, slim A-line silhouette with a corset closure. It had a sophisticated overlay of vintage lace and featured an asymmetrical satin panel that was gathered and wrapped across her waistline to create a figure-flattering effect. A simple satin bow rested gently at the side of her front hip, accentuating her wisp of a waist. As she walked down the aisle in his direction, Donovan cried, tears falling easily over his cheeks.

The ceremony attested to their faith and love for each other. With their family serving as witnesses, they vowed to love and honor each other. Gianna's tears came when Donovan recited the vows he'd written.

"Gianna, since the first day I laid eyes on you, you have made me feel more complete, more alive, and you have shown me the true meaning of happiness. I am a better man with you by my side than I can ever be without you. So today, in front of you, and those we love most, I take you to be my partner, loving what I know of you, and trusting what I do not yet know, excited to discover the woman you will become.

"I promise to respect you as my equal, and to recognize that your interests, desires and needs are as important as my own. I promise to laugh with you when times are good. To endure with you when they are bad. I will grow old with you, happily! I promise to fall more in love with you each and every day. Today, tomorrow, and every day I give you my hand, my heart and my love without condition, completely and forever."

Gianna giggled like a girl as he slipped her wedding band on her finger. She swiped the tears from her cheek and cleared her voice as the priest gestured for her to speak. Gianna had balked at writing her own vows and had only agreed after much prodding. Her vows, short, sweet and uniquely Gianna, brought joy and laughter to Donovan's heart.

"Donovan Boudreaux, I...choose...you!" She winked at him as she placed a gold band on his ring finger, then leaned down to kiss the back of his hand.

With the exchange of rings, Father Balducci pronounced them husband and wife, and the room erupted in cheers. Without giving it a thought, Donovan swept her off her feet, lifting her into his arms. He kissed her mouth as Gianna wrapped her arms around his neck. Then he carried her back down the aisle and out the church doors, their family following behind them.

The reception was held in the Martelli fields, a carpet of lush green grass surrounded by fields of red poppies. Rustic wooden tables draped with red runners sat beneath large arches of green ivy. Floral-covered spheres in bright orange, yellow and red hung from the arches, and the tables were decorated with gold-trimmed plates with the finest crystal and gold tableware. A dance floor had been set up on the lawn, and a small band was playing all of their favorite songs. The bright blue sky and the most incredible weather proved to be the perfect backdrop for their celebration.

Gathered together, the family posed for a multitude of photographs to capture the memories. Mason's wife, Phaedra, was their personal wedding photographer. Their guests dined on platters of roasted chicken, potatoes and vegetables, the meal completed with Gianna's favorite lemon-filled cake and bottles of her father's wine. Donovan and Gianna couldn't stop grinning, everything about their day sheer perfection.

Hours later Gianna pulled at Donovan's arm. "Come dance with me again," she pleaded.

Donovan laughed. "I need a break, sweetheart! I can't keep up with you."

Gianna feigned a pout. "I'll have to find another man to dance with me, then."

He nodded, pointing toward his brothers. "Take your pick!"

She leaned in to kiss his lips. As she did, she slipped a folded note into his pocket.

Slipping his hand into the jacket, he gave her a curious look. "What's this?"

"Read your mail," she said as she winked at him. She danced away, her hips twisting in a teasing shimmy.

Pulling the note out of his pocket, he stepped away from the crowd and began to read.

My dearest Donovan,
Just hours ago I became Mrs. Gianna Boudreaux, and now I wear your family name proudly. I am blessed to have your love, and I am honored to stand by your side as your partner and companion.

I pledge myself to you, heart and soul. I promise to be with you in happiness and strife. To love you in richness and debt. To be faithful, even when we are old and dull.

Thank you for trusting me with your heart. I

do not take that responsibility lightly. I will cherish you until we each take our last breath and then on into eternity.

You, my darling, have given me my happily-ever-after, and for the very first time I can honestly say I know love because of you.

Always and forever,

Gianna

PS: I think it would be good business for us to write a book of love letters. We'll call it *Tuscan Heat*. I've written the first. I'll wait for you to write the next.

Immeasurable joy painted Donovan's expression. Across the yard, Gianna met his stare and smiled. She lifted her hand and blew him a kiss. Pretending to catch it in his palm, he drew his closed fist to his heart and whispered the words *I love you!*

* * * * *

BEST FRIEND TO
WIFE AND MOTHER?

CAROLINE ANDERSON

Huge thanks to Caroline and Adam, and Bryony and Owen, who inadvertently gave me wonderful wedding inspiration, and to Shirley and Roger, Mike and Trice, who invited us to share those days with them. I love you all.

CHAPTER ONE

'ARE YOU READY?'

He eased a flyaway strand of hair from the corner of her eye, his touch as light as a butterfly's wing, his fingertips lingering for a moment as their eyes met and held. His voice, as familiar to her as her own, was steady and reassuring, but his words didn't reassure her. They sent her mind into free-fall.

They were such simple words, on the surface, but layered beneath were a million unasked and unanswered questions. Questions Leo probably didn't even know he'd asked her. Questions she'd needed to ask herself for months but somehow hadn't got round to.

Was she ready?

For the wedding, yes. The planning had been meticulous, nothing left to chance. Her mother, quietly and efficiently, had seen to that. But the marriage—the *lifetime*—with Nick?

Mingling with the birdsong and the voices of the people clustered outside the church gates were the familiar strains of the organ music.

The overture for her wedding.

No. Her *marriage*. Subtle difference, but hugely significant.

Amy glanced through the doorway of the church and caught the smiles on the row of faces in the back pew, all of them craning their necks to get a better look at her. The villagers at the gate were mostly there for Leo, hoping to catch a glimpse of their favourite son, but these people in the church—her friends, Nick's—were here to see her marry Nick.

Today.

Right now.

Her heart skittered under the fitted bodice that suddenly seemed so tight she could hardly breathe.

I can't do this—!

No choice. Too late now for cold feet. If she'd been going to change her mind she should have done it ages ago, before the wheels of this massive train that was her wedding had been set in motion. Or later, at a push—but not now, so late it was about to hit the buffers.

The church was full, the food cooked, the champagne on ice. And Nick would be standing at the altar, waiting for her.

Dear, kind, lovely Nick, who'd been there for her when her life had been in chaos, who'd just—been there, for the last three years, her friend and companion and cheerleader. Her lover. And she did love him. She did…

Enough to marry him? Till death us do part, and all that? Or is it just the easiest thing to do?

You can stop this, the voice whispered in her head. *It's not too late.*

But it was. Way too late. She was marrying Nick.

Today.

A curious calm settled over her, as if a switch had been flicked, turning on the autopilot, steadying her fall into oblivion. The voice in her head didn't care.

Just because it's easy, because you know he'll be a good husband and father and he's safe? Is that enough?

Of course it was enough. It was just nerves unsettling her. That was all. Last-minute nerves. Nick was—fine.

Fine? Like safe, steady, reliable, predictable—that kind

of fine? No chemistry, no fireworks? And whatever happened to amazing?

She tuned the voice out. There were more important things than amazing. Trust, fidelity, respect—and chemistry was overrated—

How do you know that? You don't *know that. You haven't got a clue, you've never felt it. And if you marry Nick, you never will...*

She stifled the voice again, stuffing it firmly back in its box; then, easing her death grip on the bouquet, she straightened her shoulders, tilted up her chin and gave Leo her most convincing and dazzling smile.

'Yes,' she said firmly. 'I'm ready.'

Leo felt his breath catch at that smile.

When had she grown up? Turned into this stunningly lovely woman, instead of the slightly chubby, relentlessly accident-prone girl who'd dogged his footsteps for ever? He'd turned his back for what felt like five minutes, and she'd been transformed.

More like five years, though, give or take, and a lot of water under the bridge for both of them. Far too much, in his case, and so much of it tainted by regret.

He cradled her pale cheek in his hand, and felt her quiver. She was nervous. Of course she was. Who wouldn't be, on their wedding day? It was a hell of a commitment. Literally, in his case.

'You look beautiful, Amy,' he said gruffly, looking down into the wide grey eyes of this lovely young woman he'd known so well but now hardly knew at all. 'He's a lucky man.'

'Thank you.'

Her eyes searched his, a flicker of uncertainty in them echoing the tiny tremor in her cheek, the smile on her lush, pink lips a little hesitant now, and he felt himself frown.

Second thoughts? About time. There was nothing wrong with the man she was marrying, from what little he'd seen of him—in fact, he'd liked him, a lot—but they just didn't seem *right* for each other.

There was no chemistry between them, no zing that he could see. Maybe she didn't want that? Maybe she just wanted safe and comfortable? And maybe that was a really, really good idea.

Or maybe not, not for Amy…

He hesitated another second, then took her hand in his, his thumb slowly stroking the back of it in a subconscious gesture of comfort. Her fingers were cold, trembling slightly in his, reinforcing his concern. He squeezed them gently.

'Amy, I'm going to ask you something. It's only what your father would have done, so please don't take it the wrong way, but—are you sure you want to do this? Because if not, you can still turn around and walk away. It's your life, no one else's, and nobody else can decide this for you.'

His voice dropped, his frown deepening as he struggled to get the importance of this across to her before it was too late. If only someone had done this for him…

'Don't do it unless it's right, Amy, unless you really, truly love him. Take it from me, marrying the wrong person for the wrong reasons is a recipe for disaster. You have to be absolutely, completely and utterly sure that it's the right thing to do and for the right reasons.'

A shadow flitted across her eyes, her fingers tightening on his, and after an infinitesimal pause that seemed to last an eternity, she nodded. 'Yes. Yes, of course I'm sure.'

But she didn't look sure, and he certainly wasn't, but it was nothing to do with him, was it? Not his decision to make. And the shadows in her eyes could just as easily be sadness because her much-loved father wasn't here to give her away. Nothing to do with her choice of groom...

Not your business who she chooses to love. God knows, you're no expert. And he could be a lot, lot worse.

He hauled in a breath.

'OK. Ready to go, then?'

She nodded, but he saw her swallow again, and for a moment he wondered if she'd changed her mind.

And then she straightened up and took a breath, hooked her hand through his arm and flashed a smile over her shoulder at her bridesmaids. 'OK, girls? Good to go?'

They both nodded, and he felt her hand tighten on his arm.

'OK, then. Let's do this.' Her eyes flicked up and met Leo's, her fake smile pinned in place by sheer determination, but it didn't waver and anybody else might have been convinced.

Not your business. He nodded to the usher, who nodded to the organist, and after a moment's silence, broken only by the shuffling of the congregation getting to their feet and the clearing of a few throats, the evocative strains of Pachelbel's *Canon in D Major* filled the church.

He laid his hand over hers, squeezed her fingers and felt them grip his. He glanced down, into those liquid grey eyes that seemed flooded with doubt despite the brave smile, and his gut clenched.

He'd known her for ever, rescued her from a million scrapes, both literal and otherwise; dammit, she was his best friend, or had been before the craziness that was his life had got in the way, and he couldn't bear to see her make the mistake of her life.

Don't do it, Amy. Please, don't do it!

'It's still not too late,' he said gruffly, his voice muted, his head tilted towards her so only she could hear.

'Yes, it is,' she said, so softly he barely heard her, then

she dredged up that expected smile again and took the first step forward.

Damn.

He swallowed the lump in his throat and slowly, steadily, walked her down the aisle.

With every step, her legs felt heavier and more reluctant, her heart pounding, the sense of unease settling closer around her, chilling her to the bone.

What are you doing?

Nick was there, watching her thoughtfully. Warily?

It's still not too late.

She felt Leo ease his arm out from under her hand and step away, and she felt—abandoned?

It was her wedding day. She should feel a sense of joy, of completeness, of utter, bone-deep rightness—but she didn't.

Not at all.

And, as she glanced up at Nick, she realised that neither did he. Either that, or he was paralysed by nerves, which was unlikely. He wasn't remotely the nervous type.

He took her hand briefly, squeezed it in reassurance, but it felt wrong. So wrong…

She eased it away, using the excuse of handing her bouquet to the waiting bridesmaid, and then the vicar spoke, everyone started to sing 'Jerusalem', and she felt her mouth move automatically while her mind whirled. *Her mind*, this time, not the voice in her head giving her grief, or a moment of panic, stage fright, last-minute nerves or whatever. This time it was really her, finally asking all the questions Leo's 'Are you ready?' had prompted.

What are we doing? *And why? Who for?*

The last echoes of the hymn filtered away, and the vicar did the just cause or impediment bit. *Was* there a just cause? Was not loving him enough sufficient? And then she saw the vicar's lips move as he began to speak the words of the marriage service, drowned out by her thudding heart and the whirlwind in her head.

Until he said, 'Who gives this woman to be married to this man?' and Leo stepped forward, took her hand with a tiny, barely perceptible squeeze, and gave it—gave her—to Nick.

Dear Nick. Lovely, kind, dependable Nick, ready to make her his wife, give her the babies they both longed for, grow old with her...

But Nick hesitated. When the vicar asked if he would take this woman to be his wife, he hesitated. And then—was that a shrug?—his mouth twisted in a wry smile and he said, 'I will.'

The vicar turned, spoke to her, but she wasn't really listening any more. She was staring into Nick's eyes, searching them for the truth, and all she could see was duty.

Duty from him, and duty from her? Because they'd come this far before either of them had realised it was bound to be—what were Leo's words?—a disaster?

She gripped his hands. 'Will you? Will you *really*?' she asked under her breath. 'Because I'm not sure I can.'

Behind her she heard the slight suck of Leo's indrawn breath, the rustle from the congregation, the whispered undertone of someone asking what she'd said.

And then Nick smiled—the first time he'd really smiled at her in weeks, she realised—and put his arms around her, and hugged her against his broad, solid chest. It shook with what could have been a huff of laughter, and he squeezed her tight.

His breath brushed her cheek, his words soft in her ear. 'You cut that a bit fine, my love.'

She felt the tension flow out of her like air out of a punctured balloon, and if he hadn't been holding her she would have crumpled.

'I did, didn't I? I'm sorry, Nick, but I just can't do this,' she murmured.

'I know; it doesn't feel right, does it? I thought it would, but…it just doesn't. And better now than later.' She felt his arms slacken as he raised his head and looked over her shoulder.

'Time to go, sweetheart,' he murmured, his mouth tugging into a wistful smile. 'Leo's waiting for you. He'll make sure you're all right.' He kissed her gently on the cheek and stepped back, his smile a little unsteady now. 'Be happy, Amy.'

She searched his eyes, and saw regret and relief, and her eyes welled with tears. 'You, too,' she said silently, and took a step back, then another one, and collided with Leo's solid warmth.

His hands cupped her elbows, supporting her as everything slowly righted itself. She turned to him, met those steady golden eyes and whispered, 'Thank you.'

And then she picked up her skirts and ran.

She'd done it. She'd actually done it. Walked—no, sprinted, or as close to it as she could in those ridiculous shoes— away from disaster.

Leo watched her go, her mother and bridesmaids hurrying after her, watched Nick turn to his best man and sit down on the pew behind him as if his strings had been cut, and realised it was all down to him. Appropriate, really, since in a way he was the cause of it.

He hauled in a deep breath, turned to the stunned congregation and gave them his best media smile.

'Ladies and gentlemen, it seems there isn't going to be a wedding today after all. I'm not sure of the protocol for this kind of thing, but there's food ready and waiting for you in the marquee, and any of you who'd like to come back and enjoy it will be more than welcome to do so before you head off. I gather the chef comes highly recommended,' he added drily, and there was a ripple of laughter that broke the tension.

He nodded to his father, who nodded back, pulling his mobile phone out of his pocket to set the ball rolling with their catering team, and with a brief nod to the vicar, Leo strode swiftly down the aisle and out of the church after Amy.

The sun warmed him, the gentle rays bringing the life back into his limbs, and he realised he'd been stone cold at the prospect of watching her make a disastrous mistake. He flexed his fingers as he walked over to the vintage Bentley and peered inside.

She was in there, perched on the seat in a billowing cloud of tulle and lace, surrounded by her mother and bridesmaids all clucking like mother hens, and the villagers gathered around the gate were agog. As well they might be.

He ducked his head inside the car.

'Amy?' he murmured, and she stared blankly up at him. She looked lost, shocked and confused and just a little crazy, and he could read the desperate appeal in her eyes.

'Take her home, I'll follow,' he instructed the driver tersely, and as the car whisked her away one of the crowd at the gate yelled, 'What's going on, Leo?'

He didn't answer. They could see what was going on, they just didn't know why, and he had better things to do than stand around and tittle-tattle. He turned to scan the throng of puzzled guests spilling out of the church, milling aimlessly around, unsure of what to do next, and in the midst of them he found his parents heading towards him.

'Is she all right?' his mother asked worriedly, and he nodded.

'I think so. She will be. Let's get out of here. We've got things to do.'

* * *

She'd done it.

Stopped the train and run away—from Nick, from the certainty of her carefully planned and mapped-out future, from everything that made up her life, and she felt lost. Cast adrift, swamped by a million conflicting emotions, unsure of what to do or think or feel.

Actually, she couldn't feel anything much. Just numbness, a sort of strange hollowness deep in her chest as if there was nothing there any more.

Better than the ice-cold dread of doing the wrong thing, but not much.

She tugged off her veil, handing it to her bridesmaids. If she could she would have taken the dress off, too, there and then. She couldn't get out of it fast enough. Couldn't get out of all of it fast enough, the church, the dress, the car—the country?

She almost laughed, but the hysteria bubbling in her throat threatened to turn to tears so she clamped her teeth shut and crushed it ruthlessly down. Not now. Not yet.

'Are you all right, darling?' Her mother's face was troubled but calm, and Amy heaved a shaky sigh of relief. At least she wasn't going off the deep end. Not that her mother was a deep-end kind of person, but you never knew. And her daughter hadn't ever jilted anyone at the altar before, so the situation wasn't exactly tried and tested.

'Yes, I'm fine. I'm really sorry, Mum.'

'Don't be. It's the first sensible thing you've done for months.'

Amy stared at her, astonished. 'I thought you liked him?'

'I do like him! He's lovely. I just don't think he's right for you. You don't have that spark.'

Not her, too, joining in with her alter ego and reminding her she'd been about to do the wrong thing for the wrong reasons and should have pulled out much, much earlier.

Or he should. Both of them, for everyone's sake. Oh, what a mess!

The car door opened, and she realised they'd come to rest on the drive. Gathering up her skirts, she climbed awkwardly out and headed for the front door. Her mother unlocked it and pushed it open and Amy was swept inside on the tide of her redundant bridesmaids, into the hallway of the house she'd left such a short time before as a bride on the brink of a nice, safe, sensible marriage. Now she was—she didn't know what she was.

A runaway bride?

Such a cliché. She gave a smothered laugh and shook her head.

'I need to get out of this dress,' she muttered, kicking off her shoes and heading for the stairs and the sanctuary of her bedroom.

'I'll come,' her mother said, and they all fell in behind her, threatening to suffocate her with kindness.

She paused on the third stair and turned back. 'No, Mum. Actually, none of you. I think I'd like to be alone for a moment.'

They ground to a halt, three pairs of worried eyes studying her. Checking to see if she'd lost her marbles, probably. Wrong. She'd just found them, at the absolutely last minute. *Oh, Nick, I'm sorry...*

'Are you sure you're all right?' her mother asked, her face creased with concern.

'Yes,' she said, more firmly this time. 'Yes, I'm sure.' Sure about everything except what her future held. 'Don't worry, I'm not going to do anything stupid.' Or at least, nothing as stupid as marrying the wrong man would have been. Not that she knew who the right one was, or how she'd recognise him. She seemed to have a gift for getting it wrong.

They were all still standing there as if they didn't know

what to do now their carefully planned schedule had been thrown out the window, but it was no good asking her. She didn't have a clue. She turned back to the stairs, putting one foot in front of the other, skirts bunched in her quivering hands.

'Shall I bring you up a cup of tea?' her mother asked, breaking the silence.

Tea. Of course. The universal panacea. And it would give her mother something to do. 'That would be lovely, Mum. Whenever you're ready. Don't rush.'

'I'll put the kettle on.'

Her mother disappeared into the kitchen, the bridesmaids trailing in her wake as one after the other they came out of their trances, and she made it to the safety of her bedroom and shut the door before the bubble burst and the first tears fell.

Odd, that she was crying when she felt so little. It was just a release of tension, but without the tension there was nothing, just a yawning chasm opening up in front of her, and she thought she was going to fall apart. Pressing her hand to her mouth to stifle the sobs, she slid down the door, crumpling to the floor in a billowing cloud of lace and petticoats, and let the floodgates open.

He had to get to her.

He could only imagine what state she was in, but that look in her eyes when she'd glanced up in the car—

He pulled up on the driveway of his family home, and after checking that the baby was all right and the catering was under control he headed through the gate in the fence into Amy's garden and tapped on the kitchen door.

Amy's mother let him in, her face troubled. 'Oh, Leo, I'm so glad you're here,' she said, and hugged him briefly, her composure wobbling for a second.

'How is she?' he asked.

'I don't know. She's gone upstairs. She wouldn't let us go—said she needed to be alone. I've made her a cup of tea, I was just about to take it up.'

'Give it to me. I'll go and talk to her. This is my fault.'

'Your fault?'

He gave her a wry smile. 'I asked her if she was sure.'

Jill smiled back at him and kissed his cheek. 'Well, thank God you did, Leo. I haven't had the guts. Here, take it. And get her out of here, can you? She doesn't need all this hoopla.'

He nodded, took the tea and headed for the stairs. Her bedroom was over the kitchen, with a perfect view of the marquee on his parents' lawn and the steady stream of guests who were arriving for the wedding reception that wasn't.

Damn.

He crossed the landing and tapped on her bedroom door.

Someone was knocking.

Her mother, probably. She dropped her head back against the door and sucked in a breath. She wasn't ready to face her. Wasn't ready to face anyone—

'Amy? Can I come in?'

Leo. Her mother must have sent him up. She heard the knob turn, could feel the door gently pushing her in the back, but she couldn't move. Didn't want to move. She wanted to stay there for ever, hiding from everyone, until she'd worked out what had happened and what she was going to do with the rest of her life.

His voice came through the door again, low and gentle. 'Amy? Let me in, sweetheart. I've got a cup of tea for you.'

It was the tea that made her move. That, and the reassuring normality of his voice. She shuffled over, hauling her voluminous skirts with her, and he pushed the door gently inwards until he could squeeze past it and shut it behind him.

She sniffed hard, and she heard him tutting softly. He crouched down, his face coming into view, his eyes scanning the mess her face must be. She scrubbed her cheeks with her hands and he held out a wad of tissues.

He'd even come prepared, she thought, and the tears began again.

She heard the soft click of his tongue as he tutted again, the gentle touch of his hand on her hair. 'Oh, Amy.'

He put the tea down, sat on the floor next to her and hauled her into his arms. 'Come here, you silly thing. You'll be OK. It'll all work out in the end.'

'Will it? How? What am I going to do?' she mumbled into his shoulder, busily shredding the sodden tissues in her lap. 'I've given up my job, I'd already given up my flat—we were about to move out of his flat and buy a family house and have babies, and I was going to try going freelance with my photography, and now…I don't have a life any more, Leo. It's all gone, every part of it. I just walked away from it and I feel as if I've stepped off a cliff. I must be mad!'

Leo's heart contracted.

Poor Amy. She sounded utterly lost, and it tugged at something deep inside him, some part of him that had spent years protecting her from the fallout of her impulsive nature. He hugged her closer, rocking her gently against his chest. 'I don't think you're mad. I think it's the first sensible thing you've done in ages,' he told her gently, echoing her mother's words.

She shifted so she could see his face. 'How come everybody else knew this except me?' she said plaintively. 'Why am I so stupid?'

'You aren't stupid. He's a nice guy. He's just not the right man for you. If he was, you wouldn't have hesitated for a moment, and nor would he. And it didn't seem to me as if you'd broken his heart. Quite the opposite.'

'No.' There'd been nothing heartbroken, she thought, about the flash of relief in his eyes in that fleeting moment. Sadness, yes, but no heartbreak. 'I suppose he was just doing the decent thing.'

Leo's eyes clouded and he turned away. 'Yeah. Trust me, it doesn't work.'

'Was that what you did?' she asked him, momentarily distracted from her own self-induced catastrophe. 'The decent thing? When you married the wrong person for the wrong reasons?'

A muscle bunched in his jaw. 'Something like that. Are you going to drink this tea or not?'

She took the mug that he was holding out to her, cradled it in both hands and sighed shakily.

'You OK now?'

She nodded. She was, she realised. Just about, so long as she didn't have to make any more decisions, because clearly she was unqualified in that department. She sipped her tea, lifted her head and rested it back against the wall with another shaky little sigh. 'I will be. I don't know; I just feel—I can't explain—as if I can't trust myself any more. I don't know who I am, and I thought I knew. Does that make sense, Leo?'

'Absolutely. Been there, done that, worn out the T-shirt.'

She turned to him, searching his face and finding only kindness and concern. No reproach. No disappointment in her. Just Leo, doing what he always did, getting her out of the mess she'd got herself into.

Again.

'Leo, will you get me out of here?' she asked unevenly. 'I can't stay here, not with all this...'

'Of course I will. That's what I'm here for.'

'To rescue me? Poor you. I bet you thought you were done with all that at last.'

'What, me? Change the habits of a lifetime?' he teased, and she had to laugh, even though it wasn't really remotely funny.

She glanced down at herself, then at him. He'd abandoned the tailcoat, loosened the rose-pink cravat which showed off his olive skin to perfection, and turned back the cuffs on his immaculate white shirt to reveal strong wrists above hands criss-crossed with fine white scars. Chef's hands, he called them, but the scars didn't detract from his appeal, not in any way. He'd been fighting girls off with a stick since he'd hit puberty, and the scars hadn't put them off at all.

She managed a small smile. 'We might have to change first, before we go.'

His lips quirked. 'You think? I thought I looked rather good like this.'

So did she, but then she thought he looked good in anything.

'You do, but if the press catch a glimpse of us, they'll think the nation's favourite celebrity chef's secretly tied the knot again,' she said, her mouth on autopilot, and his face clouded.

'Yeah, well, it'll be a cold day in hell before that ever happens,' he said tightly, and she could have kicked herself for blundering all over such a sensitive area. She closed her eyes and let out an anguished sigh.

'Oh, God, Leo, I'm so sorry. I can't believe I said that—'

'It's OK, it doesn't matter, and you're quite right. I don't need that sort of publicity, and neither do you.' He smiled fleetingly, then looked away again. 'So, anywhere in particular you want to go?'

'I don't know. Got any ideas?'

He shrugged. 'Not really. My house is still crawling

with builders, and I have to fly to Tuscany tomorrow on business.'

'Oh.' Her heart sank at the thought of him going, and she felt her smile slip. 'I don't suppose you want to smuggle me out there in your luggage?' she joked weakly, and propped up her wavering smile. 'I promise not to be a nuisance.'

'How many times have I heard you say that?' he murmured drily, and she felt a wash of guilt flood over her.

He was right—she was always imposing on him, getting him to extract her from one mess or another. Or she had done, back in the days when they really had been best friends. And that was years ago.

She forced herself to ease away from him, to stop leaning on him, both metaphorically and physically. Time to get out her big girl pants and put their friendship on a more equal and adult footing.

She scraped up the last smile in the bottom of the bucket and plastered it on her face.

'I'm sorry, I was only joking. I know you can't. Don't worry about me, Leo, I'll be all right. It's my mess, I'll clear it up.'

Somehow…

CHAPTER TWO

HE COULDN'T DO IT.

He couldn't desert her when her life had just turned upside down—and anyway, it might well be the perfect solution for both of them.

He'd been worrying about leaving tomorrow and abandoning her with the repercussions of all this, worrying about how he was going to juggle his tiny daughter and business meetings, and here was the answer, on a plate. Unless...

He studied her thoughtfully, searching her face for clues. '*Were* you joking about coming with me? Because if not, it could be a great idea. Not the smuggling, obviously, but if you did it could solve both our problems.'

A tiny frown appeared. 'You've got a problem?'

He nodded. 'Sort of. I've got meetings to go to, and business and babies don't mix. Normally I'd leave Ella behind with my parents, but this is going to be for several days and it's not fair on them at their age, especially on top of the wedding—and don't say it,' he added, pressing a finger lightly on her lips to stifle the apology he knew was coming.

She took hold of his hand and moved it away. 'Why not, since it's true? It *is* my fault, and they've gone to so much trouble—'

He pulled his hand back and placed it firmly over her mouth to silence her before she got back onto that again.

'I don't want to argue, Amy. Hear me out. Please?'

She nodded, and he lowered his hand and carried on. 'I like to be there for Ella every day, even if it's only for part of it, even if it means dragging her around with me. It's the only way I've been able to look after her and my business, and it's a precarious balance that so far seems to be working. I don't want to upset that balance, abandon her for days and nights on end—and anyway, shortly after I get back I start filming the next TV series for eight weeks or so, and I'm going to need my parents' goodwill for that. If you would come to Italy with us and look after her just while I'm in the meetings, it would be amazingly helpful.'

Amy eyed him thoughtfully. 'Really? You mean it? I *was* only joking, really. I didn't expect you to say yes. I was just trying to—I don't know. Make light of it, really. I don't want to be a burden to you.'

'Absolutely I mean it, and you wouldn't be a burden. Not at all. You'd be a real help. I'm trying to set up a contract with a family there to supply our restaurants. I tasted some of their products at a trade fair, and I was really impressed. I want to see how they operate, taste the whole range, negotiate the price and see if we can strike a deal. And doing all that with Ella on my hip *really* won't work.'

She laughed a little wryly. 'No, I can see that. Not exactly professional, and not really fair on her, either.'

'No, it isn't, and she's my top priority. If necessary, I'd cut the trip short rather than compromise my relationship with her, but I don't want to have to do that, because this is a really great business opportunity and it could be important for her future as well as mine.

'So—will you come? You'll have lots of free time to take photos, and it's beautiful at this time of year. You can chill out away from all this, get some thinking time, clear your head, work out what you're going to do next.

Maybe work on a portfolio of images, if that's where you think you're going.'

It sounded tempting. Very tempting, and she could see that he quite genuinely needed her help. He wasn't just making it up—and anyway, even if he was, did she have a better choice? No. And to stay here another minute was unthinkable.

She could hear the sounds of people thronging outside in the garden—not their garden, but his parents' garden next door, where the marquee had been set up for the reception.

Her hand flew to her mouth, her eyes locked on his. 'Oh, Leo! All that food…!'

She was swamped with guilt, but he shook his head briskly, brushing it aside as if it was nothing. Which it wasn't, far from it.

'It's not wasted. There are lots of people there to eat it, it's fine.'

'Fine?' It wasn't fine. Nothing was fine, and all of a sudden she was overwhelmed again. 'It was supposed to be a *wedding* present from you, and I didn't even *have* the wedding.'

'Oh, Amy,' he sighed, and pulled her head back down against his shoulder, soothing her as the tears spilled down her cheeks yet again and the enormity of what she'd done, the chaos she'd caused, the things she'd walked away from, gradually sank in and left her breathless with guilt and remorse.

'I can't even pay you back,' she choked out, but he tutted softly and cradled her head against that solid, familiar shoulder that felt so good she could have stayed there for ever.

'Hush. You don't need to. Forget it, Amy, it's the least important thing in the world right now. Don't worry about it.'

She pushed herself up, swiping the tears off her cheeks

with her palms. 'But I *am* worried about it! At least let me pay you back for it when I get a job.'

If she ever did. Publishing was in a state of flux, and she'd just walked away from a great career in a really good publishing house because she'd thought she'd have financial security with Nick and could afford to try freelancing with her photography, and now she had nothing! No job, no home, no husband, no future—and all because of some vague sense of unease? She must have been mad—

'OK, so here's the deal,' he said, cutting off her tumbling thoughts with a brisk, no-nonsense tone. 'Come to Tuscany with me. Look after Ella while I'm in meetings, so I can work all day with a clear conscience and still put her to bed every night, and we'll call it quits.'

'*Quits*? Are you *crazy*? I know what your outside catering costs, Leo!'

He gave her a wry grin. 'There's a substantial mark-up. The true cost is nothing like the tariff. And you know how precious my daughter is to me. Nothing could be more important than leaving her with someone I can trust while I'm over there.'

He gripped her hands, his eyes fixed on hers. 'Come with us, look after her while I'm in meetings, have a holiday, some time out while you work out what to do next. And take photos for me—pictures of me cooking, of the produce, the region, the markets—all of it. Your photos are brilliant, and I can use them for my blog. That would be really valuable to me, so much more professional, and certainly something I'd pay good money for. I usually do it myself and blag people into taking photos of me with chefs and market traders and artisans, and if I'm really stuck I get reduced to taking selfies, and that's *so* not a good look!'

She laughed, a funny little sound between a chuckle and a sob that she quickly stifled, and he hugged her again.

'Come on. Do this for me—please? It would be so help-ful I can't tell you, and it'll get you away from all this. You're exhausted and you need to get away, have a total change of scene. And I need you, Amy. I'm not making it up. Not for the photos, they're just a valuable added bonus, but for Ella, and I can't put a price on her safety and happiness.'

She searched his eyes again, and saw behind the reas-suringly calm exterior that he was telling her the truth. He wasn't just being kind to her, he really was in a jam, and he'd never ever asked her for help, although God knows he'd given her enough over the years, bailing her out of umpteen scrapes.

Not to mention the catering.

No. She had no choice—and she realised she didn't want a choice. She wanted to be with Leo. His sound common sense was exactly what she needed to get her through this, and let's face it, she thought, he's had enough practice at dealing with me and my appalling life choices.

She nodded. 'OK. I'll come—of course I'll come, and I'll help you with Ella and take photos and do whatever else I can while you're there. It'll be a pleasure to help you, and it's high time I gave you something back. On one condition, though.'

'Which is?' he asked warily.

'I help you with her care when the filming starts—take some of the burden off your parents. Then I'll call it quits.'

'That's a big commitment.'

'I know that, but that's the deal. Take it or leave it.'

His shoulders dropped, relief written all over him, and she felt some of the tension leave her, too.

'I'll take it. And thank you, Amy. Thank you so much.' His brow furrowed. 'Do you have a case packed ready to go?'

'Yes. I've got smart-casual, beach, jeans—will that do?'

He nodded and got to his feet. 'Sounds fine. I'll get Ella's stuff together and we'll go. I'm not sure, but we might even be able to fly out today.'

'Today!'

'Is that a problem?'

She shook her head vehemently. 'No. Not at all. The sooner the better. I was just surprised. I thought you said you were going tomorrow.'

'I was, but today would be better and I seem to be unexpectedly free now,' he added, that wry grin tugging at his mouth and making her want to hug him. 'I'll see what I can do. How soon can you be ready?'

She shrugged. 'Half an hour? Twenty minutes, maybe?'

'OK. I'll call if there's a problem. Don't forget your passport—and your camera.'

'In my bag. Just do one thing for me before you go. Get me out of this dress? I'd forgotten all the stupid buttons.'

She scrambled to her feet and turned her back to him, and he began undoing the million and one tiny satin buttons and loops that covered the zip underneath. And as he worked, button by button, he became suddenly, intensely aware of the smooth, creamy skin of her shoulders, the fine line of her neck, the slender column of her throat. He could see a pulse beating under the skin at the side, and feel the tension coming off her. Off him, too, but for an entirely different reason. Crazy. This was Amy, for goodness' sake! She was his childhood best friend, virtually his sister!

He finally freed the last button and slid the concealed zip down, and she caught the dress against her chest and turned to face him, a peep of cleavage above some transparent lacy undergarment taking him by surprise. He hauled his eyes up away from it, shocked by the sudden heat that flared through his body.

Really?

Amy?

He backed up a step. 'OK now?' he asked tersely, his throat tight.

'Yes. Thank you. I'll get changed and see you downstairs in a few minutes.'

'Good. Wear something comfortable for travelling.' Preferably something that covered her up. He backed away further, turning on his heel and reaching for the door handle, suddenly desperate to get out of there.

'Leo?'

Her voice checked him and he turned and looked at her over his shoulder, raising an eyebrow in question.

'I'm starving. Grab some food to take with us, would you?'

Food? He laughed, letting some of the tension go. Food was easy. Food he could do.

'Sure. See you in a bit.'

He called the catering manager on the way down the stairs, rang his mother to prime her and went into the kitchen.

Three pairs of eyes locked on him instantly. 'How is she?'

'She'll do. Jill, can you help her get ready? I'm taking her to Tuscany with me and we're leaving as soon as possible. I'm trying to get a flight this afternoon.'

'Tuscany? Brilliant, it's just what she needs.' She went up on tiptoe and kissed his cheek. 'Thank you, Leo. Bless you. She'll be ready.'

It was tight.

While he packed he rang the charter company he used from time to time, and found they had a small jet flying to Florence for a pick-up; he could hire the whole plane for the 'empty leg' rate, but it was leaving City Airport at three. And it was twelve forty already.

Tight, but doable, if she was ready to go. He rang to

warn her, loaded the car in no time flat and drove straight round there, reaching the front door as Amy opened it.

'I'm ready,' she said, her smile a little forced in her pale face, her eyes still red-rimmed, but there was life in them now, unlike the blank eyes of the woman he'd walked down the aisle less than an hour ago. Sure, she was hanging by a thread, but she'd make it, especially once he'd got her out of here, and he was suddenly fiercely glad that he'd managed to convince her to come with him.

'Got your passport?'

'Yes, I've got everything. What's the luggage limit?'

He smiled wryly. 'There isn't one. It's a private charter.'

Her jaw dropped slightly. 'Private—?'

He pushed her chin up gently with an index finger and smiled at her stunned expression. 'It's going on an empty leg to pick someone up—I'm only paying a fraction of the normal charge.' Which was still extortionate, but she didn't need to know that.

'Wow. Great. OK.' She turned to her mother, hugged her hard, hugged her bridesmaids and got in the car.

'Thank you, Leo,' Jill called, and he lifted a hand as he slid behind the wheel and closed the door.

'Did you get food?' Amy asked, and he leant over into the back and pulled out an insulated bag.

'Here. You can feed me en route.'

'Or I might just eat it all.'

'Piglet. Buckle up,' he instructed, but she was there already, her bottom lip caught between her teeth, the eyes that kept flicking to his filled with a welter of emotions that he couldn't begin to analyse. He didn't suppose she could, either, but there seemed to be a glimmer of something that could have been excitement.

He smiled at her, and she smiled back, but it was a fleeting parody of her usual open, happy smile, and he felt another sudden pang of guilt. What if it wasn't excitement?

What if it was hysteria? She was on a knife-edge, he knew that. Had he imposed his own feelings about marriage on her? Put doubts in her mind when they hadn't really been there at all? He hoped not—even if Nick hadn't been right for her, it wasn't his call to sabotage their wedding.

'You OK?'

She nodded. 'Yes—or I will be, just as soon as we get out of here.'

'Let's go, then,' he said, and starting the engine he pulled smoothly off the drive and headed for London.

Amy had never flown in such luxury.

From start to finish, boarding the little jet had been a breeze. They'd driven right up to the Jet Centre terminal, their luggage and the baby's car seat and buggy were handed over, and the car had been whisked away to secure parking. The security check-in was thorough but almost instant, and then they had a short walk to the plane.

At the top of the steps the pilot greeted them by name as he welcomed them aboard, gave them their ETA, a benign weather report and told them there was a car waiting for them at Florence. Then he disappeared through the galley area into the cockpit and closed the door, leaving them with the entire little jet to themselves, and for the first time she registered her surroundings.

'Wow.' She felt her jaw dropping slightly, and no wonder. It was like another world, a world she'd never entered before or even dreamed of.

There were no endless rows of seating, no central aisle barely wide enough to pass through, no hard-wearing gaudy seat fabric in a budget airline's colours. Instead, there were two small groups of pale leather seats, the ones at the rear bracketing tables large enough to set up a laptop, play games, eat a meal, or simply flick through a magazine and glance out of the window. And Ella's car seat was securely strapped in all ready for her.

Leo headed that way and she followed, the tight, dense pile of the carpet underfoot making her feel as if she was walking on air. Maybe she was? Maybe they'd already taken off and she just hadn't noticed? Or maybe it was all part of the weird, dreamlike state she'd been in ever since she'd turned her back on Nick and walked away.

A wave of dizziness washed over her, and she grabbed the back of one of the seats to steady herself and felt Leo's hand at her waist, steering her to a seat at the back of the plane across the aisle from Ella's.

'Sit. And don't argue,' he added firmly.

She didn't argue. She was beyond arguing. She just sat obediently like a well-trained Labrador, sinking into the butter-soft cream leather as her legs gave way, watching him while he strapped little Ella into her seat, his big hands gentle and competent as he assembled the buckle and clicked it firmly into place.

She hoped she never had to do it. It looked extraordinarily complicated for something so simple, and she was suddenly swamped with doubts about her ability to do this.

What on earth did she know about babies? Less than nothing. You could write it all in capitals on the head of a very small pin. He must be nuts to trust her with his child.

She heard voices as a man and woman in uniform came up the steps and into the plane, and moments later the door was shut and the woman was approaching them with a smile, her hand extended.

'Mr Zacharelli.'

Leo shook her hand and returned the smile. 'Julie, isn't it? We've flown together before.'

'We have, sir. It's a pleasure to welcome you and Ella on board again, and Miss Driver, I believe? I'm your cabin crew today, and if there's anything you need, don't hesitate to ask.'

She smiled at Amy as they shook hands, and turned her attention back to Leo.

'May I go through the pre-flight safety procedure with you?' she asked, and he delved into the baby's bag and handed Ella a crackly, brightly coloured dragonfly toy to distract her while Julie launched into the familiar spiel.

It took a few minutes, showing them the overhead oxygen, the emergency exit—all the usual things, but with the massive difference that she was talking only to them, and the smiles she gave were personal. Especially to Leo, Amy thought, and mentally rolled her eyes at yet another effortless conquest on his part. He probably wasn't even aware of it.

And then it was done, another smile flashed in his direction, and Julie took herself off and left them alone.

'Was that from me?' Amy asked, pointing at the dragonfly toy Ella was happily playing with.

Leo nodded, sending her a fleeting smile. 'You sent her it when she was born. She loves it. I have to take it everywhere with us.'

That made her smile. At least she'd done one thing right, then, in the last year or so. He zipped the bag up, stashed it in the baggage compartment, put her hand luggage in there, too, and sat down opposite Ella and across from Amy.

His tawny gold eyes searched hers thoughtfully.

'You OK now?'

If you don't count the butterflies stampeding around in my stomach like a herd of elephants, she thought, but she said nothing, just nodded, and he raised a brow a fraction but didn't comment.

'Do you always travel like this?' she asked, still slightly stunned by their surroundings but rapidly getting used to it.

He laughed softly. 'Only if I'm travelling with Ella or

if time's short. Usually I go business class. It's just much easier with a baby to travel somewhere private. I'm sure you've been in a plane when there's been a screaming baby—like this,' he added, as Ella caught sight of the bottle he'd tried to sneak out of his pocket so he could fasten his seat belt. She reached for it, little hands clenching and unclenching as she started to whimper, and Leo hid the bottle under the table.

'No, *mia bella,* not yet,' he said gently, and the whimper escalated to an indignant wail.

Amy laughed softly. 'Right on cue.'

She propped her elbows on the table and leant towards Ella, smiling at her and waggling her dragonfly in an attempt to distract her.

'Hi, sweet pea,' she crooned softly. 'You aren't really going to scream all the way there, are you? No, of course not!'

Finally distracted from the bottle, Ella beamed at her and squashed the toy. It made a lovely, satisfying noise, so she did it again, and Leo chuckled.

'Babies are refreshingly easy to please. Give them a toy and they're happy.'

'Like men, really. Fast car, big TV, fancy coffee maker… private jet—'

He gave a soft snort and shot her a look. 'Don't push it. And don't get lulled into a false sense of security because you managed to distract her this time. She can be a proper little tyrant if it suits her. You're a monster in disguise, aren't you, *mia bella*?'

He said it with such affection, and Amy's heart turned over. Poor little scrap, losing her mother so young and so tragically. Leo must have been devastated—although not for himself, from what he'd said. He'd told her that marrying the wrong person was a recipe for disaster and it would be a cold day in hell before he did it again, so it didn't sound as if his marriage had been a match made in heaven, by any means. But even so—

'I need to make a quick call to sort out where we're going to stay tonight. Can you entertain her, please, Amy? I won't be a moment.'

'Sure.' Amy shut the door on that avenue of thought and turned her attention to amusing Ella. She'd got enough mess of her own to deal with, without probing into Leo's.

But Ella didn't really need entertaining, not with her dragonfly to chew and crackle, so Amy was free to listen to what Leo was saying. Not that she could understand it, because he was talking in Italian, but it was lovely to listen to him anyway.

She always thought of him as English, like his mother, but then this amazing other side of him would come out, the Italian side that came from his father, and it did funny things to her insides.

Or maybe it was just the language doing that? That must be it. There was no way Leo talking Italian was sexy, that was just ridiculous. Not according to his numerous female fans, of course, but that didn't mean *she* had to fall under his spell. This was Leo, after all.

Yes, of course he was gorgeous, she knew that, and she'd had a serious case of hero-worship when she'd hit puberty, but she'd never felt whatever it was they all obviously felt—probably because she'd known him too long, knew all his weaknesses and irritating little habits as well as his strong points, like friendship and loyalty and generosity.

He was virtually a brother, a brother she loved to bits and would go to the end of the earth for. The best friend a girl could want. And no matter where she ended up, that would never change, but sexy? Nope—

'*Ciao. A dopo,*' he said in that delicious Italian of his, and her heart did a little back-flip to prove her wrong.

* * *

He put his phone away and smiled at Amy across the aisle.

'Well, that's our accommodation sorted,' he said with relief. 'I phoned Massimo Valtieri to tell him I'm bringing a friend to help with the baby so we'd make our own arrangements, but he wouldn't have any of it. He says there's plenty of room for you, too, and they're fine with us all staying at the *palazzo,* as from tonight. Problem solved.'

'*Palazzo*?' she squealed, and lowered her voice to a whisper. 'They live in a *palazzo*?'

Leo laughed softly at the awed expression on her face. 'Apparently. It's an old Medici villa. I've seen pictures of it, and it's very beautiful. It's been in the family for centuries, which is why I want to deal with them because it's not just a business, it's in their blood, it's who they are. The meetings will be there and they all live very close by, apparently, so it makes sense us being there, too, so if Ella kicks off and you can't cope, I won't be far away. And his wife's there, so you'll have company.'

'Oh, that's good,' she said, and a little worried crinkle in between her eyebrows smoothed away. She shook her head, her mouth kicking up in a wry smile. 'I still can't quite believe I'm going to be staying in a *palazzo*.'

She looked so flummoxed it made him chuckle. 'Well, you've got about four or five hours to get used to the idea,' he told her.

He was just relieved he'd be on hand; he didn't know what he knew about babies, but she knew almost nothing about Ella, so having a woman around who was a mother herself could only be a good thing, especially under the circumstances. He didn't want Amy feeling any more overwhelmed than she already was.

She was leaning over now and chatting to Ella, telling her what a lucky girl she was to stay in a *palazzo,* and he settled back in the seat and studied her. She was smiling, the haunted look in her eyes retreating as she fell under the spell of his tiny daughter, and for the briefest of fleeting seconds he wondered what life would have been like for all of them if she'd been Ella's mother.

It took his breath away.

CHAPTER THREE

AMY GLANCED ACROSS at Leo and frowned.

He was staring at her with the strangest expression on his face. 'Have I got a smut on my nose or something?'

'What? No. Sorry, I was miles away. Ah, here's Julie, we might be in business,' he added, and he sounded relieved, for some reason.

'We're about to take off now,' Julie said. 'Is there anything you need to ask before we're airborne?'

'I'm fine. Amy?' Leo said, raising an eyebrow at her.

'No, I'm fine, thank you.'

Julie left them, took herself off to her seat behind the cockpit, and then the pilot's voice came over the loudspeaker and they were off.

Leo strapped himself in, reached across with Ella's bottle and began to feed her as they turned at the end of the runway.

'It helps her ears to adjust to the pressure change,' he explained, but Amy didn't care right then. She leant back, gripped the armrests and closed her eyes. She hated this bit—

'Oh!' She gasped as she was forced back into the seat and the plane tipped up and catapulted itself into the sky.

'Bit quicker off the ground than a heavy commercial jet,' Leo said with a grin as they levelled out and settled into a gentle climb, banking out over the Thames estuary and towards the coast.

She looked away from him, staring blindly out of the window at the slightly tilted horizon as the reality of what she'd done kicked in. They were still climbing—climbing up, up and away from England. Away from the wedding that hadn't been, the redundant marquee on the lawn next door, the dress lying in a crumpled heap on her bedroom floor.

And she was going to Italy. Not on her honeymoon, but with Leo and Ella. Without a husband, without a wedding ring, without the engagement ring that was sitting on her dressing table at home where she'd left it.

She looked down at her hand. Nope, no ring. Just a faint, pale line where it had been.

Just to check, she ran her finger lightly over the empty space on her finger, and Leo reached out to her across the aisle, squeezing her hand.

'You OK?' he murmured, as if he could read her mind.

She flashed him a smile but it felt false, forced, and she looked away again. 'Just checking it's not a dream. It feels like I'm on drugs. Some weird, hallucinogenic stuff.'

'No drugs. No dream. You're just taking time to get used to it. It's a bit of a shock, such a drastic change of course.'

Shock? Probably. Drastic, certainly. It felt like she was falling, and she wasn't sure if the parachute would work. She met his eyes, worrying her lip with her teeth. 'I wish I'd been able to get hold of Nick. He wasn't answering his phone.'

'Did you leave a message?'

She shook her head. 'I didn't really know what to say. "Sorry I dumped you at the altar in front of all our family and friends" seems a bit inadequate, somehow.'

'He didn't look upset, Amy,' Leo reminded her softly. 'He looked relieved.'

'Yes, he did,' she agreed. 'Well, I guess he would do, wouldn't he, not being stuck with me?'

Leo frowned. 'Why should he be relieved about that?'

'Because clearly I'm an idiot!'

Leo laughed softly, his eyes full of teasing affection. 'You're not an idiot,' he said warmly. 'Well, not much. You just got swept along by the momentum. It's easily done.'

It was. And he was right, she had. They both had. Was that what had happened to Leo and Lisa when he'd done the decent thing and married her for the wrong reasons?

The seatbelt light went off with a little ping, and Leo undid his lap strap and swung his seat round slightly as Julie approached them with a smile.

'Fancy a drink, Amy?' Leo asked her. 'Something to eat?'

Amy laughed. 'Eat? I couldn't eat another thing! That picnic was absolutely amazing. I'm still stuffed.'

'Well, let's just hope everyone enjoyed it. I'll have a cappuccino, Julie, please. Amy?'

'That would be lovely, thank you.'

Julie smiled and nodded, disappeared to the galley area behind the cockpit and left Amy to her thoughts. They weren't comfortable. All those people who'd travelled miles to see her married, and here she was running away with Leo and leaving them all in the lurch when she should have been there apologising to them.

'I wonder if they're all still there having a post-mortem on the death of my common sense?' she murmured absently. 'At least a lot of them turned up to eat the food. It would have been a shame to waste it.'

'I imagine most of them will have left by now—and your common sense didn't die, it just woke up a bit late in the day.'

'Maybe.' She sighed, and smiled at him ruefully. 'The food really was amazing, you know. I'm glad I got to try

it. Do you know how long it is since you cooked for me?'
she added wistfully, and he gave a soft huff of laughter.

'Years.'

'It is. At least four. Five, probably. You did it a lot when
my father died. I used to come and hang out in your restaurant while I was at uni and you'd throw something together for us when you'd finished, or test a recipe out on
me. I've missed that.'

'Me, too. I'm sorry. My life's been a bit chaotic since
the television series.'

Well, that was the understatement of the century. 'So I
gather,' she said mildly. 'And you've opened the new restaurant. That can't have been easy with a new wife and a
baby on the way.'

A shadow flitted through his eyes and he looked away,
his smile suddenly strained. 'No. It took a lot of my time.
Too much.'

So much that their marriage had fallen apart? If they'd
even had a marriage in the real sense. It didn't sound like
it, but she knew very little more than he'd just told her
and the rest was rumours in the gutter press. They'd had
a field day, but his parents didn't talk about it, and until
today she'd hardly seen Leo since before his marriage.

All she knew was what had been in the paper, that Lisa
had been knocked down by a car late one stormy night and
had died of her injuries, and the coroner had returned a verdict of accidental death. Ella had been tiny—two months
old? Maybe not even that. And Leo had been left with a
motherless baby, a new business venture that demanded
his attention and a television contract he'd had to put on
hold. Small wonder she hadn't seen him.

'Your cappuccino, Miss Driver.'

The drink was set down in front of her, and she flashed
a distracted smile at Julie and picked up her spoon, chasing
the sprinkled chocolate flakes around in the froth absently.

His hand came out and rested lightly on her arm, stilling it. 'It'll be all right, Amy,' he murmured, which made her smile. Trust Leo to be concerned for her when actually she was worrying about him.

'I'm fine,' she assured him. And she was, she realised. A little stunned, a little bemused almost at the turn of events, but Leo was whisking her away from it all so fast she didn't have time to dwell on it, and that could only be a good thing.

She pulled out her little pocket camera and pointed it at him. 'Smile for the birdie!'

'Make sure you get my good side.'

She lowered the camera and cocked an eyebrow at him. 'You *have* a good side?'

He rolled his eyes, that lazy grin kicking up his mouth and dimpling his right cheek, and her heart turned over. She clicked the button, turned to get an interior shot while her heart settled, and clicked again.

'Day one of your Tuscan tour blog,' she said lightly, and he laughed.

She caught it, grinned at him and put the camera away.

They landed shortly before five o'clock, and by five thirty they'd picked up the hire car and were on their way to the *palazzo*. Ella was whingeing a little, so he pulled over in a roadside *caffè* and ordered them coffee and pastries while he fed her from a pouch of pureed baby food.

It galled him to do it, but it wouldn't kill her. It was organic, nutritionally balanced, and had the massive advantage that it was easy. He had enough fish to fry at the moment without worrying about Ella.

He glanced up and met Amy's eyes. She was watching him, a strange expression on her face, and he tipped his head questioningly.

'What?'

'Nothing. Just—I've never really got used to the thought of you as a father, but you seem very comfortable with her.'

He looked back at Ella, his heart filling with love. 'I am. I didn't know what it would be like, but I love it—love her, more than I could ever have imagined loving anyone. She's the most precious thing that's ever happened to me.'

Amy's smile grew wistful. 'It shows,' she murmured, and he thought of all the plans she'd mentioned that she'd walked away from, all the things she'd sacrificed. Like starting a family. And if he hadn't interfered...

She might have ended up in the same mess as him, he reminded himself, bringing up a child on her own after the disastrous end of a doomed relationship.

'Amy, it'll happen for you, when the time's right,' he told her softly, and she gave a wry little smile that twisted his heart.

'I know. But I have to warn you, I don't know anything about babies so it won't hurt to practise on Ella so I can make my mistakes first with someone else's child.'

He chuckled, ruffling Ella's dark curls gently. 'You won't make mistakes, and even if you do, you won't break her. She's pretty resilient.'

Her wry smile turned to a grimace. 'That's probably just as well. She might need to be.'

'Chill, Amy. She's just a little person. She'll let you know what she needs.'

'Yeah, if you can mind-read a ten-month-old baby,' she said drily, but the smile reached her eyes now and he let his breath out on a quiet sigh of relief. She'd been hanging by a thread ever since she'd turned her back on Nick, and it had taken till now before he'd felt absolutely sure that she'd done the right thing. Having a baby with the wrong person was a disaster, and that's what she could have done if everything had gone to plan.

Which let him off the hook a bit on the guilt front.

'Here, you can start practising now. Give her the rest of this so I can drink my coffee, could you, please?' he asked, handing her the pouch and spoon and sitting back to watch. Amy took it cautiously, offered it to Ella, and the baby obediently sucked the gloop from the spoon, to Amy's delight and his relief. Contrary to her predictions, they seemed to be getting on fine. 'There—see?' he said lightly. 'Easy.'

She threw him a cheeky grin and put the empty pouch down. 'Well, this end was easy, but I think she'll need her daddy for the other one. I can only master one skill at a time and there'll be plenty of time to learn about that later.'

He laughed, put his cup down and scooped up Ella and the changing bag. 'I'm sure there'll be lots of opportunities.'

'I don't doubt it,' she said drily, but her wry, affectionate smile warmed his heart and he was suddenly fiercely glad that she'd come with them.

By the time the sun was getting low on the western horizon, they were turning onto the broad gravelled drive leading up to the Palazzo Valtieri.

The track dipped and wound along the valley floor, and then rose up the hill through an avenue of poplars to a group of stone buildings on the top, flushed rose by the setting sun.

'I think that's the *palazzo*,' he told her, and Amy felt her jaw drop.

'What, all of it? It's enormous! It looks as big as some of the little hilltop towns!'

He chuckled softly. 'There'll be all sorts of other buildings there clustered around it. It won't just be the house.'

But it was. Well, pretty much, she realised as they approached the imposing edifice with its soaring stone walls

and windows that she just knew would have the most amazing views. She couldn't wait to get her proper camera out.

They drove under a huge stone archway in the wall
and into a large gravelled courtyard, triggering lights that
flooded the area with gold. There were several vehicles
there, and Leo brought the car to rest beside a big people-
carrier.

They were facing a broad flight of steps flanked by
olive trees in huge terracotta pots, and at the top of the
steps was a pair of heavily studded wooden doors, totally
in proportion to the building.

She felt her jaw sag again. 'Oh. Wow. Just—wow,' she
breathed.

Leo's grin was wry. 'Yeah. Makes my house look a bit
modest, doesn't it?'

'I haven't seen your house yet,' she reminded him, 'but
it would have to be ridiculously impressive to compete
with this.'

'Then it's a good job I'm not a sore loser. Unless you
count a sea view? That's probably the only thing they don't
have.'

She cocked her head on one side and grinned at him.
'That might just do it. You know me—I always wanted
to be a mermaid.'

'I'd forgotten that.' His cheek creased, the dimple appearing as he punched the air. 'Ace. My house trumps the
seat of the Valtieri dynasty.'

'I did say "might",' she pointed out, but she couldn't
quite stifle her smile, and he laughed softly and opened
the car door.

'You haven't seen my view yet.'

She met his smile over the top of the car. 'I haven't seen
theirs, either. Don't count your chickens.'

'Would I?' He grinned again, that dimple making another unscheduled appearance, and her heart lurched.

'I guess we'd better tell them we're here,' she said, but it seemed they didn't need to.

One of the great wooden doors swung open, and a tall man in jeans and a blinding white shirt ran down the steps, smiling broadly, hand extended as he reached Leo.

'Massimo Valtieri,' he said. 'And you're Leo Zacharelli. It's good to meet you. Welcome to Palazzo Valtieri.'

He spoke in perfect English, to Amy's relief, faintly accented but absolutely fluent, and he turned to her with a welcoming smile. 'And you must be Miss Driver.'

'Amy, please,' she said, and he smiled again and shook her hand, his fingers warm and firm and capable.

'Amy. Welcome. My wife Lydia's so looking forward to meeting you both. She's just putting the children to bed and the others are in the kitchen. Come on in, let me show you to your rooms so you can settle the baby and freshen up before you meet them.'

Leo took Ella out of the car seat and picked up the changing bag, Massimo picked up Leo's bag and removed hers firmly from her grip, and they followed him up the steps and in through the great heavy door into a cloistered courtyard. The sheltered walls were decorated with intricate, faded murals that looked incredibly old, and more olive trees in huge pots were stationed at the corners of the open central area.

It was beautiful. Simple, almost monastic, but exquisite. And she couldn't wait to start capturing the images. She was already framing the shots in her mind, and most of them had Leo in them. For his blog, of course.

Their host led them around the walkway under the cloisters and through a door into a spacious, airy sitting room, simply but comfortably furnished, with French doors opening out onto a terrace. The sun had dipped below the horizon now, blurring the detail in the valley stretched out below them, but Amy was fairly sure the view would be amazing. Everything else about the place seemed to be, and she just knew it would be crammed with wonderful photo opportunities.

Massimo pushed open a couple of doors to reveal two generous bedrooms, both of them opening out onto the same terrace and sharing a well-equipped bathroom. There was a small kitchen area off the sitting room, as well, and for their purposes it couldn't have been better.

'If there's anything else you want, please ask, and Lydia said she hopes you're hungry. She's been cooking up a storm ever since you rang and we'd love you to join us once you've got the baby settled.'

'That would be great, but she shouldn't have gone to any trouble. We don't want to impose,' Leo said, but Massimo was having none of it.

'No way! She's a chef, too, and not offering you food would be an unforgivable sin,' he said with a laugh. 'Just as soon as the baby's settled, give me a call on my mobile and I'll come and get you. Both of my brothers and their wives are here as well tonight. And we don't in any way dress for dinner, so don't feel you have to change. We'll be eating in the kitchen as usual.'

The door closed behind him, and Leo turned to her with a faintly bemused smile.

'Are you OK with this? Because I'm well aware you've had a hell of a day and I don't want to push it, but it does sound as if they want to meet us, or me, at least. If you don't feel up to company, just say so and I'll bring something over to you and you can have a quiet evening on your own. Up to you.'

Her stomach rumbled, answering the question, and she smiled ruefully. 'Honestly? Yes, I'm tired, but I'm absolutely starving, too, and I'm not sure I want to spend the evening on my own. And anyway, as you say, it's you they all want to meet. I won't understand what you're all saying anyway, so I'll just sit in the corner and stuff myself and watch you all.'

'I think you will understand, at least some of it. His wife's English.'

'Really?' Another knot of tension slid away, and this time her smile felt a bit more spontaneous. 'That's good news. I might have someone to talk to while you're in meetings.'

Leo chuckled. 'I'm sure you will. I'll just bath Ella quickly and give her a bottle and pop her into bed, and then we can go and meet the rest of the family.'

Ella! She hadn't even given her duties a thought, but now she did. 'Will it be all right to leave her, or do you want me to stay with her? It's you they want to meet.'

He picked something up off a side table and waggled it at her.

'Baby monitor,' he said, by way of explanation. 'They really have thought of everything.'

They had. Absolutely everything. There were posh toiletries in the bathroom, the fridge was stocked with milk, juice, butter and fresh fruit, there was a bowl of brown, speckled eggs and a loaf of delicious-looking crunchy bread on the side, and a new packet of ground coffee next to a cafetière. And teabags. Amy was glad to see the teabags. Real English ones.

While Leo heated the baby's bottle and gave it to her, she made them both a cup of tea and curled up on the sofa to wait for him. Ella fussed a little as he was trying to put her down, but it didn't take long before she went quiet, and she heard a door close softly and Leo appeared.

'Is that for me?' he asked, tilting his head towards the mug on the table in front of her.

She nodded. 'I didn't know how long you were going to be, so it might be a bit cold. Would you like me to make you a fresh one?'

'No, it's fine, I'll drink it now. Thanks. I ought to ring Massimo anyway. I don't want to keep them waiting and Ella's gone out like a light.'

'Before you call him—did you say anything to them? About me, I mean? About the wedding?'

A frown flashed across his face. 'No, Amy, of course not. I didn't think you'd want to talk about it and it just puts an elephant in the room.'

'So—no elephants waiting for me?'

He gave a quiet grunt of laughter, the frown morphing into a sympathetic smile. 'No elephants, I promise.'

'Good,' she said, smiling back as the last knot of tension drained away, 'because I'm really, really hungry now!'

'When aren't you?' he muttered with a teasing grin, pulling out his phone, and moments later Massimo appeared and led them across the courtyard and into a bustling kitchen filled with laughter.

There were five people in there, two men and three women, all seated at a huge table with the exception of a pregnant woman—Lydia?—who was standing at the stove, brandishing a wooden spoon as she spoke.

Everyone stopped talking and turned to look at them expectantly, the men getting to their feet to greet them as Massimo made a quick round of introductions, ending with his wife. She'd abandoned her cooking, the wooden spoon quickly dumped on the worktop as she came towards them, hands outstretched in welcome.

'Oh, I'm so glad you've both decided to come over and join us. I hope you're hungry?'

'Absolutely! It smells so amazing in here,' she said with a laugh, and then was astonished when Lydia hugged her.

'Oh, bless you, I love compliments. And you're Leo,' she said, letting go of Amy and hugging him, too. 'I can't tell you how pleased I am to meet you. You've been my hero for years!'

To Amy's surprise, Leo coloured slightly and gave a soft, self-effacing chuckle. 'Thank you. That's a real compliment, coming from another chef.'

'Yeah, well, there are chefs and chefs!' Lydia said with a laugh. 'Darling, get them a glass of wine. I'm sure they're ready for it. Travelling with a baby is a nightmare.'

'I'm on it. Red or white?'

Leo chuckled and glanced over at Lydia. 'Judging by the gorgeous smell, I'd say a nice robust red?'

'Perfect with it. And it's one of your recipes,' Lydia told him with a wry grin. 'I've adapted it to showcase some of our ingredients, so I hope I've done them justice.'

They launched into chef mode, and Amy found a glass of iced water put in her hand by one of the other two women. It appeared she was also English and her smile was friendly and welcoming.

'I don't know about you, but travelling always makes me thirsty,' she said. 'I'm Isabelle, and I'm married to Luca. He's a doctor, so more of a sleeping partner in the business, really. And this is Anita, the only native Valtieri wife. She's married to Giovanni. He's a lawyer and he keeps us all on the straight and narrow.'

'Well, he tries,' Anita said, her laughing words heavily accented, and Amy found herself hugged again. 'Welcome to Tuscany. Have you had a good day so far? I thought Leo was supposed to be at a wedding today, but obviously not.'

Well, how on earth was she supposed to answer that? Except she didn't have to, because Leo appeared at her side and answered for her, fielding the question neatly.

'We managed to get away early,' he said, and she only just stifled a laugh. 'The journey was great, though. Seamless. And our accommodation is perfect. Thank you all so much. It'll make it very much easier for all three of us.'

'You're welcome,' Massimo said, glasses and a bottle in hand, and he and his two brothers immediately engaged

Leo in a conversation about the wine, so Amy turned back to the women and found herself seated at the table while they poured her a glass of wine and chatted about the business and the area and their children, and asked about Leo.

'So, how long have you known him?' Lydia asked, perching on the chair next to Amy in a break in her cooking.

'Oh—for ever. Our families have been neighbours since before I was born.'

'Gosh. Literally for ever! Lucky you!'

She laughed. 'I don't know about that. He used to test recipes on me when we were kids, but I was a willing victim.'

'Victim?'

She wrinkled her nose. 'He was a little adventurous, so there were a few interesting disasters along the way. I think his palate's refined a little bit since then.'

They all laughed, even Leo, and she realised he'd been standing right behind her, listening to every word.

'Damned by faint praise,' he said wryly, and she swivelled round and looked up at him with a grin.

'Well, I wouldn't like to swell your head.'

'God forbid.'

His mouth twitched, and she laughed and turned back and found Lydia, Anita and Isabelle watching her thoughtfully. Why? They'd always behaved in this playful way, she just hadn't thought about it, but—were the three women reading something else into it? Something that wasn't there? She felt herself colour slightly and dunked a bit of olive ciabatta into the bowl of oil and balsamic vinegar on the table in front of her.

Good move. The flavour exploded on her tongue and suddenly she understood why they were there. 'Wow. This is lovely. Is it yours?' she asked, and to her relief the conversation moved on as the food was put on the table and they all piled in, and the slightly awkward moment passed.

Then as the last plate was cleared away and it looked as if they'd split up into two groups again, Ella cried out, the monitor flashing right in front of Leo, and Amy seized the opportunity to escape before the women could ask any more searching questions.

'I'll go,' she said hastily to Leo, scraping back her chair and snatching up the baby monitor. 'You stay and talk.'

'Are you sure?'

His eyes searched hers, concern etched in them, and she found a smile.

'Absolutely. We'll be fine, and if we aren't, we'll come and find you.' She turned to the others. 'I hope you'll excuse me. It's been quite a…long and complicated day.'

'Of course. We'll see you tomorrow. If there's anything you need, just ask,' Lydia said, and she nodded.

'Thanks.'

Leo reached out a hand and stopped her briefly. 'I'll be with you in a minute. I won't be long.'

She nodded back, dug out the smile again for the others, thanked Lydia for the meal and made her escape. Long and complicated didn't even begin to scratch the surface of her day, and she was only too ready to head across the beautiful courtyard to their suite of rooms, let herself in and close the door with a shaky sigh of relief.

For some reason she could feel tears threatening, and frankly she'd done enough crying this morning—no, this afternoon. Whenever. The wedding was supposed to have been at noon. So still less than twelve hours since she'd turned her back on Nick and run away.

And she would be spending her wedding night alone in an ancient medieval *palazzo* in Tuscany, instead of with Nick in the honeymoon suite of an old manor house prior to heading off to a sun-soaked beach in the Indian Ocean for her honeymoon.

She gave a tiny laugh that turned into a hiccupping sob, and ramming her hand over her mouth she headed towards the bedrooms.

And stopped, registering for the first time that the room with the travel cot in it had twin beds, and the other room had a huge double. Not that the twin beds were in any way small, but it seemed wrong for her to take the double instead of Leo and she was, after all, supposed to be here to look after the baby, even though Leo had said he'd share with Ella.

She pushed the door open a little further and peered into the travel cot. The baby was fast asleep and breathing quietly and evenly, whatever had disturbed her clearly not enough to wake her properly, and Amy turned away from the bedrooms and headed for the kitchen.

She was tired beyond belief, her brain worn out from going over and over the repercussions of her impulsive behaviour, but she couldn't go to bed until she'd discussed their sleeping arrangements with Leo, so she put the kettle on, made herself a cup of tea and settled down to wait for him.

CHAPTER FOUR

LEO STAYED IN the kitchen for a while longer, deep in conversation with the Valtieri brothers. They were fascinating men, with a passion for what they produced, for the land, for their family ties and history and also for their future—a future he realised he wanted to share.

Their business was a part of them, utterly fundamental, their enthusiasm burning so intensely that it was infectious. It was how he felt about his own chosen path, his constant striving for perfection, for excellence, and it was wonderful to meet people who produced the raw ingredients of his craft with the same passion.

He'd missed this—missed talking to people who understood what drove him and shared it, missed immersing himself in the thing he loved most in the world apart from his family. Especially his daughter—

His gut clenched. Oh, hell. Amy was looking after her, and he'd totally forgotten!

What was he thinking about? He'd let her take the baby monitor so he had no idea how long it had taken Ella to settle, and Amy had enough to deal with tonight, of all nights, without a tired and fractious baby.

He shouldn't have taken her for granted, but he'd been so wrapped up in his own agenda, so busy enjoying himself, that she'd completely slipped his mind.

How *could* he have let that happen? Especially when he was so worried about her. She'd been quiet all day, so unlike her usually bubbly self, and although she seemed to have enjoyed the evening there'd been a distracted look in her eyes—and when Ella had cried, she'd grabbed the opportunity to escape with both hands.

And he'd let her do it. What kind of a friend was he?

'Sorry, guys, I lost track of the time, I'm going to have to go,' he said a little abruptly. 'It's been a long day and I need to check on Ella.' And Amy. *Dio*, how *could* he—?

'Sure. We'll see you in the morning. Nine o'clock?'

He nodded. 'That's fine. I'll look forward to it.'

'Tell Amy we'll be around,' Lydia chipped in with a smile. 'She and Ella are more than welcome to join us.'

'Thank you. I'll pass it on. I'm sure she'll appreciate the company. And thank you for a lovely meal. It was delicious. I'll have to return the favour one evening.'

Lydia laughed. 'Feel free. I'd love you to cook for us. It would be amazing. You can give me a master class, if you like.'

He gave a soft chuckle. 'No pressure, then.'

'I'm sure you can handle it, Chef,' she said with a grin, and he chuckled again and got to his feet, shook hands with all the men, said goodnight to the ladies and crossed the courtyard swiftly, letting himself quietly into the guest suite.

Silence. No screaming baby, no sound from Amy desperately trying to pacify her, and the tension drained out of him. She must have gone to bed and left a lamp on in the sitting room for him.

He turned towards it, and then he saw her in the soft glow, curled up in the far corner of a sofa, her hands cradling a mug and her face in shadow.

'You're still up,' he said unnecessarily. 'I'm sorry, I didn't mean to be so long. I take it Ella's OK?'

'She's fine.'

He frowned. Her voice sounded—odd. Disconnected.

'Amy?' he said softly. She turned her head and looked up at him, and his gut clenched. She'd been crying. He could see the dried tracks of tears on her cheeks, her eyes red-rimmed and swollen, and guilt rose up and swamped him.

Damn.

She hadn't meant him to find her like this, and now there was guilt written all over his face. She closed her eyes, biting her lip and kicking herself for not just going to bed.

The sofa dipped as he sat down next to her, his thigh warm against her hip, his arm around her shoulders solid and comforting. She felt his breath ease out on a weary sigh.

'I'm so sorry. I got caught up in conversation and I should have been here for you, not abandoning you on your own to deal with Ella. Was she a nightmare?'

She shook her head. 'No. She was still asleep. It's not that. I spoke to Nick,' she said, and her voice clogged with tears. She swallowed and tried again. 'He rang to find out if I was OK.'

'And are you?' he asked, although she knew he could see quite clearly that she wasn't.

She shrugged. 'I suppose. I don't know. It's my wedding night, Leo. I should have been married—'

Her voice cracked, and he took the mug out of her hands and pulled her gently into his arms.

'Oh, Amy, I'm so sorry. This is all my fault.'

'What's your fault?' she asked, tilting her head back and searching his eyes. 'That I left it so long to realise it was a mistake? Hardly.'

'That you're not married. Not on your honeymoon. That you've thrown away all your carefully laid plans.'

She shook her head and cradled his cheek in her hand. It felt rough, the stubble growing out now at the end of the

day, and there was something grounding about the feel of
it against her palm. Something warm and real and alive
that made it all make sense. Or complicated it all a whole
lot more. She dropped her hand back in her lap.

'That I'm not married to the wrong man,' she corrected,
her voice soft but emphatic, needing to convince him so
he didn't carry this guilt around like a burden for ever.
'You did the *right thing*, Leo. It was me who didn't, me
who ignored all the warnings going off in my head all the
time. I thought I was just stressing about the wedding, but
I wasn't, it was the marriage, the lifetime commitment to
him that was worrying me. I just didn't realise it. So for
goodness' sake don't beat yourself up over it, because it's
not your fault, OK?'

'So why are you crying?'

She gave a little shrug. 'Because the pressure's off?
Because I feel guilty because I'm glad I'm not married
to him when he's actually a really nice guy? Take your
pick.' She tried to smile, but it was a rubbish effort, so
she sniffed and swiped the tears off her cheeks and tried
again. 'There. Is that better?'

'Not much,' he said honestly, lifting a damp strand of
hair away from her eyes with gentle fingers.

'Well, it's the best I can do,' she said, her voice choked
again, and Leo closed his eyes and folded her close against
his chest and rested his cheek against her hair. It felt a little
stiff from the products she must have had put in it for the
updo, not as soft and sleek as usual. Not his Amy.

His Amy? What was he thinking? She hadn't ever been
his Amy, even in the old days. And now was not the time
to reinvent their relationship, when both of them were
an emotional mess. However appealing it might be. And
where the hell had that come from?

With a quiet sigh he loosened his hold and sat up a little,

putting some much-needed distance between them before he did something stupid that he'd regret for ever.

'You'll feel better after you've had a good night's sleep. Why don't you have a shower and go to bed?' he murmured, and she looked up at him, her eyes lost.

'Where? Which bed? The room Ella's in has only got single beds and you can't possibly sleep in one of those, it seems all wrong. You should have the double.'

'Don't be daft. They're not small beds. You take the double, it's fine.'

'Are you sure?'

'Of course I'm sure, and I'm certainly not moving her tonight. I'll sort the luggage out, and then you go and have a shower and get off to bed. You'll feel better in the morning, honestly.'

'Is that a promise?'

She looked so forlorn that he laughed softly and hugged her. 'Yes, it's a promise. New day, new life.'

It sounded great. He just hoped it didn't turn out to be a false promise, because he was still waiting for that new life after copious new days. New weeks. New months. And there was no sign of it. He felt as if his life was on hold, in limbo, and every dawn was just as bleak as the one before...

Leo was right. She did feel better in the morning.

It shouldn't have surprised her; Leo was always right. Why hadn't she asked him about Nick before? Except of course it would have seemed disloyal, and even now it felt wrong talking to him about Nick because there was nothing *wrong* with Nick.

It wasn't about Nick. It was about her, and the fact that it had taken her such an unforgivably long time to realise she wasn't going to settle for sensible.

She sighed softly. She'd never been sensible. She only

had to look at the mess she'd made of her other relationships to know that, so she might have realised it was never going to work with Nick. Except that was the very reason she'd thought it *might* work, because for once it *was* sensible, and it had taken her far too long to realise she was wrong.

Well, at least she hadn't left it until after they were married. That would have been worse.

She threw back the covers and climbed out of the ridiculously enormous bed that Leo really should have had. She wished he *had* had it, because lying alone in the vast expanse of immaculate white linen had just underlined all the things she'd walked away from.

Still, as Leo had said, new day, new life. That was yesterday. Today was a new day, a fresh start, and she needed to get out there and embrace it.

'Bring it on,' she muttered, staring at herself in the mirror and digging out a smile. There. See? She could do it.

She could hear Leo and Ella in the little sitting room of their suite and they seemed to be having a lot of fun, babyish giggles interspersed with the deeper, soft rumble of Leo's voice. She'd go and join them, bask in the warmth of their love for each other and see if it could drive out this aching loneliness.

She delved in her suitcase for her dressing gown, and frowned. Damn. She'd completely forgotten that she hadn't brought the ratty old towelling thing that she'd had for a hundred years but a slippery little scrap of silk deliberately chosen because it was beautiful and elegant and undeniably sexy. To inject some fireworks into their honeymoon?

Maybe. It was what the garment was designed for, like the camisole nightdress she'd worn last night, and she hadn't even thought about it when she'd said that she was packed ready to go, but she should have done, she realised in dismay. Not that she'd exactly had a lot of time to think about it in the hurry to leave.

She contemplated getting dressed rather than going out into the sitting room what felt like half-naked, but she needed a cup of tea and a shower before she could put on her clothes, and it covered her from head to toe. She tugged the belt tighter and opened the door. There. Perfectly respectable, if a little on the thin side, and it was only Leo, after all.

Only?

Scratch that. He was dressed in a battered old T-shirt and jeans, his feet bare, and he was sitting cross-legged on the floor with Ella, playing peep-bo from behind a cushion and making her giggle hysterically. And for some ridiculous reason he looked as sexy as sin. It must be the bare feet, she thought, and dragged her eyes off them. Or the tug of the T-shirt across those broad, solid shoulders—

He's not sexy! She swallowed and wrapped her arms defensively around her waist. 'Hi, guys. Are you having fun?' she asked, smiling at Ella and trying to avoid Leo's eye as he turned to look at her over his shoulder.

'My daughter likes to see the sun rise,' he said drily, and she chuckled and risked another glance at him.

Mistake. His eyes were scanning her body and he looked quickly away, a touch of colour brushing the back of his neck, and she wished she'd just got dressed because now she'd embarrassed him. Oh, God. Did he think she was flaunting herself in front of him? Idiot! She should have dragged on her clothes and changed them after her shower—

'Tea?' he asked, in a perfectly normal voice that didn't for some reason sound quite normal because there was a tension vibrating in it that she'd never heard before.

'That'd be great. I'll make it.'

But he'd already uncoiled from the floor in one lithe movement and headed for the kitchen, as if he was suddenly desperate for some space between them. 'I've had two cups,' he said. 'I'll make yours, and you can sit and come round slowly and play with Ella while I have a shower, if that's OK. Deal?'

'Deal.'

He made it to the safety of the kitchen and let his breath out on a long, silent sigh of relief.

'Thank you,' she called after him.

'Don't mention it.'

He flicked the switch on the kettle, then stuck his head back round the corner while the kettle boiled, still managing to avoid her eyes by pretending to look at Ella. 'I've got a meeting at nine that'll probably go on all morning—will you be OK with her? She'll probably nap for a lot of it.'

'I'll be fine, I slept like a log. Were you OK in that single bed?' she asked.

Bed? Now she wanted to talk about the *bed*? He ducked back into the kitchen and busied himself with her mug, sending his unruly body a short, pithy reprimand. 'Fine, thanks,' he lied. 'I told you it would be.'

It hadn't been fine, but he wasn't telling her that. Oh, it had been perfectly comfortable, if he ignored the fact that he was used to sleeping in a huge bed all to himself. What wasn't fine was the fact that he'd been ridiculously conscious of her just on the other side of the wall, and swapping rooms wouldn't change that. It would also mean sleeping in her sheets, and he'd had enough trouble getting her out of his thoughts as it was, without lying there surrounded by the haunting scent of her.

He made her tea and went back through just as she was trying to rearrange the dressing gown over her legs on the floor, and he put the tea down out of Ella's reach and went on walking, keeping his eyes firmly off the slim, shapely thigh barely concealed by that slippery scrap of silk that wouldn't stay where it was put.

'Back in a minute. Don't forget to drink it while it's hot.'

He closed the bathroom door with a frustrated sigh and shook his head. Where the hell had this crazy attraction come from? Not that she was helping, flitting about in that insubstantial little silk thing, but why should that affect him now? It never had before, and Amy frankly wasn't his type.

He liked sophisticated women, and there had been plenty to choose from, especially since the first television series. But he'd used discretion, or so he'd liked to think, until Lisa. Nothing discreet or sophisticated about that. They'd brought out the worst in each other, and the only good thing to come of it was Ella. Their entire relationship had been a disaster of epic proportions, and Lisa had paid for it with her life. He'd never forgive himself for that, and there was no way he was ready for another relationship, especially not one with someone as vulnerable and emotionally fragile as Amy.

Sure, she was a woman now, a beautiful, warm, caring woman, and without a shadow of doubt if she'd been anybody else he wouldn't have hesitated. But she wasn't, she was Amy, and she trusted him. It had taken a huge amount of courage to call a halt to her wedding the way she had, and she'd turned to him for help. The last thing he'd do was betray that trust.

However tempting she'd looked in that revealing bit of nonsense. Oh, well. Maybe Ella would be sick on it and she'd have to wear something else and everything would get back to normal.

He could only hope...

By the time she emerged from the shower, he'd had breakfast and was ready to leave.

'I have to go, I'm supposed to be meeting up with them at nine,' he said, fiddling with his phone. 'Are you sure you'll be all right? Lydia said they'll be around. They all stayed over last night so you should have some company.'

'Fine. Great. And of course I'll be all right,' she said, crossing her fingers behind her back. 'Just go. We're fine, aren't we, Ella?'

He flicked her a quick glance, nodded, kissed Ella goodbye, handed her to Amy and left.

Not popular. The baby gave a little wail, and it took all the skill Amy hadn't known she had to distract her from the loss of her beloved father.

'He'll be back soon,' she promised, and retrieved the dragonfly and squished it, making it crackle. It worked, thankfully, and she ended up sharing her toast with Ella before they went to find the others.

They were in the kitchen, the women chatting at the table while the younger children played on the floor and the two oldest, both girls, sat quietly reading at the table.

'Amy, hi,' Lydia said with a smile. 'Have you had breakfast?'

'Yes, thanks, we're done. Leo said I should come and find you, if that's OK?'

'Of course it's OK. Would you like a coffee?'

'Oh, that would be lovely, if you're having one. Thanks.'

'I'm not, but it's no problem to make you one. We're all on fruit teas—caffeine and pregnancy doesn't go well together,' she said with a wry smile. 'Black, white, latte, cappuccino?'

They were *all* pregnant?

'Um—cappuccino would be lovely. Thanks.'

'I'm sorry, I'll see you outside,' Isabelle said, getting to her feet with a grimace. 'I can't stand the smell of it.'

'No, don't let me drive you out, I'll have tea!' she protested, but Isabelle laughed.

'You're fine. It'll be OK outside and we were just going out there anyway. Max, Annamaria, come on.'

They all went, leaving Amy alone with Lydia while she made the coffee, and Amy took it with a rueful grimace.

'I really wouldn't have had one if I'd known. I feel so guilty.'

'Oh, don't,' Lydia said with a laugh. 'We're used to it, and the men still drink coffee. They just do it elsewhere. One of us always seems to be pregnant and they're well trained.'

That made her smile. She couldn't imagine anything making Leo give up coffee. 'So, is this your fifth baby, or have I lost count?' she asked as they headed for the doors.

'Gosh, no! It's only my second. Massimo was widowed just after Antonino was born,' she explained, 'and I didn't know when we met if he'd want any more, but he just loves children, so this is our second, which will be his fifth, and Anita's on her second, and it's Isabelle's third—her husband's an obstetrician, which is quite handy.'

'Keeping it in the family?'

She chuckled. 'Something like that,' she said and led Amy outside onto the terrace. It seemed to wrap all around the outside of the house, giving stunning views over the surrounding countryside, and Amy was blown away by it.

They settled in the shade of a pergola draped with sweetly scented jasmine, and she cradled her cup and stared out over the beautiful valley below them, taking the time to soak up the scents and sounds that drifted around them on the air.

'Gosh, it's so beautiful here, I could take a lot of this,' she murmured. 'And the *palazzo* is absolutely fabulous.'

'Not when you have to clean it,' Lydia said with a laugh, 'but at least we have some help. And, yes, of course it's beautiful. We all feel very privileged to be guardians of it for future generations.'

'Well, there'll be no shortage of them,' she said with a smile. 'Would you mind if I took some photos of it? Leo's asked me to take some for his blog while we're in Italy, and this would be fantastic. We'd let you vet them first, of course.'

'Of course we wouldn't mind,' Lydia said. 'I'm sure the guys would be thrilled if it appeared in his blog. Just make sure he gives us a plug!'

'Oh, I'm sure he will. I haven't seen him look as fired up and enthusiastic as this in ages. Not that I'm surprised. It's just amazing here.'

'It is,' Isabelle agreed softly. 'It's a wonderful place to live, and it really doesn't take very long to fly home, which is great for keeping in touch with our families. Well, you know how long it takes, you've just done it.'

'Yes, but it doesn't really count. Our trip was ridiculously easy because Leo wangled a private charter from City Airport—'

'No!' Lydia said, laughing. 'Really? That's where I met Massimo! I was in a truly awful wedding dress, trying to blag a flight to Italy for a runaway bride competition—'

Amy sucked in her breath sharply, and Lydia stopped and frowned at her, her expression appalled. 'Amy—what did I say?'

She laughed. She had to laugh, there was nothing else to do really under the circumstances apart from cry, and she'd done enough of that. Time to introduce the elephant.

She gave them a brief précis of her impulsive actions, and Isabelle reached out and rested a hand lightly on her arm, her eyes searching. 'Oh, Amy. Are you sure you're all right?'

'Yes, of course I am,' she said lightly. 'Or I will be once the dust has settled.'

'Much more all right than if you'd married the wrong man,' Anita put in wryly. 'I wish more people had the sense to pull out instead of making each other miserable and putting their children through hell.'

Just as she and Nick might have done. She felt sick, thinking how close she'd come to it, how devastating it would have been for all of them.

Then Ella toppled over trying to pull herself up, which gave Amy the perfect excuse to leave the conversation for a moment and regroup. Not that the women had been anything other than kindness itself, but she just didn't want to talk about her not-quite wedding or their relentlessly burgeoning happy families. The full extent of what she'd turned her back on was still sinking in, but, although the shock was receding, in its place was a terrifying emptiness that she wasn't ready to explore.

Was Nick feeling the same sense of loss? Maybe. Or maybe not. He'd asked if she minded if he went on their honeymoon alone, and of course she'd said no, but she wondered now if it was a good idea for him or if it would just be making it worse.

Not that it could be much worse than her running full tilt down the aisle away from him. God, the humiliation!

She groaned quietly, and Lydia shot her a thoughtful look and got to her feet.

'I need to make lunch. Are you two staying or going?'

'We're going,' Isabelle said briskly, standing up too. 'Anita and I are going to plan a shopping trip for baby stuff.'

Anita frowned. 'We are?'

'Yes, you know we are. We talked about it the other day.'

Or not, Amy thought, because Anita looked confused for a micro-second and then collected herself, scooped up her baby and went, leaving Amy alone with Lydia.

Two down, one to go, she thought with relief, and Lydia had to make lunch, so she could excuse herself—

'Come and talk to me while I cook.'

'Ella could do with a nap,' she said hastily, using the

now grizzling baby as an excuse to escape, but Lydia just shrugged.

'Put her down, then, and come back. Bring the baby monitor. She'll be fine.'

Of course she would, and she went down like a dream, so Amy had no justification for not going back to the kitchen and facing what she felt was going to be an inquisition.

It wasn't, of course. Lydia was far too sensible and sensitive to do something so crass, and her smile of welcome was just that. There was a jug of what looked like homemade lemonade in the middle of the table, alongside two glasses, and Lydia was sitting there chopping vegetables while her children played outside the doors.

'That was quick. She's a good baby, isn't she?' she said as Amy sat down. 'Have you had much to do with her, or is she just good with people?'

'She must be. I haven't really been around recently and nor has Leo, so I haven't seen either of them much. I've been busy planning the wedding and working in London, and since Leo's wife died...' She gave a little shrug. 'Well, he hasn't had a lot of time for anything but work and Ella,' she trailed off awkwardly.

Lydia slid a glass of lemonade towards her. 'Yes, I can imagine. It must have been awful for him, and it must be a nightmare juggling his work with Ella. I know what it's like running one restaurant, never mind a group like theirs, and raising a baby is a full-time job on its own. I'm surprised he hasn't got a nanny.'

'I don't think he needs one at the moment. His parents are close by and they've helped him a lot, but he likes to be hands on. Even so, I think it's been a real struggle.'

'It was good of you to offer to help him.'

She gave a little laugh that hitched in the middle. 'Well, I didn't have anything else to do, did I? And he didn't have to try hard to convince me. I love Italy, and I owe him big time. He's done a lot for me over the years.'

Lydia's eyes searched her face for a second before she turned her attention back to the vegetables. 'Like making sure you didn't marry the wrong man?'

Her smile felt a little twisted. 'Absolutely. That's probably the biggest single thing he's ever done for me. He was giving me away—or not,' she said, trying to laugh it off, but the laugh turned into a sigh. 'My father died eight years ago, just after I went to uni, and I suppose I could have asked my uncle or his father or someone, but I wanted Leo, because he knows me better than anyone else on the planet. So I'm really rather glad I did or I might have ended up married to Nick and it would have been a disaster. Not that there's anything wrong with Nick, he's a lovely guy, it's just…'

'You weren't right for each other?' Lydia said wryly, meeting her eyes again.

She returned the understanding smile. 'Pretty much. Although why it took me so long to work out I have no idea. Probably because there *is* nothing wrong with him!' She gave a wry chuckle.

'And it's nothing to do with you and Leo?' 'No! Absolutely not!' she protested. 'I've known him all my life. It would be like marrying my brother.' Except it hadn't felt like that this morning, seeing him on the floor with Ella, when he hadn't been able to look at her, or her at him…

Lydia shrugged and gave a rueful smile. 'Sorry. It's not really any of my business, but—there just seems to be something, almost like some invisible connection, a natural rapport between you,' she said gently. 'Like with Anita and Gio. It took them years to work out what we could all see. And you seem to be so good together.'

Amy shrugged. 'He's just a really great friend. Or he was, but then Nick came along just after Leo's career took off, and then of course he got married, and Nick and I got engaged—and you know the rest. As I say, we've hardly seen each other recently, but he's still just Leo and I know if I ever need him I only have to ask. He's always got time for me, and he's still a really good friend. The sort you can lean on.'

Lydia nodded slowly. 'Well, I'm glad for you that you've got him. Going through something like this, you need a good friend to lean on. There's nothing like being with someone you don't have to explain yourself to, someone who knows you inside out and loves you anyway. I couldn't want a better friend than Massimo by my side.'

She threw the chopped vegetables in the pot, gave them a quick stir, put the lid on and turned back with a smile.

'So, tell me, what do you do when you're not running away from bridegrooms and being Leo's guinea pig?'

Amy laughed, as she was meant to, and the conversation moved on to safer, less turbulent waters, but Lydia's words echoed in Amy's head for the rest of the day.

Sure, she and Leo were the best of friends, but did that have to mean they couldn't be anything else to each other? Not now, of course. She was an emotional mess, and he was still dealing with the fallout of Lisa's death, but maybe, some time in the future...

...someone who knows you inside out and loves you anyway...

Like Leo?

And it suddenly occurred to her that for all these years, like Gio and Anita, they could have been missing something blindingly obvious that was right under their noses.

CHAPTER FIVE

THE MEN CAME back at lunchtime, and she found herself looking at Leo in a new light.

She could see just from the look on his face how much he'd enjoyed the morning, and their discussions continued for a few minutes, standing outside the kitchen door on the terrace with long, cold drinks in their hands, and they were all talking Italian.

It was the first time she'd heard them together like that, and it dawned on her with blinding clarity that, yes, it was a musical language but, no, they didn't *all* sound sexy. It wasn't the language, it was *Leo* talking the language.

Which changed everything.

They switched back to English as they came into the kitchen, but his voice still did things to her that no one else's did, and when he scooped Ella up in his arms and smiled the smile he reserved for her, Amy's heart melted all over again.

The conversation over lunch was very animated, but that didn't stop him juggling little Ella on his lap while he ate, and after lunch he handed her back to Amy reluctantly.

'I'm sorry. We're going out again to look at the olive oil processing plant this afternoon, if that's OK? Has she been all right?'

He looked a little worried, but Amy just smiled and shook her head slowly. 'She's been fine, Leo. Just go and do what you want to do. We're OK here. Lydia's been looking after us, haven't you, Lydia?'

Lydia smiled reassuringly. 'Leo, don't worry about us. Amy and I are getting on like a house on fire, and Ella seems perfectly happy. Just go. Shoo. We're fine.'

He frowned fleetingly, then gave a brisk nod, kissed the baby and left with the others, and to her relief the baby didn't cry this time.

'Have you got swimming things with you?' Lydia asked as the door closed behind them. 'We've got a heated pool, just in case you were wondering.'

Amy frowned. 'Yes, I have, but I don't know if Ella has.'

Lydia flapped a hand. 'She doesn't need one. I've got loads of swim nappies and arm bands and things. She'll be fine, and it'll only be us and the kids,' she said with a smile, and Amy felt herself relax.

'It sounds lovely. Really inviting.'

Lydia laughed. 'Oh, it is. I think we'd die without it when it gets really hot. At the end of a scorching day in the summer, it's just gorgeous to sink under that water in the evening when the kids are in bed and the stars are glittering overhead. So romantic.' She grinned mischievously. 'You and Leo should try it one night.'

She laughed awkwardly. 'I think the romance might be rather lost on us,' she said, trying not to picture herself and Leo alone under the stars.

Lydia found her a swim nappy, and they all changed and made their way to the pool set down below the terrace at a lower level. The water felt blissful on her hot skin, and Ella seemed to love it, so they spent hours playing in the pool, and it was lovely.

Ella, finally exhausted by all the fun, got a little grizzly, so Amy gave her a bottle and put her down to sleep in a travel cot strategically situated in the shade. She went out like a light, leaving nothing for Amy to do except chill out.

She should have brought a book with her, but she hadn't thought of it, so she settled herself on a sun lounger, arms wrapped round her knees, basking in the late afternoon sun and watching Lydia and the children playing in the water under the shade of a huge hanging parasol. Their squeals of delight washed over her as she gazed out over the beautiful valley below and soaked up the sun, and for the first time since the wedding that hadn't happened she felt herself relaxing.

Till the men appeared.

'The girls must be swimming,' Massimo said, and led Leo across the terrace to the railings. He could hear splashing and shrieking, and he leant on the railings beside Massimo and looked down at them.

Lydia was on the side with the youngest, wrapping him in a towel, and the other children were still in the water, but Amy was sitting on a sun lounger and he could see Ella sleeping in a travel cot in the shade just below them.

'Well, hi, there,' he said, and she looked up, her eyes shielded from him by her sunglasses.

'Hi,' she said, and wrapped her arms around her knees a little self-consciously. Not surprising. He could tell from here that her bikini was pretty insubstantial, and he felt himself willing her to unfurl her body so he could see it.

She smiled up at them, but it looked a little forced. Because of the bikini? Another honeymoon special, he thought, and his body cheered.

'Had a good time?' she asked, and he nodded.

'Great. Really interesting, but quite hot. That water looks very tempting.'

'Feel free, Leo. We've just finished,' Lydia said, gathering up the children's things and heading up the steps with the baby, the older children trailing in her wake, 'but help yourself. You're more than welcome to use it any time you like.'

'Yes, do,' Massimo agreed. 'I'd love to join you but I need to make a few calls before I can escape.' And taking the baby from her arms, he went inside with Lydia and the children, leaving Leo alone with Amy.

She didn't look any too thrilled. Because of the bikini? She would have worn it in public with Nick, he felt sure, so why did the fact that she was alone with him make any difference? Except of course it did. It certainly made a difference to him.

He went down the steps and crossed over to her, sitting on the edge of the sun lounger beside hers and pushing his sunglasses up onto his head so he could study her better. 'You've caught the sun,' he said with a slow smile. 'Just here.'

And because he couldn't resist it, he trailed a finger over her shoulder, and the heat that shot through him should have blistered his skin. Hers, too.

Why? It wasn't as if her skin was that hot. 'Mind if I join you for a swim?' he asked, and she shifted, straightening up so her shoulder was out of reach and giving him a perfect view of her cleavage.

'Actually, I'm going to go in, if you don't mind. I've been out here quite long enough,' she said, and swung away from him, getting to her feet on the other side of the sun lounger and wrapping the towel round herself quickly—but not before he'd been treated to the sight of her smoothly rounded bottom scarcely covered by a triangle of fabric, and his body reacted instantly.

She gathered up her things with indecent haste and turned to him, not quite meeting his eyes.

'Do you mind watching Ella till she wakes up? I could do with a shower.'

He swallowed. 'No, that's fine. How long's she been asleep?'

'I don't know. Half an hour? Bit more, maybe. She was pooped after the swimming. She's had a bottle.'

He nodded. 'OK. You go ahead, I'll take care of her.'

She walked slowly up the steps and across the terrace, resisting the urge to run away. She had been doing a lot of that recently, and look where it had got her, but the heat in his eyes had stirred something inside her that she couldn't trust herself not to act on, and she couldn't get away from him quick enough.

Because it echoed what she felt for him? Or because she feared it was just the knee-jerk reaction of a healthy adult male to a woman in about three square inches of fabric? In which case doing anything other than retreating could just embarrass them both.

She went in through the kitchen, across the courtyard and into their suite, closing the door behind her with relief. She didn't know how long he'd be before he followed her, but she wasn't going to hang around.

She showered quickly, opened her suitcase to look for some after-sun lotion and found the sheet of contraceptive pills that were part of her morning routine. She lifted them out slowly, staring at them without seeing while all thoughts of Leo drained away.

It was to have been her last course before she and Nick started trying for a baby, and she felt an aching sense of loss that had nothing to do with Nick and everything to do with the unfulfilled promise of motherhood.

Ironic that she'd never had much to do with babies before, and yet here she was now, surrounded by pregnant women and small children, so that just when it was suddenly out of reach she saw exactly what she'd be missing.

She hesitated for a moment, then popped the now purposeless pill out of the sheet and swallowed it, simply because she didn't want her cycle messed up.

She found the after-sun lotion, smeared it on her shoulders where she could still feel the tingle of Leo's fingertip, pulled on clean clothes and emerged from the bedroom just as he appeared, Ella grizzling unhappily and arching backwards in his arms.

'She's a bit grumpy, aren't you, sweetheart?' Leo murmured gently, his voice rich with the warmth of his love. He looked up from the baby and smiled at Amy, and the vague sense of loss she'd been feeling was overlaid with another, much more complex emotion that was much more troubling.

'I don't suppose you fancy putting the kettle on, do you?' he suggested. 'I could murder a cup of tea.'

'It was my next job,' she said lightly, and walked past them into the kitchen, wondering how on earth, when her world was steadily imploding, the scent of Leo's skin warmed by the sun could possibly be so intoxicating…

The next morning Lydia dropped the children off at school and ran a few errands, so Amy followed her suggestion and spent a while exploring the grounds with the baby in the buggy, taking photos either for Leo or possibly her own portfolio. Assuming she could find an outlet for them, which was by no means certain. Still, just to be on the safe side, she kept clicking, and she took lots of photos of Ella for Leo.

He checked in on his mobile from time to time, just to make sure that everything was OK, and then Lydia collected the children from school and the men came home for lunch, and after that they all went in the pool to cool off before the men went back to work.

It was stiflingly hot, so Amy joined them, but it didn't take very many minutes to realise that frolicking about in the water in her skimpy little honeymoon bikini in front of Leo wasn't clever. It had been bad enough yesterday when she'd just had to stand up and wrap herself in a towel, but in the water everything seemed to take on a life of its own and she'd had an embarrassing wardrobe malfunction when Ella had grabbed her bikini top. It was only by a miracle that no one else had noticed, but Leo had, and she vowed never to do it again, no matter how tempting the water was.

Then Ella started to fuss, so she grabbed the opportunity and climbed out of the pool, swathed herself in her towel and took the baby from Leo in the water, towelling her gently dry and putting a nappy on her before giving her a drink and settling her in the travel cot for a nap.

Leo swam to the side and folded his arms on the edge of the pool. 'Coming back in?'

'No, I don't think so,' she said without looking at him. 'I thought I could take some photos of you all for the blog.'

'Sure?'

'Sure.'

She forced herself to meet his searching gaze, then he shrugged and sank back under the water, leaving her to it.

She stayed resolutely on the side, wrapped in her towel and perched on a sun lounger, and spent the next hour capturing images of them all playing in the water with the children—ostensibly for Leo, since a disproportionate number of the photos were of him, but mostly so she didn't have to frolic about feeling hopelessly under-dressed.

Then Ella woke, so Leo swam to the side and vaulted out, water streaming off his lean, muscular frame and plastering his shorts to strong, straight thighs, and her heart somersaulted in her chest. She clicked the shutter, capturing the image for posterity, then put the camera away in its case, giving him time to grab a towel and knot it loosely round his hips.

'Your turn to swim, I'll look after Ella,' he said, but she shook her head and glanced back at him.

Not better. Not better at all. To her all too vivid imagination it just looked as if he had nothing on under the towel, and it was too much for her.

'I'm going to shower and get dressed, and then I'll download the photos,' she said, getting hastily to her feet, and with a smile and a wave to the others, she picked up her camera and headed for the sanctuary of the house.

She hardly saw him on Tuesday because the men didn't come back for lunch and then had a meeting after dinner, but then on Wednesday afternoon Massimo and Gio had a prior commitment and the women and children were at a birthday party, so they were left to their own devices.

'How about playing tourists?' Leo suggested, so they went out in the car with the baby and explored a nearby hill town Lydia had recommended for its food shops, and while he investigated them she clicked away on her camera, recording the day for Leo's blog.

It made her smile, watching him interacting with the shopkeepers. He went all Italian, of course, smiling and laughing and waving his hands all over the place, and she realised that he was always like that when he was fired up about something, and she just hadn't registered it until now, when it was slightly more exaggerated.

He'd always been just Leo, and she'd never really analysed him before, but she was doing it now, constantly, with every click of the shutter. Every move, every smile, every frown, every gesture, all logged and recorded in a little part of her brain labelled 'Leo', and her feelings were getting utterly confused.

Inappropriate? No, maybe not that, but certainly different, threatening the platonic status quo that she'd just realised was so fragile, and because of that, and because she wasn't going to repeat the fiasco with her bikini, when she spotted a likely-looking shop she took the opportunity to check it out.

'Can I have five minutes?' she asked him. 'I need another swimming costume if we're going to swim every day.'

A muscle twitched in his jaw and he nodded. 'Sure. I'll wait here for you.'

The shop was perfect, and she found a ludicrously expensive but utterly plain black one-piece swimsuit. She didn't bother to try it on. Whatever it was like, it had to be better than the bikini, and there was a limit to how many photos even she could take of Leo in and around the water. And anyway she wanted to swim; she just wasn't going to risk another disaster.

She picked up a pretty little pink swimsuit for Ella, as well, because it was irresistible, and she didn't even look at the price. She'd hardly given the baby anything, only the crackly dragonfly that was her constant companion, so she could easily justify it to herself.

She managed to pay without flinching, put her purse away, scooped up her shopping and went out into the sunshine to find Leo and Ella.

He wondered what she was looking for. Hopefully something that covered her up a little more successfully than that bikini, which had already given him two sleepless nights since Ella had grabbed it.

He was trying to keep an eye on the shop door, but an elderly matron who should have known better had cornered him and was flirting outrageously, so he was relieved to see Amy emerge.

'Got what you wanted?' he asked, and she nodded and waggled the bag at him.

'Yup. Are you done?'

'Definitely. We need to make a move.'

He turned to the woman to excuse himself, and she caught him by the shoulders and kissed his cheeks, laughing as she let him go with an outrageous parting shot and a cheeky pat on his behind.

He felt the colour run up his neck and walked hastily away, shaking his head in despair.

'What did she say to you?' Amy asked, eyeing him curiously as she struggled to keep up.

'Nothing,' he mumbled. 'Just goodbye.'

'I don't believe you. She was flirting—and she groped you.'

'No, she didn't. It was just a little pat. She recognised me, that's all.'

Amy rolled her eyes. 'I wasn't born yesterday, Leo. Most people don't pat you on the behind, and even I can tell a starstruck old biddy when I see one. She was hitting on you.'

He fought the rising tide of colour, and lost. 'OK, OK. She said if she was twenty years younger, she'd give you a run for your money. I didn't think it'd be wise to point out that we're not together. She might have dragged me off on her broomstick.'

Her chuckle was delicious, and he couldn't help but join in.

'You're such a babe magnet, Zacharelli,' she teased. 'They all hurl themselves at you, it doesn't matter how old they are.'

All except Amy.

The thought popped into his head without warning, but it was true. If he was such a babe magnet, how come she'd never even noticed him in that way? Well, not since she was fourteen and had come down with a serious case of hero-worship, and that didn't really count. Although God only knows he'd noticed *her* recently. Like Monday, with the bikini top that Ella had so helpfully dragged out of the way and that she'd now seen fit to replace. He'd certainly noticed that.

'Can we change the subject, please?' he muttered, to himself as much as Amy, and headed back to the car with Ella, leaving Amy to follow, still chuckling, in his wake.

The next day the men were out again, visiting the cousin who made the gorgeous balsamic vinegar that appeared with oil and bread at every delicious meal, and she and the three wives were left to their own devices for the whole day.

It seemed odd now, not seeing him at all for such a long time, and she seemed to miss him more than the baby did, which was a bit telling. They went to Isabelle's for lunch, for a change, and then retreated to the pool in the afternoon, and then at five, as they were just getting the children out of the water, Massimo, Gio and Leo reappeared, making her profoundly glad she'd bought the new one-piece.

Leo walked towards her, his eyes shielded by sunglasses, and she turned, the baby on her hip, to point him out.

'Hey, look, baby, it's your daddy!' she cooed to Ella, and Ella held her arms out to him, little starfish hands opening and closing as she jiggled with excitement.

Amy could identify with that. She watched Leo's face light up as he reached out for the baby, and felt a pang of envy. What would it be like, to have a little person so very pleased to see you?

Wonderful. Amazing.

He slid the sunglasses up onto his head and held his arms out, and she could see the wonder in his eyes.

'She's wet,' Amy warned him, but he just shrugged.

'I don't care. I need a shower anyway. Come here, *mia*

bellissima bambina,' Leo said, reaching for the baby, but his fingers brushed Amy's breast and she sucked in her breath. It was barely audible, but he heard it, and their eyes clashed and held, his darkening to midnight.

For a moment they both froze. She couldn't breathe, the air jammed solid in her lungs, and then with a muttered apology he lifted Ella out of her arms and turned away, laughing and kissing her all over her face, making her giggle deliciously and freeing Amy from his spell.

After a second of paralysing immobility, she grabbed a towel and wrapped it firmly round herself, then gathered up their things and headed for the steps, Leo falling in beside her at the top. They walked back together to their apartment, Ella perched on his shoulders with her little fists knotted in his hair, while he told her a little about his day and they both pretended that the moment by the pool hadn't happened.

'Sounds like it was worth going,' she said lightly as they went in and closed the door behind them, and he nodded.

'It was,' he said, prising the baby's fingers out of his hair and swinging her down into his arms. 'We had a lot to talk about, and we still have. And they're all off to visit their parents tomorrow. It's their mother's birthday and they can't reschedule, there isn't another time they're all available, which means we can't finalise the deal until after they're back on Sunday. Will that be a problem for you?'

A whole weekend alone with Leo? She felt a flicker of trepidation—anticipation? She didn't know. All she knew was that she couldn't refuse him and she didn't want to. 'No—why should it?'

He shrugged. 'I don't know. I said maybe a week, but we won't leave now until at least Monday or Tuesday and I don't know if you can give me that long or if there's something you need to get back for.'

She stared at him blankly. 'Leo, I can give you as long

as it takes. That's why I'm here. I owe you so much, for so many things—really, don't give it another thought. Do what you need to do. It's fine. I have nowhere else to be.'

'Sure?' he asked, but she could see the relief in his eyes and she wondered if he'd expected her to refuse.

She rolled her eyes. 'Of course I'm sure. Anyway, I'm having fun,' she said, keeping it light. 'So I'm going to be forced to spend a few more days in a medieval Medici palace with a beautiful swimming pool and a view to die for, playing with a cute baby and being fed by a celebrity chef. What a tragedy!'

He laughed softly, shrugged acknowledgement and put Ella on the floor on her towel, crouching down to peel off her costume. 'This is lovely, by the way. Really cute. Where did it come from? Did you borrow it?'

'No, I bought it yesterday in the shop while you were being chatted up by Methuselah's mother—and before you say anything, it's a present. So, are we going to be completely on our own, then, while they're away?' she asked, striving for casual while her hormones were having a field day.

'I believe so. They're going to give us keys and we'll have the run of the place till Sunday lunchtime, so we'll be able to just chill out, which is lovely. I really need that. It'll be like being on holiday, and I'll have a chance to try out some recipes using their ingredients. I'm actually really looking forward to it. I'm cooking for them all on Sunday so they don't have to do it when they get back, and I want to play around with some ideas for that.'

'Can I be your guinea pig?' she asked hopefully, latching onto the safe and familiar, and he tilted his head to look at her and grinned, suddenly looking like the old Leo.

'I'm relying on it. You have a terrifying gift for honesty where my food's concerned. And I'll try not to poison you.'

'You do that,' she said, secretly flattered by his back-handed compliment and relieved that the conversation had steered them seamlessly into safer waters.

'So how was your day?' he asked, straightening up with the naked baby in his arms. 'I felt I'd abandoned you. Were you both OK?'

'Leo, we were fine, and we've had a lovely day together. She's gorgeous. I didn't realise what fun a baby could be.'

His smile softened his features. 'Nor did I,' he murmured, brushing Ella's head with a gentle kiss, and the tender gesture turned her heart to mush.

Oh, Leo...

She showered and changed, then took herself outside, sitting on the bench in the cool shade of their east-facing terrace and leaving him to deal with Ella while she took advantage of a few moments to herself when she didn't have to pretend anything.

She'd tipped her head back and closed her eyes, but then she heard the gravel crunch, then the slight creak of the bench as he sat down beside her.

'Here. I've brought you a drink.'

She opened her eyes and sat up, taking the glass of sparkling water with a slice of lime floating in it, the outside beaded with moisture.

'Just what I wanted. Thank you. Is she asleep?'

'Yes, she's gone out like a light. The swimming must have tired her out. Look, I wanted to talk to you about this weekend. Are you OK with me doing all this cooking?'

Amy looked at him in astonishment, puzzled that he would even ask. 'Why wouldn't I be? You're the one doing all the work and it's not as if I won't get to eat it. It's not down to me.'

'It is in a way,' he pointed out. 'If I'm cooking, you'll need to look after Ella, and it's not really why you're here. I should have checked with you instead of just assuming.'

'Of course I don't mind,' she said, puzzled that he would even ask her. 'You know I don't. Ella's lovely, and, anyway, I am here to look after her.'

'Only when I'm in meetings. That was the deal.'

'Leo, it's fine, and, as you said, you need to play around with their produce, try out some recipes, and I'm more than happy to help you in any way I can. I owe you so much—'

'You owe me nothing,' he said softly, his eyes curiously intent. 'I've told you that.'

She shook her head briefly to free her from the magnetic hold of those mesmerising eyes. 'I do. Not just the catering. I'm OK with that now. That's just money, really, but—well, without you I would have married Nick, and it would have been a disaster. If you hadn't said what you did…'

His sigh sounded weary and dredged up from his boots. 'I had to, Amy. You just didn't seem happy enough for it to be right, and there was no way I could let you sleepwalk into a doomed marriage.'

'Like you did into yours?' she asked rashly, and then bit her lip and waited for his reply.

It was quiet on the shady terrace, the valley stretched out below them, the doors to his bedroom open so he could hear Ella if she woke. A light breeze whispered over Amy's skin, welcome after the heat of the day, and she pressed the cold glass to her face to cool it.

He glanced at her, then looked away. 'I didn't sleepwalk into it,' he said at last. 'Lisa did, to a certain extent, but I was railroaded into it by my own sense of decency. Lisa was pregnant, I was the father, I was responsible for her and the baby. I did, as they say, the decent thing. End of. Except that wasn't the end of it,' he added bleakly, 'and I don't know if it ever will be.'

He was staring out over the rolling hills, his eyes remote and shuttered, and she reached out and laid a hand on his shoulder.

'Oh, Leo, I'm so sorry,' she said softly. 'Want to talk about it?'

He glanced briefly back at her, then away again. 'Not really. Why would I? What's the point? It won't change anything.'

It was a less than subtle hint to drop the subject, but somehow she couldn't, so she pressed on. 'I know that, but you always used to talk to me, get things off your chest. I thought it might help you. You must be so sad, for Ella if not for yourself.'

'Sad?' He gave a bitter little laugh that made her wince. 'I don't think sad even scratches the surface. Gutted? Wracked with guilt? Ashamed?'

Ashamed...?

He turned his head to look at her, and in the depths of those beautiful amber eyes she could see an unfathomable despair. And then the shutters came down and he looked away, glancing pointedly at his watch.

'It's time we went over for dinner,' he said, changing the subject so emphatically now that there was no way she was about to argue with him. And that was that—the end of anything deep and meaningful, at least for now.

Just as well. She was getting altogether too interested in Leo and his thoughts and feelings, and it was time she remembered that it was none of her business, and that he was just a friend.

It's not wrong to take an interest in your friends. You were only asking because you care.

No, she wasn't. She was being nosy, delving into parts of his psyche that were absolutely none of her business, friend or not. If he wanted to tell her about his disastrous marriage, no doubt he'd do it in his own time, but it wasn't down to her to ask.

He got up and went inside, leaving her sitting alone on the terrace. She closed her eyes, tilted her head back against the worn old stone and sighed softly.

There had been a time, not all that long ago, when he'd told her everything. He'd poured his heart out to her on numerous occasions; break-ups with his girlfriends, rows with his parents—all manner of things. She'd done the same with him, and there'd never been anything they couldn't talk about.

And there'd been the good things, too, like the time he'd won the TV cookery competition when he was only nine-teen, and his first job as a head chef when he'd scarcely finished his training, and his meteoric rise to success as a TV celebrity chef.

That was when his ageing father had handed over the reins of the company restaurant business, and he'd raised his game and gone from strength to strength.

But all the time he'd talked to her. She'd been part of all his ups and downs, but not any more, apparently. Not since Lisa, and the marriage that had left him, of all things, ashamed.

Why? Why *ashamed*? Of his choice of bride? His be-haviour towards her? Because she'd died in such tragic cir-cumstances? Hardly his fault—unless there was something about her death that she didn't know. And she wasn't likely to now, because apparently he wasn't prepared to share anything more intimate than a menu, and she couldn't be-lieve how much it hurt.

CHAPTER SIX

As THEY WERE seeing the others off the following morning, Massimo apologised for abandoning them.

'Don't worry about it, we'll be fine,' Leo said. 'Can I raid your vegetable garden, Lydia?'

'Oh, feel free, you don't have to ask,' she said whole-heartedly. 'Use anything you want, there or in the kitchen. Are you sure you don't mind doing lunch for us all? I don't want you to feel you have to.'

He laughed. 'Don't be silly, it'll be a pleasure and I love a family party. It'll be fun. And don't worry about us, we'll be fine, won't we, Amy?'

'Of course we will,' Amy said, but the butterflies were at it again at the thought of forty-eight hours alone with him. His accidental touch yesterday by the pool was still fresh in her mind, and they'd been surrounded then. What would have happened if they'd been alone?

Nothing, probably, and if there was another awkward moment like that she'd only have to mention Lisa and he'd back off at the speed of light. She let out a quiet sigh and waved goodbye to the family.

'Right,' he said, watching the dust trail thrown up by their car as they drove away. 'I need to do some food shopping. There's a market on where we went the other day. Want to come?'

'Sure.' She flashed him a cheeky smile. 'I can defend you from all the old women who want to grope you.'

He chuckled and rolled his eyes. 'Oh, Amy, how would I cope without you?' he said softly.

'Well, aren't you lucky you don't have to?' she quipped straight back at him, and turned away so he didn't see the yearning in her eyes.

Ella fell asleep in the car, so he put her carefully in the buggy and plundered the produce stalls while Amy followed with Ella and captured the atmosphere on her ever-present camera. He found the butcher Lydia had recommended and got into an earnest conversation, which as usual brought out his lovely Italian side that was so irresistibly sexy.

He bought a shoulder of mutton, not something readily available in England, and three racks of lamb. 'I'm going to do lamb two ways for Sunday lunch,' he told her when he finally got away. 'Easy for the numbers, and tender enough for the kids to eat.'

'Yummy.'

'It will be. Even though you have no faith in me.'

She laughed. 'I never said that.'

His mouth twitched but he said nothing, just hung the bag on the back of the buggy and carried on, wandering along the stalls, chatting to people and picking up this and that as they went, and she strolled along behind him with Ella in the buggy, taking photos and pretended to herself that they were a couple.

'Right, I'm done here. Anything else you want to do before we go back?'

She shook her head, so they walked back to the car, him laden with bags, her pushing the buggy with that surreal sensation that somehow it was her place to do it. If only...

'It's getting hot,' he said, tilting his head back and looking up at the sun. 'It'll be a scorcher later.'

'It's hot enough now,' she said, happy to walk in the

shade and wondering if everyone was looking at them and speculating, because everywhere they went he was recognised, and not just by women old enough to be his grandmother. She hadn't realised his fame was so widespread in Italy, but apparently it was.

And mostly he tolerated it with good grace, but she could tell that for once he would have liked to be able to walk around without people saying something to him, or nudging each other and staring. At him, or them together? Would it spark a whole lot of media speculation about his private life? She hoped not, for his sake, and she was glad to get back to the car and away from prying eyes.

He stashed everything in the boot, strapped Ella into her seat and drove home.

No. Not home. They didn't have a home, and there was no 'they', either. Just him and Ella, and her.

'I fancy a dip,' he announced, putting the last things away in the kitchen. 'Want to swim, baby?'

She opened her mouth to answer and then realised he was talking to Ella. Well, of course he was! Why wouldn't he be? He'd never called her baby. Never called her anything except Amy. And brat, on occasions, when she had been, which had been quite often all those years ago.

'Going to join us?'

Was she? She turned her head and met his eyes. They told her nothing. 'Do you want me to?'

He shrugged. 'Only if you want to. It's easier with Ella if there are two of us, but it's not strictly necessary if you'd rather not.'

Of course. He just wanted help with the baby, and put like that it was hard to refuse. Besides, she couldn't think of anything she'd rather do than dive into the cool, refreshing water, so they changed and went over to the pool, and he rigged up the tilting parasol so it hung across the water and they played in the shade with Ella until it was time for her lunch.

'Stay here a bit longer if you like. I'll get her dressed and feed her and then I might put her down for a bit,' he said, handing the baby to her for a moment while he vaulted out of the water, rubbed himself down roughly with a towel and then bent and took Ella from her and walked away.

She let out a long, slow, silent sigh of relief as he went up the steps and disappeared from sight onto the terrace. She'd put on the one-piece again that she'd bought on Wednesday, but she'd felt every bit as naked and as aware of him in that as she had in the bikini.

Because his hand had brushed her breast yesterday afternoon? It meant nothing, she told herself, just an accidental touch.

So why couldn't she forget it, and why couldn't he look at her straight in the eye any more? Or, at least, he hadn't in the past hour or so, since she'd been wearing it.

Stupid. So, so stupid. And it was changing the dynamics of their relationship.

She kicked away from the end of the pool, gliding under the surface with her arms stretched out in front of her until her fingertips hit the other end, and then she tumble-turned and swam back again, up and down, up and down, pushing herself harder and harder until her arms and legs were shaking with the effort.

Even Leo hadn't worked her that hard the summer he'd coached her to swim for the school relay team. And she was thinking about him *again!*

She swam two more lengths to get him out of her mind, then gave up and rolled onto her back and kicked lazily into the centre of the pool, floating with her face turned up to the sun and her arms and legs outstretched like a star.

It was gorgeous. The heat of the sun warmed her where the water had cooled her skin, and she felt all the tension of the last few days soaking out of her body and drifting away across the surface of the pool.

Bliss. Utter, utter bliss—

Something cold splashed onto her face, and she gave a startled shriek and jack-knifed up, frantically treading water while she looked up into Leo's laughing eyes.

'How long have you been there?' she asked indignantly, righting herself and glowering at him.

'Only a moment or two. You looked so peaceful it seemed a shame to disturb you, but I've brought you a nice cold drink.'

'Yes, I rather got the *cold* when you tipped it on me.'

'Drizzled. Not tipped.'

'Semantics,' she muttered. She stood up, cupping a handful of water and hurling it at him. It hit him right in the middle of his chest, and he folded in half and backed away, laughing as he tugged the wet material away from his midriff.

Oh, for the camera…

'I've only just put this shirt on!'

'You should have thought of that before you tipped my drink all over my face. At least I threw warm water at you.' She folded her arms on the side of the pool and grinned up at him cheekily. 'Well, come on, then, let me have it.'

He gave a soft huff of laughter and dangled the glass just out of reach. She stretched up, and just too late she caught the mischief in his eyes.

She should have seen it coming. She knew Leo well enough to know he wouldn't let her get away with soaking him. Even so, the icy flood down her arm and over her chest caught her by surprise, and she gave a strangled shriek and ducked back under the warm water for a second, coming up further away, out of reach.

She swiped the wet hair back off her face and tried to glare at him. 'That was so mean!'

Leo just smiled, set the glass down on the edge of the pool and retreated to a sun lounger a safe distance away. Wise. She swam over to the half empty glass and sipped cautiously.

Gorgeous. Ice-cold sparkling water with a dash of lime. Pity it was only half a glass now, but she wasn't going to pick a fight with him over it. She knew she'd never win. Leo always, always had the last word. She drained the glass and set it down.

'Where's Ella?'

'Napping. She was pooped after the swimming so I stuck her in the travel cot the second she'd finished eating and she went out like a light.' He tipped his head on one side and eyed her thoughtfully. 'Your shoulders have caught the sun again. Are you going to stay in there until you look like a fried prune?' he asked mildly.

It was tempting. The alternative was to get out of the pool in front of him, and she felt curiously, ridiculously naked, even in the one-piece, but she couldn't stay in there for ever, so she swam over to the steps where her towel was waiting, climbed out and wrapped herself in it before she turned round to face him.

'Happy now?'

'I was quite happy before,' he said deadpan. 'It was you I was worried about.'

'You don't need to worry about me, Leo. I'm a big girl now. I can take care of myself. And don't worry about Ella. I'll look after her, if you want to play in the kitchen. I could do with downloading today's photos and sorting through them.'

Anything to keep herself out of his way.

Picking up her empty glass and the baby monitor, she headed up the stone steps to the top of the terrace and left him sitting there alone, hopefully oblivious of the trembling in her legs and her pounding heart and this crazy,

absurd awareness of him, which seemed to have sprung
out of nowhere in the last few days...

Leo let her go.

Not that there was anything else he could do, short of
grabbing her and hanging on, and that didn't seem like an
immensely good idea right now. So he settled for watching the slight sway of her hips as she went up the steps,
the beads of water on her shoulders sparkling in the sun.

His eyes tracked down to linger on those slender ankles
below the smooth, gleaming curve of her calves. Her legs
were browner. Even in the last few days she'd acquired a
delicate tan from the glorious Tuscan weather. It was early
June, hot yet still bearable, and Amy was flourishing, like
a flower turning its face up to the sun.

And he was getting obsessed. He had ingredients to
experiment with, the Sunday lunch menu to finalise, and
he was wasting the precious time he had while Ella was
asleep. He should be using that time wisely, not staring at
Amy's legs as they disappeared up the steps and behind
the parapet wall and imagining them wrapped around him.

And he should *so* not be thinking about her like that!

He groaned. He wasn't interested in Amy.

At all.

So why was he still watching her?

She vanished from sight and he closed his eyes and
dragged his hand down over his face as if he could wipe
away the image from his mind.

Not a chance. With a sigh dredged up from his boots,
he picked up his glass, got to his feet and took her advice.
Time to go and have a look at the vegetable garden, and
then do something useful in the kitchen, instead of fan-
tasising the day away. And from now on he was going to
keep his distance and hope that also meant he could keep
his sanity.

* * *

'So, my little guinea pig, are you ready for this?' Leo asked.

He was lolling against the kitchen cupboards, lean hips propped on the edge of the worktop, arms folded, a slight smile playing around the sides of his mouth, and he looked good enough to eat. He also looked more like the old Leo, to her relief, so she played along, trying hard not to be distracted by how downright gorgeous he looked.

Not your business! Nothing about him is your business, especially not that. Only Ella, and her care, and taking photos for his blog. Nothing else. He couldn't have made it clearer if he'd tattooed 'Back Off' all over himself...

'Are you ready for my honesty?' she said drily.

His warm chuckle filled the kitchen and made her insides melt. 'Oh, ye of little faith,' he teased, eyes crinkling at the corners and making her heart turn over. 'I just fancied playing around with some ideas and I didn't know if you were up for it.'

She shook her head slowly. 'Leo!' she said reproachfully, trying not to think about playing around with him or what she might be up for. 'When have I ever said no to you?'

'Oh, now, let me think—when I tried to kiss you?'

A distant memory stirred, and she laughed. 'I was eight!'

'I think you were nine, actually, and I was nearly thirteen—and as I recall, you told me not to be gross.'

She bit her lips to stop the smile. 'I remember. I also remember when I was fourteen and wanted you to try again, but you never did.'

His eyes changed, becoming curiously intent. 'You were a child, Amy, a minor, and I was an adult by then, so, no, I never did,' he said.

'I'm not a child now,' she said, her mouth on autopilot.

The soft caramel of his eyes darkened, the pupils flaring as he gave her a slow, slightly wry smile.

'I had noticed,' he murmured slowly, and pushed himself away from the worktop, heading towards the fridge. 'So—are you up for this, then? I promise not to poison you.'

She let her breath ease out on a sigh. 'You've tried before.'

'I have not!' he said indignantly, but it didn't work because she could hear the laughter underlying it and her lips twitched.

His laughter was so infectious she gave up the struggle and joined in, the sensual moment pushed into the background as their old banter resumed. 'Oh, all right, if you insist,' she relented.

'Ah, see? You still love me, really.'

Her heart crashed against her ribs. Love him? *Really?* She *loved* him? *Like that?*

'In your dreams,' she said drily, and wondered if he could see her heart pounding in her chest.

She couldn't—could she?

Still grinning, he wandered over to her and hugged her briefly, swamping her in that brief moment with a welter of scents and sensations that sent her emotions into a tailspin, before letting go all too soon to open the fridge and examine the contents.

'Do you fancy a glass of fizz while I cook?'

'Now you're trying to get me drunk and kill my taste buds,' she said, her heart still jiggling after the hug, the word *love* echoing in her head like the aftermath of a thunderclap.

He just rolled his eyes and plonked a bottle down on the table. 'Some people are never satisfied,' he said, then set two flutes down in front of her. A quick twist, a soft pop and he filled the glasses with pale, delicately foaming Prosecco, put the bottle back in the fridge and starting pulling out ingredients.

She sat back in her chair, twiddling the glass, watching condensation bead on the outside as the bubbles rose and popped on the surface.

Did she love him? As in, *in love* with him?

Well, at last! You've taken your time to work that one out.

She ignored her inner voice, took a slurp of the Prosecco and tried not to sneeze when the bubbles went up her nose, then swivelled round to look at him, camera in hand.

'So, what exactly are you planning to experiment with?'

He shrugged, his broad shoulders rising and falling and grabbing her attention. How had she never noticed them before this week? Had she been utterly blind? Evidently. But not any more. She clicked the shutter for posterity. Or her private collection, which was growing at an embarrassing rate.

'I'm not really sure. I haven't come up with anything concrete yet.'

'Concrete? How about your rock buns?' she added to get a rise out of him.

He rolled his eyes. 'They were fine.'

'They were rocks, and you know it.'

He sighed softly, but his eyes were brimming with laughter. 'So they were a little over-baked. I was—what? Nine? And you've never let me forget it.'

'You must have been more than that.'

'Not much. Ten at the most. And you had trouble biting into them because you didn't have any front teeth, I remember that.'

'Yes, and you teased me constantly about it.'

'And you rose to the bait without fail. You always did. Still do.' He stopped teasing her and shook his head slowly, a soft smile playing around his mouth. 'That was a long time ago.'

'It was. It feels like another lifetime.'

'Maybe it was.' The smile faded, a fleeting sadness in his eyes, and he turned his attention back to the fridge, effectively changing the subject.

'So, what are you going to kill me with tonight, then?' she asked lightly, swirling her Prosecco in the flute and following his lead.

He shrugged away from the worktop and shoved his hands into the back pockets of his jeans, drawing her attention in a way that did nothing for her peace of mind. She captured the image. Not that she needed to. It was burned onto her brain, alongside all the others.

'I don't know. I just want to play around and get a feel for their oil and cheese, amongst other things. I've had a look at Lydia's vegetable garden, which has given me some ideas. I think tonight's going to be pretty tame, though, so you're safe.'

She didn't feel safe. She felt—confused. As if her world had slipped on its axis, even though, in reality, nothing had changed.

Nothing? You ran away from your bridegroom at the altar! This is not nothing!

But it was nothing to do with Leo.

Or was it? Was that why she hadn't married Nick? Because of Leo?

The thought held her transfixed, and she watched him blindly while her thoughts cartwheeled in the background.

He diced an onion at the speed of light, pulled cupboards open, inspected spices and herbs, chose some, rejected others. She could almost hear him thinking on his feet. A slab of bacon appeared out of the fridge, and he cut a thick slice and diced it rapidly into lardons and tossed them into a sizzling pan with the onion.

The aroma of frying bacon began to fill the kitchen, and her mouth was watering. Rice appeared, a glug of wine, some stock—

'Are we having risotto?' she asked hopefully.

'Looks like it,' he said with a grin.

Her stomach grumbled. 'Sorry. Smells good.'

'Twenty minutes,' he said, and while he stirred and added a glug of this and a drop of that, he pressed thin slices of ciabatta onto a griddle and stirred something else in another little pan that he piled onto the crispy bread.

'Here, try this,' he said, sliding a plate across to her. 'Tell me what you think. I've used their oil and olives.'

'Gorgeous,' she mumbled, and had to say it again because he didn't understand her first attempt.

'Didn't your mother ever tell you it's rude to speak with your mouth full?' he said, laughing at her, and she poked her tongue out at him.

'Is this all for me?' she asked, and he leant over and snatched the plate back.

'No, it's not!'

'Pity,' she said, watching as his almost perfect white teeth bit through a slice of the delicious *bruschetta* topped with some gorgeous sundried tomato and olive concoction topped with anchovies. She didn't know what she wanted more, the *bruschetta* or the man.

She stifled a laugh and picked up the camera again. If she had the *bruschetta*, she'd eat it this once and that would be the end of it. If she had the man, she could have the *bruschetta* any time she asked for it. And not just the *bruschetta*—

Heat shot through her, stealing her breath and leaving her gasping.

There was a squeak from Ella over the baby monitor, and she shot back her chair and got to her feet. 'I'll go, you're busy,' she said, and left the kitchen hastily, glad of an excuse to get away from him while she reassembled her jumbled thoughts.

Closing the door of their apartment softly behind her, she leant back against it with a quiet sigh.

Whatever the change in direction of her feelings, and probably his, it was perfectly obvious that Leo wasn't in the slightest bit interested in a relationship with her other than the one they already had, a friend helping him out by looking after his daughter. That was all she was here for, and she had to remember it and keep her overactive imagination under control before it got them both into a whole heap of trouble and embarrassment.

Or her, at least, because for all the banter Leo wouldn't even talk to her any longer about anything personal, far less take advantage of her shaky emotional state. Which, she was beginning to realise, was more to do with Leo than it was with Nick and the abandoned wedding.

She pushed away from the door and crept over to the bedroom, but all was quiet. Ella was lying on her front with her bottom stuck up in the air, and she was fast asleep.

And Leo would know this, because the monitor had gone silent. She closed her eyes briefly, sucked in a deep breath and made herself go back to the kitchen. Nothing had changed, nothing was any different, and it wouldn't be if she kept a lid on it. Yes, she loved him, but just in the way she always had. Nothing more, nothing less, and certainly not like *that*—

Liar!

'Gosh, that smells lovely,' she said brightly, walking back into the kitchen and ignoring the nagging voice that had far too much to say for itself. 'Really yummy.'

'Is she okay?'

'Yes, she's fine. Fast asleep.' She picked up her glass and peered at the dribble in the bottom. 'Any more Prosecco in the fridge?'

He glanced over his shoulder. 'There should be, unless you've already drunk it all. You can top me up while you're at it. I've been working hard.'

She arched a brow at him and chuckled. 'Don't give me that. You could make that risotto in your sleep.'

His lips twitched, drawing her attention to their soft, ripe fullness, and she had an overwhelming urge to get up and walk over to him and kiss them.

No! What was she *thinking* about?

She did get up, and she did walk over to him, but only so she could top up their glasses. Then she retreated back to the table, sat herself down and concentrated on the power of mind over matter. Or head over heart, more likely. The last thing she needed was to allow herself to fantasise about being in love with Leo. Not that she was even thinking about love. Nothing so ethereal. Just at the moment, she was quite preoccupied enough with thinking about kissing him senseless.

She stifled a groan of frustration and impatience at herself, chewed her way thoughtfully through another slice of the delicious *bruschetta* and tried not to down the wine so fast that she fell off her chair. Getting drunk would *not* be an asset to the situation!

In the nick of time a wide, flat bowl appeared in front of her, heaped with risotto drizzled with green-gold oil and scattered with torn basil leaves, and Leo leant across her and shaved some slender curls of a wonderful hard pecorino cheese over it. She sniffed appreciatively, and got a touch of Leo in the fragrant mix.

'Wow, that smells amazing,' she said, bending down to hide the sudden flush of colour that swept her cheeks. 'Utterly gorgeous.'

Leo, sitting down opposite her in front of his own plate, couldn't agree more. She was. Utterly gorgeous, and he'd never really noticed it before the last few days. When it had happened, he couldn't work out, but it had, and he was finding it quite difficult to ignore—especially since the incident with her bikini top earlier in the week.

He frowned, picked up his fork and plunged it into the steaming pile of creamy rice and tried to blank the image of the pale swell of her breast out of his mind, but the delicate rose pink of her nipple, puckered with the cold, was seared on his retina, and he could still feel the soft jut of it on the back of his hand when he'd brushed against her yesterday, taking Ella from her.

Spending time with her was awakening something that had been dormant for months—years, maybe. Something hungry and a little wild and beyond his control that was flaring to life between them. Maybe he didn't need to ignore it. Maybe he needed to talk to her about it?

But not now, if ever. She was a friend, a good friend, helping him out when he was in a bad place and so was she. The last thing either of them needed was him muddying the waters at this point in their lives, but his body had gone stone deaf to the pleading from his mind.

'So what do you think of it?' he asked, watching her demolish the risotto. 'I like the pea and mint with the bacon, and I think their oil and cheese really lend something interesting.'

'Mmm. Not going to argue,' she said, scraping the bowl. 'Is there any more?'

CHAPTER SEVEN

WELL, HE'D MANAGED to keep the conversation on track, he thought with relief as the door closed behind her.

They'd finished their meal, and then he'd told her he needed more time to play with the flavours so she'd gone to do some more work with the photos, which didn't surprise him because every time he'd looked up for the past few days she'd had that wretched camera in her hands.

But at least she was taking his request seriously, he thought as he worked. She must have recorded every last breath he'd taken, but he wasn't going to complain because the results that he'd seen so far were far better than anything he'd ever managed.

He fiddled around in the kitchen for another hour or two before it dawned on him that he was just keeping out of the way until he was sure she was asleep. Then he cleared up the kitchen, which meant there was nothing else for him to do tonight apart from test every type of wine they produced.

Which would be a waste, he thought morosely, staring at the opened bottle on the table in front of him. It was far too good to use as anaesthetic, and the last thing he needed was a hangover in the morning. He folded his arms on the table, dropped his head down and growled with frustration.

He should have been tired—not tired as in just finished a nineteen-hour shift in one of his restaurants, but tired enough to sleep, at least. Instead, he felt restless. Edgy.

He glanced at the baby monitor. She'd left it behind when she'd gone, and he'd heard her go in to check Ella, heard the gentle murmur of her voice when Ella had cried out once, but now there was nothing. He could let himself back in there, pick up his shorts and a towel and have a swim without disturbing them. That was what he needed. A long, hard swim, to burn off that excess restless energy. And maybe then he'd be able to sleep.

Something had woken her. She wasn't sure what, but she realised she was hot and thirsty. Maybe it had just been that?

But her bedroom door was still wide open. She'd left it open so she'd hear Ella, as Leo had the baby monitor in the kitchen, but she would have expected him to close it, or at least pull it to.

She lay for a while and listened, but there was nothing, no creaks or snores, not a sound even from Ella. She slid her legs over the edge of the bed and picked up her phone, checking the time. Twelve thirty-four. He must be back, she just hadn't heard him.

She tiptoed out into the hall and peered into Ella's room, but his bed was undisturbed, and there were no lights on anywhere except the dim glow of Ella's nightlight and the slanting moonlight through the French windows. The baby was sleeping peacefully, bottom in the air as usual, one little arm flung out to the side, and otherwise the apartment was deserted.

Surely he wasn't still cooking?

Tugging on her robe, Amy walked barefoot across the moonlit courtyard to the kitchen and found it empty, the room in darkness. She switched the light on and looked around.

It was spotlessly clean, everything cleared away, the

fridge humming quietly in the background. And the doors to the terrace were open.

She stood in the open doorway and listened. There. A rhythmic splash, barely a whisper, but continuous.

He was swimming.

And suddenly there was nothing in the world she wanted more than a swim. She went back to her room and realised the more modest black costume was still wet, so she put the bikini on, grabbed her towel and the baby monitor, and crossed the terrace.

She could see him now in the moonlight, every stroke leaving a sparkling trail of ripples on the surface, and she picked her way carefully down the steps, dropped her towel on a sun lounger and slipped silently into the water.

It was cool, the air around sweetly scented with jasmine, and she let her breath out on a quiet sigh of pleasure. There was something magical about it, about swimming in the moonlight with Leo, the soft water lapping gently around her, the drift of jasmine in the air. Beautiful.

Romantic.

That was what Lydia had said to her. *'It's just gorgeous to sink under that water in the evening when the kids are in bed and the stars are glittering overhead. So romantic...you and Leo should try it.'*

Her heart hitched a little in her throat. It wasn't meant to be romantic. She'd just wanted to join him for a swim, but suddenly it didn't feel like that, with the moonlight and the silence. She was playing with fire, crossing a boundary into dangerous territory, and she had to go. Once he'd turned and was swimming away from her, she'd make her escape and he need never know she'd been there.

Except, of course, he didn't turn.

The best-laid plans and all that, she thought as he slowed his pace and coasted in right beside her, standing up as he reached the end, sluicing water off his face and hair and knuckling the water out of his eyes.

The water streamed off his shoulders, turning to ribbons of silver in the moonlight, and she wanted to reach out and touch them.

Touch him.

No! Why hadn't she stayed inside, left him alone, kept out of his way, instead of surrendering to this magnetic attraction that had sprung out of nowhere in the last few days and taken her completely by surprise?

She must have moved or taken a breath, done something, because he turned his head towards her, his eyes black in the moonlight, a frown creasing his brow.

'Amy?'

'Hi,' she said awkwardly, the word a little breathless and utterly inadequate somehow in these odd circumstances.

His head tilted slightly. 'What's the matter?'

'Nothing. Ella's fine, she's fast asleep. I came to find you,' she explained, hoping it sounded more plausible than it felt at that moment. 'It was late, and I woke up and wondered where you were, but then I realised you were swimming and I thought it seemed like a good idea. You know, as it's a hot night…'

She floundered to a halt, trying to bluff it out when all she wanted to do was run away. Or throw herself into his arms. Neither exactly brilliant options. Oh, why on earth had she been so stupid?

Leo let out a quiet sigh and sank back into the water, stretching his arms out to grasp the edges of the pool as he faced her from his position in the corner.

What sneaky twist of fate had made her wake and come down here to torment him? His fault, most likely, going in there to pick up his shorts and towel. Damn. Well, thank God he'd got the shorts on and hadn't decided to skinny-dip. At least this way he could hide his reaction.

'Sorry, I didn't mean to disturb you. I just didn't feel tired enough to sleep, and I was hot and sticky, and the thought of the water just tempted me.'

That, and the fact that he hadn't trusted himself to go back into their apartment until he was too tired to act on the physical ache that had lingered long after she'd left the kitchen. And he'd just about done it, and now here she was to undo it all over again.

'It's the middle of the night, Leo,' she said, her voice troubled. 'You must be exhausted.'

Apparently not. Not nearly exhausted enough if his body's reaction was anything to go by. 'And you're not? Why are you here, Amy?' he asked, a trifle desperately. It was a rhetorical question, since she'd already told him, but she answered it anyway and perhaps a bit more truthfully.

'I was concerned about you. You just seemed—I don't know. Not you. Sometimes it's fine and then all of a sudden there's this great gulf that opens up between us and it's as if I don't know you at all.'

She gave a soft, disbelieving laugh. 'And I don't know why. All the time I feel as if I'm walking on eggshells with you, as if anything I say can upset you, and you just won't talk to me. It's like you're avoiding me or something and I don't know why.'

Because I want you. Because it's inappropriate, messy, and I'm not going there—

'I'm not,' he lied. 'I do talk to you. I've been talking to you all day.'

'Not about anything that matters. And that's not like you. You've always told me what's wrong, and now you won't. So what is it? Is it me? And if so, why? What have I done to hurt or upset you, Leo? Just tell me.'

He sighed softly. 'You haven't done anything, Amy. It's nothing to do with you.'

'So why won't you talk to me? You always used to; you

said it helped you sort through things, cleared your mind. I only want to help you…'

Her hand reached out and rested on his arm, her cool fingers burning him with a river of fire that scorched through his veins and threatened all his hard-won control. His eyes closed, shutting out the image of her fingers pale on his skin. 'You can't help me, Amy. You're just adding another complication.'

She whisked her hand away, her voice puzzled. 'I'm a *complication*?'

'That wasn't what I meant—'

'So what did you mean? What's going on, Leo? What's changed? Because it's not just me, is it?'

He let his breath out, a long, silent exhalation, and dragged a hand through his hair.

'No. No, Amy, it's not just you, and I don't know where it's come from or why, but I can't let it happen. I *won't* let it. You're emotionally fragile at the moment, and I'm a complete mess, but we're both adults, we've got needs, and what we're feeling is just a knee-jerk response. We feel safe with each other, we can trust each other, but it isn't safe, not for either of us.'

He gentled his voice, not sure how to handle this situation and desperate not to make it any worse. 'I'm sorry it's all gone wrong for you, and I know it should have been your honeymoon, but I'm not the guy you need to choose for your rebound affair, Amy, so don't humiliate either of us by asking me, please.'

Rebound affair? For a moment she was so shocked she could hardly reply. 'I don't want—'

'No? So why are you *really* here now, then?' He shook his head, his harsh sigh slicing through the air. 'I'm not doing this, Amy. There's no way I'm adding you to the list of things in my life that I'm ashamed of.'

Pain ripped through her, making her gasp. *He was* ashamed *of her?*

Like he'd been ashamed of Lisa?

He turned and vaulted lightly out of the pool, the water streaming off him in ribbons as he picked up his towel and the baby monitor and walked away towards the steps, leaving her standing there, her lips pressed tightly together, her eyes stinging with tears as she watched him walk away.

They scalded her cheeks, searing their way down, and she closed her eyes, turning away from him and holding her breath until the heavy silence told her he'd gone. Then she folded her arms on the side of the pool, rested her head on them and sobbed her heart out.

It was a good hour—no, scratch that, a lousy hour—before he heard her enter the apartment.

He'd towelled himself roughly dry and pulled on his boxers and a T-shirt, then gone out onto the terrace, sitting on the bench against the wall and staring out over the moonlit landscape while he drank the wine he'd picked up on the way over. Not a wise move, but he didn't care any more. He was over being wise. It didn't seem to be working, not for either of them.

The valley was flooded with a cold, eerie light, and he felt oddly chilled. Not that it was cold, it was just that the moon drained all colour from the surroundings and turned it into a mass of stark white, interspersed with menacing black shadows.

Under other circumstances, it would have been romantic. Not tonight, when he was sitting here waiting for Amy and wondering how long he could leave it before he went to find her. Because he would have to, he knew that.

Oh, Amy. What a mess.

What was she doing? What was she thinking? He

shouldn't have left her like that, but he hadn't trusted himself to get closer to her, to reach out to her, because if he once let himself touch her, that one touch would never be enough and there was no way—*no way*—that he was going there. Not with Amy. He was a mess, his life in tatters, the last thing she needed when she was so emotionally fragile. Not even he with his appalling track record could betray her trust to that extent.

He heard a door creak slightly, the click of a latch, water running, the muffled sound of her bedclothes as she got into bed a few moments later. The doors of her room were open to the terrace, as were his, and he listened for any further sound.

Nothing. Then a soft, shaky sigh, followed by a dull thump—punching her pillow into shape?

He put his glass down, got up and crossed the gravel, standing silently in the open doorway. She was lying on her side, facing him. Her eyes were open, watching him, waiting for him to move or speak, to do something, but he couldn't. He had no idea what to say to her in these circumstances, so he just stood there and ached with regret. He couldn't bear to lose her friendship, and he was horribly afraid that was the way it was heading.

'What have I ever done to make you ashamed of me?'

Her voice was soft, barely a whisper, but it shocked him to the core.

'I'm not ashamed of you,' he said, appalled that that was what she'd been thinking. 'Amy, no! Don't ever think that! I'm not ashamed of you, not in the slightest, and I never have been.'

'But—you said…'

She trailed off, sitting up in the bed, arms wrapped around her knees defensively, and in the good old days he would have thought nothing of climbing on the bed and hugging her. Not now. Not with this demon of desire stalking them both. He rammed his hands through his hair and gave a ragged sigh.

'I didn't mean it like that. Really. Believe me. I'm sorry—I'm really so sorry—if you misunderstood, but it isn't, and it never has been, and it never will be you that I'm ashamed of. It's me, the things I've done, the people I've hurt.' He sighed wearily. 'I need to tell you about Lisa, don't I?'

'Yes, you do,' she said, her voice stronger now, making his guilt twinge, 'because I don't know who you are any more and I can't help you like this. Not really. Sometimes I think I understand you, but then you say something, and— it just confuses me, Leo. Tell me what it is that's happened that's destroying you,' she pleaded, her eyes dark holes, featureless in the faint light, unreadable. 'Help me to understand what's hurting you.'

He hesitated for a moment, then gave another quiet sigh. 'OK. But not here, like this. Come outside. Have some wine with me. I picked up a bottle from the kitchen on the way back and I need help drinking it or I'm going to have a killer hangover. I'll get you a glass.'

He checked Ella as he passed, fetched another glass from the kitchen and went back out to the terrace and found her waiting for him.

She was curled into one corner of the bench, her arms wrapped round her legs. He recognised it, that defensive posture, shielding herself from hurt, the wide, wary eyes and wounded mouth making her look like a child again. A hurt and frightened child, but she wasn't a child. Not any more. And that just made it all the more complicated.

He sat down at the other end of the bench at a nice, safe distance, put the wine glass down between them next to his and filled them both.

'Here.'

She reached out and took it from him, her fingers brushing his, and he felt them tremble. 'So—Lisa,' she said, retreating back into the corner with her wine glass. 'What happened between you that's changed you so much, Leo?'

'It hasn't changed me.'

'It has. Of course it has. It's taken the life out of you. Most of the time you're fine, and then, bang, the shutters come down and you retreat. The only time you really relax is when you're with Ella, and even then there's something wrong. I thought at first it was grief, but it isn't, is it? It's regret, but why? What happened that you regret so much, that you're so ashamed of?'

How had he thought she looked like a child? She was looking at him now with the eyes of a sage, coaxing him to unburden himself, and once he started, he found he couldn't stop.

'I didn't love her,' he began. 'It was just a casual fling. She was part of the team on the last TV series. I'd never spoken to her, but she must have decided she'd like a piece of me as a trophy so she engineered an invitation to the party to celebrate finishing the filming, cosied up to me and—well, she got pregnant. I thought I'd taken care of that, but she told me much later she'd sabotaged it, and she didn't show a shred of remorse. And at the time she didn't seem shocked or upset by the surprise pregnancy. Far from it. Not until the whole situation became much more of a reality, and then she just went into meltdown.'

'So you didn't love her? You married her just because she was pregnant?'

He gave her a wintry smile. *Just because?*

Amy found herself smiling back, but she wanted to cry for him, for what she'd heard in his voice. 'You could have said no to her instead of doing the decent thing.'

'Except that it was my fault. She'd had too much to drink, I shouldn't have done it.'

'Was she very drunk?' she probed.

'I thought so, but she might have been acting. But then, to be fair, I wasn't exactly sober so it's hard to tell. It was quite a party, and I suspect my drink was being well and truly spiked by her. And that was only the first time. She stayed all weekend—'

'You took her back to yours?' To his flat over the restaurant? The place they'd sat and talked long into the night, over and over again? She knew it was ridiculous, knew he must have taken countless women there, but still she felt betrayed.

'The party was at the London restaurant. I lived above it. Where else would I take her?'

'Anywhere in the world?' she suggested, and he gave a rueful laugh.

'Yeah. Hindsight's a wonderful thing. But after the weekend I told her I wasn't interested in a relationship. I had the new restaurant opening coming up in Yoxburgh in a few months, so much to do to prepare for that, and I was trying to consolidate the business so I could afford to abandon it for a while to get the new restaurant up and running smoothly before the next TV series kicked off, and a relationship was the last thing I needed.'

'So—she left you alone?'

'Yes, she left me alone, sort of, for a few weeks, anyway. And then she turned up at the restaurant late one night and said she needed to speak to me, and she told me she was pregnant. I didn't believe her at first, but she had a scan six weeks later and the dates fitted, and she was adamant it was mine. And she was delighted. Of course.'

'What did your family say?'

He snorted softly. 'Have you never met my grandmother?' he asked unnecessarily, and Amy smiled wryly.

'Nonna told you to marry her?'

'She didn't need to. She listened to my side of the story, told me I'd been a fool to let it happen, but that I owed my child the right to have its father in its life. And she was right, of course. I already knew that. I also knew that the business didn't need the media circus that would follow if I walked away from a pregnant woman, and I knew she wouldn't keep it quiet. So we had a quiet wedding and moved up to Suffolk, into a rented house, so I could concentrate on the new restaurant.'

'Don't tell me. She didn't like it?'

'She didn't like it one bit. She'd thought we'd have a glamorous life in London, and she didn't take kindly to being imprisoned in a tinpot little backwater like Yoxburgh. Her words, not mine. And then Ella was born, and she was even more trapped, and she started drinking.'

'Drinking? As in—?'

'Heavy drinking. Getting utterly bat-faced. Night after night. I told her to stop, promised her a new house, said we could go back to London, split our time between the two, but that wasn't enough. To be honest, I think the reality of the whole thing—the pregnancy and birth, the move, the amount of time I was giving to the restaurant—it was all too much. It would have been too much for anyone, but she was so far out of her comfort zone that it was just impossible. And then...'

He broke off, the words choking him, and Amy shifted, moving the glasses out of the way and snuggling up against his side, one hand lying lightly over his heart. He wondered if she could feel it pounding as he relived that hideous night.

'Go on,' she said softly, and he let his arm curl round her shoulders and draw her closer against him, her warmth reassuring.

'She came to the restaurant. She'd left Ella at home, six weeks old, and she'd driven down to the restaurant to tell me she was leaving me. It was a filthy night, sheeting down with rain, the waves crashing over the prom, and she'd been drinking. I took the car keys off her and told her to go home and wait for me, but she started swearing and screaming in front of the customers. I called her a taxi, told her to wait, but she walked out of the restaurant into the lashing rain and straight into the path of a car. The driver didn't stand a chance, and nor did she. She died later that night in hospital, and all I felt was relief.'

Amy's arms tightened round his waist, hugging him gently, and he turned his head and rested his cheek against her hair. 'I didn't love her, Amy, but I didn't want her to die. I just wanted the whole situation to go away, but not like that.'

'Is that why you're ashamed? Because you wanted her gone, and when she was you were secretly relieved? Do you think you're to blame in some crazy way?'

'I *am* to blame,' he told her emphatically, pulling away slightly. 'I should have made it clearer to her what our life was going to be like, but I knew she'd got pregnant deliberately, knew that she'd set a trap for me that weekend, so I suppose I felt she'd got what she deserved. But she didn't deserve to die, and I didn't deserve to have to go through all that, and Ella certainly had done nothing to deserve anything that either of us had done. Nor had my family, and the media had a field day with it. Don't tell me you didn't know that because I don't believe it.'

'Oh, Leo. I read things, of course I did, and I was worried about you. I tried to call you several times, but you weren't taking any calls, and your parents were really protective so I couldn't get through to you and I gave up. I shouldn't have done. I should have come and seen you.'

Her voice was soft, filled with anguish for him, and she turned her head and lifted her face to his, touching her lips gently to his cheek. 'I'm so sorry. It must have been dreadful for all of you.'

Her lips were inches away. Less. All he had to do was

turn his head a fraction, and they'd be there, against his mouth. He fought it for seconds, then with a shuddering sigh he turned his head and moved away from danger. Not far. Just enough that he could still rest his head against hers but with his lips firmly out of the way of trouble.

'Leo?'

'Mmm?'

'I wasn't trying to seduce you earlier,' she said, her voice a fractured whisper. 'I really wasn't. I was just concerned about you.'

He sighed, his breath ruffling her hair, and his arm tightened around her. 'I know. But things are changing between us, and I don't want them to. I love you, Amy. I love you to bits, but I'm not going to have an affair with you, no matter how tempted either of us might be—'

She pushed away, tilting her head to stare up at him, her eyes wide with something that could have been indignation. Or desperation? 'When have I asked you to do that? *Ever?* When have I *ever* suggested that we—?'

'You haven't. Not in so many words. But it's there in your eyes, and it's in my head, and I'm not doing it, I'm not going to be drawn in by it, no matter how tempting it is to turn to each other for comfort. Because that's all it is, Amy. Comfort. And it would change everything. We've been friends for ever, and I don't want to change that. I need it, I treasure it, and I can't bear to think I could do something stupid one day to screw it up, because I will. I'll let you down—'

She moved abruptly, shifting so she was facing him, holding his face in her hands and staring intently into his eyes.

'No, you won't,' she said slowly and clearly. 'You've never let me down, Leo. I've let myself down, plenty of times, and I expect you've done the same, but you'll never let me down. You've just stopped me making the biggest mistake of my life—'

'Yes, I have, and I'm not going to let you—or either of us—make another one when your emotions are in chaos and you're clutching at the familiar because your life's suddenly going to be so different from what you'd planned.'

He took her hands in his, easing them away from his face and closing his fingers over them, pressing them to his lips before he let them go. He tucked a damp strand of hair behind her ear and gave her a rueful smile. 'You just need time, Amy. Time to let the dust settle and work out what you want from life. And it isn't me. It really isn't. I'm no good for you—not in that way. You don't really want me, you just want what I represent—the familiar, the safe, but I'm not safe, and I can't replace what you've lost by not marrying Nick. I know what you want, what you've lost, but I'm not it.'

She nodded, shifting away a little, turning her head to stare out over the valley. After a moment she gave a shaky sigh.

'I know that—and I know I'm not ready for another relationship, especially not with you. I mean, how would that work?' she said, her voice lightly teasing now, but he could still hear the hurt and confusion underlying it. 'I wouldn't have my sounding board any more, would I? How would I know it wasn't another awful mistake? I made the last mistake because I didn't talk to you. I don't want to do that again.'

She turned back to him, throwing him a sweet, wry smile. 'Thank you for telling me about Lisa. And don't blame yourself. It wasn't your fault.'

'It was. I should have driven her home instead of calling a taxi—handed the restaurant over to the team and left, taken care of her, but I didn't, I didn't realise she was that fragile, that unstable, and because of that she died.'

'No, Leo. She died because she got drunk and did something reckless, with far-reaching consequences. Everything else stemmed from that. You were her husband, not her keeper. She was an adult woman, and she made bad decisions. And on the last occasion it killed her. End of.'

'Except it's not the end, is it? I've got a motherless child and a career I've neglected for the past nine months— more, really. And there's nothing I can do about it. What's done is done. All any of us have to do is take care of the future, and I have no idea how. All I can do is survive from day to day and hope it gets better.'

'It will.'

'Will it? I hope so, because I can't go on like this.'

He stood up, tugging her to her feet and wrapping her in his arms and holding her tight, his face pressed into her hair. 'Thanks for listening to me. And thanks for being you. I don't know what I'd do without you.'

'You aren't without me. You won't be without me.'

'Promise?'

'I promise. Just keep talking to me.'

He nodded, then eased away. 'I will. Now go to bed. You need some sleep and so do I. I'll be up at the crack of dawn with Ella.'

'Well, good luck with that,' she said ruefully. 'Look at the sky.'

They stared out across the network of fields and hills, still leached of colour by the moon, but on the horizon there was the faintest streak of light appearing in the sky.

'It's a new day, Leo. It *will* get better.'

He looked down at her, her eyes shining with sincerity, the one person he could truly trust with all his hopes and fears. He bent his head, touched his lips to her cheek and then, as he breathed in and drew the scent of her into his body, he felt his resolve disintegrate.

He let his breath out on a shuddering sigh and turned his head, as she turned hers, and their lips touched.

They clung, held, and with a ragged sigh of defeat he pulled her closer, feeling her taut limbs, the softness of her breasts, the warmth of her mouth opening like a flower under his, and he was lost.

He couldn't get enough of her. One hand slid round and found her breast through the slippery silk of that tormenting gown, and he felt her nipple peak hard against his hand.

She moaned softly, arching against him, her tongue duelling with his as he delved and tasted, savouring her, learning her, aching for her.

Her hands were on him, learning him, too, their movements desperate as she clung to his arms, his back, cradling his head as he was cradling hers, her fingers spearing through his hair and pulling him down to her.

He groaned, rocking his hips against hers, needing her for so much more than this, and she whimpered as his hands slid down and cupped her bottom, lifting her against him.

Amy...

Amy! No, no, no, no!

He had to stop. She had to stop. One of them had to stop. He uncurled his fingers and slid his hands up her back, but he didn't let go. He couldn't. He needed her. Wanted her. He had to...

His hands cradled her face, the kiss gentling as he fought with his warring emotions. And then she eased away and took a step back, out of reach, and he felt bereft.

Their eyes met and locked, and after an agonising second he dragged a hand down over his face and tried to step back, to put more space between them while he still could, but his feet were rooted to the spot, his chest heaving with the need that still screamed through him, and he

tilted his head back and stared blindly at the pale streak
of sky that promised a new tomorrow.

Could he trust it? Could he trust her?

She reached out, her hand finding his, their fingers tangling, and he lowered his head and met her eyes again, and
saw nothing in them but honesty.

'Make love to me, Leo,' she murmured, and the last vestige of his crumbling self-control turned to dust.

CHAPTER EIGHT

AMY LAY ON her side, one leg draped over his, her head pillowed on his chest, her lips tilting into a smile of utter contentment and wonder as his hand stroked idly over her back.

So that's what the fireworks were like. The chemistry she'd dismissed. The 'amazing' that she'd never, ever found before.

His lips brushed her hair, his breath warm against her scalp, and she turned her head so she could reach his mouth.

He kissed her slowly, lazily, shifting so he was facing her, his hand sliding round her ribcage and settling on her breast, and she snuggled closer, feeling the jut of his erection against her body as her leg curled over his hip and drew him up against her.

He groaned, deep in his chest, the vibrations resonating through his breath and into her like the faint tremors of an earthquake. 'I want you,' he breathed raggedly. 'I need you—so much. Oh, Amy—'

He rolled her onto her back, their bodies coming together instinctively, surely, and she felt the first quivers of another shattering climax ripple through her body. 'Leo…'

'I'm here. I've got you…'

His head fell forward into the curve of her neck, his mouth open, his breath hot against her skin as he said her name over and over again while she fell, spiralling down

and down, reaching out, clinging to him as his body caught
up with hers and took them both over the edge.

Their muted cries tangled in the soft light of dawn, their
bodies blurring into one, and as their hearts slowed and
their breathing quietened, he rolled to the side, taking her
with him into sleep.

Leo lay beside her, staring at the ceiling and trying to make
sense of his tangled emotions.

All these years, he'd been so careful to preserve their
friendship, to keep it platonic, to treasure the bond they
had without crossing the invisible line between them. It
had been so vitally important to him, his respect for Amy's
friendship so deeply ingrained that it hadn't ever occurred
to him to muddy the waters by sleeping with her. Other
women had fulfilled that need for him, women who didn't
trust him or depend on him or need him, women who
wanted from him only what he wanted from them. Women
who weren't Amy, or anything like Amy, because Amy
was sacrosanct, untouchable.

Well, he'd certainly touched her now, the line well and
truly crossed, and there was no going back. What he didn't
know was what lay ahead, because he had nothing to offer
her except the few scraps of himself that were left over
from work and from caring for his daughter. And it hadn't
been enough for Lisa, so why on earth did he imagine it
could be enough for Amy?

He groaned silently.

He should never have kissed her, never have let her lead
him into her bedroom, never peeled away the flimsy bar-
riers of their clothing and with them the protective layers
of their friendship, exposing the raw need and desperate
hunger that lurked beneath.

He'd made a catastrophic mistake by doing that, but
what an incredible, beautiful, exquisite mistake it had been.

Because he loved her, in every way, without reservation, and what they'd done had felt so right, so good, so pure and simple and innocent and—just *right*.

Oh, Amy. His lips moved silently on the words, his eyes drifting shut against the tears of joy and regret that welled in them. *Don't let me hurt you. Please, don't let me hurt you.*

But he knew he would. Somehow, some time, sooner or later it would happen. And it would break his heart, as well as hers.

Ella woke her, the baby's wail cutting through her dream and dragging her back to reality, and she stretched out to Leo but he was gone.

Oh.

She stretched and yawned and lay there for a moment waiting, sure he must have gone to her, but there was no sound from him and the baby was still crying, so she threw back the covers, found her nightdress and went to investigate.

'Hello, sweetheart. Where's your daddy?' she murmured, lifting the baby out of the cot and cuddling her close.

'I'm here. Sorry, I was in the other kitchen but there was something I couldn't just drop. Come here, poppet.'

He took her out of Amy's arms, his eyes brushing hers fleetingly, warm and gentle but troubled, and she gave an inward sigh.

'I know what you're thinking,' she said, sitting down on the bed while he put Ella down on the changing mat at her feet and knelt down. 'But don't.'

He shot her a sideways glance. 'How do you know what I'm thinking?'

'Because I know you inside out, Leo. You might have changed a little, grown older and wiser—'

His snort cut her off, but she just smiled and carried on, 'But you're still the same over-protective person you always were, and you're beating yourself up at the moment, taking all the blame, wishing you hadn't done it—'

'No.' He sat back on his heels and looked up at her, his eyes burning. 'No, Amy, you're wrong. I'm not wishing I hadn't done it. I just wish I could give you more, wish I could offer you a future—'

'Shh.' She leant forward and pressed a finger to his lips, silencing him. He kissed her finger, drew it into his mouth, suckled it briefly before he pulled away, and she nearly whimpered.

'You were saying?'

'I can't remember.'

His eyes were laughing. '*Shh* was the last thing.'

'So it was.' She smiled, and carried on. 'Forget about the future, Leo. It's far too soon to think about that. Forget everything except the here and now. We've got a few more days. Let's just enjoy them, get to know each other better, the people we are now, and have some fun with Ella. Have a holiday—'

'I have to cook.'

'You have to cook one meal.'

'And try out their stuff.'

'You're making excuses. I thought it was supposed to be a simple lunch?'

He smiled crookedly. 'I don't do simple, apparently. I want to do something that tastes amazing.'

'All your food tastes amazing.'

He arched an eyebrow. 'What happened to my critic?'

'Oh, she's still here, she'll come out when necessary,' she said with a laugh, and then sighed and threw up her hands. 'OK. I concede. Cook, play in the kitchen, and Ella and I'll play with you when we can, and you'll play with us when you can, and I know when they get back you'll be in meetings, but we'll still have the nights.'

She heard the suck of his indrawn breath, saw the flaring of his pupils as he straightened to look at her again, the jump of a muscle in his jaw. 'And then?'

She shrugged. She didn't know. And maybe it was better that way. 'What happens in Tuscany stays in Tuscany?' she said softly, and their eyes held.

'OK. I'll buy that for now.'

'Good. Oh, and by the way, you were amazing last night,' she said casually, and stood up to walk past him.

'So were you. Incredible.' His arm snaked out, his hand sliding up under the short hem of her nightdress and curving round her naked bottom, drawing her in against him. He rested his head briefly against her, his breath hot on her body through the fine silk, and then he let her go, his hand sliding down her leg and leaving fire in its wake. She sat down again abruptly.

'So, what are you doing today?' she asked when she could speak, but her voice was breathy and he tilted his head back and speared her with his eyes.

'I don't know. I know what I'm doing tonight. That's as far as my thoughts have gone for now.' A lazy, sexy smile lit up his face, and she felt heat shiver through her.

'OK,' she said slowly. 'So—assuming we're going to do something a little more practical in the meantime, shall I shower first, or do you want to?'

'I've showered. You were sleeping the sleep of the dead,' he told her, that lazy smile still lingering on his delectable and clever, clever mouth. 'If you could shower now and take Ella from me so I can get on, that would be great. I'll make us all breakfast if you like.'

'I like. I definitely like. I'm starving.'

He rolled his eyes and got to his feet, Ella cradled in one

arm, and he turned Amy and pushed her gently towards the bathroom door. 'Shoo. I've got a lot to do.'

'So, little Ella, what are we going to do while Daddy's busy this morning?' she asked. 'A walk? That sounds like a great idea. Where shall we go? The olive groves? OK.'

Ella grinned at her, a toothy little grin with a gurgle of laughter that made her heart swell in her chest until she thought it'd burst.

'Was that funny?' she asked, and Ella laughed again, so that by the time she was strapped in her buggy they both had the giggles.

'What's the joke?'

He'd stuck his head out of the kitchen door, and she turned her head and grinned at him. 'No joke. She just started laughing, and it's really infectious.'

'Tell me about it. Are you off for a walk now?'

'Mmm. Ella thought we might like to go down to the olive groves.'

'Did she now?' he asked, coming over to them and crouching in front of Ella.

'She did.'

He chuckled softly, bent and kissed the baby and then, as he straightened and drew level with her, he kissed Amy. It caught her by surprise, the sure, gentle touch of his lips, the promise of heat in his eyes, the lingering warmth of his hand against her cheek.

'Have fun. I'll see you later,' he murmured, and waggling his fingers at Ella he headed back to the kitchen to carry on.

They had a lovely walk, the air full of the buzzing of bees and the scent of the olive blossom as they strolled along beneath the trees, and predictably the rocking motion of the buggy sent Ella to sleep, so Amy's mind was free to wander.

And of course it wandered straight to Leo, and stayed there.

Not surprising, really, after last night. She'd never felt like she had then, but it wasn't because of anything in particular that he'd done, it was just because it had been him—his touch, his kiss, his body. It had just felt—right, as if everything in the universe had fallen neatly into place when she had been in his arms.

And today the sun was brighter, the grass greener, the birdsong louder. A smile on her face, she turned the buggy round and headed back up the hill to Leo. It was time she went back, anyway. She'd been out in the sun too long and her shoulders were burning.

She left the buggy with Leo and went to put after-sun lotion on, and when she got back Ella was awake, so they played outside the kitchen until Leo called them in for lunch, then Amy took her back in the garden under the shade of the pergola until she yawned again.

'I'm going to put her down in her cot,' she told Leo. 'Do you need any help?'

He shot her a warm but distracted smile. 'No, not really.'

'I'll sort some more photos, then,' she said, and going up on tiptoe she kissed his cheek and left him to it.

She couldn't quite believe how many pictures she'd taken of Leo.

Leo cooking, Leo swimming, Leo laughing, frowning, smiling, winking at her cheekily—hundreds. Hundreds and hundreds. Lots of Ella, too, and the two of them to-gether. They brought a lump to her throat.

There were others, of the family, of the *palazzo* and its grounds, the olive groves, the vineyards, the chestnut woods—anywhere he'd gone and she'd been with him, she'd taken photos. And she'd lent him the camera so he could take some when she wasn't there, and she scrolled through those with interest.

He'd certainly have plenty to choose from for his blog, she thought with relief, so she didn't need to feel she owed him anything, not by the time she'd added in the babysitting this week and for the eight weeks of the filming.

Eight weeks in which they'd do—what? She'd said what happens in Tuscany stays in Tuscany, but if they were together, at home, would that still apply? Or would it be awkward?

Was their relationship going to end when they left Italy? She didn't know, and she didn't want to ask him, because she wasn't sure she'd want to hear the answer.

Then Ella cried, and she shut down her laptop and went to get her. She was sitting up in her little cot, rubbing her eyes and wailing sleepily, and she held her arms up to Amy.

'Hello, baby,' she murmured. 'It's all right, I'm here.'

She scooped her up gently and hugged her, and Ella's little arms snaked round her neck, chubby fingers splayed against her sunburnt shoulders. The tousled little head snuggled down into the crook of Amy's neck, and she squeezed the baby tight, deeply touched by the little one's affection. She'd formed a real bond with her in this short time, and it would be such a wrench not to see her again every day, not to be part of her life when this was done.

She was such a sweet child, and it was so sad that she would grow up without her mother. How would that feel? For all her gentle interference, Amy's mother was a huge part of her life. How would it have been never to have known the security and warmth that came with being so deeply, unreservedly and unconditionally loved by the woman who'd given you life? Even the thought of it made Amy ache inside for her.

Could she take that woman's place? In a heartbeat.

Would she be invited to? As his wife?

'It'll be a cold day in hell before that happens.'

Oh, Leo...

She gave a quiet sigh and changed Ella's nappy, put her back in the little sun dress she'd been wearing in the morning, picked up her pretty, frilly sun hat and went to find him.

There was no sign of him in the kitchen, but there was a bit of paper propped up on the table with 'In veg garden' scrawled on it in Leo's bold hand.

She plonked the sun hat on the baby's head, went out through the open French doors onto the terrace and followed it around until she spotted him on the level below, in a sheltered spot amongst the orderly rows of vegetables.

She went down the steps and walked towards him. He was crouched down, balancing on the balls of his feet as he studied the lush mounds of greenery all around him, and he turned and squinted up at her in the sun. It would have made a brilliant photo, but for once she didn't have her camera.

'Hi, there. Everything okay?'

'Yes, fine. We just wondered what you were doing.'

Ella lunged towards him, right on cue, and said, 'Dadadad,' her little face beaming, and of course he couldn't resist that.

'Ciao, mia bellisima,' he said, his face lighting up with a smile for his little daughter. He straightened up, his hands full, and bent his head to kiss Ella, his eyes softening with a love that made Amy's heart turn over.

He was standing close enough that she could smell him, her nose tantalised by a slight, lingering trace of aftershave overlaid by the heady scent of warm male skin, and he turned his head and captured her mouth with a slow, lingering kiss. Then he lifted his head, and she took a step back and pointed in the direction of his hands.

'What are those?'

He glanced down. 'Zucchini flowers—courgettes. They're so pretty, and they're delicious stuffed. I thought I might do them as a vegetable. Heaven knows, Lydia's going to have enough of them,' he said, waving a hand at the rows of rampant plants he'd been inspecting.

'I'm sure she'll think it's worth the sacrifice. So what are you going to stuff them with?' she asked, trying to focus on something other than the scent of his skin in the warm sunshine, and the lingering taste of him on her lips.

'I don't know. I've got a few ideas. I'll try them out on you this evening.'

He picked up a basket overflowing with the things he'd raided from the garden, plucked the baby off her hip, settled her on his and headed back to the kitchen, nuzzling Ella and blowing raspberries on her neck and making her giggle.

He was so good with her. Good enough that the loss of her mother wouldn't matter? And what about when they got back to England and *she* wasn't around any more? Would that matter to Ella? Would she even notice?

Don't borrow trouble.

Amy followed them, the taut muscles of Leo's tanned calves in easy reach as he walked up the steps in front of her. His long shorts clung to his lean hips, giving her a tantalising view of muscles that bunched and stretched with every step, and she wanted to reach out her hand and touch them, feel their warmth and solidity, test the texture of rough hair over smooth tanned skin. Taste the salt on his skin—

Later...

He crossed over to the kitchen, dumping the basket of vegetables on the big table. 'Tea or coffee?' he asked, turning his head to look at Amy over his shoulder.

'Something cold?' she said, and he pulled open the

fridge and took out the spring water. 'So what's the plan for the rest of the afternoon?'

He shrugged, those broad, lean shoulders shifting under the soft pale blue cotton of his shirt, the cuffs turned back to reveal strong, tanned forearms. He'd always tanned really easily, she remembered, part of his Latin heritage.

'I don't know,' he said, jiggling Ella on his hip. 'It rather depends on madam here and what she'd like to do.'

'I'm happy to look after her, if you want,' Amy volunteered, but he shook his head.

'No, it's okay, I haven't seen her all day and I'm going to need you tomorrow morning so I'm keeping you sweet for that,' he said with a grin. He unscrewed the bottle and poured two glasses of fizzy water, added a slice of lime to each and handed her one. 'Has she had her bottle?' he asked, and Amy shook her head.

'No, but it's in the fridge there. I thought I'd come and find you first, see what you're doing.'

'This and that.' He took the bottle out, hooked out a chair with his foot and sat down with the baby. 'So how have you been getting on?' he asked as he gave Ella her bottle. 'Did you look at the photos?'

'Yes. There are some really good ones that'll be great for your blog. They're on my laptop. There's a ton of dross as well, of course, but you can have a look later.'

'I'd love to, but probably not until after tomorrow. I've got enough on at the moment.' He gave her a wry grin. 'I hate to ask, but would you be able to keep an eye on Ella for a while later on so I can do some more prep? You can stay in here so she can see me, but I could just do with an hour or two to make up a marinade and get some risotto under way. I'll put her to bed.'

'It's why I'm here, Leo.'

His mouth softened into a smile. 'So you keep saying. I tell you what, how about a swim first?'

* * *

She wore the bikini, and when Ella grabbed the top again, he just smiled and gently disentangled the baby's fingers, which of course involved his own getting nicely into the mix.

He eased Ella away, met Amy's eyes and winked at her, and she blushed, which made him laugh softly.

'Later,' he promised, and her mouth opened a fraction and then curved into a smile that could have threatened his sanity if he hadn't already lost it.

And before he knew what she was doing, she slipped beneath the surface and swam towards him, nudging his legs apart with her hands before twisting through them like a mermaid. She'd done it before, hundreds of times when they were growing up, but not now, when he was so aware of the brush of her body against his.

'Boo!' she said, surfacing right behind him, and Ella squealed with laughter, so she did it again, and again, and again, and every time her body slid past his, grazing intimately against him until he called a halt.

'Right, enough. I need to get on.'

'We'll come out, too.'

She went first, reaching down to take Ella from his arms and treating him to the soft, lush swell of her breasts threatening to escape from the bikini that was proving so rewarding.

Never mind mermaid. She was a siren, luring him onto the rocks, and tonight was so far away...

'Are you sure you don't mind?'

'Positive,' she said patiently. 'Leave her with me and go and make a start, and I'll change her nappy and then we'll follow you. I can take photos of you cooking, and give you the benefit of my considerable expertise as a guinea pig while I play with her. And at least that way

I'll get something to eat, because I know what you're like when you start something like this. You get totally focussed and forget everything else, and supper will just go out of the window.'

He smiled, as he was meant to, and went.

'So what's that you're doing now?' she asked, carrying Ella into the kitchen a few minutes later and peering over Leo's shoulder.

'Broad bean, mint and pecorino risotto—it's the stuffing for the zucchini flowers, a variation on what we had last night.' He stuck his finger into the pan, scooped out a dollop and held it out to her lips. 'Here. Try it.'

He'd done it so many times before, and yet this time seemed so different. She opened her mouth, drew his finger into it and curled her tongue around the tip, sucking the delicious, creamy risotto from it without ever losing eye contact.

'Mmm. Yummy. You've put more mint in it. So are they going to be cold or hot?' she asked.

Leo hauled in a slow, quiet breath and tried to concentrate on anything other than the sweet warmth of Amy's mouth, the curl of her tongue against his finger, the gentle suction as she'd drawn the risotto into her mouth all too quickly. He turned away to check the seasoning of the risotto and gave his body a moment to calm down.

'Warm. Things taste better that way, often, and they need to be deep fried in tempura batter and served pretty much immediately, which rather dictates it.'

'They'd go well with the lamb,' she suggested, and he nodded.

'They would. And I could cook them at the last moment when everything else was ready to go. Here, try this. I've been playing with the topping for the bruschetta.'

He handed her a dollop—on a spoon, this time, since

he really couldn't afford to get that distracted, but it was nearly as bad. 'OK?'

'Lovely. Really tasty. So what do you want me to photograph?'

He shrugged, his shoulders shifting under the shirt, drawing her attention yet again to his body. 'Anything you like. You tell me, you're the photographer.'

'I don't know. What are you doing now?' she asked, casting around for something to take her mind off his body, because even framing the shots for the camera wasn't helping. If anything, it was making it worse because it meant focussing on him and she was having trouble focussing on anything else.

'Marinade for the mutton.' He'd set the vegetables on one side and was pounding something with a pestle and mortar, grinding garlic and herbs together with a slosh of olive oil and a crunch of salt and pepper, his muscles flexing as he worked. 'I'll smoosh it all over the meat, leave it till later and put it in the oven overnight so I can shred it and shape it first thing in the morning.'

He stopped pounding, to her relief, pulled out the shoulder of mutton from the fridge, stabbed it all over with a knife and smeared—no, *smooshed*, whatever kind of a word that was—the contents of the bowl all over the outside of the meat, dropped it back into the oven tray on top of the chopped vegetables, wrapped it in foil and stuck it back in the fridge.

'Right. Mint jelly.'

She watched him while Ella was playing contentedly with some stacking blocks, clicking away on the camera to record it all for his blog. Most of the shots were probably underexposed, but she didn't have any lights or reflectors so she was relying on the natural light spilling in through the open French doors to the terrace, and the under-cup-board lights that flooded the work area with a soft, golden light that worked wonders with his olive skin.

And as a perk, of course, she got to study him in excruciatingly minute detail.

The mint jelly setting in the fridge, he moved on, pulling together the ingredients for a dessert that made her drool just watching him.

'Tell me it's going to be your panna cotta?'

He threw her a grin over his shoulder. 'Was there a choice?'

Of course not. It was one of his signature dishes, and she'd never eaten a better one anywhere. Technically difficult to produce reliably—or for her to produce reliably, at any rate; she doubted Leo had any problems with it—he was making it with the ease of long practice, talking as he worked, and he was a joy to watch. But then, he was always a joy to watch…

'I'm going to turn them out and serve them with a compote of freshly sliced home-grown strawberries in their cousin's balsamic vinegar. I'm hoping I can talk them into letting me have a few bottles a year. It's amazing. It's almost a syrup, and it's—oh, it's just lovely with fruit. Beautiful. Works perfectly with it. I'll make a few spares. If you're really good, I'll give you one later.'

'I'll be really, really good,' she vowed, and he turned, holding her eyes for a second or two.

'Is that a promise?' he murmured, and it turned her legs to mush.

He finished the panna cotta, poured it carefully into the moulds and slipped the tray into the fridge.

'This kitchen's a joy to work in,' he said, and turned back to her with a grin that wiped the promise of dessert right off the menu and made her think of something much, much sweeter, powerful enough to blow her composure right apart.

And his, if the look in his eyes was anything to go by. Which was not a good idea when he was busy.

'I'll take Ella out in the garden in the shade. She's bored, and she loves the little sandpit.'

And scooping up the baby, she headed for the French doors to give him space.

Leo watched her go, let his breath out on a long sigh and braced his arms on the worktop. Why was he suddenly so intensely aware of her, after so many years? What was it that had changed for them? She wasn't a child any more, not by a long shot, but she'd been a woman for some considerable time, and it had taken this long for the change to register on his Richter scale.

And how.

But it wasn't for long. They only had a few more days here in Tuscany, by which time he would have sealed the deal with the Valtieri brothers.

Because he was going to. He'd decided that on the first evening, but he'd needed to know more about them and what they produced. And now he did, they could sort out the small print and he could go home.

He just had no idea where that would leave him and Amy.

CHAPTER NINE

'So I WAS RIGHT, then,' she said, trying to keep it light. 'No supper.'

'Don't worry, you won't starve.'

'I didn't think I would for a moment, but I have no doubt I'll have to sing for it.'

He gave a soft huff of laughter and carried on fiddling at the stove. 'Did she settle all right?'

'Yes, she's fine.'

'Good. Thanks. Here, try this.'

He put some things on a plate and set it on the table in front of her. Several slices of bruschetta—with the new topping, she guessed—and a couple of the stuffed zucchini flowers, dipped in the most delicate batter and briskly deep fried, then drained and drizzled in more of the heavenly olive oil.

'Try the *bruschetta*. I think this topping works better.'

She picked it up and sank her teeth into it, and sighed as the flavours exploded on her tongue. 'Gorgeous,' she mumbled, and looked up and caught his cocky grin.

'Did you expect anything less?' he said, with a lazy smile that dimpled his right cheek and an oh-so-Italian shrug that nearly unravelled her brain. 'Try the zucchini flowers. I tweaked the risotto filling again. Here—rinse your mouth first.'

She obediently drank some of the sparkling water he

passed her, then bit the end off one of the little golden parcels and groaned. 'Mmm. Yummy. Mintier?'

He nodded. 'I thought it might work with the main course as you suggested, instead of potatoes.'

'I don't suppose you've cooked any of the meat yet, have you, so we can try them together?' she said hopefully, and he chuckled.

'Not a prayer. It's going to take hours.'

He picked up the second zucchini flower and bit into it, and a little ooze of the risotto filling caught on his lip and she leant over, hooked her hand around the back of his neck to hold him still and captured it with her tongue.

He swore softly in Italian and shook his head at her.

'How am I supposed to concentrate now?' he grumbled, putting the rest of it in his mouth, but he was smiling as he took the plate and slid it into the dishwasher.

'I don't suppose the panna cotta's set yet?'

'You want some, I take it?'

'Absolutely. With the strawberries. And the balsamic. I want the whole deal. A girl has to eat. And you wanted my terrifying honesty, anyway.'

He sighed and rolled his eyes, muttering something about demanding women, and she smiled. It was just like old times, but not, because now there was something new to add to the mix, and it just made it even better.

She propped her elbows on the table and watched as he dipped the mould briefly in hot water, tipped the panna cotta out, spooned some sliced strawberries in dark syrup over the edge and decorated it with a mint leaf and a dust of vanilla icing sugar, and then shoved the plate in front of her, his spoon poised.

'I have to share it?' she joked, and then nearly whimpered as he scooped some up and held it to her lips.

It quivered gently, soft and luscious, the strawberries smelling of summer. She let it melt on her tongue—the sweet, the sour, the sharp, the…fiery?—and let her breath out slowly. 'Oh, wow. That's different. What's it got in it?'

'Pink peppercorns. Just a touch, to give it depth and warmth, and mint again for freshness. So what do you think of their balsamic? Good, isn't it?'

'Lovely. Beautiful. The whole thing's gorgeous.' She took the spoon from him and scooped up another dollop and felt it slide down her throat, cool and creamy and delicious, with a touch of lingering warmth from the pink peppercorns and the fresh richness of the ripe strawberries soaked in the glorious balsamic vinegar waking up every one of her taste buds. She groaned softly, opened her eyes again and met Leo's eyes.

And something happened. Some subtle shift, a hitch of breath, a flare of his pupils, and she felt as if she'd been struck by lightning.

For long seconds they froze, trapped in the moment, as if the clocks had stopped and everything was suspended in time. And then he leant in and kissed her, his mouth cool and sweet from the panna cotta, a touch of heat that lingered until he eased away and broke the contact.

'OK, I'm happy with that. Happy with all of it, so that's it for the testing,' he said, backing away, his voice a little rough and matter-of-fact, and if it hadn't been for the heat in his eyes she would have thought she'd done something wrong

'Can I give you a hand to clear up?'

'No, you're fine. I'll do it. I've got more mess to make before I'm done.'

'Shall I wait up for you?'

He shook his head, and a slow smile burned in his eyes. 'No. You go to bed. I'll come and find you.'

She hadn't even made it to the bedroom before he followed her in. 'I thought you had more to do?' she said softly.

'It'll keep. I have more pressing concerns right now,' he murmured, and tugged her gently into his arms.

She heard him get up, long before the sun rose, when the sky was streaked with pink and the air was filled with birdsong. She propped herself up on one elbow and groped for her phone, checking the time.

Five thirty.

He must be mad. Or driven. This meal was important to him, a chance to showcase his skills to the Valtieri team, and of course he was driven. There was a lot riding on it, and he wasn't going to derail it just because they'd fallen into an unscheduled affair. Even if it was amazing.

At least she didn't have to get up yet. She could sneak another hour, at a pinch, before Ella woke up. She flopped back onto the pillow and closed her eyes again, and the next thing she was aware of was the sound of knocking, then something being put down on her bedside table. She prised her eyes open and Leo's face swam into view.

'Tea,' he said economically, his voice gruff with lack of sleep. 'Ella's up and I need to get on. Can I drag you out of bed?'

She blinked to clear her eyes. 'Time?'

'Nearly seven.'

Rats. 'Give me five minutes,' she mumbled, and closed her eyes again. Mistake. She felt a wet trail across her forehead and opened them again to see Leo dipping his finger in her water glass again.

'Noooo,' she moaned, and forced herself to sit up. 'You're such a bully.'

His smile was strained, his eyes tired. 'Sorry,' he said, sounding utterly unrepentant. 'I really need you. Five minutes,' he repeated firmly, and went out, closing the door softly behind himself.

She looked longingly at the pillows, then sighed, shoved

them up against the headboard and shuffled up the bed. Five minutes, indeed. She groped for the mug, took a sip, then a swallow, and gradually the fog cleared from her brain. She had to get up. Now. Before temptation overwhelmed her and she slithered back down under the covers.

With Leo?

'Don't distract him,' she growled, and dumped the empty mug down and threw off the covers, just as Leo came back in.

His eyes flicked to her legs, then up again, and he zoomed in for a hot, quick kiss. 'Just checking you weren't asleep again.'

'I'm not,' she said unnecessarily, trying not to smile. 'Shut the door on your way out and go back to work.'

He backed out, pulling it to as he went. 'I'm taking Ella to the kitchen to give her breakfast while I carry on. That should give you time for a shower.'

The latch clicked, and she sighed and went over to the French doors and stared out at the valley.

Today was a big day for him, but it was also nearly the end of their stay. She knew Leo needed far more from her than a random fumble when he was too tired to think straight, but if she was going to be there for him for the next few weeks at least, to help him through the disastrous fallout from his doomed marriage, then her feelings and his had to remain on an even keel, which meant playing it light and not letting herself take it too seriously.

And certainly not distracting him when he needed to work, even if it killed her.

She showered rapidly and pulled her clothes on before heading for the kitchen. It was still only half past seven. How on earth was he functioning on so little sleep?

She found them in the kitchen, Ella mashing a soldier of toast all over the tray of the high chair, Leo doing something fast and dextrous with a knife and a rack of lamb.

There was a pile of zucchini flowers in the middle of the table, and the air was rich with promise.

'Smells good in here,' she said.

'That's the mutton,' he said tersely. 'I got up at three and put it in the oven, and I've shredded it and rolled it up into sausages in cling film and it's chilling, and I'm just prepping the racks. She could do with a drink and a handful of blueberries. They're in the fridge.'

She opened the door and was greeted by shelves crammed with goodies of all sorts, including the lovely, lovely panna cotta. 'Which shelf?'

He turned and pointed, then went back to his prepping, and she gave Ella the blueberries and put a slice of bread in the toaster for herself.

'Do you want a coffee?'

'I've had three,' he said. 'Not that it's helping. I'll have another one.'

'Or I could give you a glass of spring water with lemon in it and you could detox a bit for half an hour?'

'Just give me a coffee,' he growled, and gave an enormous yawn. 'My body's finally decided I'm tired. Talk about picking its moments.'

She laughed a little guiltily and handed him a coffee, weaker than he would have made it, longer, with a good slug of milk, and he gave her a look but took it anyway.

'Thanks.'

'You're welcome.'

He took a gulp and carried on, and she sat down with Ella, leaving him to it while she ate her breakfast and tried to stop the blueberries escaping to the floor.

'Tell me if there's anything you need me to help with,' she said, and he nodded.

'I'm fine. You're doing the most useful thing already.'

'I've brought my camera.'

'To catch me at my worst?'

She turned her head and studied him. His hair was tousled and spiky, his eyes were bleary and he had on yesterday's shirt and ancient jeans cut off at the knee, showing off those lean muscular calves that she'd recently realised were irresistible. His feet were bare, too, the toes splayed slightly as he leaned over, strong and straight and curiously sexy. Why had she never noticed them before?

She dragged her eyes off them.

'I think your fans will be able to cope,' she said drily, and pulled out her camera. One for her personal folder...

The family arrived back at eleven thirty, and Lydia came straight into the kitchen to ask if he needed help.

'No, I'm fine,' he said. 'All under control.' Unlike his emotions. 'What time do you want to eat?'

'Twelve thirty?'

He nodded. 'I thought we should eat in the garden under the pergola, unless you'd rather be in here?'

'The garden would be lovely. So, can I ask what's on the menu?'

He told her, and her eyes lit up. 'Fabulous,' she said. 'Bring it on—I'm starving! And I *will* be picking your brains later.'

He couldn't help but laugh. 'Feel free. Now leave me alone so I can concentrate.'

Not a chance. The kitchen became party central, but it didn't matter. He was used to working in chaos, and Lydia made sure they all stayed out of his way and she helped him unobtrusively, taking over the stuffing of the zucchini flowers while he checked on the other things.

Which was fine, except of course Amy was there, and his eyes kept straying to her, distracting his attention from the core business.

He forced himself to focus. The last thing he needed was the lamb rack overcooked or the zucchini flowers burnt in the hot oil when he started to cook them in a few minutes.

But it seemed that although she was pretty much ignoring him, Amy was very much aware of what he was doing, and with twenty minutes to go she chivvied them all outside into the garden to leave him in peace. He stopped her as she was following them.

'Amy?'

'Do you need me?'

What a choice of words, after all that had happened last night. He held out a serving plate piled high with bruschetta.

'Could you give them these—and try and make sure you don't eat them all yourself,' he added, grinning.

She took the plate from him with an unladylike snort and a toss of her head, and he chuckled. Still the same old Amy. 'Thank you,' he called after her, and she relented and threw him a smile over her shoulder as she went out of the door.

She checked her watch. Any minute now, she thought, and leaving Ella in Lydia's care she slipped back into the kitchen.

'Anything I can do?'

'Take the plates out and make sure they're all sitting down ready and then help me ferry stuff in a couple of minutes? I'm just frying the last of the zucchini flowers and everything else is done. The lamb's resting, the mutton's keeping warm and the veg are steaming.'

He was working as he talked and she glanced at the clock on the kitchen wall. Twelve twenty six. Bang on time. She felt her mouth tug in a wry smile. He'd never been on time for anything in his life until he'd started cooking professionally.

'OK. Nothing you want me to do except ferry?'

'No, I'll be fine. And, Amy?'

She turned and met his eyes.

'Thank you. For everything. I couldn't have done it without you. You've been amazing.'

She felt his warmth flood through her.

'You're welcome. And I know you'll be fine. They'll love it. You have some serious fans out here. Just don't burn the zucchini flowers.'

He *was* fine.

Everything was fine. More than fine, and he was in his element.

The food was amazing, and everyone from the babies upwards loved it. The zucchini flowers he'd finally chosen as the starter were beautiful and utterly delicious, and once the lamb two ways—*agnello in due modi* as Leo called it for the benefit of their Italian hosts—was on the table, he looked utterly relaxed. And by the time he brought out the panna cotta and strawberries, he was Leo at his best.

This was his dish, the thing he'd made his own, and Lydia, who by now was muttering things about how on earth she was expected to feed the family after this, was begging him for a master class or at the very least a recipe.

'Any time. It's so easy.'

'Easy to make, but not easy to make taste like *that*,' Lydia pointed out, and he laughed

'But it's nothing without the right ingredients.' His eyes swung to Massimo.

He was leaning back in his chair, wine in hand, his eyes on Leo, and he nodded slowly. 'We need to talk. Heaven knows my wife's an excellent chef, and I'm used to amazing food on a daily basis, but you've taken our ingredients and lifted them into something incredible. We have to do a deal. I want our produce on the table in your restaurants.'

For a moment Leo said nothing, but then a slow smile

started in his eyes and lit up his whole face. 'Thank you. I was going to say the same thing. I don't know what it is about your produce—maybe the care you take, the land, the generations of expertise, but I've been able to find a depth of flavour that I've never found before, and I really want to work with you. And I want that *balsamico* on the list,' he added with a wink.

They all laughed. 'I'm sure that can be arranged. Nine o'clock tomorrow. We'll sort out the fine print,' Massimo said, and drained his glass.

She was sitting on the terrace nursing a cup of tea and watching the swallows when he appeared. Ella was in bed and the families had all gone their separate ways, and they were alone.

He dropped onto the other end of the bench and let out a satisfied sigh. 'Well, that went OK.'

She laughed softly. 'Did you ever doubt it would?'

'Absolutely. There are always doubts, but it looks as if I've achieved what I'd come for.'

'With bells on. They really like you, Leo. And if they hadn't, it wouldn't happen.'

'I know. Tell me about it. And I really like them, too. I trust them, and I couldn't have wanted more from this trip.' He turned his head, his eyes seeking hers. 'And I couldn't have done it without you.'

She looked away, suddenly awkward. 'I haven't done that much—'

'Yes, you have,' he said sincerely. 'I needed to know that Ella was all right, and she was, which left me free to see everything there was to see and take my time getting to know them. It's an important deal, and I wanted to be clear about what I was getting.'

'And are you?'

'Oh, yes. I imagine they'll want to tie up the loose ends

tomorrow, but we're pretty much done. Time to go home. I've neglected my business long enough.'

Home.

Whatever that meant.

Amy stared out over the rolling hills and felt a stab of apprehension mingled with regret. She'd always known this was just for a short time, but it had been a wonderful time, cocooned in a dream world of sunshine and laughter and playing happy families. And now it was almost over. Eight weeks with Leo and Ella, and then she had to find something to do, some way of earning a living until her photography took off, and she had no idea where to start.

Whatever, it meant an end to her time with them in this magical place, and the thought left a hollow ache in the centre of her chest. Things had changed now for ever and, whatever the outcome of their affair, it would never go back to that easy, loving friendship it had been.

'So, what's next for you?' he asked, as if he could read her mind, and she gave a little shrug and dredged up a smile.

'Oh, you know. This and that. I'm sure something'll crop up. I imagine there'll be wedding stuff that still needs dealing with, and I've got a lot of work to do on the photos for your blog, and pulling a portfolio together. I'll need to do some studio shots, clever things with lighting, that sort of thing. Arty stuff. Maybe I can do that while they're filming and the lights are there. And then I'll have to market it. Or myself.'

He nodded thoughtfully. 'I just wondered—I've been thinking I ought to do some cookery books ever since you first nagged me about it, but it's never seemed like the right time before.'

'And it does now?'

'Yes, I think it does. It will be a lot of work, but it might tie in well with Ella. And if I do, of course, I'll need a photographer.'

'You will. And you're right. I told you years ago you should do it but it just wasn't right for you at the time.'

'I don't suppose you want to take it on?'

'Being the photographer?'

Would she? It would mean seeing him again. Over and over again. Which would be fine if they were still together, but torture if they weren't. 'Mind if I think about it? I don't know where I'll be or what I'll be doing.'

'No, I understand that, but bear it in mind. I'd be really grateful. Your photos are amazing.' He gave a huff of laughter. 'There's just the small matter of a publisher, of course.'

'Now there I can definitely help you. I've got contacts, remember?'

'Great. Sound them out, by all means.'

He smiled at her, and her heart flipped over. Could it work? It would mean working with him again, spending time with him, helping him move on with his life. And moving on with hers. She knew a cookery book by him would fly off the shelves, and it would ensure her success, too, but more than that it would give them a better chance to find out if they could forge a future together.

'I'll see what I can do. I'd have a vested interest, of course, in getting this off the ground,' she reminded him. 'Always assuming I'm free.'

'I know. There's no rush. I've got the TV contract outstanding, and that'll have to come first.'

'They might want to tie them together—launch the book of the series, as it were. They do that a lot. Ask them.'

'I will. I'll sound them out, but they're getting impatient. The producer wants to see me like yesterday. I've told him I should be back by Tuesday and I can't deal with it until then.'

'Assuming tomorrow goes to plan.'

'That's right. So we need to fly out on Tuesday morning at the latest. Earlier if we can. I'd rather go tomorrow.'

'Another posh plane?' she asked drily, ignoring the sinking feeling in her gut, and he laughed.

'Probably. It's less stressful than killing time at an airport with Ella, and we need to pick the car up. It's easier. But we'll get whatever we can whenever we can.'

'See how it goes,' she said. 'I'll make sure all our stuff's packed ready first thing in the morning.'

'OK.' He reached out, threading his fingers through hers. 'I think we ought to turn in now. It's been a busy day and I need my business brain working for the morning.'

'Don't you trust them?'

He laughed, his eyes creasing up at the sides, that fascinating dimple flirting with her near the corner of his mouth. 'Of course I trust them, but they'll want the best deal and so do I. I need to be able to think clearly. I'm not going to sign my life away without realising it.'

He got up.

'Come to bed,' he said softly, and she nodded.

'Just give me a couple of minutes. You go first in the bathroom. I want to say goodbye to the valley.'

'Crazy girl,' he murmured, but his voice was full of affection, and he crunched softly over the gravel and went in through the French doors.

She let her breath out slowly. Less than forty-eight hours ago, they'd sat there together while he'd poured his heart out. And then he'd kissed her. Or had she kissed him? She wasn't sure, but she knew that from that moment on everything had changed.

Could she work with him on a cookery book? Maybe, maybe not.

She sat there a little longer, knowing they'd most likely be leaving in the early afternoon and this would be her last chance to soak up the time between day and night, that wonderful time when the swallows went to bed and the bats woke and took over the aerial display in a carefully orchestrated shift change.

She'd miss this. Miss all of it, but most especially the family, Lydia in particular. The warmth of their welcome had been amazing, and she knew it wasn't just because Leo was a celebrity. It was because they were lovely, decent people with a strong sense of family and loyalty, and she'd miss them all.

But most of all she'd miss being with Leo and Ella in this stolen moment in time. The little girl had crept into her heart when she'd least expected it, and Leo...

She sighed softly. Leo had always been massively important to her, but this holiday had changed things, shifted the delicate balance of their friendship from platonic to something she'd never anticipated.

She had no idea what the future would bring, but she knew it would be a long time before she'd be looking for any other man. Her emotions were a mess, her judgement was flawed, and it was far too soon for her to be thinking about another relationship, even with Leo.

Not that he was in any better shape than her emotionally, and probably a whole lot worse. The pair of them were a lost cause. Could they save each other and build a future together?

She desperately hoped so, but she had a feeling the answer would be no, once reality intruded.

She watched the swallows depart, watched the bats dart in to take their place, and when her eyes could hardly make them out in the darkness, she got to her feet and went inside to Leo.

Tomorrow would be here all too soon. It was time to go back to the future.

CHAPTER TEN

'SOON BE HOME.'

She glanced across at him and found a smile. 'Yes. Not long now.'

Not long enough. He'd booked another charter, not getting the benefit of the empty leg rate this time but there were bigger fish to fry, she guessed, like the meeting with the TV series producer tomorrow.

She wasn't complaining, though. This flight, like the last, had been seamless, the car ready and waiting when they arrived, and they were cruising steadily towards Suffolk as the light faded, Ella fast asleep in her car seat behind them.

She glanced over her shoulder at the little girl she'd somehow fallen in love with, and felt a sudden pang of loss at the thought of parting from her. From both of them.

Leo's face was expressionless, his hands relaxed on the wheel, his eyes on the road. He flicked a glance at her and smiled. 'You'll get a lie-in in the morning,' he said, with something like envy in his voice, but she'd swap her lie-in for a cuddle with Ella any day.

'Yes, I will,' she said evenly, trying not to dwell on how much she'd miss those special moments. She'd be going back home to her mother and he to his parents, at least until his house was finished, so at the very least their affair was on hold for now.

'So, when do you want to look at the photos?' she asked, clutching at straws. 'Shall I download them onto a memory stick for you? Obviously they'll need some work before you can put them in your blog, but you'll want to choose some initially for me to work with.'

'Yeah, that would be good. Maybe we could go over them one evening this week? I need to write it, too. I made some notes while we were over there, but to be honest I've had so much to think about my mind hasn't been on it at all. Not to mention certain other distractions,' he added, and she could hear the smile in his voice.

'Going through the photos will help,' she said. 'Will you be staying with your parents?'

'Initially, which'll make life easy when I go to London tomorrow and have to leave Ella behind. I guess you'll be with your mother?'

She would, at least for a little while, and they'd be next door. Her heart gave a little leap of joy. 'Where else?' she said, trying to keep it light. 'In case it's slipped your mind, I no longer have a home.' Or a job, after the next eight weeks. Or Leo?

'It hasn't slipped my mind.'

His hand reached out and found hers, his fingers curling around it as it lay on her lap. 'It'll be all right, Amy. Everything'll work out, one way or the other.'

Would it? She desperately hoped so, but she didn't like the sound of 'other'. The uncertainty of her future was thrown into sharp focus by the raw reminder of her homelessness. And joblessness. Not to mention the touch of his hand.

'Does that apply to you, too, or is it only me you've sprinkled fairy dust on?'

He gave a short huff that could just have been laughter, and put his hand back on the steering-wheel. 'I'm a lost cause,' he said, which was just what she'd thought last night, oddly, but hearing him say it gave her a hideous sinking feeling.

'You're not,' she argued gently, her own situation forgotten because his was far, far worse. 'You've just been in a bad place, Leo, but that'll change. It's already changing. You need to start working again, doing more at the restaurant, getting back into the filming, focussing on your USP.'

'Which is what, exactly?'

She shifted in the seat so she could study him. He hadn't shaved today—or yesterday, probably, either—and the stubble darkening his jaw gave him a sexy, slightly rakish air. How on earth had she never noticed before this week just how gorgeous he was?

'You have great media presence,' she said truthfully, avoiding the obvious fact of his sex appeal in the interest of their mutual sanity. 'Everyone loved your first two television series. Another one will raise your profile, and you can cash in on that with the cookery book. You're a great communicator, so communicate with your public, charm the punters in your restaurant, flirt with the camera, sell yourself.'

His brow crunched up in a frown. 'But I'm not the product. My food's the product.'

How could he really be so dense? 'No. You're inseparable. You, and your enthusiasm for food, your quirky take on things, your energy—that's what people love.'

What she loved. What she'd loved about him since she'd been old enough to be able to spell 'hormone'. She just hadn't realised it until now.

'Well, how on earth would I market that?' he asked, and she laughed. He really didn't get it.

'You don't have to market it! You just have to be you, and the rest will follow. The TV, the cookery book idea, your blog—all of it showcases you. The food is secondary, in a way. You were doing all the right things already. Just keep doing them and you'll be fine.'

He grunted, checked over his shoulder and pulled out to overtake. 'Right now I'm more worried about where we're going to do the filming. The plan was to do it in my new house, in my own kitchen, but it's not ready and time's running out. I won't do London again, and they want more of a lifestyle thing, which will fit round Ella, but that's no good without the house.'

'So how long will it be before it's done?'

'I have no idea,' he said, and he sounded exasperated. 'The builder's running out of time, even though there's a penalty clause in the contract, but of course I've been away over a week so I haven't been on his case and I don't know how well they've got on.'

'What's left to do?'

'It's mostly done, it's just the finishing off. They were fitting the kitchen, which is the most important thing as far as filming's concerned, and it should be straightforward, but every time I think that it all goes wrong, so who knows?'

'Could you use the restaurant kitchen in Yoxburgh?'

'Not without disrupting the business, and it's going well now, it's getting a name for itself and it's busy. I don't want to turn people away; I have to live in the town, it's where I'll be working, so it's the flagship restaurant, and that makes it hugely important to the brand. It would be career suicide and I'm doing pretty well on that already.'

'So push him.'

'I will. I'll call him in the morning, on my way to London, see how far off finishing he is.'

He turned off the main road, and she realised they were nearly home—if family homes counted, and at the moment they both seemed to be homeless, so she guessed they did count. He drove slowly through the village, turned into her mother's drive and pulled up at the door.

He didn't cut the engine, presumably so he didn't wake Ella, but he got out and by the time she'd picked up her bag and found her key he was there, holding the car door open for her.

'I'll get your stuff. I won't stop, I need to settle Ella and I've got a million and one emails to check tonight. I've just been ignoring them.'

He opened the back of the car and pulled out her bag, carrying it to the door for her. She put her key in the lock and turned to thank him, but he got there before her, reaching out a hand and cupping her face, his thumb sweeping a caress across her cheek.

Her eyes locked with his, and held.

'I don't know what I would have done without you, Amy,' he said softly, his voice a little gruff. 'You've been amazing, and I'm so grateful.'

Her heart thumped, her face turning slightly as she looked away, her cheek nestling into his hand so his thumb was almost touching her mouth.

'Don't be,' she murmured. 'You saved my life, getting me out of here. I don't know quite what I would have done if you hadn't.'

'You would have been fine. Your mother would have seen to that.'

She felt her mouth tip in a smile, and she turned her head again and met his eyes. 'Yes, she would, but it wouldn't have been the same. Thank you for rescuing me for the umpteenth time. I'll try not to let it happen again.'

And without checking in with her common sense meter, she went up on tiptoe and kissed him. The designer stubble grazed her skin lightly, setting her nerve endings on fire and making her ache for more, but before either of them could do anything stupid, she rocked back onto her heels and stepped away.

'Good luck tomorrow. Let me know how it goes.'

'I will. Enjoy your lie-in and think of me up at the crack of dawn with my little treasure.'

Think of him? She'd thought of very little else for the past week or more. 'You know you love it.' She turned the key in the door, pushed it open and picked up her bag. 'Goodnight, Leo.'

''Night, Amy. Sleep tight.'

It was what he said to Ella every night, his voice a soft, reassuring rumble. *'Goodnight, my little one. Sleep tight.'*

She swallowed the lump in her throat, walked into the house and closed the door behind her.

Time to start sorting out her life.

Her mother was pleased to see her.

She was in the sitting room watching the television, and she switched it off instantly. 'Darling! I didn't hear the car, I'm sorry. Is Leo with you?'

'No, he's got to get Ella to bed and he's got an early start in the morning.'

'Oh. OK. Good journey?'

'Yes, fine. It seems odd to be home.'

Odd, but good, she thought as her mother hugged her tight and then headed for the kitchen. 'Tea? Coffee? Wine?'

She laughed and followed her. 'Tea would be great. I've had a lot of wine this week. Wine, and food, and—'

Leo. Leo, in almost every waking moment, one way or another.

'So how was Tuscany? Tell me all about the *palazzo*. It sounds amazing.'

'Oh, it is. I've got a million photos I've got to go through.

I'll show them to you when I've had time to sort them out a bit. So how's it been here?' she asked, changing the subject. 'I'm so sorry I ran away and left you to clear up the chaos, but I just couldn't face it.'

'No, of course you couldn't, and it's been fine. Everyone was lovely about it. I went next door and spoke to them all, and the family came back here and it was lovely, really. We had quite a good time, considering, and Roberto made sure we had plenty to eat, so it was fine.'

'What about the presents?' she asked.

'No problem. I spoke to the store, and they agreed to refund everyone. They just want to hear from you personally before they press the buttons, and people will need to contact them individually, but it'll be fine. Nothing to worry about.'

That was a weight off her mind. There was still Leo's gift, of course, but she'd done what she could about that, and there was more to come. Looking after Ella for a week had been a joy, and photographing Leo had been a guilty pleasure, but she'd promised her help for eight weeks to help during the filming, and if that didn't come off, for any reason, she could give him those photos, edit them until they were perfect for what he needed, so even if she couldn't help him with a cookery book, he shouldn't come off too badly from their deal.

'Mum, are you OK with me staying here for a while?' she asked, before she got too carried away with the planning. 'Just until I get my life sorted out?'

Her mother tutted and hugged her. 'Darling, it's your home. Of course you can stay here. You're always welcome, and you always will be. And don't worry. Things will sort themselves out. I just want you to be happy.'

Happy? She felt her eyes fill, and turned away.

'I don't suppose there's anything to eat?'

'Of course there is! I knew you were coming home so I made curry. I'll put the rice on now.'

Ella wouldn't settle.

He couldn't blame her. She'd been trapped in her baby seat for a long time today, one way and another, and she'd slept for a lot of it. Not surprisingly, she wanted to play.

With him.

Again, he couldn't blame her. She hadn't seen nearly as much of him as usual in the past week, and she'd been in a strange place, with a strange carer. Not that she'd seemed to mind. She adored Amy.

His daughter had good taste. Excellent taste.

He covered his eyes and wondered how long it would take to get her out of his system. A week? A month?

A lifetime?

'Boo!'

Ella giggled and crawled up to him, pulling his hands off his face again and prising his eyes open. He winced, lifted her out of range and opened them, to her great delight. Another giggle, another bounce up and down on his lap, another launch at his face. She was so easily pleased, the reward of her smile out of all proportion to the effort he was putting in.

He reeled her in and hugged her, pushing her T-shirt up and blowing a raspberry on her bare tummy and making her shriek with laughter.

His email was squatting in his inbox like a malevolent toad, and he had phone calls to make and things to do, but he didn't care. The most important thing was checking in with the restaurant, but they were shut on Monday nights so that wasn't a problem for today.

She pulled up her little T-shirt again and shoved her tummy in the air, and he surrendered. Ella wanted her father and, dammit, he wanted her, too. The rest would keep.

* * *

She stood at her bedroom window, staring across at Leo's family home. The light was on in his bedroom, and through the open window she could hear Ella's little shriek of laughter and Leo's answering growl.

They were playing. That wouldn't please him, with all he had to do, but they sounded as if they were having fun, or at least Ella was.

She couldn't help smiling, but it was a bitter-sweet smile. She already missed them so much. Watching him playing with Ella, focussing all that charismatic charm on his little girl, not caring at all that he was making an idiot of himself.

Oh, Leo.

It was warm, but she closed the window anyway. She didn't need to torture herself by listening to them. It was bad enough without that.

She turned and scanned the room.

Her wedding dress was gone, of course, hung up in another room, she imagined, together with the veil and shoes. And her ring? She'd left it on the dressing table, and that was where she found it. Her mother had put it back in the box, but left it out for her to deal with.

She'd send it back to Nick, of course. It was the least she could do, it must have cost him a fortune. Not that he was exactly strapped for cash, but that wasn't the point.

She got out her laptop, plugged in the memory card from the camera and propped herself on the bed against a pile of pillows. She'd have a quick look through the photos before she went to bed, but she wasn't even going to attempt her emails. No doubt her inbox was full of sympathetic or slightly sarky comments about the wedding fiasco, and she might just delete the lot. Tomorrow.

Tonight, she was looking at photos.

* * *

'Are you busy?'

Busy? Why should she be busy? All she'd had to do today was draft a letter to all the guests, hand-write them and take them to the post office. Preferably not in the village so she didn't have to stand in the queue and answer questions or endure sympathetic glances. And sort through the photos.

So far, she hadn't even got past first base.

'No, I'm not busy. Why?'

'I just wondered. I'm back, I've put Ella to bed and I've got a site meeting with the builder in half an hour, but then I thought we could go through the photos.'

Ah. She hadn't got far last night. About five minutes in she'd been reduced to tears, and she'd had to shut her laptop. 'I haven't had time to go through them yet and delete the dross.' Or extract the ones that were for her eyes only. There were a lot of those. And it had been nothing to do with time.

'That's fine. We can do it together.'

'Here, or yours?'

'How about the new house? The builder said it was habitable, pretty much, so we could take the laptop over there.'

She could always say no—tell him she was tired or something. Except that so far today she'd done almost nothing. A bit of laundry, a lot of wallowing in self-pity and kicking herself for being stupid didn't count. And at least it would deal with the photos.

'Fine,' she agreed, dying to get a look at his house and too weak to say no.

'Great. Come round when you're ready, and we'll go from here.'

That meant seeing his parents, and they'd been the ones with the marquee in the garden, the catering team crawling all over the place, the mess left behind afterwards. And all for nothing.

She'd been going to take them something by way of apology, but now he'd short-circuited her plans and she wouldn't have a chance.

She shook her head in defeat.

'OK. I'll be round in a minute.'

'We're in the kitchen. Come through the fence.'

So she did. Through the gate in the fence that their fathers had made together years ago, and into their back garden where just over a week ago there had been a marquee for her wedding. You couldn't tell. The garden was immaculate, a riot of colour and scent. The perfect setting for a wedding.

She turned her back on it, walked in through the kitchen door and straight into Mrs Zacharelli's arms.

'Welcome home, Amy,' she said, and hugged her hard.

Amy's eyes welled, and she swallowed hard and tried not to cry. 'I'm so sorry—' she began, but then the tears got the better of her and Mrs Zach hugged her again before she was elbowed out of the way by her husband. He hauled Amy into a bear hug and cradled her head like a child.

'Enough of that,' he said. 'No tears. It was the right thing to do.'

'But you did so much for me,' she protested.

'It was nothing. Sit. Drink. We're celebrating.'

He let her go, pushed her into a chair and thrust a glass into her hand. Prosecco? 'Celebrating what?'

'Leo hasn't told you? They're starting filming the new television series next week.'

She turned her head and met his eyes. 'Really? So quick? What about your house?'

'We'll see. The builder says it'll be ready. Drink up, or we're going to be late.'

* * *

It was beautiful.

Stunning. She vaguely remembered seeing the cliff-top house in the past, but it had been nothing to get excited about. Now—well, now it was amazing.

While Leo poked and prodded and asked the builder questions about things she didn't know anything about, she drifted from room to room, her eyes drawn constantly to the sea, wondering how on earth she'd thought that Palazzo Valtieri could trump this. Oh, it was hugely impressive, steeped in history and lovingly cared for, but there was none of the light and space and freedom that she felt in this house, and she knew where she'd rather live.

He found her upstairs in one of the bedrooms. 'So, what do you think?'

'I think you need to give me a guided tour before I can possibly judge.'

His mouth kicked up in a smile, and he shook his head slowly. 'Going to make me wait? I might have known it. You always were a tease. So...' He waved his arm. 'This is my bedroom.'

'I see you chose the one with the lousy sea view.'

He chuckled and moved on. 'Bathroom through there, walk-in wardrobe, then this is the principal guest room—'

'Another dreadful view,' she said drily, and followed him through to Ella's bedroom.

'Oh! Who painted the mural? It's lovely!'

He rubbed his hand over the back of his neck and gave a soft laugh. 'I did. I wanted her room to be special, and I thought it was something I could do for her, something personal. I'm sure I could have paid a professional to do it much better, but somehow that didn't seem right.'

Her eyes filled, and she ran her fingertips lightly over the intertwining branches of a magical tree that scrambled up the wall and across the ceiling, sheltering the corner where she imagined the cot would go.

'It's wonderful,' she said, her voice choked. 'She's a lucky little girl.'

'I wouldn't go that far, but I do my best under the circumstances.'

He turned away, walking out of the room and down the stairs, and she followed him—through the hall, a sitting room with a sea view, a study fitted out with desk and shelves and storage facing the front garden and the drive this time, a cloakroom with coat storage and somewhere to park Ella's buggy—and then back across the hall into the main event, a huge room that opened out to the deck and the garden beyond.

Literally. The far wall was entirely glass, panels that would slide away to let the outside in, and right in the centre of the room was the kitchen.

And what a kitchen! Matte dark grey units, pale wood worktops, sleek integrated ovens, in the plural—and maybe a coffee maker, a steam oven, a microwave—she had no idea, but a bank of them, anyway, set into tall units at one side that no doubt would house all manner of pots and pans and ingredients as well. There was a huge American-style fridge freezer, still wrapped but standing by the slot designed to take it, and he told her it was to be plumbed in tomorrow.

'So—the verdict?'

She gave an indifferent shrug, and then relented, her smile refusing to hide. 'Stunning. It's absolutely stunning, Leo. Really, really lovely.'

'So who wins?'

She laughed softly and turned to face him. 'It grieves me to admit it, but you do. By a mile.'

His eyes creased into a smile, and he let out a quiet huff of laughter. 'Don't ever tell them that.'

'Oh, I wouldn't be so rude, and it's very beautiful, but this…'

'Yeah. I love it, too. I wasn't sure I would, because of the circumstances, but I do. I started planning it before Lisa died, but she had no interest in it, no input—nothing. And it's changed out of all recognition.'

'So she's not here.'

'No. And she's never been here. Not once. She wouldn't set foot in it. And now I'm glad, because it isn't—'

He broke off, but the word 'tainted' hovered in the air between them.

She took a breath, moved the conversation on, away from the past. 'So, will it be ready for filming on Monday?'

He shrugged, that wonderful Latin shrug that unravelled her every time, and his mouth quirked into a smile. 'He tells me it's done, all bar the fridge-freezer plumbing and the carpets, which are booked for tomorrow. I've gone over everything with him this evening to make sure it's OK, and I can move in whenever I want.'

'Oh. Wow. That was quick,' she said, and was appalled at the sense of loss. She'd thought they'd be next door with his parents, but now they wouldn't. He and Ella would move into their wonderful new house a few miles up the road, and she'd hardly see them.

Oh, well. It had to happen sooner or later.

'It had to be. The series team liked the Tuscany idea, by the way, and it's a brilliant opportunity to showcase the Valtieri produce, so they won't be unhappy with that. I just need to knock up some recipes, bearing in mind the schedule's pretty tight.'

'So you're going to be really busy setting it all up this week. Do you want me to look after Ella from now on?'

He ran his hand round the back of his neck. 'Yeah, I need to talk to you about that. We'll be filming all day from Monday, and I need to spend some time in the restaurant in the evenings, and I can't do that and look after her. She loves you, she's happy with you—but I don't know how you'd feel about moving in.'

'Moving in? Here? With you?'

He shrugged. 'Not—with me. Not in that way. I just think it would be easier all round if you were here, but you don't have to do it. You don't have to do any of it. It was never part of the deal.'

'I changed the deal. And you agreed it.'

'And then we moved the goalposts into another galaxy. You have every right to refuse, if you want to.' His face softened into a wry smile. 'I'm hoping you won't because my parents need a holiday and I'd like to cut them some slack. They've been incredible for the past nine months, and I'm very conscious that I've taken advantage, but I know that moving in with me is a huge step for you, and I'm very conscious of what you said about what happened in Tuscany—'

'Stays in Tuscany?' she finished for him. 'That's not set in stone.'

'But we could still do that. Keep our distance, get to know each other better before we invest too much in this relationship, because we're not the people we were.'

'So what do you want to know about me?'

'Whether or not you can live with me would be a good start.'

'We seem to have done a pretty good job of it this week.'

'We haven't shared the toothpaste yet,' he said, his mouth wry.

'We've done everything else.'

'No, we haven't. We haven't been together while I've been running the business, which takes a hell of a lot of my time, and what's left belongs to Ella. And that's not negotiable.'

'I know that, Leo, and I can handle your schedule. I've

already proved that. I'm not a needy child, and I'm not
Lisa. I haven't been transplanted into an alien environment. I've got friends and family in the area, a life of my
own. Don't worry, I'll find plenty to do.'

'I still think we need to try it. And to do that, I'd need
you living here, at least while my parents are away, and
preferably for the whole time we're filming. If you could.'

She hesitated, part of her aching to be there helping him
and spending time with Ella, making sure she was safe
and happy, the other part wary of exposing herself to hurt.

No contest.

'So how long is it? Is it eight weeks, as you thought?'

'I don't know. They're talking about eight episodes.
Probably a couple of days for each, plus prep and downtime
for me while they cut and fiddle about with it. I reckon a
week an episode. That's what it was last time. Or maybe
six, at a push. It's a serious commitment. And it's a lot
to ask—too much for my mother and father, even if they
weren't going on holiday.'

Eight weeks of working with him, keeping Ella out of
the way yet close enough at hand that he could see her
whenever he had a chance. Eight weeks of sleeping with
him every night? Maybe. Which meant eight more weeks
to get to know him better, and fall deeper and deeper in
love with both of them.

And at the end—what then?

She hesitated for so long that he let out a long, slow sigh
and raked his hands through his hair.

'Amy, if you really can't, then I'll find another way,' he
said softly. 'I don't want to put you under pressure or take
advantage of you and it doesn't change things between us
at all. I still want to get to know you better, but if you aren't
sure you want to do it, I'll get a nanny—a childminder.
Something. A nursery.'

'Not at such short notice,' she told him. 'Even I know

that. Anyone who's any good won't be able to do it, not with the restaurant hours as well.' She sighed, closed her eyes briefly and then opened them to find him watching her intently.

'So where does that leave us?' he asked.

'With me?'

'So—is that a yes?'

She tried to smile, but it slipped a little, the fear of making yet another catastrophic mistake so soon after the last one looming in her mind. 'Yes, it's a yes. Just remind me again—why it is that you *always* get your own way?' she murmured, and he laughed and pulled her into his arms and gave her a brief but heartfelt hug.

'Thank you. Now all I have to do is get the furniture delivered and we can move in and get on with our lives.'

Well, he could. Hers, yet again, was being put on hold, but she owed him so much for so many years of selfless support that another eight weeks of her life was nothing— especially since it would give them a chance to see if their relationship would survive the craziness that was his life.

She'd just have to hope she could survive it. Not the eight weeks, that would be fine. But the aftermath, the fallout when the series was filmed, the crew had left and he'd decided he couldn't live with her?

What on earth had she let herself in for?

CHAPTER ELEVEN

THEY WERE IN.

He looked around at his home—their home, his and Ella's and maybe Amy's—and let out a long, quiet sigh of relief. It had been a long time coming, but at last they were here.

Ella was safely tucked up in her cot in her new room, his parents had stayed long enough to toast the move, and now it was all his.

He poured himself a glass of wine, walked out onto the deck and sat down on the steps, staring out over the sea. He was shattered. Everything had been delivered, unpacked and put in place, and all he'd had to do was point.

In theory.

And tomorrow the contents of the store cupboards in the kitchen were being delivered and he could start working on some recipes.

But tonight he had to draft his Tuscan tour blog. Starting with the photos, because they hadn't got round to them on Tuesday night and he hadn't had a spare second since. Amy was coming round shortly with her laptop, and they were going through them together. Assuming he could keep his eyes open.

The doorbell rang, and he put his glass down and let her in. He wanted to pull her into his arms and kiss her, but with what had happened in Tuscany and all that, he really wanted to give their relationship a chance.

'Did she go down all right?'

He smiled wryly. Typical Amy, to worry about Ella first. 'Fine. She was pooped. I don't know what you did with her all day, but she was out of it.'

She laughed, and the sound rippled through him like clear spring water. 'We just played in the garden, and then we went for a walk by the beach, and she puggled about in the sand for a bit. We had a lovely day. How did you get on?'

'Oh, you know what moving's like. I'll spend the next six months trying to find things and groping for light switches in the dark. Come on through, I'm having a glass of wine on the deck.'

'Can we do it in the kitchen, looking at the photos? There are an awful lot. And can I have water, please? I'm driving, remember.'

'Sure.' He retrieved his glass, poured her water from the chiller in the fridge and sat next to her at the breakfast bar overlooking the sea. 'So, what have we got?'

'Lots.'

There *were* lots, she wasn't exaggerating. And there were gaps in the numbers, all over the place.

'What happened to the others? There are loads missing.'

'I deleted them.'

He blinked. 'Really? That's not like you. You never throw anything out.'

'Maybe you don't know me as well as you think,' she said.

Or maybe you do, she thought, scrolling down through the thumbnails and registering just how many she'd removed and saved elsewhere.

'Just start at the top,' he suggested, so they did.

Him laughing on the plane. She loved that one. Others in their suite, in the pool—still too many of them, although she'd taken bucket-loads out for what she'd called her private collection.

Self-indulgent fantasy, more like.

She knew what she was doing. She was building a memory bank, filling it with images to sustain her if it all went wrong.

There were some of her, too, ones he'd taken of her shot against the backdrop of the valley behind their terrace, or with Ella, playing. She'd nearly taken them out, too, but because nearly all of them had Ella in, she hadn't. He could have them for his own use.

'Right, so which ones do you want me to work on?'

He didn't hold back. She got a running commentary on the ones he liked, the ones he couldn't place, the ones he'd have to check with the Valtieri family before they were used.

'How about a *short*list for the blog?' she suggested drily, when he'd selected about two hundred.

He laughed. 'Sorry. These are just the ones I really like. I'll go through them again and be a bit more selective. I was just getting an overview. Why don't you just leave them with me so I'm not wasting your time? Did you copy them?'

She handed him the memory stick with the carefully edited photos that she'd deemed fit to give him. 'Here. Don't lose it. Just make a note and let me know.'

'I will. Thanks. Want the guided tour?'

'Of your furniture? I think I'll pass, if you don't mind. I still have stuff to do—like writing to all my wedding guests.'

'Sorry. Of course you do. And I've taken your whole day already. Go, and don't rush back in the morning. I should be fine until ten, at least.'

She moved in on Sunday, and the film crew arrived on Monday and brought chaos to the house—lights, reflectors, a million people apparently needed to co-ordinate the shoot, and Ella took one look at it all and started to cry.

Amy ended up taking her home for the day more than
once, which would have been fine if they'd stopped filming at her bedtime, but sometimes it dragged on, and then
she'd be unsettled, and he'd have to break off and read
her a story and sing to her before she'd go back to sleep.

'I'm sorry, this is really tough for you both,' Leo said
after a particularly late shoot. 'I didn't know it would dis-
rupt her life so much. I should have thought it through.'

'It's fine, Leo,' she assured him. 'We're coping.'

And they were, just about, but it was like being back in
Tuscany, tripping over each other in the kitchen in the morning, having breakfast together with Ella, doing all the happy
families stuff that was tearing her apart, with the added
bonus of doing it under the eyes of the film crew.

And because of the 'what happened in Tuscany' thing,
the enforced intimacy was making it harder and harder to
be around each other without touching and she was seriously regretting suggesting it.

Then one night Ella cried and she got up to her, but Leo
got there first. 'It's fine. I'll deal with her, you go back to
bed,' he said, but the fourth time she woke there was a tap
on her door and Leo came in.

'Amy, I think she needs the doctor. She must have an
ear infection or something. I have to take her to the hospital. They have an out of hours service there, apparently.'

'Want me to come?'

The relief on his face should have been comical, but it
was born of worry, so she threw her clothes on and went
with him. It took what felt like hours, of course, before
they came home armed with antibiotics and some pain relief, and Leo looked like hell.

'I feel sorry for the make-up lady who's going to have
to deal with the bags under your eyes in the morning,' she
said ruefully when the baby was finally settled.

'Don't you mean later in the morning?' he sighed,

yawning hugely and reaching for a glass. 'Water? Tea? I've given up on sleep. Decided it's an overrated pastime.'

She laughed softly and joined him. 'Tea,' she said.

'Good idea. We'll watch the sun come up.'

Which wasn't a good idea at all. Tuscany again, and sitting on the terrace overlooking the valley with the swallows swooping. Except here it was the gulls, their mournful cries haunting in the pale light of dawn.

'Thank you for coming with me to the hospital,' he said quietly.

'You don't have to thank me, Leo. I was happy to do it. I was worried about her.'

She stared out over the sea, watching it flood with colour as the sun crept over the horizon. It was beautiful, and it would have been perfect had she been able to do what she wanted to do and rest her head on his shoulder, but of course she couldn't.

'How's the filming going?' she asked, and he sighed.

'OK, I think, but I'm neglecting the restaurant, and I haven't even touched the Tuscany blog. On the plus side, we're nearly two weeks in.'

Really? Only six more weeks to go? And when it ended, they'd have no more excuse to be together, so it would be crunch time, and she was in no way ready to let him go. She drained her tea and stood up.

'I might go back to bed and see if I can sleep for a few more minutes,' she said, and left him sitting there, silhouetted against the sunrise. It would have made a good photo. Another one to join the many in her private collection.

She turned her back on him and walked away.

The filming was better after that, the next day not as long, and Leo had a chance to catch up with the restaurant over the weekend. Ella was fine, her ear infection settling quickly, but she'd slept a lot to catch up so Amy had helped him with the blog over the weekend, edited the photos, pulled it all together, and she showed it to him on Monday night after Ella was in bed.

'Oh, it looks fantastic, Amy,' he said, sitting back and sighing with relief. 'Thank you so much. The photos are amazing.'

'Better than your selfies?' she teased lightly, and he laughed.

'So much better!' He leant over and kissed her fleetingly, then pulled away, grabbing her by the hand and towing her into the kitchen. 'Come on, I'm cooking you dinner.'

'Is that my reward?'

'You'd better believe it. I have something amazing for you.'

'That poor lobster that's been crawling around your sink?'

'That was for filming. This is for us. Sit.'

She sat, propped up at the breakfast bar watching him work. She could spend her life doing it. What was she thinking? She *was* spending her life doing it, and it was amazing. Or would be, if only she dared to believe in it.

'The producer was talking about a cookery book,' he told her while he worked. 'Well, more a lifestyle-type book. Like the blog, but more so, linking it to the series. It would make sense, and of course they've got stills they've taken while I've been working so it should be quite easy.'

So he wouldn't need her. She stifled her disappointment, because she was pleased for him anyway. 'That sounds good.'

'I thought so, too.'

He was still chopping and fiddling. 'Is it going to be long? I'm starving,' she said plaintively.

'Five minutes, tops. Here, eat these. New amuse-bouche ideas for the restaurant. Tell me what you think.'

'Yummy,' she said, and had another, watching him as she ate the delicious little morsels. The steak was flash-fried, left to rest in the marinade while he blanched fresh green beans, and then he crushed the new potatoes, criss-crossed them with beans, thinly sliced the steak and piled it on before drizzling the marinade over the top.

'There. Never let it be said that I don't feed you properly. Wine?'

He handed her a glass without waiting for her reply, and she sipped it and frowned.

'Is this one of the Valtieri wines?'

'Yes. It goes well, doesn't it?'

'Mmm. It's gorgeous. So's the steak. It's like butter it's so tender.'

'What can I say? I'm just a genius,' he said, grinning, and hitched up on the stool next to her, and it would have been so natural, so easy to lean towards him and kiss that wicked smile.

She turned her attention back to her food, and ignored her clamouring body. Let it clamour. They had to play it his way, and if that meant she couldn't push him, so be it. He was turning his life around, getting it back on track, and she wasn't going to do anything to derail his rehabilitation. Or her own.

And Leo was definitely derailing material.

'Coffee?' he asked when she'd finished the crème brûlée he'd had left over from filming today.

'Please.'

And just because they could, just because it was Leo's favourite thing in the world to do at that time of day, they took it outside on the deck and sat side by side on the steps to drink it.

He'd turned the lights down in the kitchen, so they were sitting staring out across the darkened garden at the moonlit sea. Lights twinkled on it here and there, as the lights had twinkled in Tuscany, only here they were on the sea, and the smell of salt was in the air, the ebbing waves tugging on the shingle the only sound to break the silence.

She leant against him, resting her shoulder against his, knowing it was foolish, tired of fighting it, and with a shaky sigh he set his cup down, turned his head towards her and searched her eyes, his arm drawing her closer.

'Are we going to be OK, Amy?' he asked, as if he'd read her mind. His voice was soft, a little gruff. Perhaps a little afraid. She could understand that.

'I don't know. I want us to be, but all the time there's this threat hanging over us, the possibility that it won't, that it's just another mistake for both of us. And I don't want that. I want to be able to sit with you in the dark and talk, like we've done before a million times, and not feel this…crazy fear stalking me that it could be the last time.'

She took a sip of her coffee, but it tasted awful so she put it down.

'I'm going to bed,' she said. 'I'm tired and I can't do this any more. Pretend there's nothing going on, nothing between us except an outgrown friendship that neither of us can let go of. It's more than that, so much more than that, but I don't know if I can dare believe in it, and I don't think you can, either.'

She got to her feet, and he stood up and pulled her gently into his arms, cradling her against his chest. 'I'm sorry. Go on, go to bed. I'll see you in the morning.'

He bent and brushed his lips against her cheek, the stubble teasing her skin and making her body ache for more, and then he let her go.

She heard him come upstairs a few minutes later. He hesitated at her door and she willed him to come in, but he didn't, and she rolled to her side and shut her eyes firmly and willed herself to sleep instead.

* * *

The film crew interrupted their breakfast the next morning, but she didn't mind. The place stank of coffee, and she couldn't get Ella out of the house fast enough.

She strapped her into the car seat, pulled off the drive and went into town. They were running short of her follow-on milk formula, so she popped into the supermarket and picked up some up, and then she headed for the seafront. They could go to the beach, she thought, and then they passed a café and the smell of coffee hit her like a brick.

She pressed her hand to her mouth and walked on, her footsteps slowing to a halt as soon as they were out of range. No. She couldn't be. But she could see Isabelle's face so clearly, hear her saying that she couldn't stand the smell of coffee, and last night it had tasted vile.

But—how? She was on the Pill. She'd taken it religiously.

Except for the first day in Tuscany, the Sunday morning. She'd forgotten it then, taken it in the afternoon, about four. Nine hours late. And it was only the mini-pill, because she and Nick had planned to start a family anyway, and a month or so earlier wouldn't have mattered. And she'd hardly seen Nick for weeks before the wedding. Which meant if she was pregnant, it was definitely Leo's baby.

She turned the buggy round, crossed the road and went to the chemist's, bought a pregnancy test with a gestation indicator and went to another café that didn't smell so much and had decent loos. She took Ella with her into the cubicle which doubled as disabled and baby changing, so there was room for the buggy, and she did the test, put the lid back on the wand and propped it up, and watched her world change for ever.

He hadn't seen them all day.

The filming had gone well and the crew had packed up early, but Amy and Ella still weren't home.

Perhaps she'd taken Ella to her mother's, or to a friend's house? Probably. It was nearly time for Ella to eat, so he knew they wouldn't be long, but he was impatient.

He'd been thinking about what Amy had said last night, about their lives being on hold while they gave themselves time, and he'd decided he didn't want more time. He wanted Amy, at home with him, with Ella, in his bed, in his life. For ever.

Finally the gravel crunched. He heard her key in the door, and felt the fizz of anticipation in his veins, warring with an undercurrent of dread, just in case. What would she say? Would it be yes? Please, God, not no—

'Hi. Have you had a good day?' he asked, taking Ella from her with a smile and snuggling her close.

'Busy,' she said, heading into the kitchen with a shopping bag. 'Where are the film crew?'

'We finished early. So what did you do all day?'

'Oh, this and that. We went to town and picked up some formula, but it was a bit hot so we went to Mum's and had lunch in the garden and stayed there the rest of the day.'

'I thought you might have been there. I was about to ring you. Has she eaten?'

'Not recently. She had a snack at three. Are you OK to take over? I've got a few things I need to do.'

He frowned. He couldn't really put his finger on it, but she didn't sound quite right. 'Sure, you go ahead. Supper at seven?'

'If you like. Call me when you're done, OK? I might have a shower, it's been a hot day.'

She ran upstairs, and he took Ella through to the kitchen, put her in her high chair and gave her her supper. She fed herself and made an appalling mess, but he didn't care. All he could think about was Amy, and what was wrong with her, because something was and he was desperately hoping it wasn't a continuation of what she'd said last night.

What if she turned him down? Walked away and left him?

On autopilot, he wiped Ella's hands and took her up to bath her.

'Amy?'

'Yes?'

He opened her bedroom door and found her sitting up on her bed, the laptop open on her lap. She shut it and looked up at him. 'Is supper ready?'

'It won't take long. Can you come down? I want to talk to you.'

'Sure,' she said, but she looked tense and he wondered why.

'Can I go first?' she said, and he hesitated for a moment then nodded.

'Sure. Do you want a drink?'

'Just water.'

He filled a tumbler from the fridge and handed it to her, and she headed outside to the garden, perching on the step in what had become her usual place, and he crossed the deck and sat down beside her.

She drew her breath in as if she was going to speak, then let it out again and bit her lip.

'Amy? What is it?'

She sucked in another shaky breath, turned to look at him and said, 'I'm pregnant.'

He felt the blood drain from his head, and propped his elbows on shaking knees, the world slowing so abruptly that thoughts and feelings crashed into each other and slid away again before he could grasp them.

'How?' he asked her, his voice taut. He raised his head

and stared at her. 'How, Amy? You're on the Pill—I know that, I watched you take it every morning.'

'Not every morning,' she said heavily. 'The first day, I forgot. I didn't take it until the afternoon.'

'And that's enough?'

'Apparently. I didn't even think about it, because it didn't matter any more. I wasn't on my honeymoon, and we weren't—'

He was trying to assimilate that, and then another thought, much harder to take, brought bile to his throat.

'How do you know it's mine?' he asked, and his voice sounded cold to his ears, harsh, uncompromising. 'How do you know it isn't...?' He couldn't even bring himself to say Nick's name out loud, but it echoed between them in the silence.

'Because it's the only time I've taken it late, and because of this.'

She pulled something out of her pocket and handed it to him. A plastic thing, pen-sized or a little more, with a window on one side. And in the window was the word 'pregnant' and beneath it '2-3'.

A pregnancy test, he realised. And 2-3?

'What does this mean?' he asked, pointing to it with a finger that wasn't quite steady.

'Two to three weeks since conception.'

The weekend they'd been alone in the *palazzo*. So it *was* his baby. Then another hideous thought occurred to him.

'When did you do this test?'

'This morning,' she told him, her voice drained and lifeless.

'Are you sure? Are you sure you didn't do it a week or two ago?'

Her eyes widened, and the colour drained from her face.

'You think I'd lie to you about something as fundamental as this?'

'You wouldn't be the first.'

She stared at him for what seemed like for ever, and then she got to her feet.

'Where are you going?'

'Home. To my mother.'

'Not to Nick?'

She turned back to him, her eyes flashing with fury. 'Why would I go running to Nick to tell him I've been stupid enough to let you get me pregnant?' she asked him bluntly. 'If you could really think that then you don't know me at all. It's none of Nick's business. It's my business, and it could have been yours, but if you really think I could lie to you about something so precious, so amazing, so beautiful as our child, then I don't think we have anything left to say to each other. You wanted my terrifying honesty. Well, this is it. I'm sorry you don't like it, but *I am not Lisa!*'

He heard her footsteps across the decking, the vibrations going through him like an earthquake, then the sound of the front door slamming and the gravel crunching under her tyres as she drove off.

He stared blindly after her as the sound of her car faded into the evening, drowned out by the cries of gulls and the soft crash of the waves on the shore below, and then like a bolt of lightning the pain hit him squarely in the chest.

Her mother was wonderful and didn't say a thing, just heard her out, hugged her while she cried and made them both tea.

'Do you know how wonderful you are?' she asked, and her mother's face crumpled briefly.

'Don't be silly. I'm just your mother. You'll know what I mean, soon enough. It'll make sense.'

Her eyes filled with tears. 'I already know. I'm not going to see Ella again, Mum. Never.'

'Of course you will.'

'No, I won't. Or Leo.' Her voice cracked on his name, and she bit her lips until she could taste blood.

'That's a little difficult. He has a right to see his child, you know.'

'Except he doesn't believe it is his child.'

'Are you absolutely certain that it is?'

'Yes,' she said, sighing heavily. 'Nick was away, wasn't he, for five weeks before the wedding. I only saw him a couple of times, and we didn't…'

She couldn't finish that, not to her mother, which was ridiculous under the circumstances, but she didn't need to say any more.

'You ought to eat, darling.'

'I couldn't. I just feel sick.'

'Carbs,' her mother said, and produced a packet of plain rich tea biscuits. 'Here,' she said, thrusting one in her hand. 'Dunk it in your tea.'

Was it really his? Could this really be happening to him again?

He'd sat outside for hours until the shock wore off and was replaced by a sickening emptiness.

The pregnancy test, he thought. Check it out. He went up to her room and opened her laptop, and was confronted by a page of images of him. Images he'd never seen. Ones she'd lied about deleting. Why? Because she loved him? And he loved her. He could see it clearly in the pictures, and he knew it in his heart.

He searched for the pregnancy test and came up with it.

As accurate as an ultrasound.

Which meant if she *had* just done it, the baby was his—and he'd accused her of lying, of trying to pass another man's baby off as his.

And he knew then, with shocking certainty, that she hadn't lied to him. Not about that. As she'd pointed out at several thousand decibels, she wasn't Lisa. Not in any way. And he owed her an apology.

A lifetime of apologies, starting now.

But he couldn't leave Ella behind, so he lifted her out of her cot, put her in the car and drove to Jill's. Amy's car was on the drive, and he went to the front door and rang the bell.

'Leo.'

'I'm an idiot,' he said, and he felt his eyes filling and blinked hard. 'Can I see her?'

'Where's Ella?'

'In the car, asleep.'

'Put her in the sitting room. Amy's in her room.'

He laid her on the sofa next to Jill, went upstairs to Amy's room and took a deep breath.

'Go away, Leo,' she said, before he even knocked, but he wasn't going anywhere.

He opened the door, ducked to avoid the flying missile she hurled at him and walked towards her, heart pounding.

'Get out.'

'No. I've come to apologise. I've been an idiot. I know you're not Lisa, and I know you wouldn't lie to me about anything important. You've never really lied to me, not even when you knew the truth was going to hurt me. And I know you're not lying now.' He took another step towards her. 'Can we talk?'

'What is there to say?'

'What I wanted to say to you when you got home. That I love you. That I don't want to wait any longer, because I do know you, Amy, I know you through and through, and you know me. We haven't changed that much, not deep down where it matters, and I know we've got what it takes. I was just hiding from it because I was afraid, because I've screwed up one marriage, but I'm not going to screw up another.'

'Marriage?' She stared at him blankly. 'I hate to point this out to you, but we aren't exactly married. We aren't exactly anything.'

'No. But we should be. We haven't lost our friendship, Amy, but it has changed. Maybe the word is evolved. Evolved into something stronger. Something that will stay the course. We were both just afraid to try again, afraid to trust what was under our noses all the time. We should have had more faith in each other and in ourselves.'

He took her hand and wrapped it in his, hanging on for dear life, because he couldn't let her go. Let them go.

'I love you, Amy. I'll always love you. Marry me. Me and Ella, and you and our baby. We can be a proper family.'

Amy sat down on the edge of her bed, her knees shaking.

'Are you serious? Leo, you were horrible to me!'

'I know, and I can't tell you how sorry I am. I was just shocked, and there was a bit of déjà vu going on, but I should have listened to you.'

'You should. But I knew you wouldn't, because of Lisa—'

'Shh,' he said, touching a finger to her lips. 'Lisa's gone, Amy. This is between you and me now, you and me and our baby.'

'And Ella,' she said.

'And Ella. Of course and Ella. She won't be an only child any more. I was so worried about that.'

'You said it would be a cold day in hell before you got married again,' she reminded him, and his eyes filled with sadness.

'I was wrong. It felt like a cold day in hell when you walked out of my life. Come back to me, Amy? Please? I need you. I can't live without you, without your friendship, your support, your understanding. Your atrocious sense of humour. Your untidiness. The fact that you do lie to me, just a little, on occasions.'

'When?' she asked, scrolling back desperately.

'The photos,' he said with a wry smile on the mouth she just wanted to kiss now. You told me you'd deleted them, but you haven't. They're still on your laptop. I saw them just now. I opened your laptop to check up on pregnancy tests and I found them. Photos of me. Why?'

She closed her eyes. 'It doesn't matter why.'

'It does to me, because I know why I would want photos of you. Why I took them. So I can look at the images when you're gone, and still, in some small way, have you with me. Amy, I'm scared,' he went on, and she opened her eyes and looked up at him again, seeing the truth of it in his eyes.

'I'm scared I'll fail you, let you down like I let Lisa down. My lifestyle is chaotic, and it's not conducive to a happy marriage. How many celebrity chefs—forget celebrity, just normal chefs—are happily married? Not many. So many of their marriages fall apart, and I don't want that to happen to us, but I need you in my life, and I'll have to trust your faith in me, your belief that we can make it work. That I won't let you down.'

'You already have, today. You didn't listen.'

He closed his eyes, shaking his head slowly, and then he looked up, his eyes locking with hers, holding them firm.

'I know. And I'm sorry, but I'll never do it again. I love you, Amy, and I need you, and I've never been more serious about anything in my life. Please marry me.'

He meant it. He really, truly meant it.

She closed her eyes, opened them again and smiled at him. She thought he smiled back, but she couldn't really see any more. 'Yes,' she said softly. 'Oh, yes, please.'

He laughed, but it turned into a ragged groan, and he hauled her into his arms and cradled her against his heart.

'You won't let me down,' she told him. 'I won't let you. Just one more thing—will you please kiss me? I've forgotten what it feels like.'

'I've got a better idea. Ella's downstairs with your mother, and she needs to be back in bed in her own home, and so do I. Come home with us, Amy. It doesn't feel right without you.'

It didn't feel right without him, either. Nothing felt right. And home sounded wonderful.

'Kiss me first?' she said with a smile, and he laughed softly.

'Well, it's tough but I'll see if I can remember how,' he murmured, and she could feel the smile on his lips...

EPILOGUE

'Are you ready?'

Such simple words, but they'd had the power to change the whole course of her life.

Was she ready?

For the marriage—the *lifetime*—with Leo?

Mingling with the birdsong and the voices of the people clustered outside the church gates were the familiar strains of the organ music.

The overture for their wedding.

No. Their *marriage*. Subtle difference, but hugely significant.

Amy glanced through the doorway of the church and caught the smiles on the row of faces in the back pew, and she smiled back, her heart skittering under the fitted bodice that suddenly seemed so tight she could hardly breathe.

The church was full, the food cooked, the champagne on ice. And Leo was waiting for her answer.

Her dearest friend, the love of her life, who'd been there for her when she'd scraped her knees, had her heart broken for the first time, when her father had died, who'd just— been there, her whole life, her friend and companion and cheerleader. Her lover. And she did love him.

Enough to marry him? Till death us do part, and all that?

Oh, yes. And she was ready. Ready for the chemistry, the fireworks, the amazingness that was her life with Leo.

Bring it on.

She straightened her shoulders, tilted up her chin and gave Leo her most dazzling smile.

'Yes,' she said firmly. 'I'm ready. How about you? Because I don't want you feeling pressured into this for the wrong reason. You can still walk away. I'll understand.'

'No way,' he said, just as firmly. 'It's taken me far too long to realise how much I love you, and I can't think of a better reason to marry you, or a better time to do it than now.'

His smile was tender, his eyes blazing with love, and she let out the breath she'd been holding.

'Well, that's a relief,' she said with a little laugh, and he smiled and shook his head.

'Silly girl. Amy, are you sure you don't want my father to walk you down the aisle? He's quite happy to.'

'No. I don't need anyone to give me away, Leo, and you're the only man I want by my side.'

'Good. You look beautiful, Amy,' he added gruffly, looking down into her eyes. 'More beautiful than I've ever seen you.'

'Thank you,' she said softly 'You don't look so bad yourself.'

She kissed his cheek and flashed a smile over her shoulder at her bridesmaids. 'OK, girls? Good to go?'

They nodded, and she turned back to Leo. 'OK, then. Let's do this,' she said, and she could feel the smile in her heart reflected in his eyes.

'I love you, Amy,' he murmured, and then slowly, steadily, he walked her down the aisle.

And when they reached the chancel steps he stopped, those beautiful golden eyes filled with love and pride, and he turned her into his arms and kissed her.

The congregation went wild, and he let her go and stood back a little, his smile wry.

'That was just in case you'd forgotten what it's like,' he teased, but his eyes weren't laughing, because marrying Amy was the single most important thing he would ever do in his life, and he was going to make sure they did it right.

* * * * *

LET'S TALK

Romance

For exclusive extracts, competitions
and special offers, find us online:

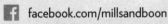 facebook.com/millsandboon

@MillsandBoon

 @MillsandBoonUK

Get in touch on 01413 063232

For all the latest titles coming soon, visit
millsandboon.co.uk/nextmonth

MILLS & BOON

MODERN

Power and Passion

Prepare to be swept off your feet by sophisticated, sexy and seductive heroes, in some of the world's most glamourous and romantic locations, where power and passion collide.

Eight Modern stories published every month, find them all

millsandboon.co.uk/Modern